Hawk was prepared this time.

He lifted Amber off her feet and trapped her body against the wall with his weight. She jerked up, struggling to loosen her hands, trying to use her legs for leverage.

Hawk pushed in between them, lifting her higher against the wall and pressing down on her. Her eyes glared at him. She wrapped her legs around his waist.

"I believe we've done this position before," he told her softly as he watched her eyes slowly close. Her legs slid off him.

Shifting his hand down to hold her so he could lower her to the floor, Hawk made contact with bare skin. He suddenly realized that the skirt she wore had ridden up to her waist when she had lifted her legs. He moved his hand down the side of her thigh, felt silky skin and a strap. Following it to the front, he encountered a holster holding a small weapon.

Note to self: The woman was always armed when her legs were open. He followed his instincts and checked the other thigh.

"I'll be damned," he murmured. The lady had a small knife there. Not a good idea to tick her off. His grin grew wider.

Too damn late.

By Gennita Low

THE HUNTER
THE PROTECTOR
FACING FEAR
INTO DANGER

Gennita Low

THE HUNTER

AVON BOOKS
An Imprint of HarperCollinsPublishers

This is a work of fiction. Names, characters, places, and incidents are products of the author's imagination or are used fictitiously and are not to be construed as real. Any resemblance to actual events, locales, organizations, or persons, living or dead, is entirely coincidental.

AVON BOOKS
An Imprint of HarperCollins*Publishers*
10 East 53rd Street
New York, New York 10022-5299

First Avon Books paperback printing: July 2005

Avon Trademark Reg. U.S. Pat. Off. and in Other Countries, Marca Registrada, Hecho en U.S.A.
HarperCollins® is a registered trademark of HarperCollins Publishers Inc.

Printed in the U.S.A.

10 9 8 7 6 5 4 3 2 1

To Mother and Father,
to my Stash, the true one among the decoys,
and Mike, my Ranger Buddy,
the ultimate warrior.

Special hugs to Melinda Hutchenberger.

Acknowledgments

This book was written under the crossfire of Charlie, Jeanne, Ivan and Francis.

Special thanks to Maria "HoF" Hammon and Melissa Copeland, two operators navigating the no-man's-land of my mind; the sea mammals that taught me swimming isn't all about floating; Erika Tsang, my editor, who panicked through four hurricanes with me; and Liz Trupin-Pulli, my agent, the best huntress out there!

And always, the ladies at Delphi TDD, especially Sandy "Sadista" Still, Mirmie Caraway, Karen King, Angela Swanson, Teena Weena Smith, and Katherine Lazo, the most supportive BSHes in the world.

Thank you RBL Romantica for all your support!

There are numerous sources for more information about human trafficking, but these official reports and news articles speak for themselves:

www.spacewar.com/2004/040506172314.wol6yurc.html

www.taipeitimes.com/News/world/archives/2004/05/08/2003154608

www.news.bbc.co.uk/1/hi/world/europe/1028249.stm

1

Velesta, Macedonia

Hrana. A zena.

There were two universal truths when it came to man and his manhood. Both had to do with hunger. And when a man was hungry for both *food* and *woman*, he tended to expend a lot of energy in search of getting what he needed. Not just any kind of food. Or woman.

Ja sam gladna.

Hawk opened his eyes. Meditation worked. But not when one was hungry.

He had discovered that he enjoyed meditating—it slowed the heart down and helped to put things into perspective. And allowed him to keep his cool while living against his code of values for two months. Of course, knowing that any slight betrayal of the truth would put a bullet in his head helped the transition.

But still, his lessons in meditation had pulled him through a few tough moments. He had seen his share of horror in his time—in bloody battles and their aftermath—but he had always been on the "good" side, if one could call war good. This time, he had to play a part, and he had to watch the horror and filth of crimes being committed in front of him without being able to do anything about them. He couldn't stop them . . . and it sickened him at night when he lay in bed, with images of girls being raped and used like toilet paper.

He couldn't stop them. And so he had used his new training—meditation. For the first time in his life as a SEAL, he had to start learning a new weapon that had nothing to do with aiming and shooting.

But Hawk was hungry. He wanted real food. A big thick hamburger dripping with juice, everything on top, the kind that squished out in a mess when one had his mouth around it. He didn't want the generic Mickey D's that were in every corner of the world, with their cardboard taste and thin meat patties. He wanted the real thing, down-home cooking, grilled to perfection the way only a man knew how. Good old American *hrana*.

So far, there was none in Velesta, Macedonia.

And he wanted a real woman. Not these half-pints parading in front of grown men in darkened *kafenas*—or "fashion houses"—as they were called here. Not females with brutalized eyes that looked older than their real age.

He hungered for a real woman who hadn't been shared by a dozen men a night, who hadn't been kidnapped or tricked into slavery, and who wasn't looking for a husband to get out of her situation. So far, in the limited world he had been shuffled through in this, the most notorious crime city in Europe, there were none.

Hawk uncurled from the lotus position. He stretched his legs, scooting forward on the soft featherbed until his feet found the thinly carpeted floor. He got up and strode to the huge antique window, unconcerned that anyone would glance up and see his naked form looking down on them. It was snowing outside. Who would be out there in this weather?

And who would be thinking of hot hamburger meat on a grill? He gave a short bark of laughter. He was used to the harshest of conditions under which to operate. His training had assured him of that. He'd gone from extreme heat to this early winter clime in a space of a few months; he missed the sticky sweaty conditions of jungle warfare, but he'd anticipated the change of venue to Velesta, and he had been mentally prepared.

Tough SEAL. Top covert operative. The local kingpin's newest best friend. Money, drugs, and women handed to him on a platter. And all he really wanted right now was a thick flavorful piece of ground beef between a sesame bun. And a real woman. He laughed again. He was getting a hard-on while thinking about meat. Pathetic.

He looked outside at the first snowstorm of the year. The snow was falling down fast and silently. An early surprise to even the locals. The weather forecasters had made jokes about global warming on the news tonight, saying that God and scientists had forgotten about Macedonia. His lips twisted. They didn't know how close to the truth they were.

If there were different levels of hell, he was in one of the hidden ones. He preferred the war zone to this—a place where the devils were running the show and appeared to be winning. At least from where he stood.

A whoosh and a thud. Hawk turned quickly, sidestepping the shadowy figure's attack. He swung up, jamming the opponent's hand against the wall. The intruder was wearing black and the material felt cold and damp, indicating that he had come from outside.

Surprisingly nimble, his attacker dodged Hawk's other hand, countering with a kick aimed for his privates. Hawk twisted, but he didn't release the captive hand, even when the kick connected with the side of his thigh. He yanked the arm hard, swung the attacker's body over his shoulder onto the floor, trapping him beneath his own body.

A sharp stabbing pain hit Hawk on the chest. He grunted, reaching up with his free hand to pull the weapon out. It was a hypodermic needle; he could feel the drug's immediate effect even as he grasped the stranger's wrist, bending it back. A pair of legs wrapped around his waist like a steel vise, stopping him from pulling away from the needle. Ignoring the floating sensation rising like thick fog, Hawk tried to press down on the nerve in the wrist, but the other man held on to the needle determinedly, pushing in the plunger. Hawk released the imprisoned hand and reached for the man's throat. Break his neck. That was his . . . only . . . hope. . . .

Amber opened her mouth and immediately tasted warm male flesh. Her face was buried against the man's neck and every breath she took in emphasized his clean scent, slightly tinged with cologne. She finally turned her head with some difficulty, feeling the scrape of stubble against her cheek.

God, he was a heavy guy. And . . . She moved her hand experimentally, then closed her eyes in disbelief. And naked.

"Shit," she announced softly.

"I won the bet. Told you he wouldn't be easy to take down." Her friend's voice, far above in the darkness, was wry and amused.

"I took him down, didn't I?" Amber retorted, her voice strained. The man's dead weight made it hard to breathe as she squirmed beneath, trying to free herself. She almost yelped when her lower body connected with something . . . no, she didn't want to think about *that*. Trust a stupid American to walk around naked in this weather. Why hadn't that crossed her mind?

"Need some help?"

"No!" Her reply was quick and breathless. Not if she could help it. No need to let her friend know that she was trapped underneath a naked man. Especially when her legs were still wrapped around his waist in a rather compromising position. She released them quickly, but that didn't solve the problem that he was still very much on top of her, still very much touching her everywhere.

She pulled at one numbed hand trapped between them and was astonished to find him tightly holding on to it in his drugged state. She already knew where her other hand was and would rather not move it around too much. Damn it. She was going to have to get Llallana to help her.

"You're taking too damn long," Llallana said. She sounded closer. Amber moved her head and saw her friend standing nearby. It was too dark to see her face, but the welling of amusement was very evident in Llallana's voice. "My, oh my, do you look comfy."

"Oh, shut up. Help me move him."

"Thought you didn't need help," Llallana snickered.

"Okay, I lied. Happy now?"

"Hmm." Her friend crouched down. "Here, I'll pull at the legs while you scoot upward, okay?"

"'Kay." Amber arched her back as Llallana pulled, and smothered a shriek.

Llallana stopped. "What's the matter?"

"Uh. Nothing. Can we . . . umm . . . turn him over instead?" She was *not* going to go into details about why sliding upward while arching her back was a problem.

There was a short pause. Llallana started to chuckle. "Oh my. Oh shit, I'm going to burst out laughing and get someone in here for sure."

Amber glared into the dark shadows of her friend's face. "Don't you dare laugh."

"Not here," her friend agreed, her chuckling barely contained. "It isn't time for us to die yet. But you can at least share with me how big he feels."

That was one detail Amber was definitely not going to share. The man might be out like a light, but she could feel him through the thin stretched material of her cat-burglar outfit, and to make it worse, she wasn't wearing any underwear. At the moment, he felt big and heavy against a part of her that was wide open because of her spread legs, and when she had arched upward just now . . . that was when she had almost shrieked. She had felt the tip of his penis pushing against the soft material. That was too damn close.

When her friend still didn't move, Amber demanded, "Are you going to help or not? What the hell are you doing?"

"I'm patting his butt. He's got . . . wow . . . a nice butt."

Amber released a sigh of impatience. "Lily, if he wakes up now, what do you think will happen to us?"

"Nah, he's out for a good two hours if you used the entire dose. If not, I have another needle right here. And his butt is nicely exposed. Wow, I like the feel of his back."

"Will you stop?" Amber said through clenched teeth. "We came here to check out how good an operative he is, not how nice his bod is."

"Well, he was pretty good, from my angle. So you're wrong about him being just another pretty face. He would have gotten you if not for the drug."

"I still won. He's down like a sack of potatoes and . . . Lily . . . will you please do something?" She was beginning to panic that her friend might leave her here. Llallana had a dark sense of humor and just might think it humorous enough, in spite of the danger of discovery.

To her relief, she felt the weight on top of her shifting as her friend began to push and roll the body over. She helped as much as she could, using her one hand to press against the bare hard wall of his pecs. He moved a few inches and she found her face tucked against his chest. God, the man was hot all . . . over. She swallowed a curse. There was no getting around it; she had to arch up.

"What did you say?"

"Nothing," Amber muttered against heated skin. She braced her legs on the floor and pushed up, trying to ignore how a certain big part of the male anatomy was grinding against her, at the moment, very sensitive nether region. She couldn't believe this was happening. She gasped out, "You aren't really helping, are you?"

"I am, too. He's just a solid guy, Amber. Push some more so I can get some leverage."

Easy for her to ask. She didn't have a penis almost penetrating the crotch of her pants. Amber gave a sigh of frustration, took a deep breath, and pushed up with her legs as hard as she could. Her eyes almost crossed at the hard and intimate contact happening between her legs. She was supposed to be the assailant, so how come she felt like she was being attacked right now?

"I cannot believe this is happening," she repeated out loud. As the body on top of her slowly turned over, she felt his hold on her hand tightening and gasped as she followed the rolling momentum.

"Oooooomph. He's heavy. What's wrong now?"

"He's holding my hand and not letting go."

"Really?" A small narrow light appeared from the slim flashlight in Llallana's hand. "He's determined to hold on to you even in his drug-addled state . . . how interesting." The light moved slowly down the length of the exposed body. "Oh my."

"Lily!"

"Check that out, Amber. No wonder you made all that noise. He's . . . ummm . . . happy."

"Damn it, stop taking liberties like that. It isn't fair to the guy." In spite of her protests, Amber found her eyes drawn to the small spotlight her friend had made. She rubbed her wrist absentmindedly as she stared down. Good Lord. No wonder she had felt him. The man was still semi-aroused. "Why didn't I think of these things? That he would be naked and . . . horny? It's the middle of the night, after all."

"It looks beautiful. Makes me want to wait for him to wake up."

"Lily!" She reached out and jerked her friend's arm away. "That's it. We're leaving now."

"What about the test and all that stuff you were talking about?"

"Oh." Amber had forgotten the reason why they were there. They had wanted to make sure the new operative was good. She worked her hand free from the man's tight grasp. "Okay, let's tuck the note where he can see it without too much difficulty."

"Where? The man is naked, for God's sake. You wanted to piss him off, you said. Well, he's going to be when he wakes up half frozen."

Yeah. She had wanted to piss off Jed's man to test him. She smiled in the dark. There was definitely a way to do that. "Go get the blanket. We don't want him to catch a cold. I'll make sure he gets the note."

While Llallana went off to the bed in the corner, Amber took out the note in her side pocket. She checked another pocket, where she had a few loose things that were useful to open locks, and grinned triumphantly when she found what she was looking for—a long piece of string. Quickly, she poked a hole in the note and pulled the string through. She thought for a moment, then took out a pen and scrawled quickly before reaching out into the darkness.

"Now what are you doing?"

"Tying the note around his wrist. There. Got the blanket?"

"Yes, here."

Amber tucked the thick feathered blanket over the sleeping man. "There. Let's go."

They switched on their nylon lines from their belts. One wonderful thing about hundred-year-old buildings converted for modern living—they still had high ceilings with walkways and turrets. It took a few minutes before they reached the small ventilation hole where they had crawled in. Their winter jackets were on the other side, fifteen minutes away. It would have been difficult to maneuver around with heavy garments on.

Llallana climbed in first, then turned abruptly. She turned on the flashlight again, almost blinding Amber. "You didn't tie it around his wrist, did you?"

Amber never underestimated her friend. She kept her face expressionless. "Of course I did. Where else would I tie the note?"

Hawk didn't open his eyes immediately. He strived to keep his breathing even, as if he were still out. He could feel some kind of cover over his face; moving his fingers slowly, he felt around him. Hard surface—on a floor? He was surrounded by some thick material—did they stick him in a sack?

He finally opened his eyes. It was pitch-black. He mentally checked his body—no pain anywhere, just a slight soreness around the right thigh. He remembered the kick. His heart wasn't racing anymore. The drug must have been some kind of sleeping agent; he didn't remember any hallucinatory dreams. There was a slight crick in his neck from lying on a hard surface, but other than that, he appeared to be fine.

So, where had his assailant taken him? It couldn't be too

far; Dragan Dilaver's building was very heavily guarded. Recalling the attacker's small build, Hawk doubted his ability to carry him out of a room, down several flights of stairs, through the huge foyer, and outside into the snowy open without a single soul seeing him. So that left only one simple conclusion—he was still in his own room, on the floor where he had been drugged.

Hawk lifted one hand and very slowly pulled at the material on him. He frowned, clutching the soft thickness several times. It felt like—his blanket. He drew his arm out from under it and encountered a lighter layer of cloth. This must be the one covering his face; the feathered blanket could have smothered him while he was out. What did you know, a thoughtful captor.

Part of him was pissed at the fact that he had been captured so easily. He couldn't afford to let down his guard ever, and here he was, lying naked without any weapons, taken by surprise, and seemingly left—he cocked his head, listening— unguarded. Slowly, he inched the cloth down from his face.

Emerging from his warm cocoon, the air felt cold against his face. He *was* still in his room. His instincts told him that he was all alone, but caution told him to not move, just in case someone had a sick sense of humor and had wired a bomb nearby.

Hawk's mind went over the events that he could remember. The attack had happened here, at the most open of the Dilaver holdings. Whoever his assailant was, he was cocky enough to do it, and was very sure of not being caught. And he was skilled in martial arts, so not just some dumb thief. He had deliberately attacked Hawk, so there was a message here somewhere. Conclusion: Explosives unlikely. Besides, why bother with the blankets if he had just wanted Hawk to die?

He was a SEAL. He sure wasn't going to lie here and call for help so Dilaver's men could come up to check around his naked body. Fuck that.

He rose up, letting the thick protective blanket fall away. It was still dark, so he couldn't have been out more than an hour or two. The first thing to do was to turn on the light to see exactly what the dark stranger had left behind.

Turning on the bedside lamp, he squinted and adjusted to the sudden glare. Except for the blanket and spread on the floor, nothing appeared out of the ordinary. There was no sign of their fight at all. No hypodermic needle, nothing broken, not even a telltale shoe print. His attacker had been exceptionally careful not to leave any souvenirs for him to find.

Hawk started to head back to pick up the blanket. Something lightly scratched his thigh. He looked down. He softly cursed. Souvenir found.

Amber didn't look up from her task when she heard Llallana coming into the kitchen. She arranged the freshly baked cookies in the jar, popping one into mouth. There was always a lot to do for the café, and her customers, both Americans—mostly peacekeepers these days—and locals, seemed to love her cookies the best.

Llallana, as was her custom, poured herself a cup of coffee and sat down in her chair by the window. Her visits seemed to be less and less frequent these days, and Amber was beginning to worry about her friend. She knew how hard Llallana's job was to one's psyche, and wished she could offer more help, but in their business, each had to worry about her own assignment.

"You still won't admit it," Llallana finally began, voice filled with amusement.

"Nope," Amber said, calmly closing the lid to the jar and reaching for another one. "No idea what you're talking about."

"You touched a man's erection and won't even tell your best friend."

"I did not!" Amber munched on another cookie, not looking up but knowing her friend had an evil smile on her face that would make her break out laughing. "Besides, it wasn't a full erection."

"Aha. You at least admit to checking, then," Llallana came back wryly.

Never mind checking, she had *felt* it in the most intimate way possible. She wondered how the poor man was going to react to her little present. "Can't help it, he was naked," she pointed out, finally looking up to meet her friend's twinkling eyes. "At least I didn't shine a flashlight on it and ooh and ahh over it like it's the eighth wonder in the world."

Llallana laughed. "Of course, blame it on me and my wicked ways." She took a long sip of her coffee, then lazily settled back in her chair, cradling the cup in both hands. She watched Amber through half-closed eyes. "Unlike you, I'm not ashamed to admit to liking what I saw."

Amber sighed. She reached for a cloth to wipe the flour from her hands. "Lily, darling, I think we both agree that shame isn't in your genetic makeup. If we're to work with this man, how could I look at him in the eye if I'd checked him out as thoroughly as you had?"

"Ahem . . . you're the one working with him, not me, so I guess what I did was okay." Llallana laughed again. "I think, either way, you're going to be in trouble with the guy right now. He should have woken up by now and found your little present."

Amber tried not to smile at the thought. "Maybe so. Maybe we shouldn't have done what we did."

Llallana arched her eyebrows. "Regrets? To hell with them if they can't take it, and to hell with this new operative if he can't take a little joke."

"It isn't a joke. It's a test," Amber corrected. She suppressed the thought of how *not* little he was.

"Oh yeah, tell his erection that." Llallana took another sip of her coffee. "I've a feeling he's going to be oh-so-mad with you."

"You, too."

"Ah, but he doesn't know I was there, Amber. You're all alone against his wrath."

Amber crunched on her cookie. "*If* he can find me."

Everything about their world was dreary and painfully serious. They had decided to seize every opportunity to have some laughter. So why not with the new operative in town? The CIA had sent him here to steal secrets. What a joke. Amber and Llallana had been working together for four years. Four freaking years watching the bloodbath around them. And now here comes some hotshot operative to take charge. Oh, really? Amber licked the crumbs from her fingers. In Macedonia, they had a saying: A foolish fox is caught by one leg, a wise one by all fours. Everything took time. And a lot of planning.

"What if he is better than the last one they sent?" Llallana interrupted her thoughts.

Amber rolled her eyes. "He has to be."

"Okay, so the last one was a real bozo, but you said this time it involved a man named Jed McNeil. Is he showing up here, too, then?"

"No, Jed doesn't just show up, Lily. He's sort of like the cleanup guy in his outfit, so if we see him at all, it's endgame time. But I did talk to him for a few short minutes."

"What did he tell you, besides that it's a CIA-sanctioned operation?"

"Jed never says anything, but the fact that he's in on this thing makes it more interesting. And you know the CIA. Sanctioned? Pffft. We're sanctioned, but that doesn't stop them from betraying us if necessary. We're still of use, that's all." Amber shrugged. "Back to this new guy—what's our boy after that has Jed calling me up personally?"

"To warn you that he's his boy?" As usual, Llallana chose not to address the subject of a CIA betrayal.

Amber nodded thoughtfully. "Lily, if he's Jed's boy, he's not really CIA, you know that. There's more going on than trying to find out coordinates."

Llallana finished her coffee, placed the empty cup on the table, and stretched out her legs. "From what you told me about this Jed McNeil, he and his outfit are even grayer than our CIA, with lots of leeway. So what do you think is so damn important that everyone's after? That Dilaver has?"

Amber had wondered herself. "Let's find out," she said. "If it's that damn important, maybe we can get it for ourselves. Hell, possession is still nine-tenths of the law, even in these parts."

2

Ubijati. To kill. Or not.

Hawk was a member of an elite black operations team, but this time he was handling an operation all by himself, with many different choices to make. No one to report to. No one to account for. Just his own life. No one would question his actions as long as he achieved the operation objective. No one to come in after him if things went to hell.

He didn't move from his lazy lean against the door as he watched Dilaver smash up the furniture in the room, his tirade a mixture of Serbian and Croatian curses, with a healthy dose of Macedonian threats. No one else in the room made a move to stop their boss. Hell, they were probably happy Dilaver wasn't in a truly mean mood. When that happened, furniture wasn't the only thing that got broken.

Killing was a daily choice here. The careless disposal of life would be appalling to many, but not to this group of Macedonians. Velesta was an international crime center, and he was watching one of its most ruthless prime movers throw a tantrum.

Hawk understood most of the angry man's diatribe, although sometimes the accent and the local dialect threw him off. Someone had done the impossible—challenged the most notorious crime lord in the most notorious crime city. His interest perked a little. Maybe this was an opening for him to get on track for his own mission. Right now he observed the men keeping out of their boss's way. A good idea. *Ubijati* wasn't the only thing fate could ask of one . . . sometimes it was *ubijen*. From killer to the one killed.

"Three trucks in a month! That's thirty-six girls. Do you know how much our loss is, especially with the peacekeepers in town? Eight hundred Euro dollars per girl a night. That's fucking thirty thousand dollars times thirty days. That's practically nine hundred thousand missing dollars that I should have in my account. And you're telling me you can't catch the culprit?"

Dragan Dilaver was a large man. Like many in the region that was once Yugoslavia, he was a mixture of Macedonian and Asiatic genes. He was built like a boxer, with the same brutish strength and ability to withstand pain. Hawk had seen it himself. A few months earlier, in Asia, he had "helped" Dilaver flee from a firefight in which the drug kingpin had been intentionally "injured." Many of Dilaver's men had been killed or captured, allowing Hawk to move in to help him escape. All part of Plan A conducted in a joint mission by Hawk's STAR SEAL team and GEM, a group of contract agents. They had, after all, been after the same man, and Hawk had been assigned to make sure of two things—that Dragan Dilaver stayed alive and to get the location of a certain cache of weapons dropped just before their joint operations.

If it were up to Hawk himself, he would have killed the man yesterday. He despised the son of a bitch. Not only was Dilaver an illegal arms dealer and a mercenary, he was also a sex-slave trafficker, especially of underage girls. As a seasoned operative, Hawk had taken the lives of others, but it had always been in the heat of battle. He had never had the chance to sit and plan the death of a human being the way he sometimes did whenever he watched Dilaver and his men during their rampages.

Violence was violence. He understood the context in which it was necessary. When one agreed to walk into a battlefield, one signed up for what violence stood for—war in all its horror and glory. He lived with the knowledge that he was, in spite of his love of all things civilized, a violent man, and sometimes, in the darkest of hours, he sat alone wondering what made him that different from a man like Dilaver.

But moments like those very quickly disappeared when he had a weapon in his hand and his life was in danger. Training took over, absolving him of the guilt of having to take lives. He was efficient at giving back to his opponents as good as they gave. He had always been focused like that. He had learned that a long time ago while watching a bird of prey while out hunting with his father and brothers. A hawk had sighted something he wanted in another bird's beak and went after both bird and prey, shadowing the screeching bird in flight—dipping and soaring, swerving and gliding—until he had gotten what he was after. Hawk remembered thinking how beautiful and exciting the hunt was. And thus began his fascination for violence.

In a family of mostly men in Colorado, he had plenty of opportunity to be active in hunting and sports. His brothers and cousins were always around and, boys being boys, there were plenty of fights and competitiveness in everything. He had joined the Navy, following the footsteps of several members of his family, and learned there were different kinds of violence.

Hawk had never been part of this side of violence, where he had to take in instead of give out. He couldn't compromise his job by walking away. And worse, he couldn't do a thing about it. He had discovered something new lately—he was starting to take every violent crime Dilaver committed against young girls very, very personally. So much so, he wished that he had killed the crime lord instead of "saving" him. There was nothing, nothing that could have stopped him if he had known the things he was to see in Velesta.

That usual regret was replaying again in Hawk's head as he stood there. He knew nothing in his stance or expression betrayed any of his violent thoughts. Besides, someone had done something pretty interesting—disrupted Dragan Dilaver's business. Whoever it was had Hawk's silent congratulations. Not many around here would dare lift a finger against the powerful man, let alone steal something from under his nose.

"You're all fuckers—all of you! I can't leave anything for you to take care of without some total fuckup. You think just because I'm walking around with a limp that I can't kick all of your bloody asses from here to Skopje and back? I lose a fucking load of cargo in Asia and come home to find that you've been losing more of our cargo here, with all of you, supposedly my captains, in charge. Give me a good reason not to kill every one of you!"

Dilaver's ranting grew more winded as he began to tire. He had been swinging his cane at every available piece of breakable furniture. Unable to kick because of his injury, he had resorted to tearing apart the room with his bare hands, scattering pieces of wood, china, cloth—anything that caught his line of fire.

Dilaver's injury would have incapacitated a smaller man, but he had toughed it out like the mercenary he was. His guide gone, his cache of illegal weapons lost, he had to cut his losses and get the hell out of Dodge. He had finally worked out a deal with Hawk's "boss," Stefan, for Hawk's services to guide Dilaver and his men out of Asia.

Hawk himself had sustained a slight "injury" to his arm, and although not as serious, it still needed time to heal. Dilaver had been impressed that the other man had saved him from being caught, despite having been shot himself, and sometimes introduced him as his "blood" brother. All part of the game, of course. Get close to Dilaver. Establish a bond. Find the locations.

And the past few months . . . life as Dragan Dilaver's new best friend couldn't have been more hellish.

"And what are you thinking of, my American friend, with that smirk on your face?"

Hawk unhooked his leg and kicked a nearby piece of broken china by his feet. "I'm glad there isn't any food in here or you'd have made quite a mess by now."

Dilaver stopped pacing and stared across the room. "Are you making fun of me?"

Hawk shrugged. "Would I dare?"

The big Slavic man dropped down on a battered chair, rattling his heavy cane against the side of the table. "Of course you would, you crazy son of a bitch. I've been observing you the last few months and have yet to see you back down from a fight when someone challenged you, and then you egg on the stupid bastard after he's lost. With the same smirk that you have now."

That was Dilaver's version of friendship. Around here, one fought for fun. With real knives. Hawk had discovered that was a form of entertainment as well as a pressure release for some of these men. So far, he had handled the few who had wanted to try out the new American. Fights were nothing; Hawk fought with his brothers and cousins all the time at home.

He shrugged. "Sometimes they make it too easy."

"Now you think my men are easy, huh? Where the hell are the drinks?" Dilaver snapped his fingers and everyone seemed to heave a quiet sigh of relief at the sight of their leader relaxing back in his chair. "You're one man here under my protection, Hawk. Never forget that. We don't like or trust Americans here."

"You don't like or trust Albanians, either, but you do business with them," Hawk pointed out.

"Money talks. And it's all business."

"And I'm here to do business, that's all. I have my own monetary concerns, Dragan. I got you home and as soon as I'm done, I'll be out of your hair."

"You know, that's what I like about you—everything is all about you, your work and money. You haven't relaxed once since you helped me get back here. No girls, no drugs, no partying. Don't you want anything else besides finishing your job?"

Dilaver's eyes were curious and challenging. Hawk knew that his refusal to be part of the other man's carousing party had been the topic of discussion several times. Sorry, he didn't like young girls. Reluctant young girls, at that.

"Yeah, I want something," Hawk said softly.

"What, my friend? Anything I can get you?"

"I want to know where the best place is in Macedonia to get a real hamburger."

Caught off guard by his answer, Dilaver stared at Hawk in astonishment. "A . . . what?" Then he laughed. He looked around at his men. "I lost a million dollars and all he thinks of is a hamburger!"

"Not just any hamburger," Hawk replied. "I'm jonesing for the real American thing."

"You're insulting Macedonian food, too?" Dilaver accepted a bottle of beer from one of his men. "What's with some mashed-up meat that looks like a pancake?"

"It's a matter of taste, I guess," Hawk said.

"Yes, like your . . . sexual preferences, I suppose."

Hawk cocked a brow but didn't say anything. He wasn't going to start on *his* distaste of Dilaver's toying with very young girls.

"Either you're a homosexual, like some of my men have suggested, or maybe you just like something different. You're a handsome devil, Hawk. Even some of the girls at the *kafenas* wouldn't mind servicing you. You have even refused my offer of free females and it's been a few months. It's not as if you were shot near the vital parts like I was. A man has needs, you know . . . real men anyway."

Hawk laughed. How ironic that his enemy was echoing his thoughts from the night before. And look what happened when he was busy thinking about his needs. Someone attacked him and . . . he was still pissed that someone got that close to his naked body. He pushed his anger away. He would deal with *that* soon enough.

"No, my *friend*." Hawk emphasized the word so that everyone in the room could hear it. He deliberately added a touch of sarcasm in his voice. "I don't need you to supply me with boys, either. But if any of your men want to try me out, I'd be happy to tear them a new asshole."

Dilaver roared with laughter. For the time being, his rage at the loss of revenue had dissipated. "Must be a new American sport. You come up with the funniest lines." He reverted into heavily accented English. " 'I am happy to tear them a new arsehole.' I must remember this one. What was the other one? 'He sucks' . . . what . . . ?"

"He sucks canal water," Hawk said obligingly.

Dilaver laughed again and repeated the phrase. His amusement and eagerness at collecting catchy clichés would have made him almost likable, if Hawk hadn't known firsthand the ruthlessness behind the façade.

What would his team say if they knew that he spent his days teaching the enemy their favorite insults? He thought of Cucumber, the big SEAL who would have a few choice lines of his own about Dilaver and his kind. And Jazz, his best friend, who would have given Dilaver more than a limp, had he known, at the time Hawk ordered him to shoot, about the punch the bastard had landed on his girlfriend's face. No, none of his SEAL brothers would understand this charade he was playing.

Life as a covert agent, Hawk was discovering, was too damn much skirting around the main issue. He had done some undercover work before. A seller looking for some quick cash. A businessman paying for an informant. Fast drug deals to pinpoint drug routes. Even a robbery in bright daylight once to prevent the sale of a bomb. But those were a cakewalk compared to what he was doing now.

His lips quirked at the term. Cakewalk. Another Americanism he could throw at Dilaver. He must buy a Macedonian book of aphorisms when he got a chance. Sometimes his American phrases didn't translate very well. Not that any of the usual communication problems around here couldn't be solved with a big weapon.

"Actually, there's a good—how you say it—'happening' place right here in Velesta," Dilaver said. "The peacekeepers love to go there, especially the American ones, and they say it's the food. I say it's the owner. She is"—he drew the hourglass outline in the air—"stacked. Just like the Americans like their women. In fact, she's one."

"An American running a restaurant in Velesta?" Hawk doubted that fact.

"Not just a restaurant, my friend. She pays for my protection, just like anybody else."

"How?" Many business owners had to pay so their stores didn't get bombed or robbed by the different gangs. It was all very old-fashioned. "Is she a friend of yours?"

Dilaver shook his head. "No, I think she dislikes me, but she is very polite about it." His laugh wasn't friendly. "But she's very intelligent. She's got my protection so her restaurant gets business, and she's got the head of CIVPOL's protection so I don't get too close."

"I didn't know that you're afraid of CIVPOL," Hawk said casually. He had heard that the new man in charge of the drugs and sex-trafficking department of CIVPOL, the UN international police force, was looking for Dragan Dilaver. This woman's friendship meant she had something over Dilaver that she was threatening to expose if he didn't play nice. Interesting. He liked someone who could hold the Macedonian by his balls.

Dilaver made a rude noise. "Afraid? I'm afraid of no one. And unlike in Asia, I'm the one who speaks the local languages around here. You and that UN puppet are the foreigners. He's like a fly, this new man in town. Not worth my time."

"A bothersome one," one of Dilaver's men chimed in. "I suspect he's behind our trouble, boss. He would like nothing better than to have a showdown with us so he can put us out of business."

Dilaver nodded, a speculative look entering his eyes. "Yes, I suppose when you're new, you want to make some big catch, and . . ." He paused to take a swig from his mug. "I'm the biggest in Macedonia."

"So why not kill him?" Hawk asked, curious about how the other man's mind worked. He had made it a point to study all of Dilaver's moves and motives.

"I would, but the UN has done so much for the Balkans," Dilaver said, with a smile like a satisfied devil. "It'd be ungrateful to start killing their law enforcers when they are all providing such a safe haven for business."

His roar of laughter was joined by the rest in the room, mockery-filled and contemptuous. Hawk didn't join in, but he understood the sentiment, and his heart filled with resigned anger. The Balkan wars had gone on for centuries. In many ways, the recent UN intervention had freed the thugs, arming many of the fighting factions. The Kosovo Liberation Army was one of them, a brutal group of mercenaries that had nothing to do with liberation. Now that they had solidified their power base, the KLA had become the crime syndicate in this part of the world in drugs, sex, and arms trafficking. Dragan Dilaver headed one of its powerful factions.

And he, Hawk McMillan, was in this nest of human trash. He felt dirty among them because, for the first time, he couldn't come to the defense of things he held precious. He had to stand by and watch these scumbags hurt women, children, and helpless people. And his anger had expanded more each day till his own self-control was tested.

He swallowed it in, accepting a mug of beer from one of the men. He waved it at Dilaver. "Maybe you can buy him off?" he asked, affecting a cynical expression.

"No, he's still in the fresh stage . . . has already refused some tactfully worded bribe offers. No, no, this man—his name is Sun—is going to have to learn the hard way. Besides, with him being interested in that restaurant owner, I can keep an eye on him and his activities. Her information has been good so far." Dilaver shrugged. "She keeps him happy and me happy. Very smart businesswoman. I think you'll like this American chick."

"But an American woman alone in Velesta? What do you think of that?"

"Suspicious, I know, but she's still useful. I'm sure you've already found out that everyone around here has hidden motives, Hawk." Dilaver's eyes narrowed. His lips curled into a sneer. "She's been here for four or five years, building her little café restaurant into quite a gathering spot for the UN peacekeepers. I guess, like you, they all want real hamburgers."

"What's her name?" Hawk asked. How odd—to have thought of hamburgers and now his wish was granted.

"Amber Hutchens. The restaurant's called The Last Resort."

The woman on the other end of the line sounded professional and pleasant. *"Hallo, dobar dan."*

"Dobar dan. Jeste li dobili moje pismo?" Hawk asked the question to signal the request to speak to Jed. He had been instructed to dial this number the moment the source established contact. To ask whether the person received his letter was a clue for Jed.

"Kada ste poslali pismo?"

"The letter was sent late," Hawk replied in Serbian. Late. In the dark. Tied to his—

"Are you positive it's the right communication?"

"Oh, quite," he said, barely keeping the sarcasm out of his voice. The *communication* was very obvious.

"Please hold."

He knew they were making sure his line was secure before putting Jed through. The man was an enigma—the last time he'd called this number, the woman had spoken Vietnamese. And the time before that, Jed had picked up on the first ring.

The woman came back on the line. "I'm sorry, but the letter isn't here. You must have sent it to the wrong address."

The line went dead.

"Shit." Amber immediately turned off her laptop.

"Got caught, huh?" Her back against the wall, Llallana crossed her arms. "Can they trace back to us?"

Amber shook her head. "Don't think so."

"How do you think they know about the chip you put in our American boy's cell phone?"

"It was a gamble," Amber admitted. "Jed McNeil has some of the most advanced tech toys on his side. But as tests go, we're getting plenty of answers."

Llallana cocked her head, her eyes thoughtful. "They sure were being very careful. Coded conversation. Tracer satellite signals."

"Not to mention an intermediary. That woman who answered him wasn't just some secretary. She was probably at a different location with her own satellite tracer just in case someone was trying to locate Jed's current position." Amber reactivated her laptop. "So even if he's been compromised, no one would have found him."

"But now he knows someone has bugged their man's phone. Now what?"

"He'll know it's us," Amber replied dryly. There was very little that escaped Jed.

"No, everything points to you, my dear," Llallana retorted. Straightening from the wall, she sauntered to the door. "Can't say I didn't warn you. You're the one who wanted to test the guy."

Amber swung her chair around, watching her friend as she headed for the door. Lily was in a strange mood. She had been reluctant about this particular operation since Amber hatched the idea of testing the new man in town. "So you just want me to help him and then what? What do I get for my generosity?"

Llallana stopped and turned back, combing her hands through her short jet-black hair as she stared at the computer screen for a few seconds. Amber let the silence draw out. Something was definitely troubling her friend.

"It's up to you," she finally said. "Why do you want to help this man out?"

"It's Jed's man," Amber explained. "Jed did me a favor and I owe him one. Besides, I'm curious . . . what's the hot stuff this time that is so damn secured?"

"Hot stuff" was their code for a wanted item, be it goods or information. It was their way to finance their own personal operation. The non-CIA-sanctioned one, that is.

Amusement entered Lily's dark eyes. "Are you sure it isn't because you saw this man's hot stuff?" Her voice was teasing. "You practically felt the entire package."

Amber felt her cheeks heating up. She was never going to live that down. "I don't need that kind of hot stuff."

"Oh yeah, I forget. Your love life's so full. How's Mr. Sun?" There was a studied casualness in Llallana's voice.

Amber raised an eyebrow. Bradford Sun, a powerful man working for the UN peacekeeping department, was a friend, nothing more. But sometimes it helped to let the local thugs think she and the tall striking man had a closer relationship.

"Brad's fine. Busy as always. Anything else you want to know?" She studied Lily closely, but her friend was very good at hiding her true feelings. "You can join us for a late dinner tonight if you like."

Llallana shook her head. "I'm busy."

"Uh-huh. Why do I get the feeling you're avoiding Brad?"

Llallana gave her a bland look. "Me? Let me get the facts right. I just came into town, remember? You called to tell me about the new CIA guy."

"I also called to tell you that Brad has found a few more girls in need of help," Amber reminded her soberly. "You have to find time to talk to him about them."

Without warning, Llallana swung around again and headed for the doorway. "Get some info for me at your dinner tonight if I don't show up, Amber," she called over her shoulder.

Amber settled back in her office chair, biting her lower lip thoughtfully. Llallana steadfastly avoided Brad. If she didn't know her friend, she would think Lily was afraid.

Hawk frowned. That had never happened before. Being cut off so abruptly could only mean one thing. He had been compromised—someone was tapping into his conversation with Jed's personnel. Dilaver? He dismissed the suspicion.

No, it had to be last night's assailant, of course. Leaving that note was just a distraction. The real intent had been to tap his phone. Hawk looked down at the small cell phone in his hand. Radio frequencies were easy to capture, but his had a built-in voice modulator that automatically changed frequencies to avoid being captured on radio. To trace calls from his cell, one would need a microchip specifically made to send wireless frequencies to a satellite source that would then send the signals back to the motherboard. Not an easy thing for the layperson, which meant his attacker from last night was not only good at martial arts but at electronics and, no doubt, computer programming.

Hawk unscrewed the top of the antenna, pulling it out of the phone. He inspected it closely for a minute and slowly, with thumb and forefinger, lifted a sliver of hairlike material attached to it. Some kind of fiber optics. His lips quirked, part of him filled with astonished admiration. That was one small delivery guy. Where would the tracer chip be hiding?

Carefully laying the sliver onto a piece of white paper, he returned his attention to the cell phone, flipping it open and closing it, trying to figure out what was done to it. For the tracer chip to copy and relate the dialed numbers to the thief-antenna, it would need to use energy for power. Stored memory. Of course, the battery.

He turned the phone over and pressed on the release button to the backing. Pulling out the battery, he found another, longer sliver of fiber optic, following it to the SIMM chip which stored the information for his phone. They had his number now, of course, and perhaps the number he had dialed. He wasn't sure whether Jed had pulled the plug quickly enough to escape being traced.

Hawk cursed softly. His fault. He had let his guard down somehow and could have put Jed in danger.

He had been in Macedonia for a few months and hadn't been challenged mentally or physically quite this cleverly till now. Being a friend of the top gangster had given him a measure of freedom that few foreigners here had—he had gone in and out of places that would have gotten other people into trouble with local KLA members.

This was his first visit to Velesta and he had been warned, even by Dilaver, to be on his guard. And look what had already happened on his first night here. Not only was he attacked at night, in his own bedroom, but he'd been assaulted and compromised. He thought of the note in his pants pocket. Sexually assaulted, he corrected grimly. He was damn lucky it wasn't more than a note tied to his dick. Except that it was.

Fuck. Disgusted at his own carelessness, Hawk stared at the pieces of fiber optics, barely visible against the whiteness of the paper, weighing his options. He could get to Jed from another phone; that wasn't his immediate problem. What he really wanted to do was get out of Dilaver's crowd for a day and track down this *problem* and exact revenge. Hell, he was alone in Macedonia. He didn't have to follow team protocol and wait for instructions for every move.

What happened last night made it downright personal. Hawk pinched his chin thoughtfully. He was looking forward to making it even more so.

3

Bradford Sun unclipped his official badge as he exited the UN security offices. He walked at a quick pace, unruffled by the knowing side glances and questioning looks from those outside the meeting who had heard the muffled but obviously heated exchange of words between the head of CIVPOL's Trafficking and Prostitution Investigation Unit, the operations chief of CIVPOL's Terrorist Unit, the general accountant of CIVPOL UN funds, and various other department heads.

"Too many damn heads," muttered Brad. *Speaking too many damn languages,* he silently added. The trouble with assigning personnel from different countries to be in one department was that there was no way to achieve the world peace the United Nations hoped for. Too many different opinions, too many ideological motives. Everyone was still working their own agenda to move up the diplomatic rung of their government. After all, no one wanted to be stuck in Macedonia. Not his predecessor, for sure.

His lips twisted wryly as he punched the elevator button for the garage level. He was the new head of the drug- and sex-trafficking department and technically held quite a bit of power. But he was also considered the new boy in town, and had to be "shown the way." Words like "protocol" and "procedure" had the same meaning in English, French, and German. He spoke all three languages like a native, and he knew meaningless shit when he heard it.

He gave a short bark of laughter. Meaningless shit indeed. Four hours of debating whether to take down the biggest piece of human garbage in town, and his hands were tied because three out of five votes were against him. All he needed was one more person on his side, and he'd thought he would get Cezare's, but something had happened between the meeting and the last time they'd talked at his office. Something had frightened the man badly.

Brad sighed. Probably a threat. Everyone was living under a threat of some kind in these parts. The man he himself replaced had survived two car bombs during his tenure.

The elevator doors opened and he stepped into the underground garage, half filled with cars. Out of habit, he looked around, checking for signs of trouble. One couldn't be too careful, especially in this war-torn climate.

The vote against action forced his hand. He wasn't going to sit back and let those animals continue any longer. He was going to call the newspaper reporter first thing tomorrow morning and give that interview. It would be interesting to see what happened after that.

He strode toward the section where his car was parked. He needed some food and drink. Having missed lunch today, he was hungrier than usual, and a few glasses of wine sounded like heaven right now. Good conversation, with classical music playing in the background, a friend and confidante he could trust—all very rare things in Velesta. He smiled for the first time that day as he climbed into his vehicle. He knew where to find good company and excellent food.

Once he passed the security booth, he activated his car

phone's remote dial, which allowed him to speak hands-free while he negotiated his way around the notoriously fast traffic in town. The evening sun was almost gone, and he turned the heater on higher.

"Hi, Brad." Amber Hutchens's voice was smooth and low.

"I'm thinking of dropping by earlier, if that's all right with you," he said.

"No problem. Hungry?"

"I haven't eaten," he confessed.

She laughed. "Sometimes I think you just come here for the free meals," she teased.

"And the company," Brad said with a smile. "There's no lovelier lady in town."

"Ah, a compliment. Definitely looking for a big meal."

That was what was attractive about Amber Hutchens. She could put anyone at ease with a few teasing words. He'd seen her doing it with the peacekeepers who went to her café for her home cooking. Most of them were men who led stressful lives, trying to be policemen when they were soldiers, tiptoeing the gray line between law and lawlessness, and the small café right in the middle of town was like a haven, giving them a quick break while its owner cajoled them back into good humor.

"Do you need me to bring anything?" he asked.

There was a slight pause. "Flowers would be nice." He could hear the smile in her voice. "The café was busy today, so I can afford a free meal."

She was also a very smart woman, Brad mused. No other café was more fiercely guarded by the foreigners here. The local gangsters knew if they messed with Amber Hutchens, they would have several dozen peacekeepers messing with their illegal businesses that had been previously overlooked. Thus, the safest place to hide in town was a coffeehouse appropriately named The Last Resort.

"I'll be there soon," he said, "with flowers."

"Looking forward to it."

Picking up fresh flowers at this late hour wasn't an easy task and he had a feeling that Amber knew this. He wondered what she was actually doing when he called. The woman wasn't always cooking; that was just a façade. Amber's thing was information—hot, up-to-the-minute information—that she used to finance her side business.

Brad rubbed the back of his neck. Gray line between law and lawlessness—he straddled it himself. He was aware that he was a source of information for Amber, that her easy questions were more than general interest in his job. His answers were carefully crafted, but he also knew that he had given her many clues, sometimes unwittingly. Her skill had raised his suspicion. He had checked with some of his sources and had found out she was a CIA contractor. A CIA contractor in Macedonia in the guise of a café owner, to be exact. For four years.

He had only been at his job as department head for barely a year. He knew he had quite a bit to learn, even though he was given a big file to study by both his predecessor and the UN source. But the file never mentioned Amber Hutchens or the operation she was running. He had only found out because he followed his own instincts, and when he had confronted her with it a few months ago, much to his surprise, she hadn't denied it. And now that he knew what she did, he approved. He sighed. Sort of.

Which brought up the subject of Llallana Noretski. Of which he didn't approve. The woman was trouble, what with her criminal record and . . . the way he always responded to her whenever she was present. She was Amber's close friend and partner-in-crime. From what he could gather, she did all the dirty work while Amber got together the information and packaged the jobs.

The woman didn't trust him. From the first moment they had been introduced, she had been alternately rude, sarcastic, and aloof. He understood the reason—she was a criminal and he was the law. They would always be on the opposite sides.

Brad released another frustrated sigh. This was Velesta, damn it. Opposite sides were a joke. Everything merged into a grayness that bothered his belief in what was right and wrong. That was why it was essential to step up and do something with the rampant drugs and prostitution going on. He was determined to draw a line somewhere. His jaw set at the memory of some of the *kafenas* he had raided. Girls under sixteen enslaved by drugs and force. He wasn't going to let fucking red tape stop him from saving those kids.

He swung into the parking spot in front of the florist, taking a moment before getting out of the car. Every time he thought of the scenes he had witnessed at those darkened *kafenas,* a raging anger took over that made him want to bash someone's face in. Especially anyone working under that scum Dragan Dilaver.

With limited help from his own department, Brad needed all the allies and help he could get. That's where Amber and Llallana came in. They might be playing both sides of the legal line, but they both detested Dilaver, providing Brad with needed information to get the man where it hurt him most— his bank account.

The cold air outside calmed him down somewhat. Flowers. He'd take his time choosing a nice bouquet and let Amber finish whatever she was doing. Maybe she would have some valuable information about the next Dilaver truckload of kidnapped victims coming in. It would make his week to squeeze the bastard just a little harder.

* * *

Hawk replaced the back panel of his cell phone. One thing he had learned from Jed about wireless connections—how to convert a laptop into a hacking device of those tapping into the same airwaves. Someone had hacked into his phone line, stealing his directory. They were still connected through that tiny device planted in his cell, so all he needed were a few adjustments. He wasn't a computer nerd, but he'd learned a thing or two from Jed's people. His laptop, unremarkable-looking, was no standard notebook. He punched in the code and password to access the shadow hard drive, the one with the programs he needed for his task. It was going to take some time and he didn't want any interruptions.

He locked the door to his bedroom, then picked up the old black telephone next to his bed. It was one of those rotary-dial ones from another era, the numbers on its face faded from use.

"This is Hawk. Where's Dilaver?" His lips quirked. "Furniture-shopping? How long will he be gone? Let me know when he's back, please. I'll be working out."

That should make them think he was doing his usual exercises. He had been very careful about explaining his tip-top shape, citing an interest in weight-lifting and body-training. He had exercised in different ways every week to get them used to his unusual program.

"I'm a guide," he had told Dilaver with a shrug. "Being in shape comes with the job."

"Don't smoke, don't have sex, what a boring fucker you are," Dilaver had said. "What do you do for fun—pose naked in front of a mirror and admire yourself?"

Hawk had nodded gravely. "Yes."

That had given Hawk the distraction he needed as the conversation moved on to more lewd topics.

Hawk remote-connected his cell phone to his laptop, making it easier to type text. Then he carefully screened off all the other programs behind a firewall. He unfolded the note from last night and read it again. It was written in English.

Looking for something?

Three words with a wealth of meaning. One, he needed all the locations where Dilaver hid his weapons. Two, he had to find out the latest delivered cache. Three, he had to find a specific weapon in the collection. And yeah, four, he was looking for the person who hung this note on his dick—the CIA tracker Jed had told him about.

It was just like Jed not to mention the sex of the CIA contractor working undercover. All he had said was that the contact would be in Velesta and that Hawk was not to make a move until Dilaver went there. Not that working with a woman bothered Hawk. Some of the women he admired had been very capable covert agents. In fact, now that he thought about it, he wondered whether this woman was another GEM operative.

His eyes narrowed. But of course. Hell, why hadn't he thought of that earlier? The American woman who ran a café. Jed had told him the password between him and the contractor was *ambrosia. Amber Hutchens . . . ambrosia.*

His instincts told him he had just hit the right conclusion. All he had to do was prove it to himself. He got up and picked up the black telephone again.

"What's the phone number to The Last Resort?" he asked.

Amber stared at her computer screen. Sending Brad to pick flowers at this hour should buy her some time. She needed it. Someone had called on her business phone just before he had reached her on the private line.

"Ambrosia," a masculine voice had said over the phone. "Check your computer."

He had hung up before she had recovered from her shock.

That had to be—and Brad had interrupted with his call about dinner. She was dying to get back to her laptop and when Brad gave her an opening for some time, she had quickly thought of a way to delay him. She knew he would get the hint.

Brad and she had a very pleasant relationship, and their dinner dates were like a public stance and a private friendship both at the same time. She had cultivated this from the start and had been surprised by his silent agreement, even when he had found out what she was. They had an understanding—he didn't ask her how she got her information, and in return she would give him some data that he might find useful.

Right now, though, it was another new person in town on her mind. He had found her in record time, way faster than any of the previous agents sent here.

She sat back at her desk and considered briefly, then shrugged. Why not? If he was that good, she would reward him. She reached out and turned her laptop on. Her tracer beeped, indicating that one of her tapped lines was active. She didn't have to check to know it was Hawk McMillan's cell phone. He had just called his online service. That meant he was using his computer with his phone.

Oh, trying to trace her, was he? She smiled. It wasn't that easy to bypass her firewalls. Intrigued, she typed a few commands, bringing up a window to show what he was doing. From the size, he appeared to be downloading a rather large file over the net back to his laptop. Whatever it was, she could get it, since he was using his cell phone as connection. Since he already knew she was watching, she suspected that he wanted her to zap it.

Her finger hovered over the command to pull the file. She had ample protection and safeguards from hackers who might try to infect her system. But he wasn't hacking into her system; he was luring her into his. That was just too much for her to resist. She clicked on the command key, then sat back to watch as her computer pulled in the program he was using.

Amber laughed in disbelief.

The man had connected with some sort of instant messenger and was . . . typing a note to himself—okay, really, to *her,* if she cared to reply, now that she had loaded the damn program into her network.

Hi Ambrosia. Found your note. Found you.

Oh, this was just too hard to resist. *Good to know you checked yourself. You couldn't have possibly missed my note, Mr. McMillan.*

I'll have to return the favor sometime, Miss Hutchens.

A shiver ran through her. She had a feeling Hawk McMillan hadn't liked being the victim last night. *You were careless. I was merely pointing out the dangers of being caught off guard. You want my help, you'd better be a lot more alert.*

Was I not alert enough for you last night?

Amber rested her chin on her hand. Not only smart, but a smart-ass. Of course he knew she felt his . . . She shook her head. He was doing that on purpose, putting that image back in her head. *Listen, hot stuff, I don't have time to play.*

Pity.

She admired his typing speed. *You get the coordinates and maybe we'll talk.*

Our first meeting won't be about talking. It'll be about making a point.

Threats won't make me cooperative. Remember you need my help, Mr. McMillan.

You tried to compromise me today. That's not help.

It would have been nice if she had succeeded. That kind of information would be very valuable, especially if she had found out what Jed and his team wanted so badly from

Dilaver. Or even to find out where Jed was . . . now, wouldn't that be a coup?

Jed McNeil would understand it's my job to test you. It was a half-truth. She needed to know how good this new man was before she would jeopardize her operation again.

My turn next. Signing out.

Wait! What do you mean?

Better not walk around naked at night, Miss Hutchens. Hot Stuff may bump into you. Signing out.

The window closed automatically on its own. Amber cursed out loud. For the second time in half an hour, the man had left her hanging, more intrigued than ever. Hot Stuff indeed. He had used her own code word to refer back to himself. Hawk McMillan had a big head. And was one very smart operative. He had cleverly gotten her to talk to him without even wasting any time trying to find open port holes in her system. All he had needed was her cooperation—to go into his system to see what he was doing and to reply to his baiting. It was a long enough conversation for him to trace her if he wanted to, but he already knew who she was and her business phone, so what was he doing while he was distracting her?

Damn it. She wished she had the evening off so she could play with this new program she had downloaded. But Brad was on the way and she had other business to attend to. She eyed the computer screen suspiciously, half expecting something else to happen, but the window didn't reappear.

She would have to tell Lily about this. It was clear she had underestimated this Hawk McMillan.

Hawk snapped his laptop shut. That didn't take long—Miss Amber Hutchens took the bait quickly enough. He had wondered whether she would, but evidently she was very confident about her computer firewalls.

He gathered that she was somewhat of a gambler anyhow. Anyone who did what she had done last night, taking the risk of being caught by Dragan Dilaver's men just to hang a message on him, had to have a wild side. Since he enjoyed living on the edge himself, he appreciated the woman's daredevilry. However, he didn't like knowing she had knocked him out with drugs, that it could have been something more serious.

She had a point. His attention couldn't slack. It could cost him his life.

He was also intrigued by Amber Hutchens's front. A café owner. Who would see her as some kind of tracker? And from what Dilaver had said, she sold information to get his protection. So whose side was she on?

When she had answered the phone earlier, her voice had had the oddest effect on him. Smooth and soft, it slid against his skin like silk. So this was the voice belonging to the woman who'd touched him. He had hated not having an image for a target. Now he had a voice. And he wondered whether she looked as delicious as she sounded.

Hawk made an impatient sound. His mind was wandering into territory that had gotten him into trouble again. Fuck! The curse brought a reluctant wry smile on his lips. Exactly. Months of clogged sperm. He was going to get himself killed if even a sexy voice was making him horny.

She was probably big as a house. Nope, he had fought with her last night. Okay, now he had a voice and a body. He closed his eyes, going through the events of last night, bringing up the fight in slow motion, from the moment his mystery assailant had attacked him till the last point of consciousness when he had tried to snap her neck.

Details came flooding back. She wasn't very tall; he had towered over her. She had a very strong grip and, remembering the way she held the needle, she was right-handed. He smiled again. And yeah, she had very strong thighs, too. He suddenly recalled, just before falling over, he'd thought the "man" wiry and . . . his hand had gone for the neck . . . brushing up against . . . Hawk sat up. He had touched her breast during that struggle and she had squirmed. That was when she'd decided to use that damn hypodermic needle, because she'd realized that he would discover the truth.

A fierce satisfaction came over him. She had been in trouble herself. Good. He hadn't liked thinking about how in control she had been, with this plan of tying that note in such an insulting way. That meditation training was damn good—his mind was pulling sensory details out of his unconscious that he didn't even know he had.

Hawk was definitely looking forward to exacting some kind of revenge now. It would be interesting to see how good an operative Miss Amber Hutchens was.

He spent the next few minutes removing the tracking devices from his cell phone. Then he called Jed's number again, going through the coded conversation with the woman on the other side. This time there was no sudden disconnection.

"This is Jed."

The Asians called Jed McNeil Ghost Lightning, a weather phenomena that the superstitious feared. Hawk had heard of other monikers given to the man who had trained him on and off the last half a year.

His current undercover assignment started in Asia a few months ago. He had to leave his SEAL team to work for "Stefan." Even though the other man never brought it up, Hawk suspected Jed had picked that name as a private joke in reference to Hawk's family's odd penchant to give all the sons the same name. Every one of Hawk's male relatives, including his father, was Steve, or Steven, or Stephan, or one of the other derivatives. He had learned quickly that

there wasn't much Jed McNeil didn't know about those
around him.

His commander, Admiral Madison, had sent him to Jed's
outfit when he'd found out Hawk could speak Asian languages. He could work side by side with the elusive man and
observe him.

"I want to know more about those COS commandos,"
he'd told Hawk, referring to Jed's shadowy unit. "This next
mission's a good way to find out."

So far Hawk hadn't found out too much. The COS commandos weren't exactly a group of guys one saw together
often.

"Sorry about the last call," Hawk said.

"We expected it, hence the safeguards."

"I know who it is now," Hawk said. "Why didn't you just
tell me?"

"You have to draw your own conclusions about the person
with whom you're going to work, Hawk. How did you like
her methods?"

Sneaky. Unpredictable. "Are you saying I can't trust her?"

There was a pause. "You can never trust an operative
who's been out there for that length of time," Jed said, "although Amber Hutchens has been a very useful asset to the
CIA."

"She sells information to Dilaver—how's that useful?
She's probably responsible for some of the leaks. In fact, she
might be in league with the D.C. rat's nest that's been betraying us." To find all those responsible for selling information to the enemy was one of Admiral Madison's goals. Too
many of their military brothers had been compromised by
those traitors. "Is there no other guide?"

"She's the most qualified, having been over there for four
years, Hawk. She knows that area very well or I wouldn't

use her as an asset. As for the matter of trust . . ." Jed paused, as if choosing his next words. "Her ratio for providing the truth runs about seventy percent, and that's in her dealings with me. So you can expect less than that toward you."

"That sounds encouraging," Hawk said wryly. That was one thing he had noticed about these GEM and COSCO operatives. They tended to talk in ratios and percentages, assets and losses. "So why do you think she tapped my line?"

"How did she do that in the first place? Did you meet her personally already?"

Hawk scowled. He knew Jed would want to know what happened. It wasn't easy admitting that he'd managed to be drugged. He briefly outlined the events from the night before—the fight, the needle, his few hours on the floor. His SEAL team commander, Admiral Madison, wouldn't be pleased that one of his men had been taken down so easily.

"Now you know what kind of woman you're dealing with," Jed said quietly. There wasn't any hint of humor or anger in his voice. "Amber Hutchens is a very careful woman. She was probably testing you because the last operative the CIA sent over nearly blew her cover. She's also a contract agent, not necessarily a hundred percent loyal to one agency. From her viewpoint, information is valuable and it doesn't hurt to get it in any way possible. And if you're a weak link, she made her point if she'd succeeded in tapping your phone and finding out information and about my whereabouts. It looks like she might not cooperate."

"I'll take care of her test," Hawk said. "I'll convince her I'm capable."

"How?"

"By doing something that'll catch her attention. She's into information and testing. I'll take her on her challenge and then some."

"Interesting. It's always good to show that you can do the same thing she did to you," Jed suggested. "It might gain her respect."

Hawk hadn't given the full details of where Miss Hutchens had left her message. He doubted any of his intentions would get that result. In fact, he was getting pissed off at being put on the defensive; this wasn't a usual position for him and it didn't sit comfortably.

"I intend to get to know how she works," Hawk said. "I don't care about her respect. I do need her constant cooperation, though, if she's to be my guide. I can't have an operative testing my decisions every step of the way."

"You have limited time to get acquainted with Amber while you find the locations of Dilaver's weapon silos," Jed said. "Any headway on that?"

"Dilaver has been recovering from his wound, so he's been using his cell phone a lot. But he's doing a rundown of some sort now and as a side note, there's trouble brewing in his business. Velesta is supposed to be one stop of many. I'm slowly getting the feel of his holdings and operation procedures." Hawk paused, then added softly, "His sex-slave operation's very big."

"That part of his business is his credit card. Your goal, lieutenant, is to look for the hidden weapons, especially the most recent ones that were dropped off while Dilaver was in Asia. I know he's human trash, but it isn't your job to take care of him that way."

"I know that, McNeil," Hawk said, "but I also want you to know that if I weren't doing this as part of a joint mission between your agency and my team, Dilaver would be put out of commission. I have seen enough."

Too damn much, in fact. The images of the locked-up young girls at the *kafenas* were starting to haunt his nights.

"Madison said you're one of his best men. Tell me now whether you can do this, that you won't let other things interfere with the main mission. We can't afford any misstep here," Jed said, his voice calm and assessing over the phone. "You must gain Dilaver's trust, and that means getting your hands dirty. The admiral told me you could do this."

Hawk had to give Jed credit. Bringing up his commander was good. As a SEAL, it was ingrained in him to handle anything to get the job done. Physically, he had barely any challenge—guiding the injured Dilaver and his men out of a particularly hostile Asian mountainous terrain was child's play. Mentally, he had been taught to block pain and emotion when he was in the war theater, but watching women and young girls victimized had been—he hated to admit it, even to himself—very, very tough.

"McMillan."

He realized Jed had been waiting for some kind of reply, and it had better be convincing or he'd be pulled off the job. "I have been doing it," he said crisply. "Dilaver's now going to different cities and I'm mapping out the routes. I'll find out more very soon."

"Good. I'll wait for your communication. And Hawk . . ." Jed waited a beat to get his attention. "Don't underestimate Amber. This business of ours isn't black and white. You either learn to function within a gray area or be killed."

Hawk looked thoughtfully at the cell phone after Jed rang off. As usual, he had more questions after talking to Jed. Why had Amber Hutchens been placed here for four years in the first place? And exactly what information did she sell to Dilaver? What did she get in return?

The more he learned about the lady, the more intrigued he was. Underestimate her? He hadn't been given the chance. But she had shown her disdain for him by initiating this pissing contest, introducing herself with a . . . memorable and naughty handshake.

He pocketed the phone. Gray ethics, huh? He could only misbehave in return.

Brad frowned. She was here. Amber hadn't mentioned it— would she be joining them for dinner? It had been almost six weeks since she had gone off on one of her "trips."

He stepped out of his car and locked it, his eyes trained on the little European car parked two cars down. He wasn't going to let her leave this time without first talking with him. The problem was, Llallana Noretski wasn't an easy person to corner.

The Last Resort was a small café, decorated like an American diner, with out-of-the-way things like a scarecrow sitting on a rocking chair in one corner and pictures of American movie stars and NASCAR drivers on the walls. Things from home for homesick young American peacekeepers. Even the tablecloths looked homey, with their cheerful prints of Americana.

As usual, it was bustling with activity, filled with hungry men looking for home cooking. They all recognized him, of course, and he nodded to those who made eye contact. Unlike the previous department head, he hadn't gone out partying and thus was getting to know some of these men casually. He didn't like some of the entertainment the men had gone for, and one of these days he would address *that* problem, too.

"Those are beautiful flowers, Brad," Amber said as she walked toward him.

And as usual, all male eyes followed the owner of the café. Amber Hutchens wasn't just attractive; she was strikingly beautiful, of the All-American blond and blue-eyed variety. She had pulled her shoulder-length hair into a chignon, showing off the gold loops in her ears. The smile she gave him lit up her eyes.

"I spent a fortune," he told her, as she kissed the corner of his mouth.

"Then I'd better make sure dessert's richer than usual," she said.

He smiled back and followed her to his table in the back. It was screened off from the rest of the dining area, sometimes used for private parties. It also reinforced the assumption that Bradford Sun was more than just a client to Amber Hutchens, especially when he would disappear through the door marked *"Privat"* later for what he knew others thought was more intimate time.

Amber was a superb hostess. She steered clear of politics during dinner, amusing him with anecdotes of peacekeepers' gossip. She was also a good listener, letting him bring up various topics that interested both of them—the new opera in town, the book he was currently reading, the big wedding of a mutual friend. There was not one mention of the latest bombing victim just a few streets from the café. Or the news of the restaurant downtown that had to shut down because the owner had mysteriously disappeared. Or the scandal about a number of peacekeepers caught literally with their pants down in a *kafena*.

They retired into the back room for drinks and dessert. Brad settled back in the sofa comfortably, sipping his wine, as he watched Amber bring in a covered dish.

"Did you hear that the younger prince of Modevia gave up his eligibility to be second in line so he could marry his civilian sweetheart?" Amber asked, as she served him a piece of cheesecake.

"I read it in the paper," Brad said, taking a bite of the dessert. It was strawberry cheesecake. "This is simply delicious, Amber."

"Have another piece." She smiled. "Take some home."

"Thanks. That would be . . ." Brad put down his fork. "Hello, Llallana."

Llallana Noretski was slim and tall, her dark coloring a direct contrast to her girlfriend's. She was dressed in a pantsuit, with swirling patterns that reminded him of a bright sunset. She walked slowly into the room, carefully studying everything around her. Brad knew from past observation that she never moved her head but her dark eyes were constantly darting, taking in every little thing. They were large, fanned by long eyelashes that she sometimes peered under, especially when she was pretending not to look at him.

"Hope I'm not interrupting dinner or anything," she said, without returning Brad's greeting. She sat down across on the adjacent sofa seat. "But I heard you wanted to see me?"

Brad had casually asked Amber a few weeks ago when Llallana was coming back into town, using business as an excuse. It was frustrating he couldn't bring up what she was doing because he didn't want to know. He didn't want to have any knowledge of any illegal activities. Yet, he couldn't help but wonder. The woman sitting nearby seemed incapable of doing anything illegal other than attending the art soirees in Europe to bid for her clients.

Fine, she didn't want niceties. "How did the last trip go?" he asked.

Llallana shrugged. "Didn't Amber tell you that it went fine? If there was anything wrong, I'm sure she'd have informed you."

Amber had silently retreated to a corner of the sofa. Brad suspected she was hiding a smile behind the cup of coffee. Unlike with her, he was always sparring with Llallana Noretski.

"I just wanted more details," he said.

"I thought you said before that you didn't want *any* details," Llallana retorted. "Didn't he, Amber?"

"I think Brad meant that certain things, like how you secured the passports and whom you talked to, are off-limits," Amber said smoothly. "He's interested in where the girls are and how they'll fend for themselves in their new homes, Lily."

"Is that right, Brad?" Llallana asked, her brows arching sardonically. "As long as your hands are clean, hmm?"

"We're on the same side on this," Brad said softly. "You know I want to help those girls as much as you do."

"And you've been helping," Amber assured him.

"Then why doesn't he take scum like Dilaver off the street?" demanded Llallana, her eyes blazing with sudden fire. "You have the power, don't you, Brad? Or are you just a puppet?"

He wasn't going to discuss UN protocol with her. She wouldn't understand how his hands were tied by votes and red tape. He put down his glass of wine. "We all have a job to do, although you seem to have more freedom than me because of your . . . shortcuts."

He watched as Llallana straightened her shoulders. Well, it wasn't his fault—she attacked him first.

"My shortcuts save lives," she told him.

"You're dealing with gray people and breaking international laws," he reminded her.

"I get my job done. Do you?"

Ouch. "I'm doing the best I can."

"And yet, supposedly, you have all avenues at your disposal." Llallana tilted her head. "Capture Dilaver. He's in town. What's so tough about that?"

"He's KLA."

"Oh yes, UN-sanctioned 'good' guys." Llallana laughed. "You can get around that."

"Break the laws I uphold?" Brad narrowed his eyes. "And what would that make me? There are consequences each time I compromise."

"Oh yes, it might affect your way up the diplomatic chain of command," she said, a cynical smile lifting the corners of her lips. "Who would want to stay here in this hellhole?"

Before he could reply, Amber interrupted. "Now, Lily, be fair. He's helping as much as he can, especially now that he's found out what we do," she said, leaning forward to pour more wine into the glasses, her eyes catching Brad's.

As always, he wondered about the two women's relationship, both of whom seemed to contrast so in style and manner. One was calm and assessing and the other bothered the shit out of him. Yet, he'd caught them laughing in the kitchen before, giggling like females sometimes did when they were talking naughty stuff. Maybe he just hadn't tried hard enough with Llallana. Hell, how could he be friendly with a woman who corrected him each time he called her Lily? He wasn't a *friend*. Fine. He'd stopped after the first few times.

"That's because you're contracting with the CIA and he feels obligated."

"Is that what you think?" Brad asked, curious. She wasn't wrong, but she was also assuming that he approved of the CIA. Llallana shrugged, as if the answer were obvious. He had a feeling that there was more to this than surface accusations. "Tell me how they've hurt you, Llallana."

Bingo. Something flared up in those beautiful eyes for a moment, then she dipped her head to study her fingernails. She gave him that sideways glance that always managed to hide her thoughts. "Getting melodramatic, aren't we? Now, what is it about the girls you wanted to know again? Where are they? Out of this country. How are they? Better than before. Those too afraid to go home have enough money to survive for a while. Will they get better care?" She paused. "I don't know. I hope so. Some of them are in bad shape, as you know."

Her voice had lost some of its passion, as if she were trying to control her emotions by being businesslike. Brad didn't miss the way her hands clenched and unclenched on her lap.

"When you"—he stopped to find another word for "smuggle"—"move them, don't the authorities question some of those in bad condition? I'd be suspicious if a few girls boarded my plane with bruises and cuts."

Some of them had more than bruises and cuts. And all of them were psychologically damaged.

"I try to give them some downtime, Brad. It isn't easy preparing a girl that age for a journey away from everything she's known. But then, she's already suffered a fate that's beyond anything girls her age should know. I try to prepare them. This is their chance to escape and they know this. There aren't many choices, you know."

"That's why getting them before they're destroyed by the *kafena* thugs was a good strategy," Amber said, then added with a small smile, "and it was Brad's idea."

"That's the information I can easily get without raising too many eyebrows." After all, it was his job to trace the drugs and illegal human trafficking. "And I do know the risks you take to get them to a safe place, Llallana."

He still couldn't believe the woman sitting across from him was also in charge of some team of thugs or mercenaries—she wouldn't tell and, of course, he wasn't going to ask—who literally played highwaymen, pretending to be going after the girls for their own gain. Where did she meet with these men?

"Let's drink to the success of the next road trip, shall

we?" Amber lifted her glass. "Brad has more information, Lily."

Brad picked up his glass and drank to the toast as he broodingly studied Llallana. He wanted to get her alone with him . . . like the last time. Part of him wanted to kiss her again.

4

"That went quite well," Amber said, after loading up the dishwasher. Despite the cool weather outside, she'd opened the kitchen back door that led onto the second-story deck outside. Standing by the entrance, she studied Llallana sitting on the stool outside, smoking a cigarette. A sign of nerves—Lily hardly smoked except when something was bothering her.

"Don't you have other guests downstairs to attend to?"

"That's what the staff is for," Amber replied, "and I usu-ally take the evening off when Brad comes to dinner."

Llallana turned around in the semidarkness. "Sorry to have interrupted your plans."

"Oh, come on, we've been friends for four years, Lily. You don't have to play those games with me. And Brad isn't in-terested in me, and vice versa." Amber took a deep breath. "There was choking tension in the room this evening be-tween the two of you that's new. Mind explaining the source to me?"

"I don't know what you mean." Llallana took a drag of her cigarette, then crushed it into the ashtray. "I didn't feel anything."

"When you guys didn't hit it off when Brad first came on the scene, you told me you didn't like his type. Too strait-laced, or something like that. What changed?"

"I still don't like his type," Llallana flashed.

"Uh-huh," Amber murmured. This thing between her friend and Brad had gotten more and more interesting to watch each meeting. They were antagonistic toward each other from the very beginning, yet there was a subtle hint of sexual attraction. "It's cold out there. I'm going to close the kitchen door now. Coming in?"

"I have my jacket on. In a few, okay?"

"Okay. Don't leave without saying 'bye. I have stuff to talk to you about."

"About what Brad told us?"

Amber shook her head. "We can talk about that tomorrow. There's something else." She wanted to tell her about the call and instant messenger conversation a few hours ago. "It isn't urgent, but it's something interesting."

"All right. I'll be there soon, 'kay?"

"Take your time, sweets. I have a few business chores to finish up first, anyway. It's almost closing time." Amber quietly closed the door. Llallana would confide in her when the time was right.

She turned off the main light, leaving only the twin ones over the oven and kitchen sink, then took a stairway through a side door that led down to her office. The luxury of living upstairs from where one worked was that she didn't need to worry about taking late bus rides or driving a car at night.

She collected the cash box from Katia, one of her wait staff, as she peeked into the kitchen. "Any guests left?"

"Someone walked in really late and I told him the ovens were off already. He went off."

Usually The Last Resort accommodated late customers, but Katia knew that Amber didn't like to be disturbed when the CIVPOL chief was here. On other nights, Amber would take over and let her help go home.

"Thanks, Katia. You and Dru can go now. I'll finish up. See you tomorrow."

"Goodnight."

Amber locked up after they left, turning off lights here and there. She had structured her café hours to suit her needs, keeping it open from ten to two during the day for customers who wanted to buy her cookies and have a quick coffee or tea break from their work. In the evenings she served the ever-popular American dinners that made her café a regular haunt for soldiers and diplomats. Usually she mingled with them, especially those who had been working in the area for a while. She learned a lot of useful information that way. Everyone who was around long enough knew that The Last Resort was the place to buy, sell, or pass on information. And sometimes get some free chocolate cookies, she added with mockery.

It took a while for the setup to work. An American-like café in Velesta was a good front. The CIA had told her that the soldiers were getting restless with their peacekeeping duties and needed something to distract them other than carousing at the girlie bars. It also attracted the locals who were curious about anything foreign. Then there were the *kafena* owners, who came here to make friends with the soldiers, giving them cards for "free" massages and other favors from "their" girls. The CIA liked the idea.

It was in this setting that information flowed like the beer she served. Some she bought, some she passed on to gain favors, and others . . . she gave to Dilaver as a gesture to show she was not one to take sides. By making the café a popular drinking hole for the soldiers, she avoided many of the dangers of running a business in a town owned by various other mercenary gangs. She didn't have to deal with giving protection money as long as she provided all sides with what they needed.

And no one questioned an American woman doing shady business while running a café. This was Velesta. Everyone had a shady background and ran something illegal. It would be suspicious if she had been a regular businesswoman, choosing, of all places, to settle here in this crime city. No, Amber Hutchens fitted right in, and everyone respected her very quiet ways of running an information ring.

CIA-approved information ring, Amber corrected, as she put away the cash in the safe. She looked at the stack of fake passports in there. And non-CIA approved human smuggling ring. She punched in the security codes, turned, and froze at the sight of a fully clothed Hawk McMillan before her.

"How did . . . mmmmph!" A cold cloth covered her mouth and nose.

Hawk was prepared this time. He knew the most likely first reaction was to grab the hand against her mouth, and when Amber did that, he effectively countered it by knocking her off balance with a quick sweep of his foot. Then he lifted her off her feet and trapped her body against the wall with his weight. She jerked up, struggling to loosen her hands, trying to use her legs for leverage.

Hawk pushed in between them, lifting her higher against the wall and pressing down on Amber. Her eyes glared at him, even as he felt her strength leaving her body. She wrapped her legs around his waist.

"I believe we've done this position before," he told her softly as he watched her eyes lose focus and slowly close. He kept the cloth on her mouth for a few more seconds, just in case she was pretending. Her legs slid off him. He loosened his hold and her head rolled forward, resting under his chin.

Sliding his hand down to hold her so he could lower her to the floor, Hawk made contact with bare skin. He suddenly realized that the skirt she had on had ridden up to her waist when she had lifted her legs. He moved his hand down the side of her thigh, felt silky skin and a strap. Following it to the front, he encountered a holster holding a small weapon.

Note to self. The woman was always armed when her legs were open. Hawk's lips quirked. Since the holster was strapped to her left thigh, he supposed she was right-handed. Unless she was ambidextrous. He followed his instincts and checked the other thigh.

"I'll be damned," he murmured. The lady had a small knife holster there. Not a good idea to piss her off. His grin grew wider. Too damn late. He removed the weapons one at a time, looping the knife into the back of his black tool belt and slipping the gun into a side pocket.

He let her down then and pulled the skirt back into place before lifting her over his shoulder. He turned, looking for the door to his left. He had watched her enter the room from there, so it must be a stairway to the upstairs. The waitress had told him the owner lived upstairs and would be down shortly if he cared to wait.

Oh, he was going to wait, but his way. It was easy enough to pretend to go out and then slip down a small corridor when the young woman's attention returned to vacuuming. He was in what looked like an office, and as luck would have it, it was where Amber Hutchens had appeared through the door. Jackpot. That was the access to upstairs.

There was enough lighting from the upper landing for him to climb up without looking for a light switch. It was a narrow space to maneuver a large man carrying an unconscious woman, though, and he had to be careful several times not to bump against the wall and hurt his prisoner. He reached the top, hesitated, then turned to the right. He had barely taken half a dozen steps when the light suddenly switched on. He blinked, and found himself staring at another woman pointing a weapon at him.

She was tall, with short dark hair, and her dark eyes held a cool look in them, telling him that she could use the weapon trained on him if she wanted to. She studied him for a moment.

"Well, if it isn't Hawk McMillan," she finally drawled.

"I gather you know me," he said.

"We have . . . met . . ." she acknowledged with a small smile.

"I see."

"Getting a little revenge?" she asked.

"Sort of. Mind introducing yourself? I kind of like knowing the names of women who have touched me."

"Not yet." Her voice turned serious again. "What exactly are you doing with my friend?"

Hawk patted Amber's bottom and watched the other woman's expression turn to amusement. "Her? Oh, nothing quite as humiliating as what she did to me. Want to watch?"

The smile returned and she slowly lowered her weapon. "Is it anything kinky?" she asked. "She'll hate it if you do anything kinky to her."

Hawk cocked his head. "Lady, she tied a note around my dick. That's not exactly prim and proper."

She shook her head, her smile turning impish. "I didn't see it, but suspected it from the look in her eyes. Ah well. I suppose that revenge of some sort's proper. You did pass her test, after all." She nodded toward Hawk's back. "That's where you want to go. This is the kitchen."

Hawk raised his eyebrows. "You're letting me walk in there with your friend, just like that." This was a very unusual woman. "You trust me not to hurt her."

She shrugged. "I'll just kill you if you do. She'd do the

same for me." She glanced at her watch. "Besides, from what I've heard, you need her to help you in your mission, don't you? You have fifteen minutes, Mr. McMillan. Is that enough time?"

"Plenty." He started to turn around, then added, "You sure you don't want to watch? Shouldn't you be protecting Amber?"

The woman laughed. "Honey, what's life without a little fun? I'm Lily, by the way. And watch that you don't overdo that revenge bit. I'll find you and hurt you before you can hide behind Dilaver's big ass."

Hawk gave her a smile and nodded, then turned toward the room Lily had indicated. He looked around as he walked toward a big bed that looked very comfortable. Spacious, with very few things on the walls. It didn't look anything like the feel-good-Americana décor downstairs. A desk with her laptop. A big love seat in the corner by the window. That was it. No frou-frou pillows on the bed, or hand-crafted throws, or anything that matched the downstairs persona.

He bent down and slid Amber onto the bed. She settled into the feather mattress, her blond hair loosened from its knot, leaving bright wisps against her face and the dark pillow.

Hawk sat on the edge, taking a good look for the first time. She wasn't anything like he'd imagined. He was still surprised at how small she was, although he knew this from the night before. He also knew how strong she was, yet nothing about this woman betrayed that.

She looked refined, with a peaches-and-cream complexion that made him want to touch her face, just to see whether her skin was as silky as it looked. With her mussed-up hair and her mouth slightly open, she reminded him of some sleeping princess.

Oh yeah, and he was just the prince to wake her up. And let's not forget the princess was a well-armed woman with quite a number of skills. Which reminded him. He was here to make a point, not to admire the woman's beauty.

He had never played a game of one-upmanship in quite this way before. He and his best friend, Jazz, were fiercely competitive, and had each done some pretty outrageous stuff to get the other's goat. This time was no different, Hawk told himself. Tit for tat. Even if the opponent was a woman with gorgeous skin.

Hawk gently lifted her skirt. Those legs . . . Without warning, he suddenly had a vision of them wrapped tightly around him while he was naked. The image segued into a more masculine fantasy of him on top of Amber and doing the plunging, instead of the hypodermic needle she had with her.

Damn it! What the hell was wrong with him?

Determinedly, he pulled the skirt higher, until the holsters were in sight. He hesitated for only a second, then reached down to unfasten the first one. His hand spanned around her thigh, his tan from Asia very dark against her paleness. He stared, mesmerized by the contrast, and against his will stroked the soft skin with his thumbs. He wondered whether she was smooth and silky like this all over.

A deep sigh halted his rampant thoughts. Hawk looked up. Amber was still out, but he'd better hurry before her girlfriend outside changed her mind and came in guns ablazing. He unsnapped the holsters one after the other and removed them. Then he took a permanent marker out of his tool belt and gently nudged her onto her side.

If Dilaver was right, Amber Hutchens had a boyfriend anyway. Was he ever going to be pissed off when he saw she'd been marked. He grinned. He actually pitied the poor bastard. This woman was obviously a control freak who would run her man ragged with mind games. He uncapped the marker.

* * *

Lily didn't think Hawk McMillan would really hurt Amber. Embarrass her a bit, maybe. She would respect the man a lot less if he hadn't retaliated in kind for what her friend did to him. Lily worked with a lot of men and considered herself quite good at understanding them.

Most men, she corrected, but she wasn't going to go into that again. She had done enough thinking about *him* out on the deck. And she wasn't going to throw another pity party for herself again tonight.

Life was for living, and she planned to have a good time doing it. She knew Amber could sense her moodiness and she intended to remedy that somehow. She didn't want anyone to think that she was anything but happy. Because life was for living, she repeated. She had seen enough misery to know her lot was way, way better than most women's around these parts, and she would help give some living back to the poor girls as long as she could.

Lily checked her watch. Five more minutes. If he didn't come out by then, she would go in. She wondered what he would do as revenge. Strip Amber? Hmm. How tediously boring. And if he did that, he surely knew he would have a war on his hands and Amber would kill him. No, he already knew that he needed Amber's cooperation, so he wouldn't do something too drastic.

But men were stupid and the last agent they had sent— Lily shrugged—well, that one deserved being caught. Better him than Amber or she, certainly.

She was well aware of the risks both of them were taking, but they had agreed that some of those risks were worth it, as in the case of the girls and children. Somebody had to do something. Why not them? They were in the position to do it, and if they were extremely careful, who would know?

So a CIA boy playing cat-and-mouse games with her good friend didn't bother her conscience. It should. Sometimes she thought she didn't have any feelings left, even about caring for Amber's well-being. She would protect her, even kill for her . . . but she wasn't sure whether it was because that was the thing to do or because she was just programmed that way. She just liked protecting people, she supposed.

Sixty seconds. Not that she was doing a good job protecting Amber at this moment, she admitted with a wry smile. A stranger in the bedroom with her friend. What was she thinking, allowing him fifteen minutes? That was enough time to do a lot.

She started toward the room. She supposed if she blew away another CIA agent, she would be forgiven this time if he happened to be naked and on top of Amber. The door was ajar, so she just pushed it open and walked in with her weapon.

A quick glance told her that Amber was alone. He was gone.

Wow. He was damn good.

Lily looked at her friend again, who was tucked in bed like she had gone there herself. Nothing around to show what McMillan had done. Oh. Amber's weapons were laid out neatly at the foot of the bed. Lily smiled ruefully. Ooops. She knew where those were kept.

That man was in so much trouble. That was good. "Keep distracting her for me," she murmured. "I'd hoped Brad would, but you'll do."

But she wasn't going to *think* about Brad. And what she didn't want him to do with Amber. She couldn't feel anything anymore, remember? No feelings. Not a damn one.

5

"*Dobro.* Call me back when the shipment arrives. I'm counting on you." Dilaver shut his cell phone and turned to Hawk. "Finally, some good news."

Hawk raised his eyebrows questioningly. He was sitting on the new sofa Dilaver had bought last night, his feet resting on the new coffee table. An entire suite of furniture to replace the destroyed one. He wondered how long they would last before they, too, became the victims of their owner's displeasure.

"I tell you, everyone wants a piece of the action, you know? It used to be they respected the different militias in charge and no one would contemplate going after anything that belongs to us, but lately . . ." Dilaver paused, shaking his head in disgust. "They even dare to rob me. In broad daylight! The last few months have been killing me, man, what with the missing shipments. Not enough income and too many damn lazy fuckers to feed, you know? What the hell's this world coming to when even the petty thieves don't respect us?"

Hawk almost laughed aloud. He was sitting with one of the most reviled men in the criminal world and the latter was complaining about his illegal activities like some business-man facing a market downturn. That the piece of action had to do with kidnapped girls being trafficked across borders like so many cattle was sickening enough, but Dilaver talked of them as shipments and income, not registering that these were human lives that he had destroyed. And it was ironic humor that struck Hawk because it didn't seem to occur to Dilaver that he was the biggest robber of all, as he sat there complaining about petty thieves.

"Yes, I've been watching all the bad news happening lately," Hawk said now. Here was his opportunity to plant some ideas. "You've been losing a lot of money since I met you. You need help."

"You think so, huh?" Dilaver eyed him thoughtfully. "You know, I've been thinking about how I could use you."

"You only paid for my guiding you out of Asia," Hawk reminded him. "My boss gave me orders to run my errand and then head on back."

"What if I become your boss? How much does Stefan pay you?" Dilaver asked. "You did a great job protecting me and getting my men and me through the borders with hardly any problems. I'm very impressed by your skills, especially when we were running like hell through the jungle. You trekked well, finding us shelter whenever we needed it, and in the end you got us out of that hellish place in one piece. I think you'll do extremely well here in Macedonia, Hawk."

His skills hadn't been tested much during that adventure. Getting them out of Asia had been made easier when he had been cleared by covert agencies way ahead of him and Dilaver. And now he had gained enough of Dilaver's trust that the latter wanted to hire him.

"I still have my one job to do for Stefan," Hawk said. "Meanwhile, I'll think about your offer, but only if I know what it entails."

"You're loyal and you finish your job, no matter what. I like that in a man. You deal with illegal weapons and that's what I would like you to continue to do."

Hawk raised his eyebrows. "I thought your girlie business was used to finance your weapon business. What's there to that? You don't deal with arms dealers like Stefan does."

"Ah, but I'm getting interested, you see," Dilaver said, tapping his cane on the carpet. "When I was in Asia, I heard about the weapon conference. Stefan mentioned it. Big names. Something big happening there. I want details; I want to get in on the deals, Hawk."

"Why? You got it good the way you're set up. Girls and drugs finance the weapons trade, right? And you arm the KLA and whomever you like." And had used those weapons to kill some of his fellow SEAL brothers. Hawk gestured at the map of Macedonia that was pinned crookedly on one of the walls. "Why would you want to start negotiating with other arms dealers, man? They would just want a piece of your pie."

Dilaver's smile was confidential. "Do you know how I get my weapons?"

Yeah, Hawk did, and that was why he was here in this rat's nest. "Like everyone else, I suppose. Take them off the hands of Russian small-timers."

The big man laughed. "Nope. Guess again."

Hawk shrugged. "Fuck, Dilaver, we aren't playing some fucking Macedonian Trivial Pursuit here. There are black market weapons galore everywhere these days. You have the money; you can buy anything."

"Yes, but I didn't buy some of these weapons, you see. They were free."

Hawk rubbed his chin. "That's nice but somewhat unbelievable. People don't just hand you weapons without expecting something back in return."

"But it's true, my friend," Dilaver said with a laugh. He waved his walking stick, pointing it at the ceiling. "They literally fall down from the sky."

The big man started guffawing, and couldn't seem to stop.

"Clearly, I'm missing some big joke," Hawk said wryly. "You're just dying to tell me, aren't you?"

Dilaver shook his head. "There you go again, with that odd American talk that doesn't translate well in Serbian." He frowned, slowly translating the phrase back into English. "Dying . . . to . . . tell. What the hell does that mean?"

"It means you have a secret and you want to share," Hawk explained, also reverting back to English. "Here's some more weapon phrases. You're sitting on a bomb. Or, you're about to explode. Or, you have a bee in your bonnet, if you're into skirts."

Dilaver put out a hand in helpless laughter. "Stop, you're killing me," he gasped. Then he laughed again, adding with amusement, " 'Killing me' . . . I said some stupid American phrase!"

Oh yeah, it was something Hawk dreamed about a lot, especially now, when the kingpin was behaving so damn normal, taking delight in a few slang terms like an eager student. It contrasted with the man Hawk saw beating the living shit out of a young girl a few nights ago because she dared to say no to him. He'd had to walk out of the *kafena* or risk his cover. That one still haunted his dreams. He wondered whether the image would ever go away.

"Here's my . . . bee in my . . . bonnet," Dilaver continued, still wheezing with laughter. "Do you know who gives me free weapons? Your government. The United States of America. It's all in big piles, dropped in shipments to arm the KLA, and I get first pick, of course, since they're using my territory."

"Dropped shipments. You mean, like you just said, they

are dropped out of the sky?" Hawk pretended to look incredulous. "How can that be? The UN wouldn't approve, would they?"

Dilaver shrugged. "Your government's sneaky, Hawk. They negotiated to have the KLA take over what's left of Yugoslavia, and they make the drops in big crates marked 'Relief Aid.' Some of these crates are actually filled with weapons and they're dropped at specific locations for me."

"How did they choose you? I mean, do you have a direct line to the U.S. armory?" Hawk affected a cynical look. "Come on, Dilaver. Don't tell me you're an agent for the American government."

"No, you got it backward. I have an agent in the United States. Several, actually." Dilaver sighed as his amusement subsided. "It's a long story, and a good one. If I have the time I might even write one of those spy novels, but then of course my aunt will kill me. There's that word again!"

"Your aunt?" Hawk prompted.

"She's high-level," Dilaver told him. "Got the authority to approve shipments or something. Of course, she and her people there are careful, so they only send out certain crates. She told me I can do anything I want with most of the weapons except for a few marked ones. Those are hers. That's where you come in."

Hawk knew that there had been a big blowup in D.C. the past year when several very important high-level CIA agents were indicted for selling information. Maybe this tied in somehow. "How?" he asked, getting up from the sofa to get a beer from the refrigerator. He activated a tiny recorder in his wristwatch.

"My aunt mentioned that conference before, you see, and that there'll be some big-time dealers who would love to get their hands on these special weapons. She said there's some problem moving them from her end right now and she might need my help." Dilaver settled back comfortably in the sofa, nodding his head when Hawk offered to bring him a bottle. "Anyway, you have links through Stefan and others. Must be fate to have met you, huh?"

Fate. Hawk didn't want to discuss fate with a man like Dilaver. He didn't want to be here drinking a beer and shooting the breeze at all. Something ugly and dark reared its head inside him lately whenever Dilaver and he talked about certain things—like friendship and fate, for instance. Those subjects reminded him of his best friend and teammates; those things bonded him to his SEAL brothers. *Not to a man like Dilaver.*

He was going to need an outlet for all this violence growing inside him. Soon.

"*Ja sam gladna*," he said softly.

"Yes, I am, too. Let's go eat. We'll talk more about your future over a good meal."

"Come on, Amber, tell me what he did. I'm dying here."

Amber looked up from the rows of figures she was trying to add up. "Will you quit pestering me? I haven't been able to get these numbers right for fifteen minutes now."

Lily finished drying her hair with a towel as she headed to the refrigerator. "Well, tell me! I promise I'll leave you in peace after you give me the details."

"Nope."

"Aw . . . come on. You're not still mad, are you?" Lily poured some orange juice into a glass, then pulled out a bottle of champagne.

"Isn't it a bit early for a mimosa?" Amber asked as she watched her friend adding the alcohol into her drink. "And yes, I'm still mad at you. I can't believe you let a man into my room. What kind of friend are you?"

Lily took a big sip, licking her lips. "It's never too early for a mimosa," she declared, then took another gulp. She toasted Amber with the glass. "The man had you over his shoulder and he looked so intimidating."

"Yeah, right."

Lily fluttered her eyelashes. "He did. He was tall and handsome, Amber. I mean, really, really good-looking handsome." She patted her heart. "I figure I did you a favor."

Amber put down her pencil and gave Lily a wide-eyed stare. "How do you know he wouldn't have hurt me?" She still couldn't believe that her friend had stood by while that man carried her unconscious body into her own room. She wouldn't have done that. But she wasn't Lily, who tended to enjoy sick jokes. "The man had his hands up my skirt!"

She was still angry at the way she had lost that fight. She hadn't even felt him in the office at all. The knowledge that she had the safe open and it could have been anyone was a sobering thought, but Lily had shrugged it off as if it were nothing.

"Well, you were armed. Besides, you've seen him naked. Tit for tat and all that."

"So have you. Are you going to let him see you naked, too?"

Lily shrugged, a mischievous light in her eyes. "I wouldn't mind, but I have a feeling Hawk was more interested in you last night."

"Oh, so you're on a first-name basis with him now?" Amber shook her head in disbelief. "How long was this conversation you had with him?"

"Oh no. You aren't getting any details from me till you tell me what else he did. He found your weapons and put them on the bed to let you know he could have done more. What else? I know he did something else because you were cursing up a storm in the bathroom this morning. Come on, give!"

Amber let out a sigh. She studied Lily, who was finishing up her mimosa. Champagne and orange juice in the morning. In her fake kimono dressing gown, jet-black hair still damp and uncombed, amusement lighting up those big eyes, she looked a bit like an imp out on some mischievous errand. Only Lily would see humor in such a moment.

She supposed she sort of deserved it. She had hurt the man's pride. Part of her gave Hawk McMillan thumbs-up for his method of revenge. He had said in the instant message that the next time they met, he was going to make a point.

Well, point taken. He showed that he could be as devious as she.

"Okay," Amber said. She stood up and lifted her skirt.

Lily put down her empty glass and walked over to the table, her eyes riveted on Amber's thigh. "Ho-ly snakes!" she murmured. "He wrote you a . . . what is that? A dirty message? *5MW/MTL/PF/18/69* and signed, *Hot Stuff*. He called himself Hot Stuff?"

Amber shrugged nonchalantly as Lily laughed in rich amusement. She didn't tell her that she was the one who had called him that. "He thinks he is, I guess," she said instead.

"How appropriate. I wonder whether he knows that's our code word for dangerous items?" Lily laughed again. "What does that line mean, do you know?"

5MW/MTL/PF/18/69. Oh yes, Amber knew what it was. She shook her head as she patted her skirt back into place. "Nope."

Lily narrowed her eyes. "You aren't telling."

"It's your turn to tell," Amber countered. "You talked to him. What was he like? Oh, stop giving me that lovey-dovey look."

"He was absolutely mouthwatering." Lily gave her a thumbs-up. "All in black and looking like some predator as he walked by with you slung like a Barbie doll over his shoulder. And his back was just as nice as his front, too."

Amber rolled her eyes. "I meant what you two talked about. I don't need you to describe his physical charms."

"Oh, I forget. You already *felt* his physical charms."

Amber stuck her tongue out at her friend and walked to the refrigerator. Now she wanted a mimosa, too. She had suddenly recalled Hawk's words to her just before she had passed out. Her legs were around his waist again, just like the other night.

I believe we've done this position before.

She poured champagne liberally into her orange juice. Damn that man!

"Isn't it too early for that much champagne?" drawled Lily.

Amber ignored the dig and took a gulp from the glass. "What did he say?" she asked.

"Nothing, just that this was only a little revenge thing. I could tell he wasn't going to really harm you."

"How?"

"Believe me, sweetie. I have been around some really, really rough characters. When they want to harm someone, I know it. I *feel* it. Hawk McMillan wasn't giving out those signals last night, although I must say he looked pretty capable of violence. He had a dangerous air about him."

"Lily, you can't possibly tell all that from just looking at a man."

"Oh yes I can. When you look at Dilaver, what do you feel?"

Amber visibly shuddered. Dragan Dilaver gave her the chills. He was a thug with a lot of power, and she had seen what he had done to young girls. Some of those victims had been in her care, after all. Every time she met him, it took all her willpower to keep her fury at bay.

"See? You can feel certain things, Amber," Lily continued. "Dilaver is a piece of shit. I don't even have to see what he did to know this. I have only to peek at him from our little office mirror to see that the man was violent and ruthless. And . . . he wants you, Amber, if you aren't aware of that."

She was. It was in Dilaver's eyes. Naked lust and oily intentions. "That's why Brad's presence is getting to be so useful," she said.

"Brad's presence can only protect you for so long," Lily warned. "But he'll do for now."

Amber took the chance. "What do you feel when you look at Brad, then? Is he a violent man?" She took another sip of her drink, studying her friend slowly over the glass.

Lily stared back at her challengingly, then shrugged. She adjusted the belt to her dressing gown. "Bradford Sun is a bureaucrat," she replied quietly. "He doesn't know violence if it's staring at him in the face."

"Oh, I think you're wrong there," Amber said, putting the empty glasses in the sink. "He's dealing with the situations the best way he can at the moment, but I know he's capable of action when he wants it."

"And how would you know?"

Lily sounded almost . . . jealous. Amber hid a small smile. "Because he looks at you and feels your violence toward him, and he's about to make his move any day now. Tell me, why do you act like that when you're around him? He's helping us, you know."

Lily shrugged again. "I don't know." She ran impatient fingers through her hair. "It's me, I guess. I don't like bureaucrats. He can just raid those damn places and get Dilaver just like this." She snapped her fingers. "And he doesn't."

Amber leaned over the kitchen counter. She knew there was more to this thing between Brad and Lily than his inability to act the lawman. "Sweetie, his hands are tied.

That's why he's giving us information when he can. It's his way of getting some of the girls out of Dilaver's hands. Now tell me the truth why you're so pissed off at Brad whenever his name's mentioned."

Lily pushed her hands deeply into her pockets. Her eyes had a startled awareness in them, as if she had suddenly realized something. "Because . . ." she said slowly, wonder in her voice, "he looks at me like Hawk looked last night. A determined, gonna-take-you-and-make-you-mine look. And I don't need that right now. I don't need any man to carry me off over his shoulder."

Amber stared back speechlessly at her friend.

6

      Hawk looked out of the window as the car
sped along the streets of Velesta. He had been here only a
few days and he already hated this city. They drove past the
makeshift billboard on the side of a building.

"Dancers!" It boasted in several languages. "Come Relax
with Our Beautiful Dancers."

There was a reason for the different languages. The adver-
tisements around here weren't targeting the Macedonians.
Everyone was after the NATO soldiers, the peacekeepers
around town, who had the cash and the time to spend on
women and booze. So everything was sold in German,
French, Polish, and English, and the most popular thing being sold in Velesta were girls.

The irony of it hadn't escaped Hawk. He wasn't big-
headed about it, but he knew that he had been particularly
lucky in the gene pool. He had been told most of his life
what a good-looking bastard he was and he'd never had trouble getting any woman. There were very few complaints, except sometimes he wondered whether any of the women
really cared what he was like inside. Of course, he hadn't
tried to get to know them better, either. Being a Navy SEAL

had taken away any chance of that, and by the time an operation was over, so was the relationship. But there was always another woman waiting around the corner.

And here he was in Velesta, Macedonia, a place filled with women from every imaginable country, except that most of them weren't here of their own free will. Kidnapped. Enslaved. These were terms that were alien to him when it came to getting women. He had never had the need to buy or take any female by force. It had never even crossed his mind that he would spend any time in a brothel looking at half-naked women being forced to please men.

Dragan Dilaver, the man sitting in the back of the car with him, was the last person on earth that Hawk had thought he would be hanging out with for any prolonged period of time. The thug was the antithesis of everything for which Hawk stood; he was a parasite, a bully, a user. It grated to know that Hawk had to walk into any place with this asshole and be regarded as *his friend*. He could see the fear in the women's eyes when they looked at him, and he loathed it with a growing, unfamiliar violence that ate at him.

There had never been fear in his women's eyes before. Or hatred. He had never intimidated a woman in that way before. Perhaps this was some twisted punishment for having it easy with women all his life—now he had hordes of women pretending to like him because they would be beaten if they didn't act that way.

Dilaver shut his cell phone. "These stupid things won't stop ringing," he complained.

"Turn it off."

"Then how am I suppose to know what's happening?"

"Dilemma, isn't it?" Hawk stared at another girlie billboard as the car slowed down at a red light. "Technology can suck you into dependency."

"Yes. Ten years ago, I didn't have this piece of crap hanging on the side of my hip, you know? I was out there, armed to the teeth, fighting fucking Serbs and Greeks, joining any side who would pay me, and there was no need for a cell phone to communicate."

Hawk turned to Dilaver. "So why the need now?"

"I was a mercenary then. I'm a businessman now." Dilaver let out a sigh. "Now you make me think of the good old days when my life was just about being a soldier. Have you ever been in the army in your country? You look fit enough. Not that I'd recommend that life. No money in it, unless you're a mercenary."

"No."

Hawk didn't want to compare notes about being a soldier. Dilaver was a mercenary, and therein laid the difference. At least, that was what Hawk told himself. He didn't kill for money. He went through rigorous training so he could protect his country from harm. And he didn't abuse power. Yet, he wasn't naive enough to believe that he was nothing but a tool. All he had to do was look around at the peacekeepers in Velesta. Soldiers, supposedly. Now mere policemen who broke the law by going to the brothels and taking advantage of the women they'd sworn to protect.

"Here we are."

Hawk already knew where they were, of course. After all, he had been here just the night before. He got out of the car.

He looked up at the oddly out-of-place restaurant, with its cheerful welcome banner above its name, "The Last Resort." Even the name was out of place. Velesta was hardly a resort of any kind, and probably the very last place for any of the girls in this city to want to visit.

"Popular place," he noted, as he glanced at the vehicles and mopeds parked outside.

"Oh yes, I told you, those NATO peacekeepers love this

place. The owner's pretty little ass doesn't hurt business, either."

Hawk thought of Amber Hutchen's pretty little ass. Funny how he had barely exchanged three lines with the woman, yet he knew how her ass felt smooth and silky under his hand. He wondered how she was, how she had reacted to his surprise when she'd woken up.

His lips quirked. There were few things that made him smile in this place, but the owner of The Last Resort was one of them. For some reason her appearance and little challenge had brightened an otherwise sobering few months.

"I can't wait to meet her," he said. "So you have done business with her before?"

"Now and then. She can't ignore me, you know. I'm the king around here. She's too old for my taste and has a bit more brains." Dilaver leaned on his cane, nodding to his bodyguards to follow him. "She's given me good information sometimes. I told you she sleeps with the CIVPOL chief, so sometimes she passes on to me that there's a raid coming on such and such a date, and I get to save some trouble and money by warning my *kafena* supervisors to shut down before the police comes. That's why I don't bother her too much."

"I see." Jed was right. The woman couldn't be entirely trusted, if she used information gathered from a lover like that. Hawk wondered whether there was anyone left in this town who wasn't corrupt in one form or another.

Bells jingled as soon as they opened the door, announcing their arrival. The main eating area was half filled, with most of the guests in uniform. Someone had started the jukebox in the corner and a familiar American dance tune was playing.

"We're here for lunch," Dilaver said to the woman standing behind the counter.

"I'm sorry, sir, but the restaurant is only open for dinners. We only serve American cakes and coffee in the afternoon."

"You go to the back and tell Miss Hutchens that Dilaver has brought an American guest here for lunch and he wants to try her specialty." Dilaver lifted a brow. "Don't keep me waiting."

The woman nodded and hurriedly went through a doorway behind her. Some of the soldiers in the café had already noticed the new arrivals and had started to look at them expectantly. News of Dilaver being back in town was probably making the rounds. The woman reappeared.

"Miss Hutchens said to take you to the private dining area. Please follow me."

Dilaver gave Hawk a triumphant smile as they followed the woman to the back where there was a screened-off area. The bodyguards positioned themselves in front of the screen as they sat down.

The woman handed them some menus. "She'll be with you shortly."

Dilaver perused the menu. "I hate American food. I'm only doing this for you."

Hawk wished he could eat this meal alone. "Much appreciated," he said.

"I know you've been dying for some hamburger." Dilaver laughed.

The man was fixated with dying. "You did say it's the best in town," Hawk said.

"Well, order whatever you like. You can even have the owner if you want her. She's quite a meal herself."

"Good afternoon, gentlemen," a voice smoothly interrupted.

Hawk looked up. Amber Hutchens stood near the screen, dressed casually in a work shirt and jeans. Her sleeves were rolled up, as if she had been busy in the kitchen, and he

could see flour stains on the dark material of her jeans. Her
eyes narrowed just a little at the sight of him, but otherwise
her expression didn't betray any surprise at the sight of
them.

"Amber, *kako ste*!"

"Fine, thank you, Dragan. How was your trip to Asia?"

Dilaver scowled. "I'm still limping from that fiasco. They
don't know how to do business there and the food's too
damn spicy. And they have shitwater for beer."

Amber came closer to the table, a small smile on her lips
that never quite reached her eyes. "Didn't sound like the vacation you said you were going to have, huh?" She took the
tray from a waitress who appeared, setting the glasses of water for Dilaver, then Hawk. Her eyes met Hawk's for the first
time. "And is this your new friend?"

This close, in the light of day, Hawk had time to take in
everything about Amber more leisurely. The first thing that
caught his attention was her eyes; she had the blackest pupils
set against a teal blue. Cat's eyes. The kind that glowed in
the dark. And she was looking at him the way one would,
too—as if she were deciding whether to be bored or interested with this particular human being. It made him want to
laugh out loud.

There was the slightest tilt at each corner of her lips, giving her that secretive Mona Lisa smile. Her complexion was
as silky smooth as he remembered, with the barest of lipstick. He caught a whiff of her perfume when she leaned
over to place the glass next to him. A hint of vanilla and
something else. He also noticed she didn't wear any rings on
her small, slender hands, but then she could have taken them
off while she worked in the kitchen.

"He's as American as you. Can't you tell?"

She studied Hawk for a second, then shrugged. "Not really. Does he talk?"

Dilaver laughed. "He's a shy boy, is Hawk, aren't you, my friend?"

"Very," Hawk agreed. He returned the same perusal Amber gave him. "Very nice to finally meet you, Miss Hutchens."

"Oh? Sounds like you've been planning on it."

"Yes." He left it at that. They stared at each other for a full second.

Dilaver didn't appear to hear the undercurrent of their conversation as he looked up from the menu. "This is Hawk. He hasn't eaten a good American meal in months, Amber. That's why I brought him here."

Amber nodded. "What would you like to eat? Since we don't do lunch, Dragan, you might have to wait a little longer than usual."

"That's all right. Why don't you join us for the meal?" Dilaver leaned forward, his big hands flat on the table. "I need some information."

Amber regarded him for a moment. "Would you like to try our meatloaf? We're in the middle of getting some prepared for tonight."

"Sure, sure, whatever. Don't forget the beer."

"And you, Mr. . . . Hawk? Anything you particularly miss from the States?"

"Surprise me," Hawk said softly. "I'm sure it'll be something I like."

She tilted her head. "What if it isn't?"

He smiled. "I have a bet riding on the fact that you will get it just right. Anything you cook up will be fine."

Amber blinked and turned to Dilaver. "I take it back. I like him better quiet."

Dilaver winked at Hawk and gestured suggestively as Amber walked away. "*Ona je lepa devojka.* Told you."

Hawk looked after at her departing figure. He knew she

was listening. "Beautiful all over," he agreed. He caught the glare of her blue eyes just before she slipped into the back room, and resisted from grinning. Would she?

Amber stalked into the study. Lily turned from the two-way mirror through which she had been studying Dilaver and Hawk.

"So, you finally get to talk to him," she said, smiling. "He's yummy, isn't he?"

He was devastatingly so, especially when he looked at her as if he had seen her naked before, but Amber wasn't in the mood to sigh about Hawk McMillan's good looks. He had issued yet another challenge and she couldn't find a way out of it.

Llallana followed her through the connecting door that led into the kitchen. "Well? Aren't you going to say something?"

"Tina, get the gentleman in the private area their choice of beer," Amber told one of her waitresses. She wrote onto the order sheet and clipped it above the cooking area. "Those are the orders, Ona. Prepare the meatloaf."

Llallana leaned against the refrigerator. "He's gotten to you."

"That man's too much into games," Amber said.

"Ha! Says the one who started it all!"

Amber grabbed chunks of hamburger meat from a container and started kneading it fiercely. Lily was right, of course. She started all this. She felt like growling. Ona came over, steadying the piece of order paper to read what she had written before heading off to the pantry.

"So what are you making him? Such a big man . . . hmmm . . . must have a voracious appetite. From what I overheard, he seems to trust your skills."

When Amber said nothing, Lily came closer. She bit her lip. Her friend wasn't stupid; she lived on the edge most of the time and could pick up signals most people didn't. She knew it would be just a matter of time before Lily found out the source of her irritation. She did, because she heard the familiar chuckle just behind her.

"Oh my God." Llallana was trying not to laugh too loudly. "Oh, he's too much."

"Shut up!" Amber made a face, shaping the meat into a thick hamburger. She didn't stop Lily from snatching the order off the clip above her. "I don't want to hear about it."

"5MW/MTL/PF/18/69 . . . that's what he wrote!" Llallana leaned weakly against the side counter. "He . . . ordered . . . from the menu!" She broke up laughing again. "Oh, I love him. He ordered his next meal. That was the secret code?"

Amber released a frustrated growl. Last night, Hawk McMillan had somehow gotten to look at the order pad and saw the way her girls wrote down orders from customers. He also seemed to have taken the time to check out her menu, because he was very specific with his instructions. Number 5 from the menu was the house steakburger, with a special sauce. A Number 5 Medium Well/Mayo Tomato Lettuce/Pomme Frittes/Number 18 was Coca-Cola. Of course she had understood the code—she saw variations of the same thing every day for the past four years. She knew what it was the moment she saw what he had written on her thigh. As for the other number . . .

"It isn't that funny," she muttered, turning on the fryer.

"I think he's cool as hell. It's a great way to get revenge for what you did." Llallana shook her head. "I think you've met your match, sweetie."

"You're supposed to be on my side," Amber complained. "Just because he's cute . . ."

"Hey, I'm not that shallow. Really, I'm offended." Llallana handed her a plate. "Here, let me help prepare a meal for Hot Stuff. You have to stop growling like that, Amber, or you're going to frighten Dilaver away."

Amber turned the heat on high. She lowered her voice. "I wonder what *he* wants today. He didn't just show up to get a meal for his American friend."

"Didn't he say he wanted some information? I'll bet you a double steakburger that it has to do with missing trailers of women."

Amber nodded. "Well, we already knew he would come to me sooner or later."

Llallana watched Amber for a few minutes, moving out of Ona's way when the latter passed by with the meatloaf. Unless it was very busy, she seldom helped out in the kitchen when she was in town, preferring to stay upstairs in the apartment, enjoying her time alone. Amber didn't mind. It was her downtime away from all the really dirty work in their venture—moving the girls from town to town, and making sure they were safe. She had gone along with her friend a few times and knew what a toll that was on the spirit.

"Why did you cook him what he wanted, anyway?" Llallana asked. "You didn't have to. Could have just given him good old meatloaf."

Amber glanced up briefly from preparing the dressing. "Because he said he had a bet riding on it that I'd get his order right."

"I heard that, but what does that mean?"

Amber smiled wryly. She had to give it to the man; he had her cornered. "If I didn't decode his message, it meant he won the challenge. If I decoded it, it meant I lost."

Llallana chuckled, shaking her head. "So he'd get you either way. He's got you figured out, you know. Knows that you think in terms of challenges. He's a smart one, Amber. Since he won, I guess you'll have to work with him."

Amber arranged the plates of food on the tray and handed them to Ona to take out to the guests. "He didn't win," she declared. "He gave me a choice. I prefer to lose than have him win."

"Oh, that makes sense, then. You two ought to make a good team."

Amber paused as she wiped her hands. Team. The idea of being partners with Hawk McMillan sent an unexpected shiver down her spine. He would use unorthodox methods. And he would constantly challenge her. Both thoughts excited and troubled her.

"We'll see what he wants," she said noncommittally.

"My, all these men wanting something from Amber H." Llallana sighed. "Busy girl."

Amber unrolled her sleeves and arranged her shirt. "I have a feeling that things are going to get busier. We have to really get our shit together now that Dilaver is back in town. Not going to be as easy to get his trailers."

"We'll worry about that later. Now you go and entertain them out there while I make a few phone calls. I want to make sure everything is okay."

"All right. Hey, Lily? Call Brad and tell him that Dilaver's here. Maybe he can raid one of his *kafenas*."

Amber watched as Llallana hesitated, knowing that she didn't want to make that phone call. She also knew her friend wouldn't say no, not when it had to do with saving more girls. When she nodded, Amber mouthed a silent thank-you before slipping back into the study. She took a deep breath. She could handle Dragan Dilaver. It was the new guy who would be a little harder to manipulate.

Maybe it was just all these months of thinking about it, but it was the most delicious hamburger Hawk had ever tasted. The mouthwatering smoky smell alone made his taste buds cry out in delight. It was exactly how he dreamed of one—a big fat slab of juicy hamburger, seasoned and charred, the works and squishy with mayonnaise. It dripped out in between the sesame buns as he took hungry bites.

"I think this is the most animated I've seen you yet," Dilaver observed, highly amused.

Again, Hawk wished that he could enjoy this particular meal alone. He was surprised at how much he had been looking forward to it. In his job, he'd gotten used to going without, be it food or physical comfort, and it was very rare that he allowed his needs to rise to the surface like this. It wasn't as if he were starving; he just had been dreaming about hamburgers.

"Amber! Look at how much my friend's enjoying your cooking."

Hawk looked up to see Amber walking toward them. He quickly wiped his hands and stood up to pull a chair out for her.

"Thank you," she said with a smile. "Is your meal to your liking?"

"Exactly how I wanted it," he replied.

"He's been talking about hamburgers," Dilaver said. "You must have read his mind."

Her smile widened slightly and she glanced back at Hawk. "It was incredibly easy."

Hawk didn't say anything at her dig, preferring to finish off his hamburger. She arched her brows at him, refusing to be the first to break off.

"Aren't you eating with us?" Dilaver asked.

She finally looked away. "I'm not very hungry, but I'll have a beer. What can I do for you today, Dragan?"

Dragan pointed a spoon at Amber. "You know. Missing trailers. I'm being robbed."

Amber took a sip from her mug. "I've heard about it, but

I've also heard that there's been a lot more highway robberies, so it's not just you."

"What else have you heard?" When Amber darted Hawk a
look, Dilaver continued, "Don't worry about Hawk. He's
one of us. In fact, he might give you some useful information in exchange for some . . . hot meals."

Amber smiled politely as Dilaver laughed at his own joke.
Hawk sensed her dislike of the big Slav, even though she
masked it well. The woman was intriguing as hell. Could
fight like a pro. Fine-looking, that was for sure. And man,
could she cook. If he were looking, here was his dream
woman.

"Has that CIVPOL man of yours mentioned anything of
use to me?"

Too damn bad she had a boyfriend. Too bad she couldn't
be trusted.

7

Brad poured himself another cup of coffee.
Like everything else in Velesta, the reporter was running
late. He had expected it; he needed the time to lay out exactly what information to divulge anyway. He needed to be
both careful and tactful. This was a dangerous place. He was
well aware of the risks of his job, how anything outside red
tape could jeopardize his career. The wrong move, and he'd
find himself in a worse place than Velesta.

But he had to do something. Dilaver's power was multi-
plying and the more girls he made money from, the more the
kingpin could finance his other activities. Drugs and women
were just a means to an end—weapons for the different factions in this war-torn country.

The UN knew this, of course. But their philosophy was
horrifyingly simple. Better the devil they knew than some
other factions that might mean a really major war on their
hands. At least the KLA kept some semblance of order, they
argued.

Order? Brad gulped down the bitterness along with the
coffee. Order in chaos. How perfect for Velesta. And meanwhile, thousands of young girls suffered because of behind-

the-scenes political wrangling between men with higher ambitions than he.

From day one, he had taken one look at these girls and knew he had to do something. How could anyone not? They were locked up and used like . . . animals. He shook off the images of the things he had seen in those *kafenas* he and his men had raided. The world needed to know.

But he wouldn't tell them about some brave people who took it on themselves to do something about this crime. People like Amber Hutchens and Llallana Noretski. That would remain a secret because their lives would be put in danger if Dilaver or any other crime lord knew about them.

He had no doubt that Dilaver was looking for the culprits robbing his men of their trailers. The man was losing money out his ass, and especially while he was gone for that short period, Llallana and Amber had taken the opportunity to double the raids. Brad had given them all the information he could get his hands on to help them.

He heard Dilaver was injured while he was away, that he walked with a limp now. His sources told him that an American had saved his life and was maybe helping him now. A wave of disgust rose up from the pit of his stomach. If he ever saw that man in the *kafena* touching any of those girls, he would personally take care of the sicko, American or not. *Then* he would arrest him.

His cell started buzzing, interrupting his thoughts. "This is Bradford Sun," he answered.

"This is Llallana."

Brad settled back against the leather chair. "This is an unexpected pleasure," he said. It must be something important. Lily wouldn't be calling him just to say hi. "Is anything wrong?"

"No, but Dumbo is here."

That was their code word for Dilaver. "At the restaurant?"

"Yes, he's lunching with Amber and she wants you to know. Just in case you have time on your hands to go on a raid."

Ah, they were back on familiar territory. "Sarcasm this early already? And how do you suppose I should go about telling my department to conduct a raid in the morning?"

"Morning, noon, night, what's the difference?"

"The department isn't put together that way, Lily," Brad said. He understood her frustration, though. He shared it, too. "I'm in the process of changing it, so in time we'll be able to do lightning raids any time of the day."

He had discovered that his predecessor hadn't been very vigilant in keeping the department clean. There were men on the take, and they called ahead of time so the *kafenas* were empty by the time they arrived.

There were also quite a few officials and peacekeeping units from different nations who resented the new head of the unit. They were the ones who refused to stop going to these sites on their off-hours when he demanded that they order their men not to do so. It was offensive to him to know that people under him were some of the abusers.

But things would change. He promised himself that. It would just take time, something the woman on the other end of the phone didn't want to understand.

"So you're telling me there's nothing you can do except sit in your office drinking coffee?"

Brad looked at the cup in front of him. That woman was uncanny when it came to deflating his ego. "I'm actually waiting for someone that might help us," he said. An idea flashed. "If you'll give me access to some of the girls in your care, it'd be an even better interview."

"Interview?" Llallana repeated cautiously.

"I've lined up one with a TV reporter. He's international. I was going to give him facts and figures, and he was going to go to the *kafenas* on his own to check out what's happening, but if we can get some of those girls to talk to him, Llallana, it'd be hearing the story straight from the source."

"And what has that to do with your department?"

Brad looked at the coffee cup again. He was proud enough not to want to admit to Llallana that his department was part of the problem. After all, she was doing something, in spite of his disapproval of some of her illegal methods. He, on the other hand, couldn't even get his own officers to uphold the international law.

"It'll bring publicity."

"To you?" Her voice turned cynical. "Always thinking ahead about the career, aren't you?"

"To the problem. Lily, stop it. I'm not the enemy here."

There was a pause. "How are you going to protect me and the locations where I have some of the girls?"

Brad seized at the opportunity. "Meet me for lunch. We'll go over the logistics."

"Be seen in public with me?" She laughed. "You're getting brave, Bradford Sun."

He couldn't care less if he was seen with her. This was Velesta, after all. "Will you believe it if I tell you that it's for your sake that we meet in private? The less you're seen with someone like me, the less likely you'll draw attention, right?" Sometimes he thought her baiting deliberate; at other times, like now, he wondered whether she really hated him so much she couldn't think straight. He had seen her teasing with Amber when her guard was down, so he knew she had a sense of humor under that prickly façade she put on for him. It suddenly occurred to him that these two women were best friends sharing many qualities. That meant, like Amber,

Llallana wouldn't be able to resist a challenge. He tested the theory. "Do you want to help, or not? It's going to be difficult, keeping identities and locations a secret, so if you're afraid to do it, I'll understand."

"I'm not afraid."

Brad smiled. "I don't want to cause any problems for you or Amber. Especially you," he said smoothly, "because you want to keep a low profile in this town. But you're also very outspoken and if you get yourself into the interview, you might be seen on TV all over the place."

"Are you saying I can't shut up?"

"I think you're very passionate about what you're doing and won't be able to resist making comments. Not that I don't agree with your opinions. Just that I know you'll say something really colorful and then the interviewer will want to know all about you and your background, and what it is exactly that you do to help these girls. See the risk? Maybe we shouldn't even think of doing this. Too dangerous for you."

He emphasized the last word. It would be dangerous for the escaped girls, too, but it was a risk that might bring some good. An exposé by an international television reporter, with real pictures and interviews, might make those who had voted against him yesterday change their minds about arresting Dilaver and those like him.

"Where do you want to meet to discuss this?"

Oh, he knew where would be the biggest challenge of all. "At my place. It's secured, as you know. Unless you feel uncomfortable going there, of course."

There was another pause. "I'll be there." He could visualize her clenched teeth as she said that. "Time?"

"In two hours? A late lunch."

"Fine. And it's still Llallana to you." She abruptly rang off.

Brad made a call to the reporter, who was running late, asking to postpone the meeting. He promised to get back with the man later, with more than just an interview with him. After rearranging his schedule, he got up from his desk, picked up his cup, and drained the rest of the coffee.

He had finally gotten Llallana to meet with him alone again. Somehow, in spite of the heavy subject matter they were going to discuss, he felt very lighthearted.

The man was good. Amber hated to admit it, even privately. Throughout lunch, Hawk had shown just enough interest in her during the meal to amuse Dilaver, and not so much that it caused suspicion. She understood the plan behind it—he was going to ask her out while he was in town. She would bet money on it.

There was something in the way he looked at her that made her . . . She tried to put a finger on the feeling. It wasn't comfortable at all, whatever it was. Something inside her jumped every time he caught her gaze. Even worse, whatever she was thinking would trail off, and she had to work extra hard to keep her focus on the conversation.

He seemed amused by it, too. Damn the man. He probably knew he had this effect on all women. He was too good-looking not to know.

She blinked at the sound of her name. Dilaver had asked something. Damn it. She hid her dismay as she pretended to take a drink from her mug. Now what? Damn, damn, damn.

"I'd like that. I heard there's an opera not too far from town, even an art show. It'd be great if you can do it, Amber," Hawk said, the glint in his eyes revealing that he'd known she hadn't been paying attention to Dilaver. "I'd like to see more of Macedonian culture other than the inside of *kafenas*."

Amber cocked her head. "A cultured American? I thought men like you just came here for business."

"Actually, I'm sort of on vacation," Hawk said. "Dilaver invited me for an extended stay."

She had heard that it was Hawk who had saved Dilaver's life. She wondered what the story was behind that. "Really?" Vacationing in Macedonia. She stopped herself from making a rude sound. "And what have you been doing for fun so far?"

"Nothing," Hawk replied, to her surprise.

"I can second that," Dilaver said. "The man's been following me around and hasn't had any time to really see our beautiful country, Amber. You should show him why you love it here, what made you choose to live here. You'll be doing me a favor."

The Slav appeared to want Hawk to stay here and was trying to convince him. Amber wondered how Hawk had become so close to the kingpin, and so suddenly, too. Dilaver wasn't an accessible man at all. During her four years here, she had never been able to find someone close enough to the man to bribe.

She was getting more intrigued by the minute. Information like this would be worth something, and perhaps she could use it to secure her future. Away from the CIA. Away from Macedonia.

But she had a certain reputation, too. And, supposedly, a man of her own. "I'll think about it," she said. She looked at Dilaver meaningfully. "I don't have much free time as it is."

"Oh, I know you travel about with that new man of yours and go out of town to the art shows and whatnot. You have to keep everyone happy, yes? Including me. And it's to my advantage that you enjoy a friendship with our new CIVPOL agent." Dilaver leaned closer. "But sometimes you can make a man's interest stronger by giving him some competition, my dear. He might get a bit more serious and you can get even more from him."

"How . . . devious, Dragan," Amber said dryly.

Dilaver laughed. "Aren't I? Hawk, don't you agree men like competition?"

"I think they like the chase," Hawk said lazily.

"Is that what you like?" Amber asked. "The chase?"

His answering smile was slow and challenging. "Maybe."

Amber perused his face slowly. He had the face of a cover model. Eyes the color of aged brandy, with that bold look in them that suggested intimacy. A straight nose. Strong sensual lips that would tempt a saint. She doubted the man had ever chased a woman in his life. She suspected it was easy for someone like Hawk McMillan to get any female he wanted. "I don't believe you," she said, wrinkling her nose. "I think a man like you gets chased a lot."

"Yes, women attack him all the time," Dilaver agreed. "He would be standing there and suddenly a woman would be next to him. And then they're all over him. I've seen it."

"Attack?" Amber locked eyes with Hawk.

"At the most unexpected times," he said softly.

"Maybe they just want to test you." She smiled. "Maybe they just want to see how tough you are . . . to get."

He gave a low chuckle, his amusement sending an odd tingle down her spine. "One or two of them enjoy needling me."

She blinked in surprise. Then laughed. A witty guy, too. "I'm sure most of them leave you a calling card," she mocked.

"Some do it in the most original way," he agreed, his eyes twinkling.

"Well, with all this female attention you get all the time, I suppose they have to do that to get yours." She was enjoying this verbal duel too much. "What's the most original thing a woman has ever done to get your attention, Hawk?"

"Now, that'd be telling," he said. "Perhaps I'll tell you when we meet again."

"Oh, I see the ploy," she mocked. "Keeping my interest going."

"It's part of the chase."

"But who's doing the chasing?"

"Depends on who's got the hotter stuff."

She almost choked on her beer. One thing was for sure. She'd have to be on her toes all the time if she were to work with Hawk. Dilaver was looking back and forth at them, a satisfied expression in his eyes. Obviously, he thought he was succeeding in engaging the interest of his American buddy.

"Is that how it all ends? The comparison of who's got the hotter stuff?" Amber quipped, finishing her drink and pushing her chair back so she could get up. "Speaking of hot, Dragan, I really have to get back to the kitchen. I have the oven on."

"You'll get back to me with the information?" Dilaver asked.

"I'll see what I can find out," she coolly replied. "No one reports about those kind of highway robberies to the police department, you know."

"Then you'll get the word out that there's a price for the information," he insisted.

"Of course. That's my business, Dragan. Now, if you'll excuse me . . ." She nodded to Dilaver and then turned to Hawk. "Nice to meet you, Hawk. Come back anytime. I like feeding hungry men."

Her heart skipped a beat again at the intense look he gave her. Was that the same one that Lily talked about this morning? It was the kind of look a man gave to a woman when he had something wicked in mind—heated and personal—leaving no doubt to his intentions.

She shook off the wobbly sensation in her tummy. For goodness' sake, she hardly knew the man! And when had she grown into such an expert at analyzing masculine gazes? She was about to turn to leave the table when his hand reached out, offering her a business card.

"My number," he told her, that easy deceptive smile hiding the fact that he knew she didn't need it. "Thanks for the delicious meal."

"You're welcome," she said, taking the card. Their fingertips touched and even that felt too personal. She stepped away and added, "I'll be in touch, Dragan."

As she slipped through the door back to her study, she heard Dragan snicker in a pseudo-whisper, *"Ja miris jedan osvajanje.* Now, do you like this one over my girls?"

"To je zena," she heard Hawk reply.

She sniffed in self-disgust. So Dilaver had challenged him into thinking she was a conquest, was that it? No wonder he was giving her all those looks. She stuck her tongue out at Lily. "I don't want to discuss it," she declared quietly.

"To je zena, indeed," Lily mocked. "I think he likes you, sweetie."

"He's responding to some challenge from Dilaver, didn't you hear?" She waved a hand at the two-way mirror, mimicking Dilaver's tone, " 'Do you like this one over my girls?' Ugh. They're comparing me to Dilaver's women?"

"You're such a silly goose. Girls, Dilaver said his girls." Lily shook her head. "Hawk pointed out to him that's a woman, meaning you're all woman to him, dummy. He's probably been in and out of those *kafenas* with that asshole and meant that there was a difference."

Amber narrowed her eyes at her friend. "Why are you defending him and explaining him to me? What difference does it make what he meant?"

"Did you watch him eat that hamburger? He's looking for something, that man."

Amber sighed. "Someday I'll understand your little side observations, girl, but I have a bunch of things to do today. Did you call Brad?" There was a rise in color in her friend's face. "Quarreled again?"

"No." Lily checked her fingernails. "As a matter of fact, I'm going out to meet him right now. He said he needed me to help him coordinate an interview with some international news agency."

Amber raised her brows questioningly. "Really? What kind of interview?" She was surprised that Lily had agreed to anything to do with Brad. "About the girls?"

"Yes."

"That isn't a bad idea. You'll have to be careful not to bring attention to us."

Lily looked up sharply. "Hey, that's what he accused me of! Am I that loose-lipped?"

Ooops. Looked like those two had quarreled. "No, just very noticeable, Lily." Amber smiled. "You're tall and beautiful and you get very passionate when it comes to a particular topic. I can just see you being the focus of some kind of article, that's all."

"Then maybe I shouldn't agree to help out Brad, since I don't know how to stay out of anyone's way," Lily flashed back.

"Hey, I didn't mean to hurt your feelings." Amber poked Lily with a finger. "You're an expert at being in the background. It's just that there are fireworks whenever you're near Brad and you don't seem to hold yourself together like you always do."

"Oh, look who's talking about fireworks. What about you and Hawk out there?"

Amber frowned. "What about me and Hawk? I don't even know him."

"Exactly. And already there's so many fireworks between you two, it smoked right through the two-way into this room." Lily poked Amber back. "You, my friend, are in the same predicament, only worse."

"How so?" And when did the conversation revert back to her? Amber looked at Hawk's calling card still in her hand. He had written something on the back.

"Hello? Two prior meetings and each time one of you had to sedate the other? I think that's a pretty serious chemical reaction, don't you think?" Lily laughed. "What did he write?"

"Ha-ha, very funny." Chemical reaction indeed. She had to smile at the way it sounded, though. She and Hawk *had* knocked each other off their feet. She pocketed the card. "Looks like I have a date tonight, too. Will you be out late?"

Lily shook her head. "I don't think so. What do you want me to say to Brad?" She smiled mischievously. "I can make him jealous, tell him you have a new boyfriend."

"Oh, stop. You know he isn't interested in me."

"Sometimes I wonder, Amber. He spends an awful lot of time with you, doesn't he? Maybe he wants more than friendship."

Amber gave Lily a long look. She had to answer carefully here. On the one hand, she and Brad always had a good time together, even though it was a platonic relationship. On the other hand, she didn't want to make Lily jealous about the situation. It was complicated. The setup was necessary to establish that she and Brad were a couple; yet she also knew her friend had a thing for Brad, no matter how much she denied it.

"I think he wants more than friendship with you," Amber finally said, not wanting to betray Brad's confidence.

Lily shrugged and turned away. "What he wants, I can't give. I don't have it in me." She picked up her purse. "Got to go. You enjoy your date, okay? Just stop drugging each other. You'll be fine. You can tell me all about it when you get back."

"We'll exchange girlie notes," Amber said dryly as they went into the kitchen.

"Oh, I'm sure mine will be boring, boring, boring." Lily headed to the back door. *"Ta!"*

You're running out just a bit too fast, my friend. Amber smiled. Sometimes one had to let things play out to see where things were going. She doubted there would be any boring moments in a meeting between Brad and Lily.

Which brought her back to her plans for this evening. His handwriting was small and very neat. *Meeting tonight. IM 0900 hours for instructions. Wear something hot.*

Instructions. Bah. Who did he think he was? He needed her to help him, not the other way around. One thing was certain. She would have to lay some ground rules with Hawk McMillan.

8

Hawk thumbed through the tourist bro-chures Dilaver had given to him. *Hrvatsko narodno kaza-liste. Beogradsko dramsko posoriste.* All the different national and drama theaters.

"Pick any one you want," Dilaver told him. He was comfortably lounging on his new sofa, still drinking beer. He had told Hawk that he was waiting for an international call, but meanwhile, his nonstop intake of alcohol didn't bode well. It was going to be one of those nights, the kind Hawk had to steel himself to be part of.

"One's in Croatia. The other's in Belgrade," Hawk pointed out dryly.

"I run business all through the Balkans and the former Yugoslavia, so we'll go wherever I want next. Or we'll fly to one place one day and the other the next. We'll even take Amber along to keep you company if you want."

"I don't think the lady can just take off."

Dilaver shrugged. "I'll order her to. Or kidnap her. Only if you want her along, of course."

"Out of curiosity, is there any woman you take with you

that you actually have invited, Dilaver?" Hawk asked. "I don't think I've ever seen you with anyone but a *kafena* girl."

Dilaver made a rude noise. "You've obviously been living in the civilized world too damn long, boy. Look around you. I have girls by the dozens at any time I want. Girls to break. Girls to teach. Even a virgin or two, if I'm lucky to get to her before her seller does." He leaned closer, a lecherous look on his face. "Have you ever broken a girl, Hawk? And I don't mean just a nice spread between the legs. I mean those obstinate ones, the ones who think they're better than the rest of them. Oh, I enjoy those the most. And at the end, they're obedient and willing, just like every girl I've got. Now, Amber Hutchens . . . she thinks she's better. I can see it in her eyes, in the way she looks at me, but she's smart, you see. She makes herself useful in other ways, such as sleeping with a powerful man. But one day"—He snapped his fingers—"her usefulness will be over and then I can have her, too. If I want. She's too old for my liking, but her looks . . . now, those are still very nice, don't you agree?"

It took every ounce of control to act detached whenever Dilaver got on this topic. He struggled with the urge to bash the other man's face in. Six months ago, Hawk's solution would have been easy. Pull out a weapon. Destroy the piece of shit. He usually countered his disgust by answering as truthfully as he could. That was the first thing he'd learned from his psychological training with GEM, the agency in a joint mission with his SEAL team. Truth would hide his lies, T., GEM's chief operative, had advised him.

"It's rather difficult to tell you about appreciating a woman when you're contemplating breaking and taming her, don't you think?" Hawk asked. He stretched out his legs in an attempt to release the tension inside him. "Not very appealing."

"Now it's your turn to satisfy my curiosity. I've been watching you around me for a couple of months now, and you're like a damn Boy Scout when it comes to women. Now you're interested in Amber. Don't you find it exciting that you have the power to take her whenever, wherever you want? That she can be your sex slave? You can own her, just like that." Dilaver snapped his fingers again. "I get horny imagining her all tied up for my pleasure, but you . . . all these months . . . and now you've found someone you want, why don't you go for it, as they say in America? Life's short. Seize the day."

Hawk had never met anyone who used clichés like Dilaver. But it made sense, in a warped way. Every action was explained away by some colloquial saying, be it local or foreign, even forcing a woman to be a sex slave.

Again, he was forced to hide behind the truth. "We're back to her having a powerful boyfriend," he said.

Dilaver shrugged. "Want to get rid of him? You saved my life. I'll do that for you."

Saved his life. So he'd take one for Hawk. Hawk knew he had to get out of the room soon before he said and did something that would betray his real feelings. He affected a yawn. "Nah. I didn't come here to start a local war over a woman, Dilaver. I have one errand to run for my boss and that's it."

"But you're still considering coming to work for me."

"Yes." *Then I'll destroy you somehow.* "Your offer sounds interesting."

"Wait till you see the cache. I'm meeting a middleman right after my international call. I'll let you in to watch me." Dilaver checked the time on his cell. "She's late again."

"A woman?"

"Oh, it isn't what you think. She's my aunt, the one I told you about who is high up in the States. She's been in the system so long she knows the ins and outs of their international networks better than the chief of the CIA," Dilaver boasted. "And she's my aunt. Cool, huh?"

"Dynamite," Hawk said dryly, knowing that would bring a guffaw out of Dilaver. There was a certain ironic humor in knowing that by the time his SEAL brothers caught up with Dilaver, the brutal Slav would be speaking like a regular surfing dude.

"Let's go out late, around tenish. Why don't you go and do those exercise you love so damn much while I conduct some business here? It's going to be a long night, with tons of partying. Maybe, now that Amber has gotten you all hot, you'll take some action with a girl tonight, eh?"

Hawk got up from the sofa. He had planned a long night ahead but not in that way. "Later, then," he said.

Back in his room, after a series of stretches, he changed into his warm sweats, knowing that he wouldn't have any company if he went jogging. Some of Dilaver's men had accompanied him at first, but they had given up when they'd realized he was a serious runner. And he had the training to run for a long, long time. He had a good excuse, too; he needed to keep in shape as a guide and Dilaver had seen outright how good a guide he had been, so no suspicions there.

He wanted away from the vicinity of Dilaver for a while. Meditation could only take one's mind off the dirtiness of his situation for so long. Sometimes, good physical pain did a better job. And he was going to need a good dose of fresh air before venturing back into one of those *kafenas* tonight. He knew it would be a rough one; Dilaver's drinking meant an orgy of abuse—breaking and taming girls, as he had called it.

He nodded to one of the many armed guards as he headed down the stairs and out the front door. No one bothered him. He was, after all, their boss's guest.

"You're crazy," Zeti said at the doorway. "It's cold outside! And you want to run around in all that melted snow? Wait till tomorrow, when it's warmer."

"What kind of freedom fighter are you?" Hawk mocked back. "What if you're called right now to go out and fight?"

"That's different. You're talking about running around and around like an idiot, not doing anything." Zeti showed his weapon. "With this and a few grenades and a Jeep, now, that gives me a reason to go out."

Hawk smiled and shrugged. "That's why you're a freedom fighter and I'm a guide, I guess," he said. "See you soon."

"A sniper will get you one of these days."

It was a fair warning. There was very little safety in these parts. But Hawk needed the fresh air. "I'm a guide. I'm good at evasion," he explained lightly, and nodded at Zeti before going out the door.

A cold blast of air welcomed him. He took a deep breath, then started at a steady pace.

To avoid the topic that would stir the swirl of emotions in his soul, he mentally went through his assignment and what he had to achieve for it to end. He was in Phase Three of a long operation that had taken years to come to this point. He couldn't afford to let his emotions get in the way; many people depended on him, and there were the high stakes of the loss of military lives if he should fail.

The last few months, while "recuperating" under Dilaver's care, his job was to get close to the kingpin and earn his confidence. He had done that. He needed to get certain information, but so far, Dilaver had just been showing off his "kingdom," going from province to province, different states that used to make up Yugoslavia to check on his sex-trafficking and drug business. It didn't help—although Hawk approved—that someone was targeting that part of the Slav's business. That had meant less focus on what Hawk was after—the weapons that Dilaver had hidden.

Hawk had to accompany him everywhere, of course. It was a way to map out Dilaver's routes, even though he couldn't tell whether these were where the weapons were located. He had memorized the different airports and roads, making mental connections between each city, from Belgrade in Serbia, to Sarajevo in Bosnia, to Pristina in Kosovo, and now Velesta, Macedonia. And at every stop, he had seen enough human degradation to last him a lifetime.

He clenched his fists and ran faster. No, he wasn't going to think about that. He must set his mind on the operation.

Get the locations. Find out about the hidden weapon silos. Then find out the last dropoff location. That was his target. He needed to get that. Once he had achieved this, he was to get his guide to take him there.

His guide. He still couldn't believe his guide came in the form of a petite blonde who looked as if she should be shopping in Saks rather than running around the Macedonian countryside. But he had already experienced some of her skills, so he knew she had hidden talents. Besides, Jed had picked her and had told him she was the best for the job at the moment.

However—Hawk wiped the sweat dripping from his chin with the back of a hand—how the hell was she going to keep up with him? He wasn't big-headed, but no matter how skilled a woman was, unless she had trained every day to be a Navy SEAL, her chances of keeping up with him while he tried to outrun Dilaver and his men were slim to none. Especially when Dilaver and his men would be gunning for Hawk once they found out he'd betrayed Dilaver. This was a problem.

And it wasn't the only problem. Jed had warned him not

to trust her all the way. How did one do that? He had spent his military career trusting his teammates when they were together, especially during a battle. He was so close to Jazz, they had been accused of being able to read each other's thoughts. There was never any question of loyalty in his group. Now, on top of watching his own back, he'd have to watch the woman at his side, too. He now understood his cousin's dilemma.

Steve had been in love with someone he thought was an assassin. At one point, he had to try to find out who she was planning to off, and just like Hawk's situation now, he had to pretend to be what he wasn't. But Steve fell from lust straight into love. Hawk grimaced out a smile as he sped up some more. Love and lust. He was straying back into emotional territory. *Stay the course, McMillan.*

He had known this operation would be very tough, precisely because of the lack of action in the beginning. He had to take the time to be friends with Dilaver. That meant actually talking to the man and watching him at work and at play. But he hadn't counted on this growing fury that ate at him. He had nowhere to target his own frustrations and hatred of that monster.

He started to run at full speed, aiming for a tree in the distance. He needed to stop thinking and feeling. Needed to clean his insides out. Pain in his lungs. Good. Pain in his chest. Good. Unable to stop fully, he missed slamming into a low branch by inches. He finally halted, bending over to take deep breaths.

Turn around and repeat, this time steady and slow, McMillan. Then he would be ready for Dilaver's festivities.

By the time he was showered and rested a few hours later, Hawk felt recharged. All this preparation, as if he were going into battle, when in reality it was more like sitting around and being unable to do anything that he wanted. He looked at his watch. It was almost time for his instant message session.

It had occurred to him that Amber might not come out to play. Well, there was only one way to find out.

He retrieved his small laptop, sat on the bed, and turned it on. After checking to make sure all the safeguards were activated, he opened the shadow drive. He didn't quite understand it, but just seeing her little icon made him smile. It was green, meaning she was there, waiting.

He typed in her handle. *Ambrosia.*

Hot Stuff.

His smile widened. He could even hear her using that snotty little tone of voice. *I like your new icon.*

You did order me to wear something hot.

He did, just to rile her. *Is that what you are, then, a little devil on fire? I see I'm going to have to be careful with my choice of words around you since you're so literal.*

You disapprove?

No. I'll put the fire out. Hawk hadn't meant to start flirting with her, but she was tempting and beautiful, and definitely a woman with a mind of her own. He would let her lead him for now.

You might get burned.

You're quick with the comebacks, too. And a good cook. Among other things.

There's more, and if you aren't careful you might find out.

I intend to. The unexpected memory of his hand sliding up the silky flesh of her thigh popped up. Soft skin. Strong, strong thigh muscles. . . .

Is this the way we're going to communicate now? Through IM? I checked this program you have. All data is erased when you shut the window. Impressive. I gather you didn't write it.

Hawk shook off the image of Amber's bare thighs. He was definitely in need of a meditation session; thinking about sex when he was supposed to be working was not the right SEAL attitude. He had to get his mind out of his pants and back to business.

Nope. Not my area of expertise. Yours is writing codes and putting them in specific places, isn't it?

What's your area of expertise, then?

Apparently, his mind was faster than his resolve. *Finding weapons. Haven't I already demonstrated it? Want me to do it again tonight?*

Okay, Hot Stuff, I'll let you win this time. Why are we meeting like this?

This is the place to establish contact. We don't have the privacy or time to know where or when to meet, so it's the best way. All you have to do is pop up the window to establish contact. My PDA will zip the message. But I want to see you tonight.

Why?

Hawk had decided that it was best to keep things vague. First, he didn't know how much he could trust Amber. Second, for some reason, he wanted to tempt her, as she did him. Maybe to test how much of her was real. *Certain discussions need to be done face to face. Also sometimes we'll be giving each other things.*

Like what?

Massages. I like them.

Do you communicate with all other ops like this? It isn't very professional.

I can ask the same about you. You started our comm by sexually assaulting me.

There was a slight pause before her answer, as if she were taken aback by his accusation. He had worded it that way to see how she would react.

Will it help if I apologize?

No.

That unforgiving? Come on, it was dark and I didn't see anything.

That didn't sound like it was typed by a remorseful woman. *Say that to my face when we see each other tonight. It'll be late. One a.m. or thereabouts.*

I'll be in bed by then.

I have to be with D for a while. I can come into your bedroom and wake you up, if you like. Will you be alone?

No, stay away from my room!

Thought so. Besides, I would like to challenge you one more time.

I'm listening.

D should be busy partying. You know the back alleys in this town. I need you to show them to me. Here's the addy.

Why? And why at night?

Will tell you later. IM is for establishing comm, remember? You want the rest of the hot stuff, you'll have to come, sweetheart. Hot Stuff out.

Wait! Wear something hot.

Hawk grinned. She was trying to have the last word. *I'm naked now. Is that hot enough?*

Amber went offline without a reply. He chuckled quietly. Served her right if she was thinking about his body now. Tit for tat.

He closed the program and, putting the laptop aside, leaned back against the pillows in the bed. He hadn't flirted with any woman since leaving his SEAL team behind in Asia. His SEAL brothers and he were used to months away from home and especially away from women, and when they were finally back among female company, flirtation came hard and fast as their male libidos bloomed overnight like morning glories.

However, these past few months Hawk had been among female company. Constantly. Dilaver had been checking up on his *kafenas* and Hawk had to go along. Female sexual slaves. Most of them were paraded in front of him half naked. Some were even willing.

Hawk had never experienced total rejection of something he loved—women. His natural tendency to flirt and tease had disappeared as he grew colder and angrier with everything he had to witness in the *kafenas*. There was no chance to relax, not with the feeling of helplessness that sat like a boulder on his soul, and it was a test of his willpower not to just go start a war all by himself. But he had a mission to complete and it had very little to do with these poor girls, some of whom fondled him at Dilaver's orders. Their attempts to seduce him had made Hawk even angrier as he showed nothing on the outside.

Hawk stared at the high ceiling, tracing the beams crisscrossing above him. No reaction. Until a certain woman dropped out from up there and landed on his naked body, that is. Amber Hutchins somehow made him feel alive inside again, made him feel more like himself. He didn't understand it yet, but he would love to find out what it was about her that made him regain his smile.

It would be nice to see her later tonight, after going through another session in hell.

It was half past twelve. Amber had arrived early on purpose. She wanted to scope out the *kafena* herself. She had never really been inside one while it was conducting business, had never wished to see the things that went under the boxlike flat roofs. The girls she and Lily had saved talked openly about their experiences and their stories made her shudder.

Lily wasn't home yet and Amber had left her a note. She wasn't worried. Her friend could take care of herself. She

smiled at the thought that Brad might have convinced her to
stay for dinner, too. He could lay on the charm when he
wanted, if Lily gave him half a chance. Those two—she
shook her head at the thought of them together—would be
interesting to watch, if they ever really managed to talk their
problems out.

She frowned. How ironic. Here she was, in a weird communication game herself. She remembered how it all
started, where she had hung a certain message. Ruefully, she
rubbed the side of her thigh. His retaliating message was
still faintly marking her. And then there were these odd
instant-messaging communications. So who was she, to crit-
icize her friend for avoiding talking to a man? The male
species was incomprehensibly complicated.

What was Hawk up to, that he needed her to guide him
through the back alleys of Velesta? He had kept their conversation humorous to distract her questions, as if he didn't
want to give out all the information. Wise move. After all,
nothing online was secured, no matter how safeguarded the
link was.

There were several dozen vehicles in front of the short
block of buildings. Music blared out into the night air as she
watched men enter and leave the different entrances. There
were three main *kafenas* here. Which one were Hawk and
Dilaver in?

Amber moved among the shadows, her dark outfit obscur-
ing her from view as she moved closer. She was to meet
Hawk in the rear, but she wanted to first satisfy her curiosity.
These faces belonged to men who came in and out of her
café, some of whom treated her like gentlemen. Yet here
they were, participating in the vilest of crimes—debasing
and degrading girls of a tender age.

She was close enough now to hear the lewd comments and
loud laughter coming out of the buildings. The weather had

warmed up enough to bring the "party" outside, and the windows were opened to let in fresh air. Climbing up the thick ivy grown to one side of the wall, she found she had a good view without anyone looking up at her. They were too busy enjoying themselves. Evidently, they were very sure there wouldn't be any raids tonight. Even so, she had to be doubly careful. It wouldn't be good to be caught.

Some of the entertainment had spilled out into the small courtyard in front of one of the entrances. A group of men surrounded what looked like a picnic table, a line forming all the way back through the door. Craning her neck, Amber could make out the white paint reflecting in the light . . . and someone writhing on top.

It was the naked form of a woman, with her hands and legs spread out and held down by the surrounding men. She was struggling as one of them stood between her open legs and dropped his pants. Amber watched with horror, gripping the vine in her hand tightly, as the man's naked buttocks started pumping. The girl's muffled screams cut through the air, making the hair at the back of Amber's neck stand up. He finished with a loud grunt, and before he had moved away, the next man in line was already between the girl's legs, positioning himself.

Dear Lord. This was . . . a gang rape. A victim had told Amber about this, that sometimes it was a free-for-all night for an unlucky new girl, chosen out of a bunch, so she could be initiated into her new job. Usually it was a girl who had been crazy enough to insult her new owners. This was her beginning punishment. Any customer could have her for free that whole night, any way he wanted. The victim who related the incident to Amber had spat at the memory. It was, she had snarled out, the most looked-forward to event by all the men.

Amber was unable to turn away from the horrific spectacle. Her mind screamed at the sight, ordering her to do something, but her whole body was frozen, shut down from shock. She watched as the girl was raped again and again, her gagged screams turning into high-pitched whimpers that were totally ignored by the monsters who shuffled up the line as if they were in a fast-food restaurant. The cries cut Amber to the soul. No one lifted a finger to help.

A raging fury rose like an inferno inside. She suddenly realized that she was aiming her semiautomatic at the crowd below. She had pulled it out without thinking, and her target was the current rapist. Her forefinger rested on the trigger. She had to do something. Take one out. Stop it. Tears ran down her face, blurring her vision.

"Don't do it."

The words were spoken softly from below her. The voice was flat, deadly. Amber didn't look down; her eyes were trained on another man in that courtyard, who was flipping the girl over. She was no longer struggling.

"Give me one reason why I shouldn't take out that bastard." She could hear the tightness in her own voice.

"You don't have enough shots to kill them all and they'll find you. Come down, Amber."

"No." She couldn't leave without doing something. "I . . . can't."

"Yes, you can. Climb down now." She didn't move or reply. "If you have to shoot, take out the girl. But there are always more inside. If you take out the men, the owners will just move their *kafenas* to another location, with better security. And you'll be caught. That one weapon you have isn't enough for this battle."

She slowly lowered her weapon, then turned to stare icily into the darkness below. She couldn't see anyone down there in the shadows. Putting away her weapon, she climbed down the wall in silence, forcing herself to concentrate on her hands and feet.

The moment she dropped onto the ground, a hand grasped hers and pulled her into a brisk jog before she could say anything. She was forced to keep up with his longer strides, trusting his eyes in the darkness, as she couldn't stop to see where they were going. They finally turned the corner and he slowed down. It took her a minute to catch her breath from the sudden exertion.

"That's why you wanted me to stay in the back of the building, isn't it?" She glared up at him, the outline of his face and body barely discernible.

"Yes," Hawk answered.

"You were in there," she accused.

"Yes."

He stood like some big statue as she stared at him. "You saw what happened and . . ."

He was a covert operative and very likely had to participate. Disgust snaked through her and she was about to back away when he reached out and grabbed her hand. She kicked out at him, wanting to get away.

They fought in silence. He wouldn't let go of her hand as he countered every one of her moves, pushing her back and moving closer until his body trapped hers against the brick wall of the building.

"Damn it, Hawk, let me go." She had seen enough tonight. "I don't want to see you or talk to you right now."

"You'll show me the back alleys like you're supposed to."

She stiffened at the coldness in his voice. "You can't order me around," she said, just as icily. "And I don't work with rapists and cowards. Couldn't you have done something?"

"It isn't time."

"You mean you can't blow your cover," she said bitterly.

"Yes." A finger tilted her chin up. His warm breath brushed her face. The back of his hand touched her cheek, softly wiping away the remaining wetness from her tears. "I know what you think of me right now. I can't do anything about that. But I want to be clear that I don't rape women and children, and if I could do anything without jeopardizing my mission, I would in a heartbeat. But I can't. A lot of people depend on the success of my mission. Jed told me you're the best in the tracking business and I need you to help me. Are you in or out?"

"What's in it for me?" she asked. "Money isn't everything."

"Jed told me to make you an offer you can't refuse. I've been thinking about it and was going to ask you tonight, but it doesn't matter now. I have an offer." He leaned down until his lips almost touched hers. "I'll destroy Dilaver for you, Amber. At the end of this mission. I'll come back and destroy him."

"Kill him?"

"No. I've strict orders not to do that for now. But I've traveled with him and know all his strongholds. There are ways to get a man like that. Will you trust me?"

Amber didn't—couldn't—trust any man right now, not after what she had seen. She couldn't fathom any decent human being witnessing anything like that and not doing a thing about it. Her own experience had been secondary; she had never seen the crimes, just the victims. This made it even more personal.

"I don't know. I can't feel a damn thing right now except murderous."

"It'll stay with you," Hawk told her. "It'll be there tomorrow, and the day after."

She shuddered at the knowledge in his voice. She jerked her face from his finger. "I'm going to kill Dilaver myself. *I* am not under orders."

"There you go. The woman of my dreams."

The statement was so ludicrous it made her stare at him for a moment. "That's ridiculous," she finally said.

"Not at all. I've always dreamed about a woman who would do everything for me, including kill a man I can't." Her mouth gaped in astonishment even as he dipped his head. Still reeling from his words, she barely registered his quick, hard kiss. "There, now that we've sealed the bargain, let's look at those alleys."

"What . . . have we agreed on?" Amber felt as if she were on a runaway train.

It might be dark, but the humor was back in his voice. "That you're the woman of my dreams, remember? And that I'll help you in any way I can. Come on."

She had gone through so many different emotions in the last hour, she didn't know what to say to that. His footing was sure, as if he were used to walking in unknown dark places. She was supposed to be leading, but he seemed to know where he was going at the moment. So she just let him pull her along, deeper into the shadows.

9

Amber was surprised at how well she and Hawk worked together. He was a natural tracker, moving through the darkness like a thief, able to slip in and out of the shadows like a ghost. No wonder she hadn't seen him when he was in her office the other night.

Hawk McMillan was more than an operative. She could tell. She had worked with different CIA-trained operatives before. A mediocre one would be noisy, hesitant in the strange darkness. A good one would still betray certain unease by pausing here and there. Hawk just followed her, his attention focused on the pathways she chose, and at certain points he would touch and explore a wall here or a landmark there, as if familiarizing himself with their texture. It was fascinating watching him at work, as he morphed from the man with the mocking voice, playing those games with her, into a very serious operative.

He asked a few questions—very good ones, in her book. Amber did her best to try to fill him in about the height and thickness of certain walls, the thickness of the ropes she used to scale them, the names of *kafenas* nearby, the cubby-holes that she might use to hide anything of value. The last question alone told her he wasn't an ordinary operative in need of a guide. The man had either stolen things before or had done a lot of tracking in places where he needed to hide things.

The most important thing was that he was keeping her mind busy, distracting her from thinking about *it*. He was remote, almost authoritative in his questions, as if he, too, had things on his mind. For once, she didn't object to the high-handed attitude.

"Tired?"

Amber shook her head. She felt blessedly numb. She wasn't tired at all, even though they had spent the better part of three hours tracking around the back alleys of Velesta. She had the routes memorized, since she used them often to move the escaped girls to her own hiding places, among other things. When Hawk had asked how she became so familiar with these paths, she had hedged on the truth, telling him that she met shady characters to negotiate all the time. He seemed to accept the answer.

"We're done for the night," Hawk continued. "I'll take you home now."

"This is my city, you know. I can get back by myself."

"I know that, but it'll be a good test whether I can take you back through these alleys without your help, right?"

She looked at him disbelievingly. "You couldn't have memorized all the routes with a quickie tour and some of the rough maps I drew up."

"Try me."

"And if you lose?"

"I won't."

He sounded so arrogant, she was tempted to just disappear down one of the alleys and leave him there. If he was so damn good, he could find his way back to . . . She bit down on her lower lip as horrifying images immediately popped up.

"Don't go there," he said, reading her mind.

She swerved around to face him. "How can you not be affected by it? Going in and out of those places." She jabbed his chest with a finger. It felt hard as rock through his shirt. "How can you be with Dilaver and not want to kill him?"

"It isn't what I was sent to do."

She hated simple answers. "That's it?" She didn't back away as he came a few steps closer. She had always been on the short side and big guys didn't particularly frighten her; if he was thinking of intimidating her with his size, he was in for a surprise. "That's not an answer. These are little girls suffering at the hands of men, Hawk. You can't just dismiss them by saying that you weren't sent to help them, so there's nothing you can do."

"I didn't say that," he said patiently, as if he were talking to a child. "I said, that isn't—"

"I heard you the first time," she interrupted, letting her earlier fury seep back in. The numbness was disappearing fast. "If you can stand there and watch . . . that . . . you're heartless and cruel. Even if you don't take part in it, you're just as guilty, just like they—"

Hawk moved so fast, she hadn't even had time to take a breath before she found her back against a wall. His big hands were on her shoulders, firmly holding her in place. She supposed she could maim him with a knee, but for some reason she checked her anger at being manhandled by him again. Instead she stared up into his face defiantly, even though she couldn't see his expression.

He was silent for a few seconds, then his hands gentled. He took a step back. "I'm not like them," he said, then turned abruptly and walked away. Very quickly. Without looking back.

Amber stared at Hawk as he disappeared into the shadows. *He* was leaving her? Oh no, no, no. She was a tracker, and no one left her behind like that.

She set out in the direction he took. He was already gone, even though he only had a minute's head start. She started running. There was no way she was going to lose him.

Lily didn't know what had gotten into her. She had come here to discuss the interview, yet it was now past midnight and she had stayed for dinner, wine, a video, more wine, and . . . She surreptitiously studied the man sitting next to her, legs comfortably stretched out as he watched the last few minutes of the movie. His tie was gone, the top few buttons of his shirt undone, his hair slightly mussed up.

She had always known it. Bradford Sun was a wolf in a bureaucrat's suit. He had demonstrated it tonight, slowly taking down her defenses one by one. He had first tackled business, surprising her with how prepared he had been, throwing out ideas on what to show the newsman. He had numbers and declassified papers from Amnesty International about the human trafficking business to use as quotes. He suggested how to deal with each one-on-one interview with the victims. She was privately amazed at how far he was willing to push the envelope, even to reveal that peacekeepers were contributing to the problem, that his department wasn't doing its job.

It had been such an interesting conversation, Lily hadn't noticed the hours going by. He had refilled her glass, and she had enjoyed both the wine and his company as he talked about her other favorite subject, art. She looked at the coffee table. Two bottles of wine. Two margaritas. No wonder she was feeling relaxed.

"Are you enjoying the movie?" he asked.

"Yes. I think I should be going." She was enjoying everything way too much. Usually her radar would be beeping madly by now, warning her of danger, but she hadn't heard a damn thing tonight.

"You can't drive with all that alcohol in you," he pointed out. "Stay. I have a spare bedroom, if you like."

She was tempted to stay, and not to check out his spare bed. There wasn't any room in her life for Brad, or anyone. She didn't even like him, anyway. It was just the alcohol. *You just keep telling yourself that.* She ignored the sarcastic bitch in her head.

"One would think you purposely plied me with alcohol tonight, Mr. Sun," she said softly.

Did his smile widen slightly? There was certainly amusement in his voice. "I think you once accused me of being too straightforward. Now you're accusing me of being underhanded."

" 'Devious' comes to mind. 'Underhanded' isn't calculating enough."

"I purposely chose a fruity wine. Obviously that didn't sweeten your tart tongue, damn it," he said mildly.

That was the second part of the attack, sneaking in that teasing charm over dinner. How could she have missed that? And why did she want to muss up his hair more? She wondered how he would look after hot sex. Oh, bad idea to bring that up now. Because she suddenly had a vision of him on top of her right here on the couch. She bent and picked up her glass, drinking quickly.

"It takes a lot to wear me down," she said.

"I have time," he said.

He didn't know it, but there wasn't enough time for anything in her life. A quickie here or there, maybe, but nothing that she knew would be what she wanted, if she allowed this thing happening between her and Brad to grow. She didn't need another complication, either. No room for romance, or love, or anything permanent.

Let's face it. Bradford Sun was an upcoming bureaucrat, sworn to uphold the law. She was at the opposite end of the spectrum, running illegal art booty and mingling with criminals. Oil and water, and ne'er the twain shall meet.

"I like it when we're friends and talking," Brad continued.

"We aren't friends," Lily muttered. "We're just being friendly."

"Not going to argue with you right now over semantics," he retorted mildly. "We've an agreement about the coming interviews, then?"

"Yeah." She had agreed to ask several of the girls who could speak English whether they would tell their story. She sighed, hating the fact that she had to admit it out loud. "I like the idea, Brad. And it's really good of you to facilitate the meetings. I wouldn't have been able to get hold of any big-shot newsman to run this kind of story."

He regarded her quizzically. "There, it wasn't that difficult, was it? While you're all relaxed like that, you can throw in a line or two about how wonderful being with me is and that you would like to stay the night." He laughed, then added with a wicked grin, "If it helps, here, have another drink."

More than relaxed. Lily seldom drank so much in one sitting, especially with a man around. Alcohol made her horny. There, she admitted it. And Brad wasn't helping by showing her this side of him. She had always known it was there, and she had diligently avoided being alone with him because of it, yet here she was, doing exactly that, enjoying that hidden side and wanting him more than usual. He chose that moment to look back at her and his smile was that easy masculine curve that always made her insides clench.

She was so fucked.

The man was in phenomenally good shape. He had scaled walls and run on the top of narrow ledges as if he had been living in this city of old buildings all his life. Amber had determinedly followed along, but he had managed to keep just out of reach, turning around now and then to make a show of checking his watch.

Amber scowled. He had hardly been out of breath when she had finally jumped in front of him a few minutes ago, a mile away from where they had started.

"Not bad. You'll do," Hawk said.

"There has got to be a better way for me to spend my nights than doing this," she said, trying not to breathe too hard.

"Chasing a guy can be good."

"Not if he keeps running off," she pointed out.

"Consider it foreplay. Here's your car. I've got to get back to Dilaver, and I'll be gone for a few days on a trip with him. I'll talk to you soon."

Amber looked speechlessly at his back as he disappeared in the direction of the *kafenas*. Foreplay? That was play? Her aching muscles didn't think so.

Once she reached home, Amber sat down on the bench behind the restaurant and removed her wet shoes. The wooden steps that led up to her back deck had a tendency to creak, especially when the weather turned warm after a cold night, and she didn't want to wake Lily. She stretched her legs out, ruefully wondering whether she would be able to walk on heels in a matter of a few hours. God, was she going to be tired today.

Hawk had purposely taken her on a workout. There was no question in her mind that he had been testing her stamina as she began the chase that had taken her a solid hour to catch up with him. Even then, she wasn't so sure it hadn't been because *he* had wanted to be caught.

She made a face as she rubbed the bottoms of her aching feet. One thing was for sure. Hawk continued to surprise her each time they met.

A creak from behind her made her turn around quickly, only to find Lily standing at the bottom step of the wooden stairs. Her friend stopped at the sound.

"Damn it," she whispered to herself. "Forgot to take off my shoes."

"Busted," Amber said, standing up.

Lily gasped and whirled around. "Shit! You nearly gave me a heart attack!" She cupped her hand over her eyes, trying to see Amber. "Where the hell are you?"

Amber stepped into the lighted area. "Ta-da."

Lily looked her over, taking in the tight dark outfit she had on. "Oh, you're so busted yourself," she said mockingly. "You just got home from your rendezvous with Hawk. I want all the details."

"And you just got home from yours with Brad," Amber retorted. "So let's hear your excuse for creeping in after curfew hours, young lady."

They stared at each other for a few moments, then began to giggle. Lily leaned against the banister, her shoulders shaking. Amber flopped down at the foot of the steps.

"You look dirty and tired. Doesn't look like a romantic night out," Lily noted as she joined her.

Amber snorted at the thought. "That man's idea of romance is me chasing his ass all over Velesta at top speed."

"Ooooh. You were doing the chasing, huh? Why? Where did you guys meet?"

Amber didn't feel like sharing what she saw at the *kafena*. Not right now. It would only upset Lily, especially when she herself hadn't done anything to save that girl. Guilt sat heavily inside her.

"Hey." Lily interrupted her thoughts. "You got all serious all of a sudden. What's the matter?"

"I'm exhausted," Amber said. It wasn't a lie. Now that she was off her feet and the adrenaline from the chase was gone, her energy level was near zero. "Hawk isn't much of a talker, that's for sure, but I managed to get an outline of his operation. I'll tell you tomorrow, when my brain's working again. Now tell me about your meeting with Brad. And don't lie about talking business till the wee hours in the morning."

"Well . . ." Lily studied her fingernails carefully. "We had dinner."

"And?"

"And we talked about art and stuff," Lily added.

"And?"

"And we watched a movie."

Amber sighed. "Are we going to get to the good part or not?"

"And nothing. Then I came home." Lily stood up and offered Amber a helping hand.

Amber got up slowly as her thigh muscles protested. "Normally, I would believe you," she said, wincing as she lifted one leg onto the first step. "But we're talking about you and Brad here. No quarrels, just a good old nice evening dining and watching movies. Uh-huh, sure, I believe you."

"He was very charming tonight," Lily conceded. "You sure are walking up these steps like a grandma. If Hawk's so full of energy at night outside, can you imagine his endurance indoors? Say, in bed?"

"Nu-uh, I know a changing-the-subject tactic when I see one," Amber mocked. "So, you find Brad charming, huh? I told you that he isn't all bureaucrat. That's a really interesting man once you get to know him, Lily."

"Yeah, well, I'm not exactly in town long enough to do that. His lifestyle and mine aren't going to converge anytime in the future, either."

Amber admitted that that could be a problem. Brad was all black and white, and Lily was obviously as gray as one could get when it came to the law. If there were ever an example of opposites attracting, then her friends were the prime example.

"Things have a way of working out," she said as they reached the top. She wiped her damp feet as Lily opened the door. "Maybe you'll retire from your line of work, and who knows?"

"And maybe pigs will fly." Lily turned on the kitchen light. She went straight to the refrigerator. "Want a drink? I think we have some mimosa left."

Amber closed the door behind her. "Nah. I'll just have water. I have a restaurant to run in . . . oh . . . a couple of hours." She sighed. "We'll talk sometime tomorrow, okay? Maybe I'll skip the bookkeeping in the morning, stay in bed, and curse at Hawk McMillan."

She watched Lily pour a large drink. Something had happened tonight, she could tell. She had hoped that Lily would see that she deserved Brad, no matter what her background was, but it would take time. Lily's darkness wasn't exactly something one light could brighten immediately. Anyway, Brad would talk to her later. She poured a glass of water for herself.

"Goodnight, then," Lily said, heading for the sofa. "I'm going to stay up a bit. We'll definitely have a lot to talk about today. Brad has info about a new group coming in. There's also his interview venture and our plans for that. You have this thing going with Hawk McMillan which might take up some of your time, so we definitely have to look at schedules."

So it was "our plans," was it? That was interesting in itself. Amber nodded. "It's all tied together in one big Dummy package. We might be able to use it as hot stuff."

Lily raised her eyebrows. "It looks like we all have something in common—Dilaver." She took a gulp from her mimosa. "Maybe we can get Hawk to help us with our venture."

"We'll see. The man's a bit one-track." Amber thought of how Hawk's focus was on his mission, even when there were other things that needed his immediate attention. "He might not help."

"Oh, be your persuasive self, Amber," Lily said, settling back comfortably in the sofa with a yawn. "Stop competing with one another and talk to the guy. He can be an asset to us."

"Umm, I could say the same thing about your being nice with Brad," Amber pointed out as she limped toward her room. "You must tell me the rest of this date. Girlfriends are supposed to do that, you know."

"Horrors, next you'll want us to paint each other's toenails," Lily quipped.

Amber laughed. "I'll keep that in mind for our next slumber party," she promised lightly. "Goodnight."

" 'Night."

She quietly closed the bedroom door and leaned against it. *Don't go there.* Hawk's quiet words came, sliding between her and the painful images. She took a deep breath, finished her drink, then started to undress.

As she headed for bed, the laptop by her bed caught her eye. She crawled between the sheets and purred appreciatively. Her laptop was on an adjustable table that slid over the bed at lap level. Within such easy reach, it was way too tempting. She had to check.

Yes, he was online, waiting for her, it seemed. She found it disconcerting that he read her mind and knew that she would look for him.

Don't you ever sleep? You're always up, no matter what time of the night it is!

There wasn't a reply for a few minutes. Maybe he was asleep after all. It didn't matter. Amber yawned, then grinned. Maybe he was tired out from the night's activities.

I was waiting for you. Make sure you got home safely.

Damn. So much for that thought. *I can take care of myself, Hot Stuff.*

You had a rough night. Thought you might want some company.

She was touched at his concern. He'd said it would be tough to shake off the memory of what she'd seen. She rubbed her eyes with the heel of her palms. *Will the anger ever go away?*

No.

What do you do about it? How did one live normally after watching that? She bit her lip. How did those girls she helped out live normally after going through that? She was beginning to understand that the stories she had been told before were a mere fraction of this horrific display of inhumane torture.

I meditate.

His reply surprised her. Meditate? He didn't look like the meditating type. *Like ohm-ohm-the universe is perfect? Not my cuppa.* She preferred to deal with a problem more directly. Like total destruction of Dilaver's network, for instance. *You're full of surprises, Hot Stuff.*

So are you, Ambrosia. Not just a pretty face, after all.

She could hear the smile behind the words. She had only met and talked to the guy, what—three times?—yet she could read between the lines, understand that he was trying to distract her. It dawned on her that the guy was very much a gentleman, in an odd covert operative sort of way. She laughed softly. She supposed she could reciprocate and give him the same comfort he was offering—gently teasing each other to sleep.

I'm not the only one with a pretty face, you know. But I'm sure you know that. He was, by far, the nicest-looking man she had seen in Velesta, or anywhere, for that matter. *I'm sure you hear that all the time.*

Yeah, all the time.

Must be tough. Amber almost asked him whether he had any special girlfriend waiting for him somewhere, then shook her head. Where did that come from? It was none of her business. A man who looked like him had to have lots of girlfriends, if not one. *Girls must flock around you like bees to honey.*

Actually, they make me feel like a candy bar. Or a big pizza with all the toppings.

Startled by his reply, Amber settled back against her pillow for a few moments. *Wow, do you really feel that way?*

A pause. *Sometimes.*

She didn't quite know what to say to that. She had started out teasing him and he had once again flummoxed her. She thought of how he had looked when she had first seen Hawk . . . the outline of his body against the windowpane, with outside snow flurries forming a halo around him. She hadn't known he was totally nude then, but that sight of him had caused her to pause. In fact, she realized now that it had given him the split second he needed to realize he hadn't been alone. She smiled ruefully. An assassin she was not.

Go to sleep. He interrupted her reverie. *I'll contact you when I'm able.*

Where are you going? Would he tell?

No idea. D's going on the road, and that's good. He wants

me with him on this trip, which has to do with other business, so that's good.

She understood what he wasn't saying. Dilaver was beginning to trust him more, and this trip had to do with weapons, not women. *Okay, Hot Stuff. Hamburger waiting for ya when you get back.*

5MW/MTL/PF/18/69. 'Night, Ambrosia. He signed off immediately.

Amber stared in disbelief. It was the same line he had written on the side of her thigh, but she had just realized 69 wasn't on her menu. She clicked off the program with a snort. Smart-ass.

10

Veza. **Every country has a form of exploit-**ing connections, and Hawk was finding out that the Slavic states were practically run through *veza*. The right connections could get one a good government job, or a bigger, better-equipped hospital room, or a place in the university. In the world of mercenaries, *veza* could get one freedom to move from province to province, state to state, without too much trouble.

Through his weapons and drug trades, Dragan Dilaver had accumulated and given many *vezas,* thus making him very powerful. His weapons, Hawk discovered, were very much sought-after. He hadn't been kidding when he'd told Hawk that what he had couldn't be found on the streets yet, that they were the most current state-of-the-art weaponry. Someone in the United States had been dropping these shipments for him to distribute in any way he wanted, as long as he armed the KLA. Of course, Dilaver made sure he made a lot of money while following orders.

"My aunt is a genius, isn't she?" Dilaver boasted, as they rode through the bumpy roads in a Humvee, courtesy of a *veza* with a high-end peacekeeping official. "She's coordinated this for years, you know. I'm really looking forward to meeting her again."

"When's she coming?" Hawk asked. He wanted to know who this "aunt" was, too.

Dilaver shrugged. "She says she's been delayed and will call again later. I want to get as much of the business in order as I can so she can see I can take care of bigger things, you know?"

Hence the road trip. Dilaver wanted to take care of certain gangs who hadn't been "respectful" enough. He also wanted Hawk to see how it was done over here. Hawk knew it was also a test to see how he would handle a "situation" if he were to work for Dilaver.

Hawk didn't mind. Taking out a gang was appealing, anyhow. Who cared whose side he was on? They were all alike, in the same trades, killing each other over illegal weapons and drugs. All this watching and waiting was wearing on him; he looked forward to taking a few of them out. And along the way, he would be mapping Dilaver's routes and trying to find out where the weapon depots were.

Their convoy rode boldly through the city streets onto scenic country routes. Dilaver's men were armed to the teeth, waving weapons at passing vehicles. Sometimes they shouted, their anticipation of some action ahead obvious to Hawk. He understood the adrenaline running through their blood; he felt it, too.

"Sometimes I miss being young," Dilaver commented, gesturing at the younger men leaning out of their open Jeeps. "They aren't afraid of dying. They just want to kill."

"Are you afraid of dying?" Hawk asked.

"Of course not. But I don't take stupid chances like I used to. Money and old age will make one a cautious man, Hawk."

Hawk ran his hand down the AK-47 standing between his

legs. It was on the tip of his tongue to point out that mercenary-turned-old-farts became pimps, just as Dilaver now was. Somehow, he didn't think the kingpin would like to be called that. He deliberately changed the subject. "So we're going to cautiously attack some group of militia, and then what?"

Dilaver laughed. "Cautiously attack? Damn your odd American-Serbian translations. In this country, it's all war and no caution, my friend. That's why I keep solidifying my power base. That's why I make and take care of certain friends in need of *veza*. You never know who will help you out later on, so you help out as much as you can."

"That . . . doesn't make one bit of sense, but keep talking," Hawk said.

"It's easy to demonstrate. This group we're going after has been bothering a few friends of mine. I also suspect they've been hijacking my shipments. Now, you lead my guys and take out this group, right? My friends will hear of this, and also your connection to me, and now you can get some favors done through *veza*, you see? You'll be a friend, too. Around here, you can't buy connections, like you do with the coffee money stuff in Asia; you earn it. Much more deserving, don't you think?"

In a twisted sort of way, yes, it made sense. But then, everything in this world was twisted. The talk of friendship and loyalty. The camaraderie between two "blood" brothers, talking about life and sharing locker-room jokes. All this sandwiched between bouts of violence. These were things Hawk valued in his life with his SEAL brothers. Yet now he had to function the same way with his enemies.

It sickened him to see the horrifying similarity from the other side. And now he had to go out and kill in the name of collecting *veza*. He knew the veneer of humanity was very thin in the war front, and once killing became a cheap thrill, there was very little left to distinguish right from wrong. And those young men riding open shot in the convoys were just going for the cheap thrills of bloody action and quick cash.

Hawk thought of the girl who was so violently raped last night, and the look of anguish and betrayal in Amber's eyes. He wanted to destroy Dilaver's network and take out those men one by one, not for the thrill of action, and certainly not for cash. For those girls. And to take away Amber's pain and grief.   •

He clung to the image of her crying and aiming a weapon at the group of rapists, and somehow it clicked in his mind that the sight of Amber represented reality to him. She knew and understood the twisted world she was living in was fake, that everything happening around her—the friend-ships and the bondings—wasn't real. She had been able to do this for four years and still cried at not being able to help the helpless.

"Besides, I have good reasons to get rid of them," Dilaver continued. "I want this area under my control."

The closest city was a few hours drive away. The roads had slowly deteriorated and became more like country paths.

"Why?" Hawk asked the obvious question. There was nothing here.

"You'll see."

There was a shout informing them that they were closing in, to get ready for attack. Hawk looked out the window at the pretty countryside, with the shadows and sunlight of dusk settling in, giving it a postcard effect that belied the tragic horrors of war happening in its cities. The truth was hidden in this twisted world.

So what truth was Amber Hutchens hiding? For the first time, Hawk admitted to himself that he wanted to find out because he needed something—someone—solidly real, and not some abstract reason, on which to hang his sanity.

"Ready, Hawk?"

"Ready," he said, as he watched all the men spill out of the vehicles, scrambling toward the top of the hill. Time to stop thinking.

Hawk jumped off the Humvee, grabbing his weapons in both hands, and not glancing at Dilaver, started running. No use being a sitting duck contemplating about life and death in the vehicle. He'd get himself killed.

The ground under his feet rumbled with the familiar sound of an exploding grenade. Clumps of earth flew up over the crest of the hill. When he reached the top, he went down flat on his stomach and started a belly-crawl. The scene from his vantage point showed a chaotic battle under way. Apparently, the only strategy these guys knew was pretending to be cowboys and Indians. Circle the wagons and make a lot of noise while shooting. He didn't think Jazz, the co-commander of his SEAL team, and the consummate strategist, would approve. There was nothing to do but aim and shoot as bullets whizzed past.

"Hawk!" Dilaver shouted from behind. He was limping but was still able to keep up with his men. He came up close behind Hawk. "Take a few of my men and circle around to the other side. We'll cover this side. Once they know they're surrounded, they'll surrender."

"Care to tell me first why this band of brothers is in the middle of nowhere like sitting ducks?" Hawk shouted back.

"They're guarding territory. And looking for something."

"What?" Hawk shook his head. "Never mind. I'll get rid of them and collect my *veza* points first."

Dilaver smacked him on the back. "There you go. Now you get how we do business here."

Hawk studied the area quickly, noting the landscape and impending nightfall. A barrage of RPGs and small arms fire disturbed the air. Hell, he didn't need anyone to help him. But this was a test of his skill and he wasn't going to show his hand just yet. After all, he was merely a guide who happened to be in excellent shape, not a mercenary. Or a Navy SEAL.

He signaled to two of Dilaver's men whom he'd gotten to know. They were the most skilled ones, least likely to get too excited when sneaking up toward the enemy's rear. For now, he had to view them as part of his team.

"Bring grenades," he ordered briskly. "We're going to make a lot of noise."

Amber closed the container. "That's it, that's the last one," she said. "Do you have the drinks and clothes packed?"

"Yes, and I have the car out back, ready to load." Lily taped the box she had filled up with clothes. "I think this will be enough for this and the next group."

The boxes of clothes, food, and amenities were for the young girls they had in hiding in various basements around Velesta. The girls needed a few weeks to recuperate from their injuries. Those who were stronger helped the weaker ones.

Amber stacked the containers near the doorway. "We have to be careful," she cautioned. "Our groups are getting bigger and we don't want Dilaver to start getting too suspicious."

"So it's good we have your Hawk to tell us he isn't in town, right? We can do our runs and maybe tell Brad to get in another raid."

Amber cocked her head. "So are you calling Brad again today?"

"You can."

"I will, if you'll tell me what happened last night."

Lily scowled. "I told you—nothing happened."

"Right. And that isn't a hickey on your neck." Amber grinned when Lily smacked at a certain spot on her neck and made off to the bathroom. There wasn't any hickey, but she'd tossed the lie out to see how her friend would react. Now she knew for sure that Lily and Brad hadn't just had dinner.

"Bitch! There's nothing there!" Lily yelled from the bathroom.

"Of course. Nothing happened, so how could there be any hickey?" Amber laughed when Lily reappeared, her dark eyes flashing threateningly at her. "Ooooh, busted again, huh?"

Her friend made a face at her, running a careless hand through her short tresses. Her gold ear hoops jiggled and glinted against the black hair. Her smile turned rueful. "Oh, okay, so we kissed." At Amber's raised eyebrows, she made another face. "Among other things."

"My, things are progressing between the two of you, aren't they?" Amber took a bite from a freshly baked cookie.

"Yeah, well, don't expect it to progress too much," Lily muttered as she moved some of the boxes.

"Why not? Lily, he likes you. You like him. That's a good thing."

Lily looked up. "Since when is getting involved emotionally a good thing when it comes to people like me?"

So that was her problem. Amber finished her cookie, eyeing her friend thoughtfully. "Lily, sometimes the future isn't so bleak, you know? You don't have to see yourself as a career criminal for the rest of your life."

"Right. I don't go around making illegal art bids and not have a reputation among certain people. And oh yeah, involvement with shady people who run guns, make fake passports, and are basically mercenaries looks so good on my résumé."

Amber went over to Lily and pulled her by the arms. "Look, I've known you for four years and we're friends, aren't we? You never did tell me why you chose this lifestyle. You're beautiful, know enough about art to tell me something about your background, and yet you're running around with people who are using you to make money. Why?" She gestured with her chin toward the boxes and containers. "I know it has something to do with the girls, but you make it very personal, Lily. You've never told me the reason."

Lily's eyes met hers for a long time, as if she were considering whether to tell Amber the truth or half of it. "Why are you a contract agent for the CIA?" she asked quietly. "You hate them."

"I don't *hate* them, hate them. I just know they are users." Amber released Lily's arms. "They see me as an asset because I provide them with information they need for their analyses and political games. I see them as a way to help these girls out of this hellhole. I met some of the luckier ones in the States, runaways who had stories to tell and no one who truly cared, and I wanted to make a difference. Throwing money at organizations didn't seem to help. I know this, I was part of one and all they did was hold fundraisers and play with numbers to get more funding as the kids became hopelessly lost in the system. So I opted for an unconventional way. You know this. I've already told you the story of my life."

"You have a big heart, Amber," Lily said quietly. "Don't your parents miss you?"

"They were missionaries. They know I'm just continuing their job, only in my way. Besides, they're happily retired now with their own little café in Florida." Amber missed them, actually. She hadn't called home for a while now. "You don't have to tell me anything you don't want, Lily. I know some of it is too painful for you."

Amber was, after all, a contract agent. Backgrounds were made up all the time. She had chosen to tell Lily the truth a couple of years ago, when they had become closer friends. Their partnership had started very slowly, when it became obvious Amber needed help. She couldn't run a CIA front *and* travel around the region moving girls in and out of hideouts.

"Do you remember how we met?" Lily asked.

Lily Noretski had appeared on a prayer, when Amber had accompanied a businessman to an illegal art auction out of curiosity. After they were introduced, she had dropped by The Last Resort a few times when she was in town. Amber liked her. Lily was eclectic, well traveled, funny as hell, and totally fearless when it came to handling weapons and dangerous situations. Amber had seen it herself one night when they were accosted by some thugs who had thought they had found some candidates for their *kafenas*.

Together, she and Lily had beaten the crap out of the men. Amber still smiled at that particularly satisfying memory. That had been the beginning of their getting to know each other.

"Let's see, wasn't it fighting over some man?" Amber laughed at Lily's frown.

"Bitch. That's why we get along so well. Always joking. I guess it's time to tell you a bit about me."

Through the years, Amber had discovered that Lily didn't seem to have anyone. Nor did she want to talk about her own past. It still intrigued Amber how her friend could possibly end up being an expert in the highly secretive world of illegal art. Who trained her about art? And how did she get started? And how did one go about bidding for black market art? Lily was mum about the methods, but obviously her cut was high, since she gave Amber a lot of the cash to pay for information and hideout places.

"I lost a sister this way." Lily tapped one of the boxes with a foot. "She was kidnapped. My parents didn't really care, since we didn't have enough money to support six kids anyway. No one cared, and I was really angry at them. So one day I ran away with a gunrunner who became my boyfriend. He taught me how to use weapons and take care of myself. In fact, he taught me about networking with different groups. I was his . . . asset, if you know what I mean."

Amber kept her expression bland. She knew Lily was revealing a lot more between the lines.

"Then I met a businessman who dealt in art, who told me I could be his asset. And he had better clothes, so I left my boyfriend for him." Lily shrugged. "On to bigger, better crimes. End of story. Sorry you asked?"

"No. Glad. I see now why you get so passionate about the girls."

"Yes. I hate those bastards that lure and kidnap them," Lily said fiercely. "And I'll save as many girls as I can, however long I can."

"I'm sorry about your sister," Amber said softly.

"We were very close. I couldn't save her, but I'll save the others," Lily said, then picked up a box. "Ready to load these babies in? We really should get going."

"Okay. Hey . . ."

"What?" Lily paused at the back door.

"Brad would understand, you know."

There was a flash of emotion in Lily's eyes before her face shuttered. "Would he? And what kind of asset would I be to a career bureaucrat?" she asked before walking out the door.

Amber sighed. Good point. In terms of assets anyway.

She picked up a couple of containers and headed after her friend.

They had three safe houses, two in town and one just outside. The girls were moved to the last one just before their long ride out of Macedonia. They were good hiding places. Dilaver would never guess that his missing girls were actually driven into Velesta, the very place to which they were headed.

Now there were a different group of girls—those who had been taken from the raids. They were in worse condition than the ones Lily and her mercenaries had saved while being transported, sometimes needing extreme medical attention.

"When will Tatiana and Alia be able to go?" Lily asked as she started up the car.

"I don't think they'll be well enough to make it this trip, Lily. Tatiana really needs to rest. That girl is mentally and physically exhausted." Tatiana had also not spoken a word since the rescue. The girls who had been with her said she hadn't for a long time, even when "Papa" hit her many times to make her plead. Amber's heart broke every time she saw the scars on the girl's body. "Maybe next trip."

Amber and Lily had been very careful to transport the girls by different routes so they were harder to trace. Those flying out had to be taught how to use their passports and what exactly to say at different embassies, if they were caught. Those who preferred to return to their homes were accompanied to the farthest train stations possible.

"I hope she makes it, Amber," Lily said quietly. "She . . . reminds me of my sister. I would love to get her out of here as quickly as possible, to somewhere safe."

Amber's responsibility was to get the girls ready, or as ready as possible; Lily was in charge of transportation. Amber had gone on several of these trips, after shutting the café down for vacation, to learn the different routes and meet the networks involved, and was always amazed at Lily's many connections.

Veza—who one knew to ease away problems—was the most valuable asset besides cash, and in the world of moving people without papers across borders, one needed to know many people at different levels of government *and* crime. Sometimes, watching how Lily nimbly navigated her way through them, Amber wondered whether there was any line between the two. Four years of doing this had certainly made her even more cynical.

She touched Lily's arm comfortingly. She had never lost a sister the way Lily had and could imagine how painful it had to be to see these girls and know her sister had suffered the same fate. "I'll do my best to get her ready," she said. Privately, she was worried. The girl wouldn't talk. How was she going to function among strangers?

By the time they reached the last safe house with the deliveries, it was very late in the afternoon. At every stop, Amber checked on the injured girls while Lily talked to those who were ready to leave with her on the next trip. They restocked the place. Amber gave cash to the caretakers, two nurses who had lost their jobs and families in the Balkan wars.

"You must take more away soon," one of them told her. "Too many girls."

Amber nodded. The more they took in, the more dangerous the situation. With Brad's raids, their numbers had almost tripled, and she couldn't afford to get anyone else involved in the caretaking. Too many people equaled more risk of being discovered. As it was, three safe houses was pushing it. Brad had offered to bring in international medics, but then that would mean reports would filter out. Their operation wouldn't be a secret anymore.

"Very soon," Amber agreed.

THE HUNTER \ 143

Lily burst into the room suddenly. "Amber," she said, her calm voice contrasting her expressive eyes. "Can we talk?"

Amber nodded to the nurse, who went off with a few of the containers. "What is it?"

"I just got a cell call. Dilaver's men are attacking one of the gangs that have been seizing his trailers."

"That means—"

"If Dilaver captures them alive, they'll tell him about selling the girls to me. They're mercenaries, without much allegiance."

"But you've been careful. Dilaver wouldn't be able to trace you."

"Yes, but it'd interest him to know that it's a woman who's setting a price on his trailers," Lily said. Her movements were very measured as she picked up her jacket from the back of the chair. "I have the location and I need to go there."

"Why?" Amber frowned. "They're in the middle of fire-fight and this guy calls you? Isn't that a bit odd? And what are you going to do in a battle?"

"I said the mercenaries have some allegiance, didn't I? The man owed me, so he's doing me the favor of telling me to run before Dilaver comes after me." Lily shrugged. "I'm not running. I'm going there to take the mercenaries out myself. That way there's no chance for Dilaver to interrogate them."

Amber stepped in front of Lily. "Wait a minute. You're going there alone to . . . what . . . take out a whole gang of mercenaries? Lily, you aren't the Terminator, you know. You'll get killed."

"I can't let this destroy what we're doing, Amber. It's an hour's drive from here. I can take a chance that they'll still be at it when I get there. All I need is a few grenades."

"Lily!" Amber shook her head in disbelief. The image of

Lily tossing grenades in her short top and heels was stretching her imagination. But she'd had a gunrunner boyfriend. . . . "No, no, that's too damn dangerous. We'll take the chance that Dilaver—"

"No, not with this many girls in our care!" Lily's expression turned grim. "They're my responsibility and transporting them will be dangerous if Dilaver sends the word out to look for a woman. Do you have any other ideas?"

There was no way she was going to let her friend drive out into a gang war. Amber racked her brain for an answer. "Cell phone. Cell phone!" She yelled out, snapping her fingers.

"What about my cell phone?" Lily was already buttoning her jacket.

"Let me try getting hold of Hawk. He told me last night his would be on if I needed to call him."

"He tells you to call while he's going into a firefight? Come on!"

"Well, he didn't know he was going to be in one. He told me Dilaver was taking him out to show him the weapon depots and routes. We were joking when I asked about contacting him in case I needed to instant message something . . . important." *Something sexy* was what she had said, actually. Amber went to the counter to get her handbag. "Let me give it a try."

"I can't believe it. You're going to call the guy while he's running around with a weapon in his hand."

"Your mercenary called you," Amber pointed out. "I read in the papers that the Americans did it in Somalia. Called in on the embassy for help. Collect call, too."

"That's true," Lily admitted. "Shit. Men are crazy. I wouldn't have time to call anyone while I'm in a middle of a war. Oh, go ahead, give it a try. The man's crazy enough to break into the café and carry you upstairs, he's probably crazy enough to answer a buzzing cell phone."

Despite the gravity of the situation, Amber grinned. "Maybe I'll phone in a take-out order," she said as she dialed.

The descent down the hill was quick enough, with rounds impacting all around Hawk and his men. The sound of the firepower was tremendous as they moved closer. Hawk motioned the two others that they were going to the flank.

The other side was using clumps of trees for cover. Their vehicles were parked together near a clearing behind the kill zone. To get closer, Hawk and his men would have to get nearer to the enemy's camp and line of fire. Hawk sent the two men to opposite points. "Wait till dark," he ordered. "I'll move in and get closer. If we synchronize our explosives, they'll think there are actually more of us. With Dilaver uphill, they'll give up a lot sooner."

"What about those who try to escape in their trucks?"

"Pick off as many as you can. Dilaver wants to capture them, so I'd go for the tires." He didn't know how good they were with weapon precision skills, and frankly, he would prefer to exterminate as many of these bastards as he could. He didn't care whether they were of any value to Dilaver or not. "Darkness is good cover for us, so they won't be able to see us while we can see their headlights."

"Okay. We'll wait for your first charge and then we'll toss in ours."

"Remember to get out of the way, American," one of the men said in a joking tone. "We tend to just throw in all the explosives we've got and watch the fireworks. We don't worry about who's on whose side at that point."

"Right." Hawk got the point. Dilaver might be thinking about business, but this was "fun" for the men. They were in this for the sheer adrenaline of bloodletting.

The opposing side had retreated under tree and bush cover, leaving some of their trucks in the clearing. They had evidently been caught with their pants down by Dilaver's sudden attack. Hawk wondered again why they were here in the first place. Dilaver had mentioned that he believed this gang was responsible for some of his missing trailers, so were they here to capture another? Yet the country road was so out of the way from the usual routes the gangs traversed.

He decided that as soon as it became dark enough, he would sneak up to the trucks. It would have been easier if he had a grenade launcher, then he could just take them out from a distance, but where was the fun in that? Hawk bellied up under a clump of bushes and waited, listening to the sounds of gunshots and explosions around him.

Stringing up explosives, as Jazz would say, was like making music; the more expert one became, the better the result. And a very well-done explosion could devastate the enemy's psyche. If his team were here, they wouldn't be hurling grenades at each other like these idiots were doing, making more noise than actually targeting the enemy. Hawk felt strange, removed from it all.

The buzzing in the back of his pants made him frown. He had ignored it several times now, but whoever it was kept calling. He didn't think it was McNeil calling, unless there was an emergency. What the hell? He was alone and he still had a few minutes before dark. He pulled out his cell phone.

It wasn't a number he recognized. There was a text message, too. He clicked on it. *Pick up hotstuff. Now.* Hawk stared at the message, then looked up into the darkening sky. He wasn't going to—Ah, hell. He would just have to use the earphone so his hands would be free.

Amber picked up on the first ring. "About time." Her voice came in clearly through the earpiece. "I almost gave up."

"This had better be good, Ambrosia," Hawk said, as he looked around him. "This isn't a good time to have our usual phone sex."

Even her snort came in loud and clear. "I know you're currently using your gun for other sports, Hot Stuff. That's why I called. I can hear explosives, by the way."

She knew. Hawk studied the figure darting in and out of the shadows toward him, slowly sneaking up. He briefly wondered whether he should find out whether it was "his" side or the other who was trying to surprise him. It didn't really matter. He was on neither. "Let me guess. You're concerned for my safety and are calling me to tell me you want me badly." Hawk took aim at the figure, his eye steady as the shadow popped up and down like a dummy target. "You do know that most people don't answer cell calls in the middle of a firefight?"

"The soldiers did in Somalia, so why can't you? You're probably just hiding behind a big tree while waiting for Dilaver to finish his war games," she answered sardonically. "It isn't as if you're special ops or something and have any special skills in warfare to be any help."

Hawk's lips curved reluctantly. It didn't matter how grave the situation was, but that woman always managed to put a smile on his face.

"No special skills . . . I'll have to remedy that," he said, then fired his weapon. The figure fell over. And stayed that way.

There was a pause. "Hawk? I heard a shot. Are you okay?"

"Just target-shooting. What is it you need, Ambrosia?"

"You have to make sure Dilaver won't take those men alive, especially a man named Dija." There was a pause and Hawk could hear women's voices arguing back and forth. Then Amber returned, sounding a lot more sober. "They know Lily and we prefer Dija doesn't mention anything about Lily to Dilaver."

Lily. Hawk remembered the dark-haired woman with the weapons at Amber's place the other night. "Connection?"

he asked. It was about time to make his move toward the vehicles.

"These men are mercenaries and Lily retains their services to get certain things."

He should have known. This place was full of shady dealings. "Let me guess. Highway robberies. Dilaver's shipments." The persons behind Dilaver's problem were two women. Dilaver wouldn't like that. "This all has to do with the kidnapped girls, doesn't it? I know Dilaver's after the people robbing him."

"Yes. A potential problem if Dija gets caught. He doesn't intend to be, but he claims he's surrounded and might have to give up. Dija is five-eight, scar on his left cheek, speaks English almost without an accent, and is missing a little finger."

"So what do you want me to do? Go looking for some man with a missing finger in the dark?"

"If he gets caught, Hawk . . ." There was more muffled discussion at the other end. Amber cleared her throat, then continued, "Take him out before he talks. He doesn't care which side he's on, as long as he's paid. He warned Lily because she had saved his life once, but now they're even. And you don't want Lily in danger, because then who's going to guide you around?"

Her attempt at flippancy didn't ring true. She must really need him quite desperately to make this call. He supposed, if he had to take one side, he would choose the ladies'.

Whether Amber had called or not, Hawk was going to kill tonight. But he supposed now he had a good reason other than gratuitous violence. "Are you sure?" he asked quietly.

"I wouldn't call you if this wasn't an emergency. I don't order hits," she replied just as quietly. "I have no choice."

Hawk wasn't one to let an opportunity go by without seizing on it. She was all serious right now, her thoughts on her decision. And like the other night when he had seen her staring down into the yard, he had this urge to make her sorrow disappear.

Besides, he enjoyed keeping her off-kilter ever since she'd taken him off-guard at their first meeting. "If I do this, you owe me. I want a date, with all the trimmings." He got on his feet, undoing his back pouch where the grenades were tucked.

"Trimmings?" She sounded confused.

"Yeah . . . you know, makeup, stockings, garter belt."

Another small pause. "Those are trimmings? You make me sound like I'm a meal."

"That reminds me," Hawk said as he looked through his small binoculars. "Edible underwear, preferably strawberry."

"Edible . . . you're kidding, right?"

"Nope. I do this for you and you owe me the trimmings."

"I'm not going to discuss edible underwear over the phone."

Hawk chuckled softly. "I'll call back later, Ambrosia. Tell Lily she owes me, too."

"You haven't done anything yet," she reminded him. "And it's me who's asking the favor, so Lily owes you nothing."

"Well, then, you're Lily's *veza*, and I'm yours," Hawk said, pulling out his bowie knife instead. The grenades would have to wait, since he now had to get up close and personal. "That's double-duty *veza*, so I'll have to think of more trimmings. How about the rest of the order I wrote on your thigh?"

"You—"

Hawk cut off the cell phone. He was learning how to get *veza* for future advantage.

11

Lily was surprised. She didn't think Amber
had the balls to ask Hawk to do it. Seeing the look on her
friend's face, she knew she was thinking about it now. She
didn't want Amber to dwell on it. She knew from experience
that one couldn't second-guess decisions like this or it would
eat a hole in one's head. Being the daughter of missionaries
probably didn't help. She needed a quick distraction.

"Edible underwear?" Lily drawled, arching her eyebrows.
She watched the heat rise in Amber's cheeks. "Isn't that on
our Wretched Wenches List?"

They had gotten drunk one night and made that list. A
wretched wench was a desperate woman trying to get laid.
It was done in fun to relieve the tension in the lives they
both led.

"You didn't hear that," Amber said defensively.

Lily smiled. All she had to do was bring up Hawk. She
had never seen Amber quite so flustered before.

"As long as he doesn't want me to wear them, too. I draw
the line at edible underwear." Lily unbuttoned her jacket.
"Does that mean he agrees to do it? When will we know
whether he succeeds?"

"Yes. He'll call back later." Amber became subdued again.

"Do you think he'll get to Dija?" She had an idea that Hawk McMillan was a very capable agent. Amber hadn't complained once about any of his skills. Another interesting observation.

"It's our only chance, Lily. You wouldn't have been able to drive out there and not be seen. I heard the fighting in the background."

Lily sighed. "I know, but I'd have done it anyhow, if you hadn't come up with this idea. Of course, now you'll have to delve into the Wretched Wenches List to pay up." She grinned. "He's something else. Where are you going to find edible underwear?"

"Oh, shut up," Amber said rudely. "There isn't going to be any, so you can wipe that grin off your face. He was just joking."

The woman was obviously in denial. "I wouldn't be too sure about it. After all, you two have the most unusual courtship going."

Amber looked up, startled. "What the hell are you talking about now?"

Lily cracked her knuckles. "Let's see. Playing with each other's body parts. Tapping each other's phones with shadow programs. Running around in the dark alleys of Velesta. And all of this without a first date. Definitely an unusual courtship."

"We don't even know each other!" Amber shook her head, her fingertips touching her lips as she looked away.

"Look at her, deep in thought." Lily interrupted her reverie, studying her with knowing eyes. It appeared someone else had been kissing last night. "Poor Amber. She's joined the Wretched Wenches."

Amber wrinkled her nose. "I'm going to finish up here," she said. "When we get back home, we have to make a list of girls to prep for the interview. Then you have to call Brad and make your own schedule."

Lily felt her grin fading. Brad. Damn, damn, damn. How could she face him after last night? She was a foolish, foolish woman, to get drunk and let her heart rule over her head.

She had given in and done what she had wanted to do. Had her hands into that thick blond hair and mussed it up. Ran her tongue against his and tasted him again. And again. She could feel her foolish heart start beating faster at the memory of the way he had kissed her back. He had turned her into the curve of the sofa arm and had plundered her mouth with such silky skill, he stole all thought along with control. All she remembered was how soft his hair was as she'd pulled him closer, how wonderful he'd smelled, and how absolutely, obviously hard he had been.

Lily turned around, using the excuse of taking off and folding her jacket to hide her expression. She wondered what Brad was thinking right now, especially about her. She probably deserved to be called a bitch. Or, worse, a tease.

She closed her eyes briefly. She just couldn't overcome her fear. She hated feeling out of control, especially during sex. Last night—she sighed—last night she had actually felt something more than lust, and she had panicked. Panicked and ran off.

"Well, nothing to say?" Amber asked from behind her.

Lily opened her eyes. She had to make the call first. It always felt better afterward, knowing she was in charge of something so much bigger than one man. Personal stuff didn't mean a damn thing to her. "I'll do that later," she said casually. As soon as she figured out what to say. Maybe he wouldn't bring up last night.

A tease. She hated that kind of stuff—playing around and then not delivering. That was a big no-no to her, one of the things she and Amber . . . she bit down on her lip to stop the curse threatening to spill out. Horny, unsatisfied, and a tease—who had joined the Wretched Wenches now?

The ride back to The Last Resort was a quiet one. Amber thought about what she had asked Hawk to do and how, in the middle of it all, she had still managed to flirt with the man. Like Lily had said, she and Hawk had a strange courtship.

What a strange, alien word in her world. She was attracted to Hawk—there was no denying that when she couldn't seem to stop thinking about him—but courtship? Trust Lily to come up with a word that seemed both ludicrous and yet so right.

She barely knew the man. But she wanted to know more. He seemed different. He hadn't shown any vanity like some good-looking men did around women. In fact, he projected a calm quiet confidence that had nothing to do with his outside at all; everything he did, he had done with an efficiency of someone who knew he was more than just a face.

Amber had always liked men who used their brains. Her father was a wonderful thinker and reader, and had impressed upon her that it was the mind that made men civilized. Men who think were often the contributors of enlightenment, he had said. And Hawk had told her he meditated. She wondered whether he liked to read.

Yet Hawk was also a man of action. He was in a battle right now, and she was worried. That particular emotion surprised her. He was a man capable of taking care of himself—a trained operative who was a natural tracker. What she saw last night told her a lot. How he reacted to her request told her even more. The man had killed before; it was in his eyes and attitude. That didn't surprise her; she lived in a very violent world.

She had her first rude awakening about that fact at a very

young age, when a neighboring tribe attacked the African village at which she and her parents stayed. While most little girls were at home watching Saturday cartoons, she had seen things done to humans that made her grow up fast. Then she had struck out on her own, first as a rebellious teenager and then as a contract agent, and without the protective shield provided by her parents she had discovered how dark the world could be.

Yet she had never felt the same helplessness as she did the other night. She had chosen her line of work to do *something*. The other night, she hadn't lifted a finger.

A man of action. But only at the right time. She had met a man like that once. Jed McNeil. Hawk had similar qualities. Jed had helped her out of some tight corners, showing her that sometimes, one had to dirty one's hands.

Amber looked at her own. Like Jed, Hawk was also good at hiding, appearing and disappearing at will. There was more to him than what he showed. She couldn't quite put a finger on it yet, but that was what was intriguing. That hidden side of him. That secret ingredient to that whole recipe that every cook went after. She wanted it.

But still, how combat-ready was he? He had thought Dilaver was just showing him the weapons routes. The shot she had heard on the cell phone just now—was that he who was firing or was that a shot aimed at him? Yet he had sounded so cool and detached, even mocking her. She gave a mental shake. The man was combat-ready, all right. Few men could talk about a date with—she gave a wry smile— trimmings in the heat of battle. He was definitely a deliciously dangerous man.

Her smile disappeared. And he needed her to help him track whatever it was he was after. So was he just playing her to get what he wanted? Jed McNeil had probably given him a profile of her. She knew Jed well enough to know that he would have warned Hawk not to fully trust any contract agents. After all, Jed knew about some of her riskier dealings, although she was sure he hadn't yet discovered that she was behind some of the highway hijacks of certain trailers.

One thing was for sure. She couldn't risk exposing herself just because an attractive man was playing mind games with her. A covert operative was trained in many ways, and if Hawk was one of Jed's men, he was definitely in the big leagues. She knew about some of Jed's past adventures. He would definitely be an expert in what Amber had joked with other contract agents as "sexpionage," those pillow companions who were deadly and so very real in international spy games. She'd had dealings with them before, too.

Amber sighed quietly. Things always got more complicated when feelings were involved. She glanced sideways at Lily, who also seemed deep in thought.

"I think we need a drink when we get back," she said, trying to lighten their mood.

"Why's that?"

"We've fallen into the dark side. We're now Wretched Wenches."

The corners of Lily's eyes crinkled with amusement. "Oh, please, we can't allow that to happen." She smiled. "I do know how to get hold of edible underwear."

Amber snorted. "I won't be ordering from any websites or catalogs," she declared. "And I still maintain he was just joking. He's like that."

"He's like that, huh?" mocked Lily, imitating Amber's tone. "Wretched, wretched. You're going to do it. And I will, of course, want all the details. Not that I haven't seen him naked before . . . and on top of you. . . ."

"Lily!" Amber made the turn that led to the back street to her place.

Lily laughed. "I swear, Amber, you're such a prude sometimes. You can still blush after all this time. It must be your missionary background."

She was right, of course. Her upbringing had been stricter and more conservative than most kids'. But still, it wasn't the image that was embarrassing Amber. It was the sensation of Hawk on top of her, the secret knowledge of how he had felt intimately. In her fantasies, she had him doing a lot more than just lying there naked. He was . . . Damn, she would not think about the evil, immoral, absolutely delicious things she had imagined herself doing with Hawk McMillan.

"You like him, go for it," Lily advised.

"I thought we were going to find out what he's after, remember?"

"Well, you can do both."

"I can't like a person and then turn around and steal from him!"

Lily pursed her lips. "Information isn't stealing." She opened her door. "If it's worth something and we can get more funds, why not? We can add a little time delay so your Hawk can run off with whatever it is."

Amber got out of the car, pulling her purse from the back seat. "I'll feel guilty if I like him," she said quietly.

"Then don't do it," Lily said with a quick smile. "Just enjoy it and then move on."

"Look who's talking about just enjoying it. Need I remind you that someone should follow her own advice?" Amber raised her brows mockingly.

Lily paused in midstep up the deck stairs. "Shit. I need a drink. I feel . . . wretched."

They both laughed. Amber couldn't help but wondered whether Hawk was all right. She hoped he would call soon. She wasn't used to this type of worrying.

Later that night, while she was accounting the bills for the day, the phone rang. She had been anxiously waiting for the call.

"The Last Resort," she answered, leaning forward in her chair in anticipation.

"This is Brad."

Amber slumped back, swallowing her disappointment. "Oh, hello, Brad, good evening." She looked at the clock. He usually called earlier if he was coming for dinner. "What's the matter?"

"How do you know there's a problem?"

A certain date with a certain someone. But she didn't say that. "Lucky guess?"

"I think it's more than that. Is she there?"

"Lily isn't here right now, although she'll be back soon. Do you want to leave a message?"

She could hear his sigh. "She isn't answering her cell phone, and I think it's on purpose."

Amber knew Lily had her phone on in case she needed to contact her. "Maybe she left it in her purse and didn't hear it buzzing," she said.

"You don't have to cover for her, Amber," Brad said. "She's doing it again. Every time I get too close, she runs off. Last night, I thought I had made a little headway, but I guess it meant nothing to her."

Brad was definitely frustrated if he was confiding in her about Lily. Those two were as close-mouthed about each other as the Jaws of Life.

"Maybe she just needs time," Amber said soothingly. "She sees you as a total opposite from her way of life, you know, and is afraid of what that means."

There was a slight pause. "She detests what I do."

"I wouldn't say that, but you two need to talk about this, for sure." Especially if he intended to be a career bureaucrat.

Lily was right in that sense; her shady background was a career-killer. "There's no getting around the fact that Lily is different from other women."

"She doesn't talk much, Amber. Not with me anyway. In fact, the only way to get the woman to respond to me is to . . ." There was another pause, and then a short bark of laughter. "Never mind. I'm sorry to burden you with these things when there are bigger problems at hand. Can you pass on the message that I've set up the interview time and date and that she really needs to contact me so we're all on the same page?"

"Of course," Amber replied quietly. "I can do that, Brad. And you know you can talk to me anytime about anything."

"Thanks. Goodnight."

Brad hit the red button on his cell phone and slipped it into his pocket. Damn it all to hell. He sounded like a lovelorn schoolboy obsessing about his first crush.

Different from other women. Wasn't that supposed to be why a man became interested in a woman?

He looked down at the open file on his desk. When he had first met Amber and Lily, he had used his insider contacts to find out more about them. They were, as he had suspected, not what they seemed. He studied the small photograph of Lily in the file. She was different, all right. Obsession, that must be it. Why else would he be so drawn to a woman who was so casual about breaking laws?

Europol Databank had produced quite a bit of Llallana Noretski's background. She had appeared out of nowhere, it seemed, running into trouble with the law for theft and robbery. She had been a runaway, living off petty crime. She had spent some time with mercenaries before disappearing for a year. When she showed up again, she had remade herself. Officially, she was now an art procurer for small firms throughout Europe. He didn't doubt that there was something gray going on under that business, but the files hadn't provided any more information.

Probably blocked or wiped off by certain people. However, Brad could read between the lines. Her working with Amber, who was under contract with the CIA, was enough to show that she wasn't just an art procurer. Brad traced the outline of her face on the photo.

Yet there was more to Llallana Noretski than being a criminal. She might be funding the escape of those kidnapped girls through illegal means, but at least she was doing something about the problem in her own way. He didn't approve, but part of him secretly envied her ability to skip the hurdles created by laws meant to protect the innocent, but that had become impediments. In a society where crime ran rampant and there were more criminals than law keepers, bureaucracy was useless.

Brad's lips twisted into a bitter smile. Which meant that he was fucking useless. Everything was twisted into some kind of warped justice. Lily was Robin Hood, saving the helpless. He was the fucking sheriff of Nottingham, or at least the bureaucracy was, what with so many around him on the take from the KLA. No wonder she looked at him as if he were garbage.

But not last night.

He traced the photograph again. Last night, she had that look again. She had gazed at him with the kind of yearning that made a man think of nothing but the blood pounding between his legs. There hadn't been contempt in those dark eyes then. Not the moments before he'd kissed her. Not when she unzipped his pants and put her hands inside.

Brad closed his eyes, remembering her touch. It had been years since he had made out on a living room couch, but he didn't seem to have any control at all when it came to Lily. The moment she had touched his zipper, he was a goner.

He would never be able to sit in that damn living room and simply watch a movie again. Not when he had been lying there as Lily slid off the sofa to settle between his legs, her sweet mouth driving him out of his mind. She hadn't given him a chance to say anything, her tongue and lips—

"Sweet Jesus," muttered Brad, feeling himself getting hard again.

He opened his eyes, massaging the area between his brows. What the hell was wrong with him? This was his office and he was thinking about sex. That was the problem. There hadn't been sex. The woman had taken him to the brink and wanting to be inside her, he had pulled her onto his lap. Had inserted a desperate hand between her legs and found her panties damp. Had pushed the material aside desperately. She had gasped at his touch. He had been quite sure she gasped. He had slid his fingers inside and she had leaned over him with a moan. He had been sure there was a moan, as she clenched and contracted and . . . before he even knew it, she was off his lap, panic in her eyes as she stumbled and ran off.

By the time he had gotten his wayward penis back into his pants so he could go after her, Lily was gone. All he had left was her scent on his hand.

He hadn't been able to sleep all night. Had she? What the hell went wrong? Everything had been fine until that moment. She had been soft and needy, wanting him—he knew she had wanted him.

She had driven him wild with her mouth. She had been wet for him and was close to coming herself—*he'd felt her starting to come*. And then . . . he shook his head . . . why did she stop it there, when they had both been so close?

The phone rang, cutting through his thoughts. Brad picked the receiver.

"Sir, that earlier report about a battle has been confirmed as gang warfare. NATO peacekeepers are on the way there. The commander is still waiting for orders, though."

Brad frowned. "Why?"

"On which side to take out, sir."

"Both sides," Brad said. "They are both gangs, right? Bomb them to oblivion."

"It isn't that simple, sir. NATO has an agreement with the KLA that they won't interfere with any local incidents if it's outside jurisdiction areas."

"There aren't any areas not under NATO jurisdiction," Brad pointed out. But he knew what was coming. NATO, the entity formed by European countries and the United States to defend Europe from the Soviet Union, had no power to attack unless specifically ordered by special sessions. Gang warfare outside the cities and villages technically didn't fall under the category of defending citizens. When the underling started to explain, Brad cut in, "You don't have to cite me bylaws and subarticles, Victor. At this late hour, I doubt there'll be any Orders coming down till morning, and by then, who knows what will be left of the battle? Just make sure you get some information from the peacekeepers who are heading that way. Try to find out who and what's involved. If it's an emergency, call my cell or beeper."

"Yes, sir."

Brad rang off. He had stayed in the office later than usual because he hadn't wanted to go home and look at that couch. He put away the file on his desk, picking up the thickest folder in his in-box to take home with him. Lots of work. That ought to banish the image of Llallana Noretski kneeling between his thighs, her hands and lips—Brad let out a colorful expletive between gritted teeth. Frustration didn't sit well on an empty stomach. He hadn't wanted dinner for the same reason he had avoided driving home. It was going to be a long night.

Hawk accepted the bottle of beer from the woman whose house Dilaver's men had invaded. There was fear in her eyes as she served them whatever food and drinks she had. She kept darting worried glances at her kitchen and he had a feeling that someone was hiding back there. He wanted to tell her to stop giving herself away like that, but Dilaver was sitting nearby.

"So what do you think of my loot, Hawk?" Dilaver peeled a banana, nodding curtly at the woman when she offered him a fresh bottle of beer. "I want fresh meat for dinner and not some canned shit. You'd better have something good in that larder, lady."

"Yes, of course. I'll get started immediately." She scurried off, giving another fearful backward glance before disappearing into the kitchen.

Dilaver noisily drank from his bottle. "Well?" He cocked his head at Hawk.

"It's a lot of weapons," Hawk said. "I'm still tabulating the cost and profit in my head."

Dilaver laughed. "I like the way you think. No wonder your boss was unwilling to let me have you as a guide. He knew I'd try to get you away."

Hawk shrugged. "I'm here on business for him, too. I haven't agreed to work for you yet."

"But you see how much money you can make if you take over here."

Hawk had discovered the reason for the gang war. The mercenaries they had attacked were very close to finding one of Dilaver's hidden caches of weapons. "The potential's there," Hawk said, "but too many people seem to be after your weapons."

Dilaver frowned. "I don't know how they found out the location. They were very close," he said, bringing his thumb and forefinger within an inch of each other, "too damn close."

"Could there be a leak in your organization?" Hawk asked casually.

Dilaver's frown deepened. "I have been very careful. I don't think so, but you never know. The weapons are very valuable on the black market." He leaned forward. "That's why I need you, Hawk. You can negotiate for me. Also, with your ties to Stefan, you have access to people like Maximillian Shoggi. If I could get Mad Max's attention, I'd be swimming in dough."

Maximillian Shoggi was one of the top international illegal weapons dealers. His influence in the shadowy world of politics and weapons-running was so great that he was constantly invited to elite parties given by powerful people.

"Mad Max? He has tons of the weapons you got, Dilaver."

Hawk had been briefed on him by his agency and GEM. Mad Max had been responsible for killing a group of covert agents during an ill-fated mission. Since then GEM had been on a two-year operation, slowly applying a chokehold on the weapons dealer's holdings, until he was now desperate to get his hands on any big item to replenish his coffers. GEM had plans for his future, and had informed the admiral and Hawk that under no circumstances would Dilaver be allowed to deal with Mad Max. That would give him an opportunity out of his hole.

"But I have something else besides the ones you just saw." Dilaver leaned forward confidentially. "I don't have enough information yet, but my aunt just informed me that it's going to be something really big in the market. It's in one of those hidden shipments that came down while I was gone."

"Is that why you're waiting so eagerly for her arrival?" Hawk asked, leaning back against his chair. "She can identify this weapon, right?"

Dilaver nodded. "Yes. So you just wait. It won't be too long now."

But Hawk already knew what the weapon was, and that he must get to it before Dilaver and his aunt got hold of it. "I never say no to new weapons," he said. "I'll stick around as long as I can. Meanwhile, though, it would help if you take me more on these side trips so I can see what the countryside looks like. As a guide, it'd help me to identify routes, and if I'm to work with you, that would be a big help in the future."

"Absolutely," Dilaver said. He finished his beer with gusto. "I'll draw some maps for you so you can study them. The shipments were dropped in specific locations close to aid relief areas, so that's why they are so scattered. Clever, huh? The U.S. government hasn't even realized they have been used."

Hawk drank down his beer. Once he had the maps, he would be able to find the targeted dropped shipments. Then he was going to need Amber Hutchens.

The thought of traveling and hiking through the countryside with the woman was both intriguing and worrying. When he had tested her the other night, she had kept up with him, but that was for three hours. What about a week? He had never done anything strenuous with a woman before, so he had no idea . . . he smiled despite himself . . . okay, not *that* kind of strenuous activity.

"And what are you smiling about?"

"I was thinking about the owner of The Last Resort,"

Hawk answered truthfully. "Since I might be staying longer, I thought I would get to know her better."

"Ah, Amber. I knew you would like her. She is, how do you say it . . ." Dilaver paused, gesturing with his mug, then reverted to English. "Your cup of tea. Right up your trail."

"Right up your alley," Hawk corrected.

Dilaver frowned. "Trail, alley, path, same thing," he said.

"Nuances," Hawk explained, "are very important in idioms. You know how I mess up Serbian slang and you guys laugh."

"True, but our idioms make sense. How can a woman being right up your trail mean anything sexy? Bah. Stupid. But back to Amber and her"—Dilaver waggled his eyebrows—"delicious assets. I bet you want to have a taste, huh? Are you going to ask her out?"

Hawk shrugged. He didn't want to discuss Amber with Dilaver, although he did need to show an interest in her so it would look natural if he went out with her. "If I'm staying longer, yes, it'd be nice to get a bit closer. But you said she has a boyfriend."

"Yes, she's a pretty woman! Of course she has one. And a powerful man, too. That's why you should get her between the sheets. It would please me no end to see that son of a bitch CIVPOL chief losing his girlfriend to one of my friends." Dilaver laughed. "That would be funny. I'll laugh my arse off. And don't correct me about 'ass' and 'arse.' At least I'm not using the stupid phrase 'you cracked me up.'"

It still felt strange to know that the Macedonian and he spent time teaching each other idioms in their respective languages. But then, as Jed had warned Hawk before he had taken on the mission, everything was going to be upside down when he became "friends" with the enemy. To get close, he had to establish an easy camaraderie. He hated that piece of crap sitting across the table from him but had to hide it.

"You can always say 'bust a gut,' " Hawk said lazily. Dilaver laughed, shaking his head. He looked up to see the woman coming out of the kitchen, carrying some bowls. She avoided meeting the men's eyes as she set them down.

"Hurry up, woman, we are all hungry. Do you want us to go in the kitchen to help you?" one of Dilaver's men asked.

She couldn't disguise her look of panic. "No . . . everything will be ready soon. Please, no need. . . . Make yourself comfortable."

"Hey, you can have mine first if you're that hungry," Hawk said, trying to distract the young man who was watching the woman a bit too closely. "Come join us. Here, have a beer."

The man caught the bottle Hawk lobbed at him and he twisted the cap. "Thank you. You're probably not used to killing like we are," he said as he walked over, "but there's nothing like war to make a guy horny. Right now even that old bitch looks good to me."

"I bet Hawk hasn't seen a day of fighting like the kind we do," another chimed in. Catching Hawk's eyes, he added hastily, "I mean, you're pretty good with that fucking knife, but something like today's . . . You were hiding in the bushes, Hawk. I saw you."

Hawk drank down his beer. War was his business. He had been trained for action in warfare on sea, land, and air. And he hadn't been hiding in the bushes today. But he couldn't say any of his thoughts out loud. "Yeah, well, it saved my life," he said instead.

"Too bad about our guys with you. They were good fighters. I wish we caught that fucker who killed them."

"There were quite a few of them, but I got them before they took off in the trucks," Hawk said.

"I wish they hadn't been killed that easily," Dilaver said in between bites of food. "I wanted to question them about how they knew of my weapons being there."

Hawk didn't say that he had been busy making sure that no one who was going to be captured was left alive. It had to be done that way. The few he had set free, including Dija, the leader, understood this. Dija had nodded in the dark and had fiercely whispered, "I owe you. Come collect your *veza* if you need one," before jumping into his truck with the few men left.

"Well, you know, you only gave me some grenades and an AK-47," Hawk pointed out. "I didn't know you wanted me to get up close and personal. I figure with so many trying to escape and two of the guys with me killed already, I had better do something." Like taking them all down with the submachine gun before any of Dilaver's men came for them. "I'm sorry I couldn't save your friends."

The young man shrugged and wiped his mouth with the back of his hand. "Death is every day around here. I don't care."

Dilaver leaned over and smacked the side of the man's face hard enough to catch the attention of the others in the room. Eyes wide with fright, the woman serving them stopped ladling out food from the big bowl.

"Those two who died were worth three of you, kid," Dilaver said softly. "They've been with me a lot longer than you and have enough killings than the number of girls you've fucked in my *kafenas* these last few years. They were great fighters, especially with knives, so whoever killed them must have given them quite a fight. Ask Hawk. He fought them before. They weren't easy to take down, were they, Hawk?"

"They weren't," Hawk said quietly. "They were very good with their knives. I couldn't make out how many men were fighting in the dark, but I know the battle was very fierce."

He stretched out his legs under the table. The hilt of his hidden knife rubbed against the side of his leg. He wanted to be ready, in case he had to go into the kitchen to save the woman and whoever she was hiding in there. He might have to take down a few more of Dilaver's men.

The gang war wasn't the bloodiest battle he had been in, nor was it the toughest. Usually, he and his team would swoop in on a gang such as this one and do their business and leave. They didn't take any prisoners unless they were ordered to do an extraction, and when they did, the prisoners were handed over to their higher-ups; they never did any interrogation of prisoners.

However, this group of men wasn't his team. He was working with people he didn't trust or want to work with. It didn't bother him to take out the two who were with him earlier; he had seen them in action with prisoners, especially the female ones. In his opinion, they deserved a more painful death.

Sometimes he wondered at his cavalier attitude at taking lives. It seemed ridiculous to justify that it was easier when the men he had killed were called "hostiles" and "targets"; when he didn't have to live among them and call them by names or listen to their jokes. Killing was killing. But he still wished he could just take them all out instead of living among them and watching them commit the kinds of things against which he was taught to fight.

Then there was the part of him that was horrified that he could just sit here with Dilaver and eat and drink with these men. He had just killed two of their friends. He was planning to get rid of all of them eventually. In his head, anyway. If he ever got out of this in one piece. He knew without a doubt that if Dilaver knew what happened tonight, he would be history.

It was a risk he had taken because of one woman's request. In his job, many of the risks were calculated; this one wasn't. He had done it because Amber Hutchens had asked him to. Even though she had given him an adequate reason, in most covert operations it was very rare to divert from the original plan. Short of a total disaster to the entire operation, as a team leader for his SEAL unit Hawk was a stickler for keeping to a plan once the mission was under way. To change direction suddenly could be dangerous to the team.

But this wasn't a team operation. There was a team of commandos and operatives at different levels of this huge undertaking; he, Hawk McMillan, was a lone assignment here and he was responsible only for himself. As long as he got what GEM and COS Command Center wanted, he could use any means necessary.

Decisions like the one he had made didn't come easily for Hawk. This was a calculated choice and he couldn't help but wonder at why he felt he could trust Amber enough to do what he did. She could have easily turned around and betrayed him. After all, she sold "hot" information to the highest bidder. Yet, she was going out with the top lawman in the country. The woman was a contradiction.

Hawk watched one of Dilaver's thugs whispering to another nearby, both eyeing the lone woman walking in and out of the kitchen with trays of beer and food. No time to reflect. When he saw Amber again, he would just have to get close enough to find out the real person inside. And he wasn't interested in talking anymore. Macedonia wasn't a place for long contemplation.

He got up after the woman made her last trip and stood in front of the kitchen doorway. "I don't know about you, Dragan, but I don't feel like watching a screaming woman being torn apart by the boys tonight. So, if you don't mind, any one

of your men thinking of going through here for their little
fun will have to go through me."

Dilaver bit into a piece of chicken, chewing with his mouth
open as he looked from Hawk to his men, who had also stood
up. He grinned and laughed. "Different entertainment."

Hawk nodded. He could feel the woman behind him, listening in to the conversation. She was muttering prayers as
she cowered near the door.

Lord protect us. Lord protect us. He hadn't been wrong.
There was someone else hiding in the kitchen. He casually
finished his drink and passed the empty bottle back to the
woman in the kitchen, his eyes on the watching men.

"What do you say? Drink or fight, guys?" he asked, giving
them a toothy grin. He sincerely hoped they would choose
the latter.

12

Amber smacked the dough on the table with the palm of her hand, sending puffs of flour upward. Nothing from Hawk for two days. No phone signal. She had checked the instant messenger program. Even had it on at night, just in case. Nothing. She folded in the dough and started to knead it, pressing down with her thumbs. Where the hell was he?

She made a face. He could have contacted her somehow. Even Dija, the mercenary he had helped, had gotten hold of Lily to report that he was safe. It was through Lily that she had an idea of what had happened during the firefight the other day.

She had sat listening in on Lily's speakerphone as Dija gave an account of how a man with dark hair and weird golden eyes had saved him from Dilaver's men. It was full of macho talk. He and the stranger against a dozen, all wielding weapons. He and the stranger engaging in a tough knife battle that was fiercely fought in the dark. And how he and the same man had circled back and stalked the enemy, giving all of them what they deserved, and cutting off—

It was at this point that Lily had leaned forward and cut

off the communication. Obviously the man was full of it. Hawk would never have killed so many and risked Dilaver's wrath. Dija was, Lily said with a dry smile, a very good embellisher of stories. He was lucky to be alive, and from the sound of it, Hawk was responsible for that fact.

"I'll get the real details when I see him on the way back with the girls," Lily had added. "He was just drunk. They all get drunk after a battle."

Amber frowned, her hands automatically molding and kneading the dough. Hawk could have called her. Was he in another battle? Had Dilaver found out and. . . . After all, it was a risky thing she had asked him to do. Worry niggled at her, and she paused in the middle of her task to wonder at why she would feel that way about someone she barely knew.

It was more than just a sense of responsibility in case he had been caught. She hadn't been able to sleep well the past two nights, waking up several times just to go check a blank computer screen. That didn't have to do with guilt or responsibility. It was worry, and now it worried her that she was doing it.

As if she needed more on her mind. She had enough to contend with, what with the secret interview with the girls set up by Brad with some international reporter. The reporter wanted to bring two more people with him, a cameraman and a doctor, and Lily had insisted that the doctor be from out of town. Amber had agreed with her. Anyone local could betray locations as well as identities, and the owner of The Last Resort was well known.

This interview was going to be a huge risk to her and Lily. The reporter had agreed that none of their identities would be revealed in any form of media, but one just never knew. Brad had given him fake identities just to be on the safe side, but how difficult was it to trace Brad, the head of CIVPOL, to her?

And there was Lily and Brad. Amber shook her head as she rolled the dough into a long tube, then shook a couple handfuls of flour onto the table. She slowly glided the tube over it, lightly patting the flour onto the mixture. Those two were her friends, and something had happened between them during that dinner date. Now they were acting like two mountain cats with heartburn.

Lily was probably nervous about the coming interview. Well, Amber was, too, but she didn't go around trying to bite Brad's head off whenever he asked her about the preparations. Brad, on the other hand, was mad about something else entirely. After one of their sharp exchanges, she would catch him standing back, hands in pockets, that brooding stare studying Lily's every move as her friend pretended not to notice.

Amber told herself it was none of her business. Usually she would play the peacekeeper, but this time there was a tension that wasn't there before. She absentmindedly pinched the bridge of her nose. Brad would be here later. She was determined to pull Lily out of wherever she was hiding and get the three of them up in her dining room to talk without—

The outside connecting door to the kitchen opened. Thinking it was Lily, Amber didn't look up immediately.

"I was just thinking about you," she said, pinching off dollops of the dough.

"Nice thoughts, I hope," a male voice answered.

Her gaze swung upward in startled surprise. Hawk stood at the doorway, his eyes that odd glittering color that reminded her of a wild animal. He looked like one, too, his clothes rumpled and stained, his handsome face dusty, cov-

ered by several days' stubble. There was something dangerous about him. Amber straightened from the table. Why was
her heart bursting into a smile at the sight of him?

"Don't you ever knock?" she asked. It wasn't opening
hours yet. Locks, it seemed, weren't much of an obstacle
for him.

He sauntered in slowly, his gaze traveling from her face
down to her floury fingers sticky with cookie dough. She was
suddenly very aware of how civilized her surroundings were
compared to what he must have been in the last few days.

He stopped in front of her. "*Ja sam gladna,*" he said
softly.

"Want something to eat?" she asked, conscious of the way
he was looking at her, as if he were hungry for something
else.

"Yes."

She indicated a nearby chair. He sat and watched as she
put away the dough and cleared the table. "Are you all right?
You've been away for a few days." She patted the right side
of her face, near the jawline. "There's a cut there . . . I think.
You'd better take care of that. It's caked with dirt."

"Later."

She poured a cup of coffee from the carafe. "Cream and
sugar?"

"No."

"Anything particular for food?"

His eyes gleamed and his teeth were very white against
his tanned face. She wouldn't quite classify that as a smile.
He didn't answer, either. The man was obviously not in the
mood to talk right now. Another side of him. Where was all
that sexy bantering?

She went into the huge refrigerated pantry that kept all the
restaurant food and took out anything that would heat up
quickly. She glanced back at Hawk now and then and found

him watching her with half-closed eyes. She was used to men looking at her—having grown up as the blond, blue-eyed missionary's daughter, she had been in countries where her coloring attracted all kinds of attention. Her parents had taught her to treat it like background music, sometimes noticeable, sometimes slightly uncomfortable.

The man sitting there with that intense look in his eyes couldn't be ignored like background anything. He was too still. Too alive. Too damn sexy sitting there like a wild animal in her spic-and-span kitchen.

And too dangerous to ignore.

Hawk knew he shouldn't be here. Not in his current mood. But he couldn't help himself. He was drawn here as he was to his own sanctuary, his little private place on the island back home. And he wasn't quite sure why.

His island getaway off Florida was perfect when he felt like this—a little wild, a little melancholy, the need to connect to nature in its most natural setting, without battles and strategy planned ahead by humans. He could sit for hours playing with his fishing nets and going out to sea pretending to be Captain Ahab or the Old Man. Hours and hours of just sitting there enjoying the nothingness of contemplation, his mind at rest.

But he had a fierce need tonight, after two days of going to battle for . . . nothing. He had never fought for a side he didn't choose before, nor had he ever killed just for the sake of killing. It had left a hole inside him, one that seemed to be tearing wider. He wasn't sure why, but the thought of Amber in her kitchen was on his mind.

He didn't want to talk to her on the phone or on the instant message program; he wanted to see her. So he had asked Dilaver to drop him off here when they were heading back into town.

"Doing your own celebration, Hawk, eh?" Dilaver had chuckled with a wink.

Hawk didn't feel the need to point out that there was nothing for him to celebrate. The only good thing he had done on this trip was to save that widow and her daughter, who had been hiding under the kitchen sink, from being used by the bastards. No one had dared pick up his challenge of a fight, not when they'd seen Dilaver warningly smack the young thug who had carelessly shrugged off the deaths of two of their gang. He had hoped for some outlet to the rage inside.

Worse, after that night, they had gone off to raid a rival encampment in a small village town, one not endorsed by the KLA. Dilaver was, after all, one of the KLA's own, and those illegal weapons Hawk had seen went right into their hands. That was what he was fighting for, Hawk told himself—to get hold of the one weapon that must not fall into enemy hands.

The battle had been bloody. As he was with Dilaver most of the time, Hawk had to be part of the fighting in a real way. The other side was no better than this side, he had told himself. But he couldn't help thinking what if it happened to be his SEAL brothers, and he was still undercover? What would he do then? Such thoughts were dangerous in the heat of battle, and he had cut them off almost as soon as they surfaced and had gone into combat mode.

At the end of the day, Dilaver had captured his enemies and as a warning, chopped everyone's middle finger off. And that was it. That was the fucking point of the battle—to chop off everyone's middle finger.

Driving back into town, with all the noisy aftermath of men high on adrenaline, all Hawk could think about was Amber and hamburgers. He wasn't a man who questioned his own private needs. He knew where to find both, and he went for them.

And she had been in the kitchen, looking so damn good, he had wanted to cross the room and take her on the kitchen table right then and there. There were smudges of flour on her nose and chin; her fingers looked sexily edible as he watched her knead and roll dough, a little frown on her forehead as if she were thinking unpleasant thoughts.

Something dark and wanting arose in him. The feeling fed that hole inside, a fire in his gut. His whole focus was on the woman and he had to concentrate hard on what she was saying because there was a roar in his head drowning out all superfluous noise except for what his body and mind hungered for.

Here was a woman who wasn't captured, or underage, or begging for help. Here was someone who had cried outside the way he had cried inside at the sight of those girls being gang-raped. Here was someone he'd had to talk out of *doing* something that he had wanted to do for the last few months; he couldn't forget the sight of her dangling on the side of the building with that weapon aimed at the crowd of men. There had been just enough light to see her expression as she willed herself to pull the trigger, one so fierce and sorrowful that he had wanted to hold her in his arms and comfort her, as he needed to be held and be comforted inside. Because he had understood what she was feeling and going through.

Food. She thought that was what he wanted. He waited till she placed the dishes on the table, then grabbed her by the arm. She landed on his lap without resistance. He began devouring her lips.

She was warm and soft, her lips opening willingly for his exploration. He pushed his tongue inside her mouth, tasting her. He couldn't get enough, putting his hand behind her neck and pulling her even closer.

He reached up with his other hand, caressing her jawline, her neck, then downward, until he cupped her breast. She jerked forward, a soft sound in her throat, as he ran a thumb across the thin material covering her nipple. She wasn't wearing a bra. He pulled at the shirt impatiently, trying to find an opening to get what he wanted.

Her hands stopped his progress. "Hawk," she whispered. "People can come into my work kitchen."

"I don't care. I want you now. Here, on this table. Upstairs. Somewhere, Amber. Take your pick." His hand was still on her breast and he used his thumb to his advantage. He didn't wait for her answer. Standing up with her in his arms, he started heading for the door that led upstairs. "You know, this is getting to be a habit. At least you're conscious this time."

Her beautiful eyes narrowed. "I'm going to kick your ass."

"Afterward," he said.

"Afterward," she agreed.

13

A thousand excuses to say no melted in the heat of Hawk's gaze. There was a certain look a man gave that could make a woman weak in the knees. Determined. Focused. Undressing. The eyes of a predator on what was his to take. And plenty of time to do it. Hawk had that look in his eyes. A tingle of anticipation ran down Amber's spine at the thought of the intent behind that gaze.

There was something implacable in the way he held her in his arms, as if he had every right to do as he wanted. Each step echoed the drumbeat of her heart, up the stairs, through the small landing, past her kitchen, inexorably toward her bedroom door. He didn't pause, his gaze holding hers captive, moving so nimbly as if she only weighed fifteen instead of a hundred and fifteen pounds, until he reached his goal. He nudged it open with a foot.

Amber knew that once he stepped through the doorway, it would be too late to say no. And she should, she really should. A thousand excuses and none of them popped up on her lips as she stared into his golden eyes . . . that *look* banishing every one of them to some other place in her mind, replacing them with unspoken promises that quickened her breath.

Hawk walked into her bedroom. Kicked the door shut.

And she was right. There was no more time to think as his head dipped down and he started kissing her immediately. She had never been kissed this way before, seemingly in midair, her head tucked against a man's heart as his lips locked on hers ferociously. Not releasing her lips, he slowly lowered her back onto her feet, her body sliding against his hard one, and she found her arms still around his neck as she stood on tiptoe. She gasped as his hands cupped her buttocks and molded them possessively, sexually. His fingers went between the cheeks, going lower, seeking intimately. She heard a distinct tear. His fingers were immediately inside her. Moving. Sliding. Going to the next target.

Amber thought she was weak in the knees before. She was wrong. She was under siege. Her legs parted helplessly and she lost her already precarious footing. He ignored her as she tried to free her lips, stumbling about to find her balance. It only gave him easier access to what he wanted and she gasped again as his other hand moved to a frontal attack, tearing her pants apart like a piece of rag.

"I like a woman who doesn't wear underwear," he said, his voice low and seductive, as he started walking her backward.

He backed her into a nearby wall and she grabbed his shoulders in startled surprise as he lifted her up again. It occurred to her that he wasn't just keeping her physically off balance; he was also doing it to her mentally. She was unable to think or say anything; she hung on and let him take over.

"This is our position," he murmured in her ear. She heard the sound of a zipper being undone. "I'm going to take you like this first. Teach you to do it right next time."

"Right?" That was all she managed as he pushed against

her. Oh, Lord. She had felt *that* before. Only he had been semi-aroused then. He felt as big as he had looked that first time she had seen him naked in the dark. She gripped his arms, digging her fingers into the coiled muscles.

"The right way to do it," he said, penetrating her softness with slow accuracy, "is without anything on."

Amber wrapped her legs around his waist as he drove the point home. He slid in, settling his body between her open legs, pushing her hard against the wall. He was deep inside her at the first thrust, his hands holding her firmly around her waist. He pushed her higher up the wall, his hands sliding from her waist to her hips, warm against her thighs, his fingers invading the soft flesh of her labia, opening her wider.

He slid out slightly. Thrust in again, his thumbs pressing down on her sensitive flesh in tandem with the glide of his thick penis.

"Ohhhh!" Amber felt all her strength leave her as molten hot pleasure shot up through her system. Her hands fell away from his shoulders as he rocked into her again and again, relentless in his assault, teasing the sensitive flesh around her clitoris. As he brought her higher and higher, he felt impossibly bigger. She wrapped her legs as tight as she could, holding on for dear life, as he thrust hard inside her and trapped her against the wall.

She heard another rip. He had torn off the front of her shirt. His head bent and she felt the brush of his hair against her cheek and caught his earthy masculine scent as he took her right nipple into his mouth and bit gently.

Amber gave a cry, jerking forward. He was so deep inside her now. His mouth on her breast. One hand massaging the other nipple. His other hand still on her hip, moving in slow sensual circles, making her whimper every time he stopped. His hips undulating hard as he flexed inside her.

His teeth caught her nipple again and she heard soft cries

escaping her lips as she started coming, her whole body uncontrollably shuddering with a white-hot pleasure she had never felt before.

When she opened her eyes, she was on her back on the floor. She couldn't remember how she had gotten there. He looked so big from this angle. His golden eyes gleamed down at her as she stared up, her breath still hitching. She heard more than felt the rest of her pants being torn.

"Second position," he said, "except I think this time I want the taste of you in me instead of some drug."

Before her mind grasped his meaning, he had pulled out and his mouth was already between her legs, his tongue exactly where it should be. She reached out in helpless wonder as he opened her wider for his feasting. His rough stubble scraped the inside of her thighs as his tongue did things she hadn't thought possible. His hands caressed her exposed tummy, the pads of his fingers finding every erogenous spot. Stretching down, she shaped his dark head between her hands, urging him to go faster. She gave a strangled cry when he scraped his teeth against the soft flesh, a gentle warning of his current mood, that he was doing the taking.

And he was taking his time as his tongue slowed to a frustrating glide, pushing her to the limits, only to flutter back down. Release. So close. . . . She urgently reached down again, then stopped when his mouth lifted away from that so important place.

"I didn't touch you while you looked at my body," he whispered. "You aren't allowed right now."

"I didn't touch your body!" Amber managed to gasp out.

"How would I know? I was out." His tongue teased her in between sentences. "You could have been licking me all over."

"But . . . I . . . didn't." He had taken command of all her senses. She couldn't think about anything but what he was doing to her.

"Don't believe you." He bit her thigh, then ran his tongue tantalizingly closer to where she really wanted him to lick. She groaned when he paused. "I had a hard-on then, you know. I didn't have one when I woke up. Did you do this? Or this?" He jerked away from her desperate hands. "No touching, or I stop."

Amber clawed at the carpet in desperation, using her legs to push her hips upward. Into his face. There. She groaned again when he just softly kissed her, somehow adding to the torment. She pushed up even higher, demanding more pressure. He peered up at her, his eyes glinting with deviltry, knowing what she wanted.

"Was this what you did the other night, getting yourself all excited while I was on top of you?" His hands went under her hips and she gasped as he cupped her bottom roughly. "I remember those legs wrapped around me tightly before I fell on top of you. You couldn't have moved without feeling some pleasure, honey."

His head dipped and he demonstrated what he meant. Amber squeezed the soft tufts of carpet on each side of her as his tongue and mouth kneaded her sensitive nub with the skill of a master at work at his craft. His fingers slid inside her deeply, even as his busy tongue imitated the upward movement, an arc of heat rising from her loins all the way into her chest.

Amber could hear herself starting to beg for release, stopped herself, then, unable to stand it any longer, started again as those fingers and lips and tongue continued their intimate massage, moving in and out, over and downward. Half-formed words mingled with little gasps as she strained against his mouth, the heated pressure building into a kaleidoscope of sensation.

Without warning, he jammed his tongue hard against her core. Amber's mouth opened, a silent scream forming as the first orgasmic wave locked all her muscles. He pushed her legs higher with his shoulders and his tongue delved deeper into her, as if he could drink her whole soul as she gave herself.

Hawk McMillan, Amber was discovering, knew a lot of different ways to make a woman weak in the knees.

She was melting hot in his mouth, coming apart with the sweetest sounds to his ears. He had been hungry for this—a woman in the throes of real passion, letting him pleasure her any way he wanted. A real woman to make love to.

That was what Hawk wanted. He couldn't explain the tension pulling like an arrow stretched on a bow inside him. All he knew was that he needed a release, something that would take away the hurt inside. His control was at breaking point. If he didn't do something, he would kill Dilaver and his men. In the darkest hour, between anger and loathing, Amber had called to him. And he wanted to be with her.

It was so good to hear a woman scream in pleasure, rather than in fear. Hawk had missed having a woman with whom he could have the kind of sex he enjoyed—a little rough, a little kinky, and a lot foreplay. He had found her. He wasn't going to relinquish her for a long while.

Her thighs clamped around his neck and he forced them apart again with his shoulders, straightening her legs so she couldn't use her strength. "Did you look at me like I'm looking at you now?" he murmured. She was wet and swollen, pink and aroused, and damn tempting. "Did you touch me, feel how hard I was?"

Eyes closed, she shook her head restlessly and trembled when he touched her gently with a finger. He wanted her to come again. He needed to see her hot for him, moaning in pleasure. Part of him was taking an insane delight in exacting revenge for the way she had attacked him that first night; part of him was ridiculously happy to have a willing and satiated woman in his care. The coiled tension that had been growing inside him the last few days pulled at him still—

He pushed away those dark images that rose up. Need. He ran his knuckles lightly over her swollen nub, pulling at the hood. Her body reacted immediately and her eyes opened wide, an electric blue fire that made him hot for her. And there wasn't any hurt in them, just pure desire. He needed to see more of it.

"Hawk . . ."

His name came out like a caress. He gave her a slow smile as he continued playing with her, her wetness making it easy to glide his knuckles with long, slow strokes over and over. He had started out just needing her, but now he wanted her to need him, too. Her breathing was uneven again. Those beautiful blue eyes became pools of soft womanly need. No fear in them at all. He wanted to drown in them.

"You do know what the third position is, don't you?" he asked. She licked her lips nervously and he smiled. "Remember? You tied a note around my dick."

Still caressing her intimately, he climbed over her. "*Looking for me?*, you wrote in that note." He nudged her intimately with the hard tip of his penis. She was so wet. The raging tension in him coiled in anticipation. "I believe I just found you, Amber."

His weight on one elbow, he sank into her slick heat slowly, wanting to feel her take him in. He stroked her with his knuckles and gave a hum of satisfaction as her hips undulated upward, her internal muscles milking him eagerly. Her eyes were mere slits, her mouth parted, her hair like bright sunshine against the dark carpet. She fit around him, tight as a glove.

"Hmm. It feels good to be inside you. I've wanted you from the moment I saw you in the restaurant."

"Not in the dark the first time? You did have a hard-on," she reminded him, a smile teasing her lips.

"I was thinking of hamburgers."

"Hamburgers." She laughed. "You're turned on by meat?"

He began thrusting into her in leisurely strokes. "Juicy meat." He licked a corner of his mouth. "Delicious. Hot. Dripping with juice."

She stared at him. "You're turning me on with all this talk about hamburger."

He grinned. "What were you doing a few minutes ago, darling? Reciting poetry?" He flexed deep inside her before withdrawing.

He began to thrust in earnest, closing his eyes. Pressure building. Every push brought him unbearably close. It had been so long, he knew he couldn't last the first time. He was too eager. Too desperate to be inside her. She deserved more than a sex-hungry fool trying to get months of pent-up emotion out of his system. He had intended to give her some more loving, but a man could only play so long without killing himself. He was close to losing all sense of control as it was, what with her coming so wild and sweet in his mouth. She tasted fine. Deep inside her now, she felt even finer.

Trigger point. When all thought gushed like a mental stream of pleasure, gathered into a ball of energy suspended over some imaginary precipice, and time stood still, as his whole being balanced on the razor-sharp line of consciousness. Hawk gave one final complete thrust. Breath suspended somewhere between lung and throat. He groaned as release came. Tumbled over. Free at last, like a bird floating with the wind. He fell forward, lips finding Amber's, and she tasted like the finest wine as he came hard into her.

"You know, the last time you were on top of me like this, I needed help to turn you over," Amber said, her mouth tasting salty male flesh.

He was big and heavy, a satiated sexual animal still inside her. She didn't know what to say; she had never had sex on the carpet before. Or against a wall. Or, she noted, in tattered clothes. He had touched and kissed her with such hunger; it made her shiver just remembering his mouth doing all those naughty things to her again.

"Does that mean we have to call Lily up here?" His voice was lazy now, as if he had momentarily satisfied that dangerous edge she had felt emanating from him. "Ow."

Amber had bitten him without thinking. The idea that Lily . . . No, no, she would never allow Lily to ever see him naked again. Hawk McMillan ought to be locked in a jar like a genie, to be summoned by she, and she alone. She ran a hand down his muscular back, shocked at her own possessiveness.

"Never say another woman's name while you're naked with me," she warned.

"I'm not naked."

True. He hadn't had his clothes torn apart by a sexual animal. She wanted to explore him as closely as he had her. "Easily remedied. A shower."

He finally lifted his head and she had to stop the sharp intake of breath. She had thought he sounded satiated, but he still had *that* look in his eyes. He sat back on his haunches, pulling his T-shirt over his head. "Okay, fourth position," he said, voice muffled. He wadded the shirt into a ball and cocked his head. "What is it?"

Amber closed her mouth and blinked. She couldn't take her eyes away from what had caught her attention. Running through Hawk's right nipple was a very thin but very real band of gold. She shifted her gaze upward and caught him watching her. The image fit him somehow—a secret pirate—and her eyes shifted back down again, this time a lot lower. With a very big bird boldly jutting out between the vee of his pants. She wanted to see the rest of him.

"Just admiring," she breathed out. He really was magnificent. His face might look like a male model's, but that physique didn't look gym-made. She held several belts in martial arts; she recognized a trained fighter's body. From the muscle-corded arms, to the broad chest, to those amazing cuts on his stomach, he was, simply, a fantastic specimen of a man. And all she wanted was to get a closer look at that nipple ring.

"Keep looking like that and we might not make it into the bathroom." His voice had lowered a notch. "I'm still not quite in control, Amber."

She caught something underlying in Hawk's words and returned her gaze to his face. Something had happened in the last few days to him. She was pretty sure of it. Once he had stepped into her bedroom, he hadn't even bothered to reach the bed before he had taken her.

And he *had* taken her. There was no other word for it. He had given her the kind of mindless pleasure she had only read about, had wanted to experience all her life. She was surprised by how emotionally involved it was: To allow a man to take her like that needed a bond of trust, a willingness to let the other person take the lead.

Yet this had been more than that. If he had just wanted some kind of quickie to slake his male needs, he wouldn't have taken the time to give her so much pleasure. No, he had come looking for her because he knew she would understand him.

It was ridiculous. She didn't know the man. Yet somehow, intrinsically, she had bonded with and trusted him.

She reached out and touched the half-off pants. "Fourth position?" she said, bringing up what he had said when he took off his shirt. "I never did anything to you in a shower that night."

His answering smile made her swallow. "Don't believe you," he said, his hands covering hers on his hips. He stood up, pulling her to her feet at the same time. He pushed her hands downward and his pants slid lower until they fell into a pool around his ankles. He stepped out of them.

Amber bit her lower lip as he slid her hands to his front. She automatically fisted around his arousal. His eyes narrowed as she caressed the length of him.

"Is that what you did before tying that note?"

She shook her head. "I was very . . . careful." She really had been. She hadn't touched him as she had looped the cord gently in the dark. Her naughty joke, she realized now, had really pissed him off.

"Don't believe you," he repeated, as he squeezed her hands tighter around him.

He was fiery hot in her hands.

He turned and she reluctantly released him as he pulled her by the elbow. He looked totally out of place in her very feminine bathroom, with its candles and figurines decorating the table by the ornate European tub. He turned on the tap and as hot water began filling it, he climbed in and made himself quite at home. In all her life, she had never seen a sexier picture than a naked man in her tub. She let him pull her in, even though it was a tight fit.

He put a heart-shaped soap in her hand. "Show me how

you tied the note," he invited, turning off the water. She had to smile at the sight of his penis rising up like a mast of a ship at sea. He obviously had more than bathing in mind.

"I didn't use soap and there was no water involved," she protested, still smiling.

"Don't believe you."

Amber laughed. She could see it was going to take some time to convince Hawk that if she had really touched him the way she now wanted to, he would have remembered it a lot more vividly. She dipped her hands in the water, then soaped her hands until bubbly foam engulfed them.

A few minutes later, he huskily said, "Still don't believe you. Do that again."

"Stubborn man," she observed.

Lily heard laughter coming from Amber's room as she walked by. She paused in midstep, her heart falling like a heavy stone. Unmistakably male. Her jaw clenched as she listened to the male voice amid the sounds of water and Amber's laughter. The bathroom was in the far corner of the house, so she couldn't make out what was being said.

She had a strange feeling about this. It had started right after her phone call, and she had never been wrong before.

Brad was coming here for dinner tonight. He was early. The thought of him in there with her friend gutted her like a knife. How could he . . . but why not? She had run off the other night, leaving him in a state of need, and a man had to release his frustration somehow, right? And Amber and he were close enough friends. . . .

Lily abruptly turned around. She couldn't stay here and listen to them having their little private fun in there. She looked at the clock on the wall. Yeah, and she was invited to dinner to talk about the coming interview. She hadn't answered any of Brad's or Amber's calls; they must have concluded that she wasn't showing up. That was all right. Her appetite had evaporated anyway. She didn't think she could bear them exchanging intimate glances in front of her while she played third wheel, trying to swallow down food.

You could have had him. She closed her eyes at the memory of Brad and her on the sofa. How he had felt in her hands; how he had tasted. If she had given in to her needs and stayed the night, everything would have changed. Her eyes flew open. Therein lay the problem. She didn't want any changes. She wanted to stay the course. Bradford Sun would change everything for which she had worked so hard, and she couldn't afford it.

Perhaps it was better this way. Brad made her feel too damn much. Every time he was around her, she alternately wanted to either hit out at him verbally and physically or grab him by the lapels of his expensive suits and kiss him till she forgot what she was.

What she was . . . a loud thud brought her attention back to the closed door. And murmurs, mingled with . . . Lily backed away slowly. She didn't want to think what those soft sounds meant or what two people could be doing in a small bathroom.

She abruptly turned and retraced her steps back outside. She closed the door quietly behind her and leaned against it, breathing hard. The evening air was cool, yet she felt as if she were standing naked in the dead of winter.

She shook her head violently. No, she wouldn't think about being naked right now. Too many people were naked around here. She was Lily Noretski and she had sworn never to be naked and cold in any way or form ever again. She had sworn never to feel for anyone or anything. Feelings were for weaklings, and people like her could never be weak. Or they would break. In a million pieces. As she had done once.

Running down the steps in twos, she headed for her car. It was going to be all right. She was strong; she hadn't given in to those base feelings that made women weak and men powerful. She didn't care about Amber having sex with Bradford Sun. She slammed the car door shut, fired up the engine, and jammed on her sunglasses. She looked into the rearview mirror and, taking out her lipstick, she refreshed her lips, making a moue at her reflection.

Sex was nothing. She had had plenty of that, with anyone she wanted. As long as she didn't care, or take the time to know the man's body, or let him manipulate her feelings, she was all right. She had come precariously close to doing just that the other night. She almost had an orgasm in front of a man. What an idiot. If she had done that, everything would have changed.

And Lily didn't want anything changed. She took a deep breath and backed out of the driveway. She had a cause and people like her did not sway from the path. People like her . . . her lips twisted into a bitter smile as she made a turn into the road. People like her had no place in that kind of a world.

She pressed Amber's cell number on her phone. As expected, her friend's message service came on. She affected cheerfulness in her voice. "Hiya, sweetie. Have an emergency and will probably not be able to make it tonight. Here are some details that you and Brad can discuss if he shows up for dinner. . . ."

Amber lay on top of Hawk in her bed, her face against his chest. They were still damp from the long bath they had taken. It was the most use of that tub she had had since moving here four years ago.

"You're very, very good in the bathtub," she told him lazily.

His rumble of laughter echoed in her ear. "Your being triple-jointed helped, honey."

She bit his chest. "You liked that, huh?"

"Baby, you can reach back that way in a tight space and move your sexy butt again anytime." His hand covered her derriere. "I love your ass. So perfectly round and silky. With enough meat for little bites. And the little tattoo on the right side near your thigh drives me crazy. Why did you choose to have one there?"

Heat rose in her face. "You sound like you're talking about food," she said lightly.

"And I was doing quite a bit of eating," he teased. "That trail of little roses that led the way. I felt like Hansel and Gretel eating bread crumbs."

He caressed the spot where she had her tattoo. "There you go with food again," she said.

Using his other hand, Hawk nudged her up into a sitting position, her thighs spread on either side of him. She looked down at him, enjoying his nakedness as much as he was hers. He traced the pattern of the flowers in her thigh, his finger following each rose until the stem disappeared.

"You must have done this during a vacation."

She expelled a breath when his fingers moved lower. "How do you know?"

"It was just an assumption. You must have shaved for the bikini," he said, and his smile was very wicked. "I'm just trying to imagine you lying there spread out for the tattoo guy."

Amber flushed. "It was a biker festival," she told him.

"A biker party, huh? Interesting. Somehow I don't see you as a biker mama, Amber."

She laughed. "It was the most rebellious thing the daughter of missionaries could think of to do, although to this day my parents really don't know about the tattoo. Just that I spent a whole weekend with bikers." She laughed again at the memory. "My girlfriends and I wanted to put our tattoos somewhere sinful. The tattoo place was run by a couple, and the woman there suggested this."

"I like it. It makes me want to go down on you again." His gaze traveled intimately up her body. By the time it reached her eyes, her whole body was on fire from his leisurely inspection. "Shave for me. I want to see the rest of it."

"What do I get in return?" The sight of his tanned hand on her fair skin was erotic.

"I remember another position you owe me."

She leaned forward, putting her hands on his shoulders. "For an unconscious man, you seemed to remember all kinds of things I supposedly did to your body."

His lips quirked. "You mean to say you didn't climb on top and take advantage of me, like you're going to right now?"

"I didn't climb . . . I know, I know, you don't believe me." He was already positioning her. "Hawk, if I were doing all those things, shouldn't you let *me* be in charge?"

"Later."

He was too sure of himself. He opened his legs, effectively widening her thighs. There was the sensation of pressure as he guided himself inside her with one hand and pushed her down on him with another.

"You're a control freak," she whispered as she slid down on him.

"Yes."

She ignored the arrogance of his reply as she enjoyed the thick feel of him. He lay there contentedly as she adjusted to an easy rhythm; she could feel his eyes watching her as she abandoned herself to enjoyment. He trailed his fingers along her tattoo as she moved up and down, not quite touching her, just enough to make her go a little faster.

The shrill from her private line cut through her haze of pleasure. Her eyes darted to the phone on the night table by them. The tone told her it was the direct line linked to her study. Shit. She caught the time on the alarm clock. Shit, shit. Brad. She had forgotten about the dinner. He sometimes called her from the study when he got in early.

Hawk didn't stop her from answering the phone, but his hands on her thighs made it impossible for her to disengage her body from hers. She leaned over to get the phone.

"Hello? Hi . . . Brad." She almost lost balance as Hawk began to sit up. She held on to the phone tightly. "I'm fine, just running a little . . . late."

Amber couldn't do anything as Hawk pushed her back against his raised thighs. Just in time, she stopped the groan that rose in her throat as he thrust upward. She glared up at him. His eyes had an unmistakable glint in them.

She cleared her throat again. "No, no, I'll be down there soon." She ignored, or tried to, the hands cupping her breasts. He leaned forward and she jerked forward at the feel of his mouth on her nipple. This time she couldn't stop her gasp. "Oh! I mean, have some . . . wine."

She slapped at the teasing hand traveling down from her rib cage, but there wasn't much room to maneuver, not when she was trying to have a conversation at the same time. She leaned back helplessly against Hawk's thighs as his thumb mercilessly began its external assault. Sitting on him, impaled, there was no escape. And Brad was asking about Lily.

"Don't know." Her voice came out breathless and high. "I'll come down . . . soon."

She hit the off button. Just in time. Her assailant turned over suddenly. If she had still been on the phone, Brad would have definitely heard the telltale squeak of bedsprings as Hawk began his assault.

She stared up. He had a devilishly satisfied expression on his face.

"I'll come down soon," he mimicked her words. He leaned forward and his kiss was hard and hungry. Possessive. "Come for me first, baby."

14

Hawk had never, in all his life, slept with another man's woman, but he didn't think he could hand Amber back to Bradford Sun that easily. This feeling of possessiveness was unfamiliar territory for him. He had never wanted a woman this much before.

"I need to explain," Amber said, "before you two meet."

"Are you going to tell him the truth?" he asked quizzically.

She regarded him levelly. "Do you think I'd have slept with you if I weren't ready to tell the truth?"

"I didn't give you the chance," he pointed out.

"Oh yes, you did. You carried me up here. I'd have said no if I hadn't wanted to," she came back. She patted his newly shaven face. "I'm running late, and I don't want to keep Brad waiting."

"You really think he's going to come up and have dinner with me here?" Hawk shook his head. If it were him . . . like hell. He would be running up here to break a few bones. He would feed the bones to the other man for dinner. He would . . . He shook his head again. He'd had too much violence the last few days. He continued, in a sarcastic drawl, "Sure, I'll wait here. A nice civilized European air-clearing, followed by a nice glass of wine before dinner. You don't mind if I make rude sounds now and then, do you? I'm an American, after all."

Her eyes filled with amusement. "Brad's American, Hawk. And there are things you don't know about, so that's why I'm bringing him up here. I don't have time to explain it to you and have him wait downstairs. People will wonder. There are spies all over the place. We'll be talking a little business, too, okay?"

"Okay."

Hawk sat down and impatiently studied Amber's living area. He hadn't noticed anything that belonged to another man, not even when he asked for a razor. She had given him her own. If Bradford Sun overnighted here sometimes, he didn't leave any of his stuff lying around, not even an extra pair of slippers for lounging. Well, hell, how would he know? He hadn't checked under the damn bed.

He almost got up to return to the bedroom. Took a deep breath. Relaxed back into the chair. He looked around again. There was something missing in this picture and he hadn't quite figured out everything yet, but one thing was for sure. Now that he'd had a taste of Amber Hutchens, there was no way in hell he was going to share.

He didn't share. Or poach another man's woman. He expelled a disgusted sigh. It seemed that ever since he took on this covert operation, he'd gone back on every one of his values, from protecting women and children to getting rid of the world's scum that were responsible for hurting them.

Everything was fucking backward. He didn't share. And the woman he wanted for himself was downstairs talking to another man. *Her* man. He didn't poach. And he had gone and . . . He felt tension rising in him again. She couldn't have a very loving relationship with the guy if she responded so passionately to his lovemaking. Maybe she would break off with him. Either that or Hawk would just break one more code of honor and steal her away from the son of a bitch. And then what?

Hawk scratched the back of his neck. What the hell was happening to him? He had a job to do, and shouldn't be thinking about ways to seduce a woman or steal her away from her lover. His mind was back on the two things that had gotten him in trouble that first night when he and Amber had clashed. Woman. Amber in all her naked luminous glory. And now—his lips twisted in self-mockery—food. Running a hand through his damp hair in frustration, he stood up, needing to expend energy. Where was his SEAL training to forgo all physical needs when under stress?

Concentrate on the job, man. He needed Amber's help. *Don't fuck it up.* Everything depended on him.

The stairway door opened. Hawk turned around. Amber walked in, followed by a tall man. Light hair, almost as blond as Amber's. Square-jawed. A big man in an expensive suit, carrying a bottle of wine. Hawk clenched his teeth. Unlike the other man, he was wearing his dirty pants and one of Amber's T-shirts. Certainly no competition in the suave and debonair department.

Bradford Sun looked every bit the chief of CIVPOL, in command of his world. The easy and quiet self-assurance of a man of power. He looked very good together with Amber. Hawk disliked him already. Intensely.

Amber's blue eyes narrowed just a little. Her smile was different, a smooth complacent curve that was nothing like the pouty, sassy grins she had given him. Then she broke the tension of the moment with a wink. The woman was a tease.

"Brad, this is Hawk McMillan. Hawk, this is my friend Bradford Sun."

Brad regarded him for a moment before extending a hand. "Mr. McMillan," he said, his voice cultured, his eyes keenly studying him.

What did one say to the lover of the woman he'd just bedded? Nice to meet you? A pleasure? Hawk opted for non-committal. "How do you do?"

They both eyed each other for an instant before Brad inclined his head. "I hear you're after Dilaver. That's one thing we have in common."

"Not the only thing," Hawk said, keeping his voice bland. He didn't like the way Brad smiled at Amber. "I've heard that you can't seem to put him behind bars."

He enjoyed the sight of Brad stiffening his shoulders. Hit a hot button there, hadn't he?

Amber moved in between them. "Sit down, both of you, and please, my place is too small for all this testosterone. Can both of you stop baiting each other while I get us something to drink? We'll talk like adults, and then we'll eat."

Hawk sat down again. Either something was very odd, or Brad and Amber had one of those very open relationships. Talk like adults and eat. . . .

Amber came back with three glasses. "Open the bottle of wine, Brad, and pour us some." She flipped open her cell phone. "I think Lily's not going to show. I see a message from her."

Lily was coming to dinner, too? So this wasn't a twosome thing? Hawk relaxed a little. She listened intently to the phone as she and Brad exchanged glances, her expression unreadable. Brad turned and filled the glasses, giving one to Hawk.

"Thanks." He really didn't want to talk like an adult and eat. Maybe he hadn't gotten the violence out of his system for the day because he was feeling like beating someone up again. Hawk scowled. That brought his mind back to how he had come here and what he had been doing with Amber. Brad sat down at the table, too, seemingly unperturbed that Amber's hair appeared a little damp, like Hawk's. Maybe the man wasn't as perfect as he looked; he was probably nearsighted.

"Lily has an emergency," Amber said after she had sat down between them, "but she says she'll try to make it. If not, she gave me some details to pass along."

"Do you believe her?" Brad asked. There was something in the tone of his voice that made Hawk study him closely.

"You know how important this project is to her, Brad. She wouldn't not show up when the interview can help the girls." When Brad didn't say anything, Amber turned to Hawk. "This isn't as complicated as it looks, although your being here does add one complicated factor. Brad and I are seen as an item by some people. Since I deal with information, it'll be reported to certain ears if he goes home without dinner, or doesn't stay his usual length of time, or if you were to go down and have dinner with us in our private booth."

"Okay." Seen as an item. Her choice of words was peculiar. Hawk drank down his wine. "But Dilaver knows I'm here."

Brad's eyebrows lifted. "Do you report your whereabouts to him?"

"He dislikes you," Hawk said, and looked at both of them, "so anything to do with you interests him."

"So he must have told you Amber and I are more than friends. Did he set you up to come between us? Are you reporting back to him?"

Hawk stared back at the other man, challenging him silently.

"Brad . . ." Amber cut in. She put her glass down. "Why don't I do the talking for now, hmm? This is . . . awkward." She turned to Hawk. "Brad and I are just friends, but it helps me to let Dilaver and various other gangs think I'm dating the chief of CIVPOL."

"I see." He didn't have time to wonder about the odd sense of release washing through him at the revelation. For some reason Amber wanted to include him in this secret and he was hoping to find out more. "Then you're sort of a couple so Mr. Sun can protect your outfit and you can give him information. Very good front."

"He's got some brains," Brad remarked wryly. He looked at Hawk again and added, "Don't think I won't check up on you when I get back to my office."

It was a small warning that he hadn't earned Brad's trust yet. Fair enough. He didn't care, either. As long as Amber wasn't really going out with the man, who cared what Bradford Sun thought of him? "Dig away." Hawk shrugged. "Why don't you spend some time going after Dilaver instead?"

"Brad raids Dilaver's *kafenas* whenever he has reliable information from me," Amber said, "but Dilaver, as you know, is very hard to catch."

What, the man couldn't speak for himself? "All you have to do is raid his compounds with a bunch of peacekeepers and shoot a lot of bullets," Hawk said very politely.

"We're under NATO and international laws, Mr. McMillan," Brad said equally politely. "And, if I may also point out, Dragan Dilaver appears to be under the protection of the United States government."

"Certain sectors of the U.S. government," Hawk swiftly corrected. Not *his*. He had never pretended to understand all the political games played back home, but since going under training with GEM and the COS organizations, he had a better picture of how many covert operations crisscrossed each other. Dilaver was a useful asset for now and that was why he was alive. He didn't agree with the reasoning behind it, but he was under orders and he would do his best to make sure everything went as planned.

"Nevertheless, he does have his connections," Brad said. "I arrest his minions, but that's nothing. Even if I managed to lock him up, he'd be freed too soon."

"You don't have a lot of confidence in the justice system around here."

"Hawk, you know very well there isn't much of one around Macedonia and the former Yugoslavian states," Amber said quietly. "There are a hundred *kafenas* here alone, run by a dozen or so pimps who are under the crime organizations. Human and drug trafficking are businesses around here, and the United Nations turns a blind eye to some of it because they are busy rebuilding nations." She made imaginary quotation marks to the last two words, then added, "Many UN officials have been eliminated by assassins since the war. The last chief of CIVPOL had a bomb scare before Brad was appointed."

"You don't have to make him feel sorry for me, Amber," Brad said wryly. "I think he doesn't care, as long as I'm not sleeping with you. Right, McMillan?"

"Right," Hawk agreed.

Amber's fair skin betrayed her discomfort. He supposed she had to tell Brad about why he was upstairs, and the chief probably wasn't too stupid to put two and two together. He had heard about the assassinations in between his own deployments overseas, of course. He supposed being a CIVPOL official would make Brad a big target. Dilaver had expressed his dislike for the new chief, saying that he had been targeting his holdings. If nothing else, Hawk respected Bradford Sun for causing the kingpin some grief.

"You two are determined to have a pissing contest over nothing," Amber said quietly.

"Nothing?" Hawk asked, raising an eyebrow. Her blue eyes flashed at him in answer.

"I have to make sure he's worth all the trouble he's going to cause you," Brad said, looking from one to the other. "Besides, if Lily were here, I wouldn't feel as if I were intruding."

Lily . . . Hawk remembered the tall, dark-haired woman he had met. So Brad was interested in another woman. Good. One problem eliminated. He could concentrate on more reasonable things now.

"I can talk like an adult and eat," Hawk said softly to Amber.

"Oh, goodie," she said sarcastically. "I was beginning to think I'd made a mistake."

Where was Lily? Amber wished her friend hadn't left her in this predicament. Brad was playing protector and Hawk was . . . well, she didn't know what Hawk was doing. She wasn't even sure why she felt she had to explain the situation to him. She didn't owe him anything.

But she didn't want Hawk to think that she was the kind of woman who would play around. Somehow, it was important that he respect her. It suddenly struck her as odd that she wanted him to meet Brad and Lily, her two close friends, and get along with them. It was so totally out of character for her to do this, and Brad knew because he was looking at her like she had grown another head.

She couldn't explain it to herself, so how could she do a good job of it for Brad? She did the next best thing—let Brad and Hawk meet. So far, Brad had been predictably careful, almost like a big brother giving subtle warnings. Hawk—she had to hide a smile—didn't seem afraid or care about making any impression. In fact, he was acting like he had the right to be in her kitchen, eating dinner here. He looked too comfortable sitting there, wearing her T-shirt, one that looked big on her but fit him snugly, stretching over those broad shoulders that she knew were corded with muscles, fitting around that hard body that had been on top of her own not too long ago. Damn, why did she have to think of that now? The man looked too good in that shirt. And she wanted it off.

The glint in Hawk's eye told her he knew what she was thinking about. He had accepted the story about her and Brad's façade as a couple without making any personal comments, and throughout dinner he sat listening quietly as she gave a brief outline about what she and Lily were doing. She didn't give the full version, just enough details so that he understood where she stood as far as Dilaver was concerned.

"That's why I'll help you locate the item you want," she said. "Anything that will eventually bring an end to Dilaver's control of this region is good."

"Is that a yes as my guide, then?"

Amber nodded. "That's also why I need Brad and Lily to know what's going on. I'm the facilitator to both operations and when I'm gone with you, someone will have to take over certain details. We'll have to make up some story about my being missing at the same time that you are. This is where Brad comes in."

Hawk looked at Brad. "How?"

"I'm slated to go on vacation in about ten days," Brad told him, "and I'll take Amber with me. At least, that will be what Dilaver will think. If you take off a week after that, Dilaver won't suspect Amber's in on this."

"A little over two weeks," Hawk said, thinking quickly. "That should be enough time to get all the coordinates of his dropoff points and map out his gunrunning routes."

"I'd like you to give me details of the latter," Brad said. "If your people can't stop him, I'll get him for illegal arms-dealing."

"How about illegal human-trafficking? From what Amber's saying, I'm assuming you're helping her because you can't get him through your laws. Can't be easy, what with all those peacekeepers being Dilaver's customers and all."

This time, there wasn't any sarcasm in the tone of Hawk's voice. Amber couldn't help but admire how quickly he read between the lines and saw the situation for what it was. But she had to defend Brad, who didn't seem inclined to explain that his hands were tied. "He arranged the interview so an outside party can report the extracurricular activities of some of the peacekeepers, Hawk," she said.

"It's a good strategy," Hawk said, finishing the last of the roast from his plate. "I think it would be even better if you could arrange for an interview inside the *kafena*. Say, the interviewer poses as a client. He'd get firsthand experience."

"That's risky to the girls and the interviewer," Brad said.

Hawk shrugged. "There's always risk in our chosen line of work. If that guy wants a truly hot story, he'd want to go undercover and take some on-the-scene photos. Technology is so remarkable now, one can use any number of ways to get a photo and put it online." He drank down more wine and his smile wasn't very pleasant. "I'll take great delight in taking some risk and getting the interviewer inside as my friend. That way he'll have a before-and-after kind of story and perhaps there will be more international outrage to help your cause. I hate that . . . asshole."

Amber sat back, a little stunned at how quickly Hawk had taken over. He was volunteering to put his life in danger to help those girls inside the *kafenas*. The other night, when he had persuaded her not to shoot at those men, she'd thought that he didn't want to make waves and disrupt his covert operation, but now she was no longer sure.

Brad's gaze was thoughtful. "So why don't you get rid of him yourself?"

"Why don't you?" Hawk challenged back.

"Ah . . . orders from above," Brad said with a nod. "Looks like we're in the same predicament. Something else we have in common."

"Unlike you, I don't have a whole department under me whom I can send out and cause some havoc," Hawk pointed out, then muttered, "Not right now, anyway."

"Meaning?"

Hawk paused, then shrugged again. "I have my connections. Dilaver will be taken care of eventually. Right now it's essential for me to get the coordinates. If he's terminated now, I can't do that, so, in CIA parlance, he's still an asset. But that doesn't mean I can't do a little damage my own way." He glanced at Amber. "I want to be part of this. Some of those girls are in really bad shape. I couldn't see how I could get them out of there before without compromising my cover."

It wasn't an exact revelation to Amber that Hawk had seen what went on in those places and hadn't lifted a finger to help the victims, but seeing that look in his eyes, it suddenly dawned on her how much he had been fighting the urge, and the toll it must have taken on his spirit. She had seen the same look in Lily's eyes, had watched her friend's seething anger at her own inability to stop the crimes at their roots. Yet she and her friend had really only been standing at the edge, doing what they could. Hawk was in the center of it all.

"All right," she said quietly, "if Brad and Lily have no objections, and if those newspeople want the inside story, we'll do it."

There was a short pause. Where the hell was Lily? Amber wanted to shake her friend, wondering whether there really was an emergency after all. This was so unlike her, especially when it had to do with the girls.

"So we have the next three weeks' agenda," Hawk said.

"I'll zero in on the coordinates. Sun will set up the interviews. You and Lily will work out the times for both of them. I'll bring the men into the *kafenas* at the proper time when Dilaver isn't watching too closely. Meanwhile, I also suggest that we set up a love triangle of sorts so that it appears that you'll have reason to spirit Amber away from Velesta. It'll give me a chance to get a bit upset about it and appear to take off. That should give Amber and me a head start without Dilaver suspecting."

The man did *love* ordering people around, didn't he? Amber looked at Brad to see how he was taking Hawk jumping in with all the suggestions. Not that she could tell. He had his poker face on, which meant he was thinking.

She turned back to Hawk. He was looking around expectantly. "What are you looking for?" she asked.

"Dessert," he said. "I'm hungry."

Brad opened her back door and she stepped outside onto her deck before he joined her. He closed the door behind him. She had left Hawk on the couch, placing the remote to her television in his hand. He hadn't said a word, turning the set on.

"Are you sure he isn't going to come out here just to make sure I don't lay a finger on you?" Brad's voice was amused. Their plan was to walk down to the parking lot together, like a couple on an evening stroll.

Amber breathed in the evening air, enjoying its fresh crispness. "He's got a remote, hasn't he? I thought that's supposed to turn a man into a happy control freak."

Brad laughed. "I'd never have thought you would get yourself a control freak for a love interest, Amber. You're so damn organized yourself. How are you going to take someone else taking charge, especially during this sojourn into the wilds?"

She frowned. "Love interest? Is that what he is?" she said it more to herself than to Brad.

They walked down the wooden steps. "My dear, I have never seen you as flustered as you were when you came downstairs into your study, trying to explain the whole situation. I can see why you're attracted to him, though. Good-looking, smarter than hell, and with great taste, I might add." He turned and touched her arm, then added quietly, "He isn't from the Agency, you know. I can tell."

Anyone working for Jed wasn't exactly Agency, but she didn't see any need to tell Brad that. It was better to introduce Jed's world to as few people as possible. "How?" she asked, curious as to how Brad came to that conclusion.

"The way he took over and strategized. It's very military, assigning different tasks to everyone. He's used to ordering teams. He didn't slouch once while he was sitting at the table, even when he was devouring you and your food with his eyes and mouth." Brad laughed softly. "I'll bet you a hundred Euros he's watching from the window to see what you and I are up to."

Amber stopped herself from looking up to check whether Brad was right. "You're silly. We've just met. I don't know him that well." She didn't elaborate that they had met under very intimate circumstances and that she had flirted with the man through phone and on the computer. "He's very unusual, that's all."

"You know him well enough to trust him. You have been with him a lot more than you're telling, Amber."

She knew that not much escaped Brad's notice, especially when it came to details about people he interacted with. That was what made him an excellent bureaucrat; he studied the behavior of those around him to gauge things going on under the radar.

"We've done a lot of unusual things that couples don't

normally do," she admitted with a smile. He had been practically naked the first time they'd met. She had rendered him
unconscious with a drug. His revenge. The romp around the
city when she had spent hours chasing him up and down old
walls and dark alleys. Their midnight chats. It seemed crazy,
but she did feel closer to Hawk than to any man she had
known. "But this is Velesta. It isn't like anything around here
is usual."

"I'm going to do some background-checking anyway,"
Brad said. "He's more than meets the eyes."

"But so am I, Brad."

"Yes. I must admit I felt a little envious tonight."

Amber stopped in midstride, curling a hand into the crook
of his arm. "I'm sorry about you and Lily. But you both need
to talk this out. I can't seem to reach her."

"I can't, either. What we both need is to make love the
way you guys did upstairs today. Seemed to add a lot of private electricity in the air. From where I was sitting, I was
afraid of getting zapped by all those sexy looks."

"Brad!" Amber protested, half laughing and half embar-
rassed that he saw so much. Had she really acted that unpro-
fessionally? "I'm sorry."

"Don't be," he assured her. "I'm glad to see you finding
someone after so long. It's just too bad we couldn't be a real
couple. We both seem to go after those dark-haired and tem-
peramental types."

"It'll work out for you and Lily," Amber said, crossing her
fingers in the dark.

They finally reached Brad's car. "I'll call and let you
know about the interviews. You try to talk to Lily. We need
her for these meetings."

"I know. I will." She stood on tiptoe and his hands rested
on her shoulders as she gave Brad a goodnight kiss. "By the

way, where are you taking me for vacation?" She teased him to put him in a better mood.

She could hear the smile in his reply. "Somewhere we can get totally naked on the beach. Make sure you tell everyone that part of it."

Especially Hawk, of course. She smiled and they had another friendly goodnight kiss before she turned and retraced her steps, taking her time as she pondered over what Brad had said. She did like Hawk and yes, she did trust him enough. But where was it going?

"Tell me you didn't kiss him goodnight," Hawk said from the couch when she went back upstairs.

"Of course I did," she quipped. "I kiss Brad goodnight all the time."

"Brush your teeth, or here, have some wine." He lifted the glass in his hand. "Bureaucrat breath stinks."

She flopped down beside him. "Are you jealous?"

"Yeah."

"Why? We hardly know each other, Hawk." She wanted to know whether he was feeling as close to her as she did to him. "I mean, was it all just hot sex for you this afternoon?"

He put down the glass. The lighting was just dim enough to add a golden glow to his eyes. "No, it wasn't just hot sex," he said, lowering his voice. "Hot sex is for tonight."

"So this is all just sex to you, then," Amber insisted. She really wanted the hot sex, too, but she pressed on anyhow.

He studied her for a second, then, flinging an arm around her shoulder, pulled her close to him. He crossed outstretched legs on her coffee table. "Tell you what. To show you that it isn't really just all sex, we'll watch TV for a while."

Amber looked at the screen, finally paying attention to what was on. "Sumo wrestling?" she asked in a faint voice.

Hawk looked down, a grin on his face. "Damn European TV doesn't have anything on. What's more entertaining than men in diapers groping each other, hmm?"

"Umm . . . hot sex?" she ventured hopefully.

He shook his head. "You wanted me to prove it's more than that, honey. You'll just have to enjoy some sumo wrestling."

She laid a suggestive hand on his crotch. "Can I dissuade you?"

He burped rudely. "You can try." It didn't take that long to make her point, but his eyes remained fixed on the screen. "My, what big diapers this dude is wearing."

Amber curled up next to him. Her hand teased him for a while, then her mouth. She was going to make Hawk McMillan always associate sumo wrestling with hot sex.

Brad got into his car. If he smoked, this would be a good time to light up a cigarette and go into deep thought. He wondered whether that was why people did it in their vehicles so much. Twisting a cup of hot coffee in contemplation about life needed two hands. And the image was certainly not quite so world-weary.

He undid the top few buttons of his jacket, then put on his seat belt. He wasn't lying to Amber when he told her he felt envious while watching Hawk and her together. He wished he had the opportunity to have such a relationship with Lily. Hell, he had to start one first.

He had hoped to talk to Lily privately tonight. No touching. No arguing. Just talk. Why was it so difficult to do that with this particular woman? Her no-show tonight was a message, that she was unwilling to give him a chance.

Brad started his car. He should just back off. He had kept telling himself to give her time, but maybe this thing was just not to be.

Damn it. How could he just let it go when all he could think about was the way those dark eyes had looked up at him?

He checked the rearview mirror as he made the turn. A car had pulled out from the curb, going the other way. It looked like Lily's car, but he couldn't be sure in the evening light. Probably just fanciful imagination. Why would she be sitting outside just to avoid dinner with him? That was too melodramatic, even for Lily.

15

222 / IRIS JOHANSEN

"My end's secure. Twice in one week. Must be urgent, Hawk." Jed McNeil's husky voice came over the headphones suddenly. Hawk had been waiting for a few minutes as his call was redirected through several channels. "What's all the noise in the background?"

"I'm supposed to be working out," Hawk explained as he landed a blow to the made-up punching bag in his room. "I need to work up a sweat because Dilaver wants to do a slow jog around his compound later to see how his leg's healing."

"Good. Updated Madison about your plans with Ambrosia and he agreed it was a good risk. Checked up on Sun. He's ninety percent. He'd be a good cover for Ambrosia and you."

Madison was Admiral Madison, Hawk's SEAL commander. It was good to know that his leader and McNeil were in direct contact. All this skulking around within organizations had made Hawk wary about third-party communications more than ever.

"What's the missing ten percent?" He was curious about Bradford Sun, not just because of his special friendship with

Amber, but he wanted to make sure the CIVPOL chief posed no danger to Amber and her friend.

"He has an interest in Llallana Noretski. Her credibility is at twenty-five percent." All these numbers didn't mean a thing to Hawk. He preferred concrete evidence, but GEM and COS operatives had been trained that way, memorizing codes and percentage factors to save time as well as preserve secrecy. At twenty-five percent, the file on Llallana Noretski would be thick with evidence of criminal background activity. Hawk had known about Brad's interest, but this evidence about Lily was a new surprise. As if he read his mind, Mc-Neil continued, "The CIA has had dealings with her before, so that upped her percentages. But we don't know exactly what Sun's and her relationship is, since they keep it tightly under wraps. We aren't worried about her yet, but she's an unknown factor."

"So Llallana is with the CIA? Does Ambrosia know?" Hawk and Jed always used Amber's code name.

"Negative to both. Noretski was picked up by the Agency before. The information we have pointed to perhaps an interrogation, so her experience with them might not have been a happy one. You'll have to find out yourself."

"Okay."

"Ambrosia doesn't appear to know much more. What we know of Llallana also comes partly from her when they first met. She'd checked her out then."

"They are best friends now," Hawk told Jed as he dodged the swinging bag and turned to execute a flurry of punches.

"What does she think of you?"

"We get along."

"What do you think of her?"

Hawk recalled her letting him carry Amber into her room. Their conversations this past week had been brief. She hadn't questioned his sudden appearance in her and Amber's plans; in fact, she had seemed subdued. "She has attitude," Hawk said, stopping the punching bag with a taped hand, "and a lot of secrets."

Amber had asked that his description of her and Lily's side project be as minimal as possible. Jed, she had said gravely, would use that information for his own ends. She had added, with sarcasm, that it might pull down her percentage statistics with COS Command. Hawk hadn't said anything, although he was privately amused at her direct heat.

"What's new, then?"

Hawk put the punching bag in motion again. "Be ready for an upload of coordinates."

"All of them?"

"Not sure, but enough info to map out where each drop point might be."

"Good. Then we have to figure out which load has our target."

Hawk started his routine again. "Ambrosia and I start our journey as soon as we have a map from your end."

"Fax it to her?"

"Yes."

"Are you sleeping with Ambrosia?" Jed's sudden question made Hawk pause in midstrike and the bag bumped into him. He reached out with both arms to hug it to a stop, as Jed continued in polite tones, "Got the air knocked out of you?"

"Is there a policy against that?" Hawk asked, nursing the shoulder that had borne the brunt of the hit.

"We have only one policy. Do your job."

"I'll get it done," Hawk said.

"I expect no less from one of the admiral's Standing and Ready SEALs. Call me again when Sun is ready for his vacation. I should have the map and key positions ready for you and Ambrosia. I'll also give you the name of the contact that will pick up the merchandise once it's in your hands."

After Jed rang off, Hawk gave the punching bag a quick kick for revenge before putting away the headphone. He'd forgotten what good interrogators those commandos were. By invoking his STAR status, Jed McNeil was reminding him to keep his focus on his job, which was to stay as close to Dilaver as possible, and not to a certain blonde with a sassy mouth.

He had to admit, he had been going to Amber's place too much. Even Dilaver was teasing him about it, commenting that Hawk had finally rediscovered his libido. Which brought the focus back on the main problem. He did enjoy spending time with Amber, but he was also avoiding going to the *kafenas*. It was good to get away from *that* for a while.

But Hawk could avoid it only for so long. To be close to Dilaver meant being with the Slav while he committed crimes that made his stomach turn. Thank God the big thug had the sense not to do hard drugs for recreation. Hawk had been trained on how to best avoid ending up an addict, if, in case, such a scenario cropped up, but it was tough for an in-experienced covert agent not to get into trouble when confronted with the unexpected invitation of joining the "fun." Many had ended up addicts themselves, and some had lost the fight to get clean.

Oh yeah, he was one lucky devil, standing there like an idiot and not lifting a finger when a young woman was being beaten. Or, even worse, sexually humiliated. It made Hawk ashamed of his own sex when he watched the depraved things the men made the girls do. The first time he had accompanied Dilaver to one of his "training sessions," it took every ounce of control he had not to pounce on and kill the scum who was doing the training.

He had the satisfaction of thinking that he had finally got-

218 \ **Gennita Low**

ten rid of one of them that evening during the battle by the
hillside. That man was one of Dilaver's closest aides and had
been particularly vicious when it came to breaking in the
new girls. Hawk had mentally killed him dozens of times in
the last few months. However, he hadn't found much relief
in the act; the images of the girls still haunted him.

Amber. Hawk smiled every time he thought of her. She
made him forget, at least for a while, what he had seen. Either his abstinence had sharpened his senses or she made
him feel like never before. He couldn't seem to get enough
of her. Every time they made love, he craved more. How was
it that he could want a woman so badly? Even now he
wanted her.

But he couldn't. Not tonight. He had to get back to playing Dilaver's new friend. A knock on the door interrupted
his reverie.

Hawk pushed the punching bag into a swing again.
"Come in," he said as he started punishing it. He knew it
would be Dilaver, meeting him to go jogging. Without stopping, he continued, "Ready to run?"

"Fuck, no. I can't believe I'm going jogging." Dilaver still
walked with a slight limp and sometimes needed his walking
stick after being on his feet too long. He kicked his leg out.
"It's taking me longer to heal."

"Yeah, they say it's the feet that go first, then the face,"
Hawk quipped as he stopped the moving bag.

Dilaver chuckled. "You're just saying that because you're
a pretty face," he said. "If you had pretty legs like mine,
you'd say it's the face that goes first."

Hawk started to untape his hands. "Well, let's see how
your pretty hairy legs keep up with mine today."

Dilaver tapped his foot. "I bet they are just as pretty as
Amber Hutchens's, eh?"

Hawk pretended to give it some thought. "To be honest,"

he said, "my attention isn't focused on her legs much, but I know hers are a hell of a lot less hairy."

Dilaver laughed. "You know what I like about you, Hawk? You aren't afraid to make me laugh with the most absurd observations. I can't imagine talking about my leg and comparing it to a woman's with anyone else but you."

That was because Hawk had set out to talk to Dilaver as he would to any of his SEAL teammates. It was drilled into him to be as natural he could be, as he would be with his own best friends. It was the last thing he wanted to do; by acting with the same familiarity, it felt almost like betraying his own friends. But he had succeeded, just as his GEM trainer in NOPAIN had said it would, in gaining a measure of friendship from the gunrunner. Nonphysical persuasion and innovative negotiation, a system most GEM operatives he'd met seemed to practice, both repelled and fascinated him with how good it was at manipulating human minds.

"Yeah, well, I don't know whether to feel insulted or special now," he drawled.

"Oh, special," Dilaver said. "And especially special since I have been hearing about our CIVPOL chief having a public argument with your Amber this morning."

"Is that right?" Hawk tossed the tape into a nearby pail.

"Seems like someone has informed our Mr. Sun that a certain American has been sharing Amber's bed every night for a week."

Hawk cocked an eyebrow. "Is that someone in your pay, perhaps?"

"But of course. Revenge is sweet. Mr. Sun has raided a couple of my sites and cost me quite a bit of income. This is just the beginning. One day . . ." Dilaver's voice trailed off and he shrugged. "But not yet. Can't keep ridding every one of them so quickly. I'll wait awhile till that sanguine outlook of his wears off a bit."

"Sanguine?" Hawk wouldn't use that description for Bradford Sun at all.

"He's optimistic that he can clean this region up," explained Dilaver with a humorless smile. "I find that extremely comical."

"And you say I make absurd observations?" Hawk commented as they headed out.

"You don't find it funny that the man thinks that and yet has a girlfriend who sells his secrets to people like me?" Dilaver laughed nastily, glancing at Hawk craftily. "And today his sanguine outlook was just a little dimmer when he realized that she isn't all sunshine. I heard he's taking her off for a vacation to get her away from you, my friend. What are you going to do about it?"

So far, so good. Fed information was being passed on as planned. Hawk feigned surprise. "That's news to me. When?"

"My sources say in a couple of weeks, but hell, the way you're over there all the time, it might be sooner. I don't think any man would let a woman like Amber go so easily." Dilaver nodded at his guards as they passed them. The latter kept a distance, keeping an eye on their boss and the surroundings. "So you had better spend as much time with her as you can before she's whisked off, my friend."

"I'll do that," Hawk promised. Maybe he could spend tonight with Amber after going out with Dilaver. "Better warm up first or your pretty legs might cramp up."

Even the guards behind them snickered at Hawk's joke. But his mind was already on the day's agenda. He had to ready the file to be uploaded. He wasn't sure he could get away to go with Amber to that interview. He wanted to. Tonight, at the *kafena,* he had to see which of the girls could speak enough English for the interviewer. It would be tough;

they all lived in fear. He would have to think of some way to persuade them without blowing his cover.

Amber poured tea for everyone in the room. There was an anxious excitement in the air as the three girls who had agreed to do the interview sat on the big sofa, eyeing the two newsmen with suspicion, cynicism, and hope. They were young, but they had been through enough to know that promises didn't mean anything. It was also decided that no doctor was needed to examine the victims until the girls had met the reporters and felt comfortable.

Amber and Lily had been very upfront about it. This interview was meant for them to tell the world what was going on, in their words. The reporters would try to sell the story to international cable news and other agencies. It would do *some* good—not for them, but maybe for those other girls who were still in the *kafenas*.

Of the girls they had in the safe houses, only three could speak enough English to give personal accounts, with a little help from Amber and Lily. They were also the few who were old enough to have something to say. The others were too young to give extensive interviews; some of them weren't comfortable with telling their stories to adult men. Amber had told the two men that she had compiled a list of what these girls had told her, about what had been done to them after they were kidnapped.

Brad was standing by the fireplace. He had already briefed the reporters that under no circumstances were the identities of Amber and Lily to be revealed, or their pictures taken. In fact, he had introduced them as Anna and Ludmilla.

Amber watched Hawk question the two men as they set up the taping and photo devices. He was speaking in a low voice, but she heard enough of the conversation to know that he was asking for a direct copy of the interview as well as the reporters' final copy.

"I want to compare what was said and what was written," he told them. "And if I feel you have done a poor job, I'll release my own copy of the interview as well as your direct copy."

To her surprise, Hawk showed them a recorder the size of his palm. He hadn't told her about this. Again, she was struck at how prepared he was for this sort of thing. She exchanged glances with Brad.

Lily was giving last-minute encouragement to the girls, each in her own language. They were all from different countries and Lily was the only one who understood the cultural horror of so many girls being traded like international souvenirs. Amber had sighed with relief that her friend and Brad had been very cordial with each other. Maybe they had come to some sort of understanding. She had tried to talk to Lily about it, but her friend's replies had been oddly cool.

Not that she had spent that much time talking to Lily, Amber acknowledged wryly. She had been kept very busy with Hawk showing up at her place at the oddest hours. Lily must have gotten the clue that she wasn't alone too much because she had practically been living somewhere else, only showing up during the day to help with plans and business.

All in all, it had been a heck of a week. She glanced at Hawk again. He was very comfortable with her and her friends, participating in their plans and risking his own cover. Brad would tell her if he'd found anything unusual in Hawk's background, so she wasn't worried. But neither was she blind.

Hawk McMillan was a natural at taking charge, and he did it without ordering anyone about. There was just an air about him that made her feel very safe whenever she was around him. She couldn't quite put a finger on it. Maybe it was the way he pointed out alternate ways to do things, giving sound reasons why a direct interview at the *kafena* would be even more effective as a news story. Or the way he was now handling the two reporters. Without making any verbal threat, he had subtly warned them that he would be paying attention to how they would spin the girls' tales.

It dawned on her that he was always searching for weaknesses in any situation and fortifying them before they were exposed by the other side. He had a very indirect approach about it, as shown in the way he maneuvered himself into her secret venture. But it was remarkably effective, as in the way the two reporters in the room were answering all his questions quietly and respectfully, as if his approval were essential.

She wondered what Brad thought of that. He was watching all this, too, and hadn't said anything to undermine Hawk. She sensed that he was learning as much as she was about this operative sent in to infiltrate Dilaver's nest and hunt down some kind of hidden weapon. To do that required a lot of skill. She knew from experience that nobody ever got too close to Dragan Dilaver. That Hawk had succeeded in this feat gave her an idea how really capable he was.

She approached them and refilled their teacups. "Let me know when you're ready," she told them, "so I can go talk to the girls first."

"Five minutes," The bespectacled reporter, Thomas, said.

"Do we use the girls' real names, Anna?" Hawk asked, using her assumed ID.

"First names are fine. It doesn't matter now that they are free," she replied.

Hawk nodded. "I was just thinking about the girls at the *kafenas* later. They'll want to use different names." He glanced at Thomas. "I don't have to spell out what could happen to them if somehow their pimps find out they gave interviews."

Thomas nodded soberly. "Understood. We'll be very careful."

Amber turned and walked to the sofa. She gave Lily a nod. "Five minutes."

"Okay." Lily was holding on to the girls' hands. "We're ready."

Her friend had lines of tension around her mouth, making her look older. Amber knew she was probably thinking about her lost sister, the one who had gone missing. She joined them on the sofa, giving Kia, the girl next to her, a hug. "If you feel uncomfortable, let me know. I'll stop the interview. If you don't understand or need me to translate, just turn to either me or Ludmilla." They had already briefed the girls about the fake names. "These men will get your stories out in some form of media, maybe even television."

The other two girls, Michela and Judi Kay, listened intently, then nodded along with Kia. Amber signaled and Hawk brought the men over. Brad took a seat nearby. The introductions were brief and Thomas explained about the tape recording.

"Let's start with telling where you came from and how you were kidnapped," he said.

"I'm from Bucharest," Michela began first in slow, accented English. "I was sixteen when some man approached me and told me he was looking for models to send to America. He said he would take photographs of me and put me in an album with other girls and if I was lucky, I would be picked for magazine covers. Of course I said yes, and he took pictures of me and everything was okay because he gave me money and said he would contact me again. A week later he called and told me to meet him at a café because he had good news. I was very excited. He showed me a contract that I signed and said that I was to bring my passport with me that night so I could fly to Los Angeles. He showed me the plane ticket, so I believed him. When I went to the meeting place, he put me in a car with two other girls. There were two men sitting in front. I noticed there was a plastic divider between the front and the back seats, but I didn't think much about it because I was so excited. It didn't take me long to realize we weren't being taken to the airport. We couldn't get out because the locks in our doors wouldn't open."

She paused to take a deep breath, a frown creasing her forehead. She looked inquiringly at Amber, chewing on her lower lip.

Amber nodded back to assure her that she was doing fine, hoping none of her own anger was showing on her face. She had heard versions of this story many times before, and each time it broke her heart. She also knew, from experience, that if she showed how truly upset and angry she was, some of the girls either became too emotional to speak or they shut down entirely. She wanted to help the girls stay as calm as possible for the interview.

She interjected an explanation to give Michela some time to gather her thoughts. "These men are called impresarios and they are paid about a thousand Euro dollars for each girl they photograph for the album. In turn, the girls are sold for twenty-five hundred Euro dollars to different dealers, depending on where they are heading," Amber said.

"So each destination has a different price?" Thomas asked incredulously.

"The girls are seen as goods and commodities," Lily said in a low voice. "They're taken to Bucharest, which is the headquarters for these operations. Then they are marketed to different branches in Moldavia, Ukraine, and Russia as dancers. It's a legitimate business in Bucharest, by the way, since the authorities there sanction the businesses."

"Businesses?" David, the other reporter, prompted.

"The agencies are legitimate businesses in Bucharest," Amber said. "The business license costs about twenty-five thousand Euro dollars or the equivalent in deutsche marks."

"You're saying that it's a legitimate business in which men are sitting around making bids on women being sold as prostitutes," Thomas said. He shook his head and took a gulp of tea from his cup. "How do you know this?"

"Because I have sat through such an auction," Lily said. "It isn't very different from the slavery sales held in the United States not that long ago, gentlemen."

Amber glanced over at Lily. She had never mentioned being at an auction before. She stared straight ahead. Amber could see the tension in her hand that was holding on to Michela. Looking up again, she caught Brad's hard gaze on Lily.

"Tell me about yourself now, Judi Kay," Thomas said gently.

"I'm from Chisinau, Moldavia," Judi said. Her father was American and although her vocabulary was limited, she spoke English well. "I was picked up with my two friends after we went to see a movie. The men said they would give us a ride home." She shrugged. "They took us to Bucharest. I knew we were going to be sold off; my father had told us things like this happen. From Bucharest, they drove us to Turnu-Severin, then we all crossed the border to Serbia, to Belgrade. From there, other men brought us here to Velesta, Macedonia. There are many girls from Moldavia here, all of them kidnapped and sold, like me."

"Did you see your two friends again?"

She shook her head. "No, they weren't sold quickly, like me. I heard those who don't get sold are taken to Turkey."

"They are taken through Hungary," Lily told the reporters. "Hungarian passports are easy to get, about five hundred Euro dollars per fake one."

"You appear to be very knowledgeable about these routes, Miss Ludmilla," Thomas said.

"I make it my business to know about them. I prefer to get to the girls before they are taken to the brothels and broken," Lily said calmly.

"How do you transport them in and out of Macedonia?" David asked.

"As quietly as possible," Lily replied, this time with a smile.

"Not telling, huh?"

Brad finally spoke up. "We've agreed not to go into Ludmilla's and Anna's activities because it could jeopardize what they do, David. Your story is going to be on the girls' plight."

"The ladies' cause would make a great angle to the story," David pointed out.

"No, their operation must be kept as quiet as possible or this interview won't do us any good, gentlemen," Brad said firmly. "Stick to our agreement."

"Okay, okay," David said, "but you have to agree that showing how these girls were saved would add an exciting element to the story."

Amber sat up. "Exciting?" She recalled the girl being raped by a group of men in front of the *kafena*. Anger seized her insides. "Do you know how exciting it is for these girls to be used by ten or twelve men a day? That they are chained to beds or fed drugs or even beaten if they don't please their owners? I have several girls upstairs who can't walk because of their injuries. Do you think their stories would be exciting enough for your article?"

Thomas held up a hand. "Bad word choice," he conceded, shooting a warning glance at David. "We'll do this right, Miss Anna." He looked at the girls on the couch. "Tell us about the clients. Tell us the things done to you so we can report it in your words."

Amber willed herself to relax. If this was tough on her, how much more difficult it must be for the girls to do this. Yet, she noted, it was she and Lily who were expressing anger and bitterness, not Michela or Judi Kay.

"Our clients are mostly NATO."

Thomas's head jerked sharply. "NATO? As in peacekeepers?"

The girls nodded. "Yes," Lily answered for them, sarcasm evident in her flashing eyes. "They are the brothels' main clientele."

"A lot of them?" David asked.

"Seven out of ten," Hawk replied from behind them. Like Brad, he had been quietly playing observer. "I know this from being inside the *kafenas*."

David expelled a long breath. "Wow."

Lily cocked her head. "Surely you don't think a uniform or a title would stop a man from going to a whorehouse? They're the ones with money and a lot of time on their hands."

"And NATO officers are from all over, as you know, so you want to add that this is an international problem," Brad added. "By the time my department goes off to raid these *kafenas,* they are mostly empty because the pimps have been warned in advance."

Thomas nodded again. "We'll have to be extra careful when we go to a *kafena*." He stood up. "I don't know how to say it without being blunt, but a firsthand account of the business will make the story even more marketable. Michela's and Judi Kay's stories are very touching, but even if I took photos of them here in this room, it won't quite bring across the horror of what happened to them."

"You want pictures of battered women, then? Bruises and welts from beatings?" Amber asked. She wanted to shake these two men and yell at them, but part of her understood that they needed the tactile experience to make their story different from a World Health Organization report. The latter had been reporting on these activities for a few years now, but no one had really paid any attention; reports were just that—reports. The emotional pain suffered by these women, the horrific surroundings of their imprisonment, the groups of rowdy men crowding around a naked woman— these things weren't conveyed through the cold hard facts and numbers.

"Why don't you get Tatiana to show them her injuries?" Hawk suddenly said.

Lily breathed in sharply. "No!"

"Why not?"

"Tatiana hasn't spoken a word since she was brought here," Amber said, shaking her head at Hawk. "She's not . . . exactly friendly to men."

"What happened to her?" David asked.

"She was very, very unlucky," Judi Kay said. "She fought back and Papa was in a bad mood. He stripped her and made her his personal slave and kept beating her if she didn't do what he wanted. One time, I saw him give her to a dozen men, who raped her on the pool table. And after that she had to crawl on the floor all night naked because she screamed once."

Judi Kay shuddered, closing her eyes. Thomas swallowed hard, taking off his glasses to wipe them.

"Is Papa the pimp?" David asked.

"Yes, and his favorite is called Mama. She reports to him. Our Mama was only fourteen years old, but the bitch already knew how to suck up and get favors. That way she gets her own room and cell phone, and she gets to eat three meals a day."

David muttered an expletive. "Where the hell is this place? I want to burn it down."

"Tetovo," Judi Kay supplied the name. "Please do it. Kill them all. Help us."

"Come with me to the kitchen."

Amber started to hear Hawk's whisper in her ear. When had he come up behind her? She glanced up. "Why?" she mouthed quietly.

Hawk nodded in the direction of the kitchen again and made his way there. Amber hesitated. She really didn't want to miss any part of the interview, but Lily and Brad could supply any information the reporters might need. She patted Michela's hand and whispered in her ear before getting off the sofa. The girl nodded. Amber felt Brad's gaze following her as she left the room.

Hawk was waiting for her, a grim look on his face. "What is it?" she asked.

"Take me to Tatiana."

She studied him for a moment. "You don't even know her. She wouldn't want to see you anyway. Don't tell me you're going to convince her to show those two men her injuries." She shook her head. "Hawk, she's in really bad shape."

"Take me to her, Amber. I want to ask her one question. If she doesn't answer me, then I'll just leave."

Lily would never agree. She was very protective of Tatiana. "Hawk, I really don't think it's a good idea."

"Please, Amber. This could change everything for the girl."

"How?"

"Trust me."

Crossing her arms, she narrowed her eyes. "You're being too secretive. Why can't you tell me now? How do I know what you're going to ask won't upset her even more?"

"You don't. But if I can convince her to talk to those guys out there, even for five or ten minutes, and show them her condition, it would really prepare them for what they're getting into when they head for the *kafena*. Their eyes aren't open, Amber. You know what I mean."

Amber sighed. She did know what Hawk meant. The two men out there were still in reporting mode. They needed a nudge to get them to tell the story the way Amber and Lily wanted them to. A kick in the ass, actually, she corrected. And Tatiana . . . Tatiana could be the one person to do that.

"Okay," she said, "but if you're wrong, I'll let Lily beat you up."

Hawk's lips quirked. "Aren't you going to protect me?"

"I'm your guide, not your protector," she told him, taking him by the hand. "Let's go to Tatiana's room."

Tatiana was sitting by the window in her room, staring out, even though the panes were shuttered. Her crutches were leaning against the wall. She didn't turn around when they entered.

"Tatiana? It's me, Amber." No answer. "I brought a friend. His name is Hawk."

Tatiana turned around, her eyes in her thin face widening at the sight of a man in her room. Amber squeezed Hawk's hand hard, trying to stop his advance.

"Tetovo," Hawk said very, very quietly. Tatiana reacted with a jerk of her head. "Just nod your head, Tatiana. Was Papa's name Sarunas?"

Tatiana fisted a hand to her misshapen mouth. Her eyes flashed with sudden emotion, then they became dull again. She nodded.

Hawk took a few careful steps toward the girl. Amber released her hold of him, closely watching Tatiana's reaction to him. In the few months the girl had spent under their care, she had hardly shown any emotion, even when she was in pain and needed medication. There was always a far-off look in her eyes, as if her body were just a shell and she wasn't really there. This was the first time Amber had seen Tatiana come to life. And over the name of the brothel Papa.

"He's the one? This tall. A scar here. Two tattoos shaped like skulls on his back." Tatiana nodded again. Hawk knelt down so that they were eye to eye. "Tatiana, I promise you. He can never hurt you again. I killed him not long ago."

Amber watched as Tatiana leaned closer to Hawk. Her heart was in her mouth as she watched the girl struggle to speak, as if she had forgotten how to use her tongue. "Are . . . you . . . sure?" she managed to croak.

"Yes."

"How?"

"With a knife during a battle."

Tatiana reached out and grasped Hawk's shoulder. Amber could see her nails digging into his shirt. "Long . . . fight?" she asked, and her voice was stronger, fiercer.

"Long. Long and dirty fight."

"He suffered? He must suffer first." The veins on her neck stood out. Her words came in a slow staccato through gritted teeth. "Tell me he died a long painful death."

Hawk didn't move a muscle as she continued holding on to him. "All knife wounds are painful, Tatiana," he said softly. "He suffered, but not as much as I wish he had, now that I know what he did to you."

"You don't know. You don't know everything." Tatiana sat back in her chair.

"Tell your story to the reporters downstairs, then. You know they are there. Show them the scars, Tatiana."

Amber covered her mouth as Tatiana began to cry. Oh God, it was so heartbreaking to finally see the girl showing her grief, as big teardrops rolled down her cheeks. She didn't know which she preferred—the unemotional girl or this sad creature sobbing in low moans.

"He made me feel . . . dirty. He made me lick his toilet bowl. He killed me inside," Tatiana said, her words barely audible through the sobs. "I'm glad he's dead. I wish I was there to watch him die."

Hawk reached out and traced one finger down Tatiana's wet cheeks. "There are others like him. You have to try to help the other girls by giving this interview. Michela, Judi Kay, and Kia are doing it for their friends who are still missing. Don't you want to, too?"

"I don't have any friends!" Tatiana said.

"Amber and Lily," Hawk reminded her gently.

Tatiana nodded, finally giving Amber a glance. "Yes. I'm sorry," she said.

"It's okay," Amber said. "You don't have to do anything you don't want to, Tatiana."

"I'll do it for your friend Hawk," the girl said, suddenly coming to a decision. Her voice was still hoarse from crying, but she was more composed. "He did me a favor. I'll return it now. Help me walk downstairs?"

"I'll carry you," Hawk offered.

"Careful of her ribs," Amber said, when Tatiana nodded her permission. She watched him lift the young girl up with a gentleness she hadn't seen in him. "Here's a hanky, Tatiana. I'll bring the crutches."

She followed them, listening quietly as Tatiana started to tell Hawk the things the dead Sarunas had done to her during her captivity. She wasn't waiting for any interview. Her story was pouring out of her as if Hawk had turned the tap on.

She moved ahead so she could open the door. Every eye in

the room focused on Tatiana, who ignored them all even as she continued talking. The reporters never said a word as she went on. And on.

Every horrifying humiliation. Every bruise and how she got them. Amber listened and wanted to kill all the Sarunas in the world.

16

Hawk anticipated there would be an argument afterward. He had seen it coming from the expression on Lily Noretski's face. She had barely kept her cool through the interview.

The two reporters were now gone, with three hours of taped conversation in their possession, the most powerful segments of which were Tatiana's, her hoarse voice filled with wretched hatred. Hawk didn't think he would ever forget any of it, or the expressions of growing horror on the men's faces as they listened to her halting account.

"You have no right, no right at all, to make her relive her ordeal." Lily glared at Amber.

The girls had gone back to their rooms. "I didn't make her, Lily," she said.

"What did you say to her? She hasn't said one word, not to you, not to me, all these months." Lily raked a hand through her short hair. When Amber gave her a short account of what had happened upstairs, she continued, "You don't know what you might have done to her psychologically. We agreed to be extra gentle with her."

"I'll take total responsibility," Hawk said from the doorway. He didn't want the two friends quarreling.

"You lied to her to get her to talk," Lily accused, turning to face him.

"No, I didn't. Tetovo's one of Dilaver's *kafenas* and I have seen what Sarunas can do to a girl."

"And you didn't stop him before, even when you were standing right there," Lily sneered, "so why should I believe you really killed the bastard? You and Brad, one playing on the inside, the other the almighty chief of some NATO department, both of you have the power to stop this at one time or another, yet you choose not to. How could you? And you're worse, Mr. McMillan. You're actually in that place, participating in the fun." She paused, her eyes growing flat. "I could kill you just for that."

That Hawk believed. There was a look in her eyes that reminded him of war veterans who had been in the combat theater too long, especially those who had seen and done too much that crossed the line, with no relief of downtime or family ties. Yet Lily had Amber and other friends, as well as these girls, so why did he suddenly get the feeling that she was desperately hiding something from the world? It was just a gut feeling he had, from years of having been deployed in and out of bloody arenas; he had dealt with men who had so alienated their humanity that they had turned into killing machines. Why did he get the same vibes from her?

Since he didn't reply, Amber spoke up. "Lily, you know why Hawk's in there."

"Oh yeah, right, silly me. Bigger things in the world and all that," Lily said.

"And Brad's doing all he can," Amber continued, ignoring Lily's sarcasm.

Lily cocked her head, her eyes darting from one person to another, as if she were seeing them for the first time. "It isn't enough for me," she told them, and the fierceness in her voice reminded Hawk of Tatiana's anger. "All these girls all over the continent being sold and used in a human meat market, and all perpetuated and sanctioned by the so-called authorities. They are all the same, all crooks and rapists, all guilty in my eyes. I'd take down every one of them if I could."

She gave Hawk one final glare and swept out of the room.

"I'll go talk to her," Amber said, touching his arm before slipping out, too.

"She doesn't like it when she isn't in control," Hawk remarked to Brad, who hadn't bothered to join in the argument. "She yell at you like that often?"

Brad looked at the cup in his hand. "Only when she isn't in control," he said quietly. "She usually takes off for a while and comes back a lot calmer."

"Sounds like you have heard her tirades a few times already. How do you handle the attacks on the job thing?" Hawk was curious about the relationship between Brad and Lily. From their body language, it was obvious that they were hot for each other and were in the middle of some kind of struggle. "Is this part of the quarrel between you two right now?"

Brad looked up, a wry twist on his lips. "You make all my women hot and bothered."

Hawk lifted an eyebrow. "Excuse me?"

"Lily isn't the only one reacting so excitedly to your presence. I've never seen Amber quite like this before. Doing things on her own, running off with you to do things without consulting Lily. She's never the crazy one."

Hawk thought about a certain message hung on his dick. A certain triumphant feeling surged in him when he realized that Brad really didn't know Amber. "I beg to differ," he said.

It was Brad's turn to lift an eyebrow. "Somehow I get the feeling you're happy about Amber's wild side. As for Lily, she's always been a bit unpredictable."

"Is that why you're hooked on her?"

Brad frowned. "I wouldn't say 'hooked.' I'm . . . fascinated." He shrugged. "Lot of good that does me."

"Maybe she thinks you have a thing for Amber," Hawk suggested. It was just another one of his gut feelings. Lily had been looking at Amber surreptitiously over the last week and had him wondering. He had noted that the intensity always grew whenever Brad was around the two women. "Does she know about your fascination, as you call it, for her?"

"Not that it's any of your business. She does, and she knows Amber and I are friends."

"Then there's something very wrong."

Brad regarded him from behind the cup as he took a slow sip. "What?"

"I'm sure you checked up on the women when you first got to know them," Hawk said, walking to the coffee table to refill his cup. "I'm damn sure you have or are still checking up on me. All of us have something in our background that we don't want others to know."

Jed had told him that he needed to find out more about Lily Noretski because the risk she posed was an unknown factor. Brad had the means.

"Are you saying you don't trust Lily?" Brad asked, watching him pour the tea.

"That isn't what I meant. I know my secrets. I have a lot of background info on Amber because that's who I'm supposed to work with. You're a public official, so the background is pretty open. Lily's the only one I don't know much about, except for one or two things." Hawk took a gulp from his cup. "She's a friend of yours and Amber's, so I'm not trying to bring trouble to the table, but there's something in her past that makes her tick like a bomb whenever it comes to these girls."

"You're the one we don't know about here, Hawk. If there is someone who shouldn't be trusted, it's you. These two have run their operation for a number of years."

"Want some more tea?" When Brad shook his head, Hawk settled back in the sofa. "Okay, let's say it's either your presence or mine in this operation that's grating on Lily's nerves. Amber doesn't know what it is, or she isn't telling me. You don't appear to know and aren't able to solve the problem, or you'd be in Lily's pants. I still say it's all about Lily."

Brad put his empty cup down. "You're a confident son of a bitch." Although his tone of voice was quietly mild, there was steel in his gaze. "Don't think I haven't been watching you. Been here a couple of weeks and taking charge of lives you hardly know. I wonder what's in your background that makes that second nature to you. So far, someone's definitely delaying certain files from reaching my hands, but don't think I don't have other sources."

Hawk smiled. "Dig deeper." His smile disappeared. "You have the connections. It doesn't hurt to know more about the people you're fascinated with."

Brad was silent for a moment. "I will," he said, his fingers tapping a quiet beat on the arm of the sofa.

Hawk nodded. There wasn't any handshake, but he knew Brad had agreed to find out more about Lily. He wasn't afraid that the bureaucrat would find out about his own secrets. For one thing, he wasn't the one with whom Bradford Sun had a fascination.

Nor Amber, he added. And he was glad about that, too. He

couldn't help but admire the woman. How she managed to run a café, an information service, a complicated operation of saving and transporting girls from country to country, *and* avoid being caught by all the different thugs and groups who moved around her was beyond him. He couldn't help wondering if, given the chance, she would run his own SEAL team just as capably and calmly.

One day, they might be able to tell each other things about themselves. Not that he didn't enjoy finding out about Amber with intimate contact. There were secrets about the woman he had grown particularly captivated with. Like that tattoo. And he didn't deny the male smugness that came with knowing that Bradford Sun wouldn't know about that secret.

Amber called out Lily's name. Her friend was walking quickly toward her car, talking on her cell phone. She waved at Amber, signaling that she needed a minute.

Amber slowed down, thinking about Lily's angry words in the house. There was something wrong, but she couldn't put a finger on it. Lily had been very distant the last week, disappearing more and more. She knew her friend wasn't with Brad, or both of them wouldn't look like they had toothaches.

"Everything's ready," she heard Lily said. "I'll call in when I arrive."

"Are you okay?" Amber asked after Lily ended her call. She wondered whether there was trouble about which Lily wasn't telling her. Her friend had been on the phone a lot lately.

"I suppose. You really should have asked me first."

"You were in the middle of the interview. I thought it best not to interrupt," Amber said, studying Lily. She didn't seem so angry now. "Besides, I thought it helped."

"That's not the point. You and I are partners in this and

you went off on a wild idea Hawk had. It went well, but at what cost to Tatiana? You and I don't seem to talk anymore," Lily said, turning around and walking toward her car.

"Hey." Amber reached out and grabbed Lily's elbow, stopping her in midstep. "We can't talk if you keep running off every time you're mad, which is a lot lately. Tatiana will be fine. I think her talking again is healthy, don't you think?"

Lily shrugged, refusing to meet her eyes. "So she tells you and the others what happened to her. How can that be healthy?"

Amber stared at her friend. How could it not be healthy? The poor girl had been catatonic since her arrival. "Lily, it's a start. We can't offer her psychological care. She needed an emotional outlet. Hawk somehow reached inside her, grabbed back what was still alive—"

Lily turned sharply, her temper coming back into her eyes. "Hawk this and Hawk that. What does he know about psychological pain? You're siding with him as if you know him that well. He's just like Brad, standing there doing nothing."

"They are both doing something, sweetie," Amber said gently. "Is it the guys, then? Are they what's bothering you? If you didn't want the interview, you should have told me."

"The interview's fine. It's just the way everything else is being handled."

Amber frowned. She was trying to understand what was going on in her friend's mind, but for the first time ever, she was failing to see the reasons for the anger. She had thought it had been Brad's presence, but now it was Hawk's, too.

"Tell me what's wrong, Lily."

"Look, if you can't see it, you can't." Turning away again, Lily shrugged off her arm. "It's okay to enjoy the guys, Amber, but if you get emotionally involved, it won't work."

Now it was getting even more confusing. She caught up with Lily, who seemed determined to get to her car. "Okay, what won't work? And don't keep going off every time you say something cryptic like that."

Lily pulled her car keys out of her pocket. "Okay, here's a question. I thought we were going to get information from Hawk and sell it. Now that you're involved semi-seriously with him, you aren't thinking about that any longer, are you?"

"Well, no," Amber admitted. "I told you I agreed to help him out."

"Yes, as a favor for this Jed dude that helped you before. I get the favor thing, but why can't you extract some info and use that to your advantage? It's a weapons thing, so it'll get us a lot of fresh funds. I can get help to track down more girls on the trails. The location of whatever Hawk's looking for will be worth a lot in the market, don't you agree?"

"Yes, but you know I am very selective over the sale of information. Anyhow, this information involves the CIA, so I'll have to clear it with them first."

"Since when have you followed the rules that closely?" Lily asked, her voice strangely toneless. "Or, like I said, are you getting so involved with the man that you're now abandoning our own operation?"

"Hey, wait a minute." Amber stepped in front of Lily so they were facing each other. "Why do keep you saying that as if I have been doing nothing? The girls and their safety are just as important to me. Brad and Hawk have been helping a lot and you know it. I can't just betray my friends willy-nilly for money."

She wasn't sure she liked the look in Lily's eyes. They were bright with something close to hatred. Yet, when she spoke, it was still in that strange toneless voice.

"I see, now they are friends. Brad the protector. Hawk the hunter. Yet they really haven't done anything to deserve your friendship. What am I, Amber?"

"You're my friend, too, Lily," Amber replied quietly. "I don't have to keep defending Brad. He's an issue to you, and the two of you need to sort things out. Brad is a good man and is risking quite a lot in arranging this interview. As for Hawk, I don't know about him, and you may be right that my heart's getting involved, but what he did today was done in kindness. He was very gentle with Tatiana and she opened up to him. And if that doesn't convince you, how about the risk he's taking in getting the reporters to meet the girls at Dilaver's brothels? He didn't have to offer, Lily, yet he did because what he sees in those places really bothers him."

"And he told you this, huh? When, in between bouts of hot sex?"

Amber looked up at her friend. "I like him," she said simply. She didn't have to say anything about what she and Hawk had been doing. "And I have been getting to know him."

"Well, whoopee-do. It must be great to have men eating out of your hand and talking about saving the world at the same time. Speaking of which, I'm late for an appointment to get a new replacement for our injured mercenary from last week. I do have to make this meeting because some of us like to actually take these girls out of this hellhole, you know?"

Amber stepped away so Lily could get her car door unlocked. "Will you be back tonight?" She didn't like the way this conversation was ending.

"Maybe, depends on how much negotiation I'll be doing with this new man. If he asks too much, we might not have enough funds to cover his expenses and ours." Lily got into the car, slamming it shut. When she looked up, her gaze was guarded. "Sorry to have to bail out on you, but we'll have to talk again later when I get back. Now that you're going off with Hawk and with me going on the usual trip, there's no

•

one here to run things. You see how it is when your attention is divided, Amber? Maybe after this operation we might have to split up for a while, so I can check out new avenues of saving these girls."

"Split up?" Amber repeated carefully.

Lily nodded as she started the car. "Yes. It might be good to streamline the operation. I understand about the need for men, Amber, but it isn't going to work out if you have to take off with them, too. The girls need an environment where they can depend on you or me being there when they need something."

Amber watched her friend's car pull away. She massaged the back of her neck as a headache threatened. She didn't know what to do. Something was horridly wrong and she had just made it worse somehow.

"I wish you could stay the night."

Hawk smiled. Amber's voice was sleepy-sexy, muffled against his chest. He kissed the top of her head, inhaling her perfume and scent appreciatively. He liked these moments with her the best—his arms around her, in semidarkness, her womanly curves somehow bonelessly soft under his body. He was very comfortable with Amber, with the way her smaller size fit against his, with the way she lazily kissed his chest while she was half asleep, like she was doing now.

"Me, too, but I have to be there earlier than Thomas." He and the reporters had agreed that it would look better if he didn't bring them there. "I'll point out the girls who I think will talk to them. Most of them will, but it's better to be careful anyway." He paused. "I'm sorry that Lily's upset. I didn't mean to cause any problems between the two of you."

"She and I will be okay. Will you IM me tonight and let me know what happens?"

"Keep doing what you're doing and I might return and

crawl back in bed with you instead," Hawk said. She was licking his nipple, driving him crazy with that hot tongue. She bit him in response. "And then you'd start complaining about not getting your beauty sleep."

He smiled again. They hadn't slept much whenever he had been in this room. He had made good use of her bed, her shower, the floor—hell, the four corners of this room—and he still couldn't get enough of her. Strange. All these months, he had females walking around him mostly naked, some practically throwing themselves on him, others in erotic situations that usually tempted the male libido, and he hadn't felt a thing. And all Amber had to do was walk past him with that particular sway of her hips, or look at him with those amazing eyes, or even roll dough with her very talented and strong hands, and his heart would start a steady patter that would increase. He was getting used to the way all his cells seemed magnetically charged whenever she was near, his whole body leaping to an aliveness that was so razor-sharp that sometimes making love to her became a spiritual experience.

It dawned on him that the anger he held checked inside all the time wasn't there when Amber was around. He didn't feel helpless, unable to do what he wanted to do—stop the things happening around him. Nor did he feel cold, as if part of him died every time he stopped himself from lunging at those bastards playing with a girl young enough to be their daughter.

Amber made him feel light again. And able to feel something other than anger. He gathered her deeper into his arms.

"It'd be better than instant messaging," she agreed, wrapping her arms around his neck. "All you do is tease when we IM anyway. I'd rather have you here so I can do this."

This was her teeth tugging at his nipple ring. Hawk grinned. She was insanely turned on by that little piece of jewelry. "I'll leave that here with you tonight so you can stare at it fondly," he offered. "I think you like it better than you do me, anyway."

She reached down, her hand teasing him. "Oh no, I just like things that dangle."

Hawk laughed. "Dangle? Baby, you're hurting my feelings. It's standing up very proudly. There's no way it's dangling."

"Oh yes, standing and ready." She looked up inquiringly. "What's the matter?"

"Standing and Ready"—STAR—was the name and motto of the SEAL teams under the charge of Admiral Madison. When orders were given, the teams yelled out, "standing and ready" as a war cry. Of course, among the brothers, the term also applied in reference to certain anatomical functions during male locker room talk.

Hawk missed his SEAL team. Almost three and a half months without his frog brothers. And longer than that out of water. They had been in the jungles of Asia when he had left them, playing his new role as Dilaver's guide. Hearing that phrase again made him wonder what his team was doing at the moment. He had the sudden urge to go swimming.

"Hawk?"

"Hmm?"

"Lost you for a minute there, Hot Stuff. What were you thinking?"

He wanted to tell her about his real job. He stroked her hair softly. "I was just thinking about us, and then you distracted me with that naughty hand of yours." Maybe later. After he had retrieved the weapon. Life was complicated enough for both of them at the moment without adding yet something else to discuss and analyze, as he knew by now she would. Women liked to do that too damn much. He nudged her suggestively. "I'm standing. You ready?"

He let her roll him onto his back, taking her with him. She grinned down at him. "Such a liar. You were thinking of something else and are now trying to distract me with sex."

She was too perceptive by far. "Is it working?"

She cocked her head, her startlingly blue eyes smiling down at him. "Remember you wouldn't let me move before?"

He ran his hands lazily down her back to her backside, rubbing the round silkiness gently, knowing that it turned her on. "What do you have in mind?"

"It's my turn."

Hawk was a SEAL. He knew when it was a win-win situation. "You mean, if I don't move, you're going to distract me instead?"

"Yeah. And get you to tell me a deep dark secret . . . maybe. . . ."

"Ahhh. Ulterior motive." He lifted his hands from Amber's body and cradled the back of his head. "I'm all yours, lady."

He enjoyed her love of playing games in the bedroom. Lovemaking with her was so much more personal, always engaging him in more than the physical act, a union of both mind and body. He'd never had a partner who enjoyed giving him pleasure like she did.

"Good, now lie still while I lick you all over."

"Oh, please, not that again." He shuddered in mock horror. "All that wet tongue, doing all that licking."

She pushed up, sitting on him. Her hands tiptoed up his chest, sending little shivers wherever she touched. "You know, it'd be more believable if I didn't have this thing sticking up against my behind when you say that." She reached behind her, giving him a long stroke that had him clenching his haunches in pleasure. "Maybe I won't lick you all over. Maybe I'll just lick you there."

Minx. She knew it turned him on when she talked dirty to him. "There?" He widened his eyes mockingly. "You mean . . . ? Surely you can't do that!"

Her hand moved leisurely. Up and down. It took all of Hawk's control to force his hands to stay where they were, to appear nonchalant, and to talk at the same time. He watched as Amber got on her knees and swiveled around so her back faced him. He couldn't see what she was doing, and that made him even more excited.

"You sound like you don't like this," she chided.

She was now using both her hands on him, somehow massaging him in two directions at the same time. Hawk closed his eyes, trying to visualize what she was doing. The way she wrapped one hand and stroked upward over the head of his penis while pulling down had the effect of upping the pleasure quotient to an intense level. She moved again. He opened his eyes. She was up on her knees again, her sweet little ass curving toward him. Holy . . . He laced his fingers tightly behind his head. She leaned forward, her ass teasing him. He was going to break the bones in his knuckles.

And all the while she took her own sweet time. He couldn't see the back of her head anymore. What was she doing, taking so damn long?

He must have made a sound. "What did you say?" she asked.

Her breath fanned the top of his arousal. That was even worse. Now he knew how close her mouth was to where he wanted it to be. "Not . . . h . . . ing," he managed.

"Are you sure?" she asked, her lips against his rock-hard arousal. "I could have sworn I heard you say something." He strained upward, trying to get into her mouth. She tsked-tsked. "Now, now, you said you wouldn't move."

So a SEAL cheated sometimes. Hawk parted his legs, which made her knees part, too. Out of balance, she fell forward the few required inches and he felt sweet wet heat suddenly gloving the head of his penis. Oh yes, thank you. He grunted with satisfaction.

He almost came when she tightened her grasp. Her tongue tantalized him, rolling around and around, until every muscle in his legs felt like Jell-O. He wanted to sit up. Needed to see her taking him in his mouth. He loosened his hands and was about to reach for her when her ass swayed a little as she started to get down to business and he could only stare helplessly at that sexy ass, imagining himself standing behind her.

He slid a hand between her parted legs. She was deliciously wet. He heard her gurgle of pleasure as he probed and stroked her. Her mouth started to follow his hand, stroke for stroke, until they were both moaning. He felt her trembling, slid a finger deep inside her, and felt the first wave of her orgasm hitting her. His whole being quivered like a readied arrow pulled on a bow. She tightened around his finger and her mouth suddenly took all of him even as he endeavored to keep pleasuring her.

She shuddered and her sweet release wet his hand, robbing him of the last shred of control. All sensation rushed at top speed as he let go, his own orgasm hurtling him at top speed heavenward. Her mews of pleasure were even more erotic because he was still in her mouth. Everything zeroed in on that connection. He came long and hard and her tongue prolonged it, swirling the whole length of him. He groaned. Managed to glide his finger out and up over her nub. She groaned, her mouth still refusing to let him go.

"Baby. Yeah. Like . . . that. All of it."

And he gave her everything he had.

When she could move again, she flopped down next to him. "You aren't obedient," she complained weakly. "Talk, talk, talk."

It took him a few minutes before Hawk's brain could process an answer. "You said don't move, not don't talk," he said. When Amber turned her head and went for his nipple ring again, twirling her tongue languidly, he laughed and added, "I promise to be better next round."

He kept his promise and when he got up much, much later, he kissed her as she enjoyed the sleep of a satiated woman, smiling as she reached for him still. He looked down at her for a long moment, and then left the small gold nipple ring in her hand.

17

Lily crushed the half-smoked cigarette, leaning back against the windshield of her car. Everything was falling apart. Time to discard everything. Why couldn't it remain the same?

She looked up at the night sky. It was so silent out here it made her heart ache. How many times had she stared up and made a wish? Wishes that hadn't come true. How many times had she sat in the stillness of the night just talking to herself? Alone again. She didn't mind. She worked better alone, anyway. She didn't need anybody. Life had always been that way and she had accepted a long time ago that she could do without, as long as she was in control.

She wasn't happy with the way things were turning out, anyway. She didn't like these feelings she had about Brad. She didn't want to think of Amber with him; somehow it angered her. It really shouldn't. She didn't care. Maybe he went to her that night and it was just a onetime thing, since Amber was now spending time with Hawk. She shook her head. She didn't care.

They could all go to hell. All she cared was to make sure the girls were all right, that they were safely out of harm's way. Dilaver was no dummy. He would find out about Amber sooner or later and then he'd be after her girls. No way was she going to let that happen.

Things fall apart. So she had to work alone again, formulate a new plan. She had done it before, reinventing herself, moving on from old to new. It was easy.

Lily sighed. She couldn't understand why she felt so hurt inside. She had shut down the emotions that had gotten in the way of life before. It was easier. Feelings only made life painfully unbearable.

She thought of Bradford Sun sitting there looking at her with those accusing eyes. She hadn't had a good night's sleep for weeks. All she had to do was close her eyes and she could feel the wavy thickness of his hair as she mussed it up, the way he tasted, the way . . . She jerked up from her comfortable position. Stop, stop, stop. Why couldn't she stop all this nonsense?

He haunted her, with all that golden glow, promising stupid things that she knew wouldn't come true. She was, and would always be, on the dark side. There was only one future she knew and he wouldn't be a part of it, no matter how she wished it.

As for Amber, she had help now. There was Brad and, of course, Hawk. She didn't really need Lily, not for important decisions anyway. And here she had thought they were partners in this one aspect. But like all things in her life, the usual happened.

Things fall apart. And she'd better get used to being alone again, because it was happening right in front of her eyes.

Tatiana was the last straw. How could they use the poor girl like that, just so they could get their damn interview? Didn't they see that she wasn't ready for that kind of exposure? Speaking out to the world, revealing all the depraved things done to her—she would regret it because there was no way she could understand how her life would be like an open book, with every dirty detail for everyone to read. And when she did, it would be too late; everyone would already know how she had been used and humiliated.

Lily thought about her kidnapped sister. She would never have let her sister suffer the pain all over again. With all she had seen through these years of looking for her, she would rather cut her arm off than to make someone relive those experiences, especially when they were like Tatiana's. She often thought about her poor sister lost in that evil world, how she secretly hoped that one of these days, she might see her among these girls that she saved.

But she couldn't have become what she was now without being touched by some of that evil. She had done things that crossed the line. She didn't regret it, but she'd known that when she went down that road that it would be a lonely one. She must do everything by herself. Brad, no matter how much she wanted him, was unattainable.

Her cell phone buzzed in her jacket. She was tempted not to answer it. She was just going to lie anyway. She flipped the phone open.

"Yes, it's me," she said, injecting a briskness in her voice, trying to sound busy. "Everything's on the up and up, don't worry. I'll talk to him soon. Route? Yes, I'm busy figuring it out. It'll take a while, what with all the roads being guarded these days. I'll be careful. I have to go now, in the middle of something. Talk to you tomorrow, okay?"

Lily thoughtfully tapped her chin with the cell phone. Well, that was painless. She couldn't explain why she'd find it so easy to lie to some people and yet other calls gave her a headache afterward. But there was one thing the CIA had taught—she *would* be in control. Those girls would be safely out of the way before things fell apart between her and Amber.

* * *

Brad had always prided himself in being able to handle any situation with diplomacy. It was, after all, his area of expertise. He enjoyed being in the middle of a hurricane and being the calm eye, able to see things on all sides and take action when necessary. These were the tools that had helped him advance to where he was now, and why he had been sent here to Macedonia.

So many different factions, with so many different countries involved. Everyone had to walk on eggshells while juggling all the different balls required by each side. There was his loyalty; to do everything right and yet not make his country look bad. And there was his commitment to his beliefs, that criminals should be brought to justice.

He didn't question anyone's reason in choosing to act as they did. He believed that it was action that made people think, not vice versa. People started to think only when they had to cover their tracks. Someone with nothing to hide didn't need to keep thinking about his actions, or anyone else's.

At least, that was how he had been all these years—logical, functional, and damn fucking practical. These were the qualities he had thought were good. Yet he had somehow gotten tangled with a woman who thought the complete opposite. To her, he was utterly useless.

He smiled grimly at the memory of Lily's earlier outburst at the safe house. They weren't that different—she was just as loyal, just as committed to her cause and to bringing justice, except she had the passion of someone who had been wronged.

And that revelation jolted into his awareness today—watching her, listening to her, and for once not reacting to her accusations. He sensed that she had something to hide, that there was a reason behind her actions. Hawk's conversation with him later only reinforced the suspicion that there was more than what was on the surface. He felt that he needed to understand Lily. His mistake had been going around and around her while she kept spinning the same direction, constantly facing him. What was behind her? He had her files, but he now felt that there was something missing. And Hawk had pointed out that he had the means.

He had CIA and Europol connections, and they spied on each other. He was on the board of several UN covert agencies that gave him privy to a lot of classified information. All he had to do was contact someone with the right questions about Llallana Noretski. So far he had asked about her background, but as a citizen. She had been picked up by the CIA, and from their reports they had questioned her extensively on smuggling routes, perhaps even using her several times. She had to have made a deal with them to be able to go about so freely throughout Europe. So the question was, what deal had she made? What did the CIA have over Lily?

Brad stared unseeing at the phone for a moment before picking it up. Regular channels showed that the CIA didn't have anything in their files, so that was a dead end. Time to collect a *veza* from his private contact at Europol.

"Joj! Sta jedan gomila nocas!" The young soldier, still in uniform, peered over Hawk's shoulder, a tipsy leer on his face. "It's packed like sardines in here. Must be a new batch of girls tonight, what do you think?"

Hawk shrugged. There seemed to be more people around tonight, but he thought it probably had more to do with the new arrivals from the UN divisions than anything else. The men always appeared cleaner-looking when they first came in and—he studied the groups of men cynically—more excited at the thought of visiting something forbidden. This was true of the really young American peacekeepers; some of them had never been to a brothel before. He could always pick them out, since they tended to come in groups, speaking English to everyone in that bold assuming way that Americans tended to have with every foreigner.

Thomas and his partner had arrived half an hour ago, slipping in between the peacekeepers and curious foreigners, and Hawk knew they had seen him. They had agreed not to meet up immediately, since that might call attention to them, so they were milling around, taking in the whole rowdy atmosphere. Thank God they had the sense to dress in similar colors as the younger men around them. The new visitors in town were good timing, since all these new faces were an excellent cover for the reporters.

"Hey, man, any recommendations?" another young man addressed Hawk. He smelled of alcohol, his eyes bright with anticipation. "I've seen you here before. You must like it here."

"Yeah," Hawk said noncommittally.

"So, who do you like screwing in here? My favorite's"—he snapped his fingers, trying to remember—"the little blonde, what's her name. You know, the one with that tattoo. Man, does she have a clever mouth. Why, the last time she . . ."

Hawk stared stonily as the man went into lurid details about his last visit. He had stopped listening; the physical description was too close to Amber's for comfort. Familiar anger rose like bile as he contemplated bashing in the man's face, besides rendering other parts of his body incapable of sexual function for the rest of his life. Instead he crossed his arms over his chest, leaning back against one of the giant beams that supported the building.

"Yeah," Hawk repeated.

The young man seemed intent in getting injured. "And

then there's that young thing. She's got the biggest boobs for a fourteen-year-old, man." He demonstrated the size lewdly. "Mama mia, I couldn't believe my eyes when I first saw them. No way could they be real, you know? Wonder where they found her. Can't understand a word she says. The last time they had her in some contest in the pink room, or whatever they called it. She was totally drugged out and having the time of her life, I tell ya. I've never seen such a horny girl, doing so many at the same time."

That was it. He was going to kill the guy any moment now. "I suppose you could tell she was fourteen and horny," Hawk said.

"They're in here every night, parading in those nighties. Got to be horny."

"Tell me, son, how old are you?"

"I turned twenty-one last week," the man said proudly.

So he wasn't young enough to really be Hawk's son, but these last few months seemed to have added decades to Hawk's age. "You aren't too far away from being fourteen," he said, stabbing him with a direct stare. "You think it's normal for fourteen-year-olds to run around among adults night in and night out and be horny, huh?"

There was a slight reddening in the other man's face as Hawk continued to hold his gaze. "Well, they're whores."

"Ah. And whores get horny all the time, right?"

"Well, no. Man, what's it with you? It's just the way it is around here. You know, they must need the money and all that. Why, I give them presents all the time. They like baubles, you know? Don't you give your favorite girls anything? They treat you better, I swear, give you more personal attention than just lie there with their legs—Hey!"

Hawk had lifted him off the flat of his feet, pulled him close enough that he could whisper into his ear. "One of these days, boy, if you end up in prison somewhere and you get the attention of some of the older inmates in there, remember one thing. It's just the way it is around those places. Nothing wrong with a group of men and you in the middle without a single one of them caring what language you're speaking, hmm? And don't forget the baubles. You'll collect quite a few in there, too, or so I've heard."

Hawk casually dropped him back on his feet. He had done everything in one smooth motion, as if he had something private to share with a friend, which he did. His young man's face had lost some color. Good. Maybe this one actually had some brain cells left.

He could still feel the fury roiling unabated inside. He'd better walk away before he actually beat up someone. Maybe talk to Thomas now or get some fresh air. Something.

He caught the reporter's eye and started to make his way toward him. Someone tapped him on the shoulder. He turned. It was one of Dilaver's men.

"Hey, you're wanted at Dilaver's table. He wants you to meet someone."

"Okay."

Dilaver had his own table near the back exit, usually surrounded by his guards. A quick call from any informant that a raid was coming and he would be the first out of there, leaving the scene for his men to clear out.

"Hawk, this is my aunt, Greta. She's just arrived."

Hawk turned to look at the woman sitting across from Dilaver. She was fiftyish, with short stylish brown hair. Her gaze was narrowed, sharp.

"Same build and dark looks. That's not him, but he looks very similar to Steve McMillan," she said in excellent American English. "He's an agent, Dragan. Take him. Alive."

Adrenaline rocketed through Hawk's system as Greta's

words registered. He had no idea who she was, but somehow she had seen through his cover. All the background action receded as Dilaver's men rushed at him. Hawk crouched into a fighting stance. No time to run.

18

Amber smiled as she combed her hair. The image in the mirror showed she had that silly small secretive grin of a woman who had been having naughty thoughts about her lover. She could hear Lily's mocking voice now. She hadn't told her friend about waking up with Hawk's little piece of body jewelry in her hand when she had called earlier. Nipple rings weren't on the Wretched Wench List, she would say.

She knew why he had left it with her. He wanted her to think about him while he was away. She still didn't understand why the sight of it on him made her insides clench up. It wasn't as if she hadn't seen body piercings before, but there was just something sexy about Hawk wearing it. It was totally so out of character for a macho guy, but everything about Hawk had been a surprise to her so far.

A very pleasant surprise. The more she got to know him, the more intrigued she became. He wasn't just a very good-looking man; from their conversations, she had found out he was also very quick-thinking and intellectual when he wanted to be. He could talk about anything, from opera to politics to philosophy. He had even read all her favorite books in their original languages. She suspected that it was a side of him that he didn't show to many people.

Everything was a contradiction. He opened doors for her, was very protective about women. He had all the young girls and even the two housekeepers in the safe houses eating out of his hand by treating them with unexpected gentle respect that Amber found very charming. She discovered, just by watching him interacting with her girls, that he was quite a gentleman to all women, and irregardless of age, they all responded with typical feminine flirtatiousness.

Yet she also knew he could take care of a problem with lightning-fast decisiveness. The way he had saved Lily's ass when her mercenary was in the line of fire. Tatiana, whom he had treated with such utmost care that the young girl had clung to him like she had known him all her life. Amber had seen him in action and knew, from his line of work, that he had taken lives before and that behind that smooth, teasing façade was a very complicated and at times ruthless man. There was something very sexy about a quiet, very gentlemanly male who had a very dangerous air about him.

Amber sighed, her smile fading a little. She should be afraid, really. She was in danger of falling for the man. She was too happy when he was around. Too turned on at the sight of him. Thinking of him too much when she was alone. Wanting to do things with him too much. Too everything, in fact. This was probably what was bothering Lily and had sort of bruised their friendship. She hadn't spent as much time with her friend as she usually did.

Logic told her that this happened in relationships, especially between good friends. A third one who came in always caused some friction because sharing was involved, no matter what the gender. She hoped Lily and Brad had worked out their feelings for each other. Then maybe her friend wouldn't feel so angry and left out.

She checked the time. It was too early to do anything, but she couldn't fall back asleep. Hawk hadn't left any good-night notes on the instant messenger program, so he must either still be at the *kafena* or partying with Dilaver somewhere. A shiver of apprehension ran through her. She wondered whether he had gotten hold of Thomas and helped him secure a private interview. It was a risky thing for Hawk to do, but he had assured her that he would be fine. Still, she felt uneasy about it. What if the girl reported it to her "Mama"? It wasn't unusual for the girls to tattletale on each other just so they could gain some favors.

She heard the phone extension ringing when she came out of the bathroom. It couldn't be Lily. . . .

"Amber? It's me, Brad."

"What's the matter?" She was suddenly wide awake. He would never call her at this hour. "What's wrong?"

"It's Hawk. I just got a call from Thomas. Something's happened."

Hawk struggled as they bound him up with ropes. He had taken down the first wave of Dilaver's men coming at him. They had picked up whatever was close by—bottles, chairs, anything long and deadly—trying to overpower him amid the confused customers. Surrounded, he had fought back, dodging the weapons hurled and swung at him as he tried to find a way out the front. Then someone fired a shot and bedlam ensued.

Fights broke out among groups of men, some of whom were peacekeepers. Hawk couldn't really tell; he was too busy avoiding being bashed in the head.

Screaming girls. A popping sound to his left. He had

pushed a young woman out of the way before what felt like five hundred pounds fell on top of him. He fought against the three or four men pounding on him till he couldn't move anymore.

Someone turned him over. A fist landed a punch on his jaw. Another.

Amber pulled on her shoes, her mind racing a hundred miles an hour. She must keep calm. She had never felt so afraid for someone in her whole life. She *must* keep calm. Hawk had been compromised somehow, and not by Thomas, at least not from what Brad told her.

She snatched from the bed the black lycra hood that she used to cover her head and face and stuffed it into the little tool bag attached to her utility belt. Her mind quickly went through the list of things she might have forgotten. There wasn't any time to double-check.

When he'd called, Brad had been on the way to the department from his house. She could hear his attached emergency siren in the background while he gave her a rundown of the night's events. Apparently Thomas and his friend had been already there and they had seen Hawk milling around, talking to some people. They had moved around for an hour or two, secretly photographing the place, taking notes. Hawk had been heading in their direction when someone tapped him on the shoulder and he had changed course.

From that point on, Thomas wasn't sure what actually happened. Dilaver had been there. At least, he thought he was, based on the photographs Brad had provided. Hawk was at some big table and then hell broke loose. All of a sudden, a bunch of men started rushing at Hawk with weapons.

"It didn't seem like they wanted to kill him, if that's any comfort," Brad had said.

No, that wasn't much of a comfort. She glanced at her clock on the way out. Time was of the essence.

Brad was taking his men to the *kafena*. A raid. That was all he could do. But Thomas had reported that Hawk had been dragged out the back door and taken somewhere. So raiding the brothel wasn't going to save Hawk.

"Thomas said Hawk fought like no one he'd ever seen. Took down a whole bunch of them with his bare hands. But the girls and customers around impeded his ability to escape or use some other means of saving himself. Where could they have taken him?"

"To Dilaver's compound just at the edge of town," Amber had replied grimly. "Can you send a force there?"

"Are you sure? Thomas said they went out the back way. Is there another building behind there that he could use to interrogate Hawk?"

There was, but Amber didn't think Dilaver would take Hawk there. "It's possible," she had said, "but I just have a feeling Dilaver would choose his compound. I could be wrong."

"I'm going to that building behind the *kafena,* since it's in town and closest to us. It's the most likely place, anyway. It'll look like a standard raid in the reports. If I can't find him there, I'll direct a group of my men to the compound, but Amber, it's going to take time, with all of Dilaver's guards. Be patient, okay?"

That was why she was going off to the compound. Dilaver needed time to interrogate Hawk and his heavily guarded place would give him a lot more security. She knew she couldn't tell Brad what her plans were. Besides, if he went there and engaged Dilaver in a firefight, Hawk might be used as a hostage, or worse, be killed off. She felt sick to her stomach at the thought.

"All right," she had lied.

"I'll call you."

"Be careful."

She had called Lily, but there was no answer. Left a quick message about her plans. No time to wait for her anyway. She had to save Hawk somehow.

"Stay alive, Hot Stuff," she muttered, backing the car out of the driveway, tires squealing.

Coming to consciousness after being beaten up was a very nasty experience. Hawk felt like a train had run over him. The back of his head throbbed violently and he swallowed the nausea rising in his throat.

Eyes closed, he assessed his situation. Sitting slumped over in the most uncomfortable way. Hands and feet secured tightly. He heard the familiar rumbling of a car. Okay, they were taking him somewhere. Back to the compound, he guessed.

He had escaped death many times before, but he was aware that he might not be so lucky this time. He had been outnumbered back there. The blows to his body and face took their toll after a while, and something had come down hard on his head during the fight.

That was the last thing Hawk remembered. He didn't open his eyes. He wasn't worried about a concussion. There were worse things coming up in his immediate future. Right now, lying here inside Dilaver's vehicle, he could buy a little bit of time by pretending to still be out of it. Not that any good ideas were floating in his addled brain at the moment.

Death. Well, that was one thing he could deal with. The part between now and his demise was what he was worried about. Dilaver would want to extract information from him in the most painful ways available and Hawk didn't need his imagination. He had seen some of the thug's methods with his very own eyes.

Hell, the Slav cut off fingers from a whole gang just to make a point. Hawk flexed his own. Fuck. He hoped he wouldn't die before sticking the middle one in the air at Dilaver. If it was still attached to him by that time.

He wasn't going to think about death. That felt like giving up already and that wasn't how he had been trained. As long as he was breathing, there was always a chance. The sound of his name penetrated the fuzzy haze of his thoughts and he struggled to concentrate on the conversation in the vehicle. To his surprise, it was in English, not Serbian.

"Are you sure, Aunt Greta? He's been a good friend."

"Of course I'm sure." That was the voice belonging to the woman at the table. She sounded very American. "There was a Steve McMillan in the States who came in and out of the office I was in who looked like this man. Unmistakable—tall, dark, good-looking, just like him. Same last name, Dragan. Coincidence?"

"No."

"That Steve was a plant by a very powerful Navy admiral at the task force I worked in. This Hawk is probably a plant, too."

"But why me? The Americans and I have a deal!"

"Dragan, you're an illegal arms dealer. Never forget that you're both using each other."

"I don't need your advice about how to deal with the Americans."

"Oh, stop acting like the little nephew I haven't seen for fifteen years. Think about it. I didn't spend ten years in the States and not understand its system. The CIA has an agenda politically, so it uses you to further it. In the meantime, there are departments inside the CIA as well as other agencies who are being ordered to fight people like you. Do you see the contradiction?"

Hawk heard Dilaver's snort. "I don't care about their fucked-up system as long as I get to profit from it."

"Then you'll listen to me in this one thing, my dear nephew, if you want a huge sum of money. You owe me."

"Yes, *veza*. You got it. You have made me very rich and powerful around here by picking me as the CIA go-to guy, or as Hawk would call me, a gofer." Dilaver snorted again.

Hawk suddenly understood why Dilaver was always practicing his English and improving his knowledge of American colloquialism. He wanted to speak like a native with his aunt.

"There's a reason for it. I need to talk to you later about a shipment of weapons we sent your way. I don't want it for sale, Dragan. It's a very special weapon I'm looking for." There was a short pause. "I know that's probably what your friend Hawk's after."

"If you know already, why don't we just kill him?"

"Because I don't know what the weapon looks like and exactly which shipment in which it was sent out. Rather than wait for my contact, who's been missing now that his partner's in prison, Hawk can provide us with that information. You can have your fun with him, but you make sure in the end he can at least draw a picture of the weapon."

"With pleasure."

Hawk flexed his fingers again. Well, on the bright side, he would be able to flip that middle finger before he died.

Her car hidden in an alley, Amber checked inventory in the dark. She usually was light on weapons, but this time would be different. Silencer. Semiauto. She would sneak into Dilaver's compound, but she doubted that she would be sneaking out. Wrapped-up small Uzi. Hell, maybe another one, just in case Hawk was able to defend himself. . . . She threw it into her duffel bag. Smoke bomb. Goggles. High-tech infrared glasses. Rope. She checked the back of her utility belt. Knives. She prayed that Hawk was still able to run . . . not quite sure how she was going to get him out if he was unconscious.

The main thing was to get inside the place, locate Hawk and assess what was happening, then make some really quick decisions. If he was injured, she couldn't mount a direct attack. If he was dead, she was going to . . . She mentally shook herself. Hawk wasn't dead. Not yet. They would have killed him at the brothel if they wanted him dead.

She loaded one of the weapons, pulled the car trunk down without slamming it, and slung the duffel bag over her shoulder. She started running up the alley. Off to get her man.

A few items on Hawk's new list of things he didn't like being done to him. Number one, he didn't like having his head slammed on a hard surface while his hands were tied. Number two, he definitely didn't enjoy having his ribs kicked in when his legs were tied and he couldn't retaliate by kicking back. Number three, spitting out blood wasn't a good sign to state of health.

The list got too long after five minutes. And he knew that more was to come. They hadn't even mentioned what they wanted from him yet. Dragan hadn't even lifted a hand yet. That wasn't a good sign, either.

Thank God she had cased the compound a few times before. First thing was to make sure she would be able to kill the lights if needed. That might help make escape a lot easier, especially if her appearance was a surprise. She prayed for enough time to get to Hawk, and that she remembered how to rig small explosives.

When she got in through Hawk's room, there was such a

loud commotion she didn't even have to be really quiet. From her vantage point, she could see them tearing his room apart, looking for something. She caught sight of someone walking off with a laptop. That must be Hawk's. Another man was slicing open the mattress with a knife. Another was throwing stuff out of the little wardrobe in the corner. She had to follow the first man who went out. He would be the best bet to get to Hawk's current location in this big place. She pulled out her silencer.

"What are all the favorite American sayings in this type of situation?" Dilaver asked, a careless casualness in his voice as he approached Hawk. "You disappoint me. This is going to hurt me more than it does you. You make your bed, now lie in it. I think I like that last one the best. What do you think, Hawk?"

Hawk struggled to sit up. Either he was, or the chair was propping him up, he couldn't really tell at this moment. He peered up, blinking at the brightness of the light overhead.

"Nothing to say, huh?" Dilaver continued. "Where are all the smart-aleck sayings, my friend? That's what hurts most, you know. I thought we were friends. I liked you. Part of me actually admires you now because your deception was so good, and I don't get deceived that easily, let me tell you. I repeat, where are all the smart-ass lines now?"

Conserve energy. Why waste the rest of his ability to think on that fucking scum? Hawk watched as Dilaver lay his walking stick on the table a few feet away.

"Do you know, if you get hit around the right spot on the kneecap, it would shatter in such a way that you would never walk again? I think that would be good payment for my limp, which I'm sure you're responsible for, somehow. An eye for an eye, right? Or is it a leg for a leg this time around? Let's start with that. . . . Oh wait, if you tell me what you know about a certain weapon, perhaps I won't go for that sweet spot in the kneecap, what do you say? Maybe we could just break the shinbone."

If he could, Hawk would laugh. Dilaver was a mercenary, a brute. He had seen the thug kill with his bare hands, strike fear in those around him by giving a lot of pain. But, to win information with refined threats, he wasn't going to win the Negotiator of the Year Award.

There was no humor in the knowledge that his career as a SEAL would definitely be over, even if he survived this. Swimming without a kneecap would really slow him down and underwater covert operations were all about timing, especially when they had to do with underwater demolition.

Hawk laughed, or at least a sound choked out of his mouth. It must be his macabre sense of humor surfacing, if all he could think about were ways to retain swimming speed when he was about to lose the use of his legs. He laughed again and a wracking pain followed the attempt.

Two down. Luck was on her side. The man with the laptop was going downstairs alone. Amber promised that she would appreciate old European buildings even more from now on. They were badly lit, easily allowing her to tail her quarry down three flights of stairs and giving her time to plant weapons along the way.

He turned on the landing, heading for the rooms. She looked up and down the passage as she cautiously followed. No guards. Dilaver must have left some of the men at the *kafenas*. Either that or Hawk had hurt enough of them to send them to the hospital. She hoped so.

The man slowed down as he reached the end of the passage. He knocked at the door. Amber pulled on the gas mask, then raised both her hands, taking aim.

* * *

"Untie his hands," Dilaver ordered. "Perhaps writing is easier right now, hmm? If you cooperate and draw this weapon you're after, Hawk, I'll make the end a little quicker."

Hawk took several deep breaths as the wave of pain subsided. Dilaver must have thought he had been trying to reply. Someone came up behind him and he felt the bonds that imprisoned his hands loosening. The same person pushed him hard and he fell out of the chair onto his knees. He heard laughter around him.

"He doesn't act so cool now, boss."

"He's still cute, though."

Someone kicked Hawk's ribs. He doubled over.

"Let's fuck him in the ass. Always thought he was a homo, the way he stayed away from the girls."

"I say he's still too pretty. We'll have to remedy that."

"Now, now, men, didn't you hear me tell Hawk that I'll make it quick if he helped me out?" Dilaver asked. "Come on, Hawk. They're getting restless here. Better get up and do some drawing."

Hawk pushed up with one hand, trying to sit up. If he could get the other man to kick him again, he could go for the weapon strapped at the man's side. It was time to end this bullshit. If he had to go, he preferred it to be in a blaze of bullets. At least he would be sending a few more of them straight to hell. A knock at the door and Dilaver turned to answer. Hawk stared up at his attacker, Sanu, and gave him the finger.

Everything seemed to happen all at once. Sanu came after him amid the jeers of those watching. Hawk somehow managed to dodge the kick aimed at him. He grabbed the off-balance man by the balls. At the same time, he registered a shout of surprise and gunshots coming from somewhere as he pulled the weapon from the howling man's holster. He pulled Sanu forward, using him as a shield. Someone shot out the main light.

Smoke. Jesus. Hawk recognized the instant and distinct burn of CS gas. During boot camp and SEAL training, they were required to sit in a room as it filled with tear gas and count to twenty slowly before they were allowed to strap on the gas masks by their sides. It was to help them to stay calm. Many first-timers gagged and panicked at the first fiery taste of the gas, forgetting to put on their masks as they rushed for the exits with closed eyes. It had taken Hawk two tries before he was able to sit calmly and count.

More shots. Total darkness. Everyone was yelling and scrambling, screaming for the exit. Hawk stretched out on the ground and began to crawl toward the general direction of the door. Someone at the entrance was picking off the running men one by one. Whoever it was must have a mask on. He had an idea who that might be. His eyes were hurting more and more as the gas started to waft downward. He squeezed them shut. Holding his breath, he continued his painful belly-crawl.

He wasn't going to make it. He was going to be trampled before reaching the doorway.

Suddenly the glare from a flashlight hit his eyes, blinding him even more. Something slid onto his nose. Then a familiar weight came over his face. Gas mask. He reached up to hold it in place. Forcing his eyes open, he found everything had changed from darkness to another familiar sight. He had been fitted with infrared night goggles, too. Not that he could see much when his eyes felt as if they had been scratched raw.

But he didn't need any urging. A familiar shadow stood over him. Leaned down. Hands urging him to get up. Unable to explain that he was still tied, he started to paddle hard with his arms toward the door. His rescuer pulled him by his shirt, hurrying him. He heard it tear as he tried to keep up.

At last he was out of that room and the passage light was still on. He heard the slam of the door behind him. Then his legs were freed. Knives were wonderful things.

He heaved himself up with the help of the wall. He staggered from the pain. He waved away the helping hand and started to run. He smacked into a wall. Still stinging from the gas assault, he couldn't see very well. Besides, he wasn't the one leading here. For once he had to depend on someone other than his SEAL brothers to take over. He turned to the small figure beside him. She took his hand.

19

Hawk coughed, or tried to. His lungs still burned like hell. Another thing to include in his new list of things to dislike—climbing stairs after being kicked in the ribs. They were heading to his room. He was very glad they were getting as far away from the gas as possible. He didn't think he could have taken another whiff of that without throwing up.

He saw the open duffel bag strapped over Amber's back and reached in it. Ah, more familiar things. The woman had weapons out the kazoo. He loved this woman.

They met with a few hostiles as they climbed the stairs. Blocking Amber's body with his, Hawk shot out the lights with the Uzi. The firefights were short, but they were losing more time. With the surprise element gone, he could hear the sound of more people rushing up the stairs.

Amber reached into her belt and pulled out something. "Here," she said.

Grenades. He managed a grin. The woman was something else. He pulled the pins and dropped them down the stairwell. The blast shook the building.

Hawk turned to Amber. "Problem taken care of," he said.

They reached his room. She pushed the gas mask off over the top of her head, then pulled off the small goggles. Hawk did the same, taking in the two dead bodies in his now-messy room. She pointed to her back, indicating that he should return the Uzi to the duffel bag.

"Are you all right?"

Hawk grinned. "What took you so long?"

"Oh my God, Hawk." He couldn't see her face, but her voice cracked with emotion. "Your face . . . your teeth are red. Are you in a lot of pain?"

He shrugged, and managed to hide a wince when she touched his face. "Just a little. Do you know you look like the Invisible Man with that getup?" She was covered from head to foot in dark material. "The gas mask looks really strange on a faceless person."

"Yeah, well, what about flopping around, trying to walk with just your hands and belly? What was that, your rendition of the Little Merman?"

She sounded more like the Amber he knew and he wanted to kiss her. Unfortunately, they didn't have much time for that, either. Besides, he didn't think she would be turned on by the taste of his blood. "Remind me later about the 'little' comment. So, how do we escape?"

"Can you climb?" Amber indicated the rope that she had used. "I hope so, because that's the only way out at the moment."

"Let's do it."

Something that would usually have been an easy task proved to be a formidable undertaking. Halfway up, Hawk struggled with shortness of breath as he blocked the surge of pain that accompanied every pull of the rope. He could feel the strain of his arm muscles as he slowed down from fatigue.

Amber reached the upper beam first. "Hurry," she urged

softly. "There are some kind of spikes in the beam to your left. I use them for footholds."

"Now you tell me," Hawk muttered.

He found one of the spikes with one foot, secured his hold on the rope, and then, taking a deep breath, resumed pulling himself up. He finally made it to the top that way.

Amber helped him climb onto the ledge.

"You should have let me know how injured you are," she scolded. "And don't lie now. You would have climbed a lot faster."

Hawk was too out of breath to tell her that he hadn't had time to check the extent of his injuries. At the moment, he was feeling every punch and kick that had landed on his body.

It was pitch-black up there, but she seemed to be well acquainted with the cubby space, pulling up the rope and twining it around something that he couldn't see from his angle. She had an air of quiet efficiency that reminded him of her in the kitchen. He loved to watch the way she moved so minimally and accomplished so much.

"We're going through the ventilation access. There's a breeze as we head out and it can get quite cold at this time of the year. There are different chutes and one comes out near the fireplace. That's where we usually climb down from. I didn't have time to bring us jackets. We can't run with them on anyway. Ready?"

Simple enough. "Yeah," Hawk said.

"Tell me if you need to stop," she told him.

He followed her, barely fitting through the opening of the access. They started on their hands and knees, and he found that he had to belly-crawl through parts of the chute. Again, he was struck with how capable Amber was, moving along in the cramped darkness, seemingly able to know which turns inside the chute they needed to take. A regular person would be lost inside this maze, but then she wasn't one. She was doing what she did best as a contract agent, and he finally understood that guiding had many different kinds of skills. He had at first scoffed at the idea that he needed a guide when he could, with a map and weapons, get anywhere faster than most people. He'd bought the part about the need for someone who spoke the language like a native and knew the region, but still, part of him had held on to the idea that, out in the wild, he would work better alone.

But Amber was showing him a side of being a contract guide he hadn't considered. She was trained to be a human compass and, gender aside, she must be viewed as someone who had studied every possible route in an assignment, weighing every aspect that might affect the people she was assigned to guide, including timing and conditioning. That was why she had kept asking him how injured he was. Her job was to go from point A to point B with the least possible impedance. He realized now that he should have told her he was a SEAL, that he could take a lot more than the usual covert agent. She needed this information, especially in a dangerous situation.

"You okay?" she asked.

"I'm right behind you, babe," he replied softly. "Keep going. I'll keep up."

"We're almost to the chimney. Once outside, the descent is roughly ten meters. The chimney is very old, so there are plenty of footholds. I don't know how many guards are down on the ground, what with our little grenade fun back there, but I'm sure some of them are busy looking for us."

"They'll turn on the spotlights," Hawk said.

"No, I disabled them at the main generator."

"How? There was still electricity when you came in. I was shooting out the lights as we went upstairs."

"Plastics," Amber explained, finally coming to a stop. "I

278 \ **Gennita Low**

activated that when we started climbing. I figured if I started a fire of some sort, they'd have to call the fire department and all the commotion would give us an even better chance to escape."

"Do you know I get turned on by brainiacs?" he asked. He reached out and took her hand. "You saved my life."

"Not yet, love. We need to get out of the compound and to my car, then to my place, and then you can show me how grateful you are. Besides, I thought you were turned on by hamburgers."

She squeezed his hand before pushing open the flap that led to the outside. A blast of cold air hit them.

"Cooking and brains . . . I just might marry you," Hawk quipped.

She suddenly went still and his face almost smacked into her cute behind. He was actually as shocked at his own words as she was. It was probably the most inappropriate time and place, and he didn't know where that came from, but it sure felt right when he said it.

"Hawk, did they hit you in the head with something?"

He remembered the mild concussion he had suffered earlier. "Why?"

"Because we're going to descend really fast and you're making me light-headed with that marriage proposal."

He remembered his resolve to tell her about anything that would make her job easier. "I was knocked out of it during the fight. Probably with a bottle. I've been knocked out before, by the way. Still single."

"Did a woman rescue you those times, too?"

He could hear the smile in her voice. He grinned back. "No."

"Okay, then. Think you can handle thirty meters down?"

It wasn't as if they were underwater and that he might suffer the bends. "You'll know soon enough," Hawk told her. "I'll be down there either on my feet or on my back."

She hesitated for a second. There was really no other choice—they both knew that—and she silently started her descent. Far below, the faint sound of sirens broke through the night air. Hawk patted his rib cage lightly. This was going to hurt just a little.

Keep your focus. She mustn't think about how horribly bruised and abraded Hawk's face was. She knew he was hiding the amount of pain he was going through, but she had heard the shortness of breath, and the way he coughed didn't sound good, either. Internal injury. Her heart sped up again when she recalled how close she'd been to being too late.

Don't think. She had to get them out of there. There was one big problem coming up—how to get out of the compound without being killed. Dilaver and his men would be searching for them. The advantage was that they wouldn't know yet that there were just two of them. The disadvantage was . . . the same. The two of them against possibly a dozen or more men. It was small comfort to know that the grenades probably took out a bunch of them and that most of the thugs were still at the other *kafenas* at this time of the night.

The fire was a good distraction, but she doubted that would stop them from looking, especially if she had shot Dilaver in that room. She hoped that she had. That scumbag deserved to die, but she had been aiming at blobs of heat seen with her goggles, so she couldn't be sure. Her main concern had been to get at Hawk, so when she had knocked at the door, she had gone in with the focused intent of looking for only one familiar figure before she started shooting.

Once she had both her goggles and gas mask on, she had had to locate Hawk without actually being able to see him.

As luck would have it, he was lying on the floor, being kicked by one of Dilaver's thugs. That was the perfect place to be when CS gas was released. She'd committed the spot to memory before throwing in the canister of gas.

She heard Hawk's sharp intake of breath above her and wished she could carry him over her shoulders. She had to smile at the image. Somehow, short of being knocked unconscious again, she didn't think he would actually allow that. She couldn't describe the relief and joy that had engulfed her at the sight of him, still fighting his captors.

Now her job was to keep him alive. No, it was more than a job. She looked into the darkness below. Life was so strange. Why did she have to be hanging in midair and being chased by gangsters when she realized that she was in love?

She jumped the last five feet and immediately readied her weapon, looking for signs of Dilaver's men. She could hear shouts from somewhere not too far away. She heard Hawk's landing behind her and another sharp intake of breath, but he was reaching for her duffel bag already, pulling out the Uzi and some other weapons she had in there. He reloaded the Uzi as she scanned the area.

"Ready," he whispered.

"Okay, we keep running that way, no matter what," she said. "There's a bush there and a ditch grating in the wall behind there. That's the target."

"Ten-four."

They rounded the corner. Dilaver's men had turned on all their car lights and there was no way Amber and Hawk could sprint across the grounds without being spotted.

"I have one more grenade left," Amber said.

"Let me have it, since you're the leading the way. I'll use it once when they get closer."

"All right. Here. Ready?"

"Affirmative. Go!"

Amber took off. She heard shouts and the crack of weapons. Bullets zinged through the air past them. She ducked behind as many trees as she could.

"There!" she heard someone yell. "Get in the car and go after them! Keep the headlights on them!"

But she was heading for the bushes, not the driveway, and their pursuers would have to go on foot as soon as they caught up to where she and Hawk would be. She reached the wall that surrounded the compound and looked for the shrubbery she had marked. There was a metal grate behind it that covered the storm drain leading out of the property. She turned to find Hawk not too far behind. As soon as he saw the wall, he turned and heaved the grenade at their pursuers. A loud initial blast silenced the firing weapons.

"Right through here, Hot Stuff," Amber said, moving the heavy grate with both hands.

"You know, I now fully appreciate all the trouble you took to see me that first time," Hawk said as he helped her.

His breathing was uneven and Amber frowned. She had seen him run for miles when he was exploring the alleys with her. He must really be injured. "Not too far now," she said, although they still had to hike to her parked car.

They jumped into the storm drain and he took up a lot of the space. He turned and, to her surprise, kissed her hard on the lips. "Couldn't resist," he said. "Not after watching your butt wiggle inches from my face."

"You're one crazy man," Amber said, shaking her head. They were far from being safe and he still wanted to banter. The crazier thing was, she felt perfectly safe with him, for no apparent reason. "Come on, Hot Stuff, before they realize we aren't coming out from behind the bushes."

The base of the wall was very thick, constructed centuries ago, with newer walls built on top of it. A natural sound barrier, the trench was strangely quiet compared with the noise from a few minutes ago, and this time, Amber's worry grew as she really heard Hawk's hitched breathing as they made their way out on the other side.

She jumped up and pushed out of the drain, cautiously looking around in the darkness. It was a side street, on the west side of the compound. The two main front and back driveways were in the north and south. She knew from checking that a car driving out from inside the compound would take at least five minutes to turn into the alleyway.

"My car is down the end of the road," she told Hawk.

"Okay. I think they've discovered where we went down, by the way. I can hear them behind us."

"We have a five-minute head start if someone's smart enough to run and get a car," she said. Her concern grew as she watched Hawk getting out of the deep trench. She knew a healthy person would easily push off with his hands and climb out; instead, he was using his elbows.

They barely reached the other side of the street when two cars turned into the road from opposite ends, their headlights shining straight at them.

Amber looked to the left, then right. "Shit. They're smarter than I thought," she said. "And we're out of grenades."

"Where's our target route?"

"Down that way, then a side alley." She pointed in the direction of one of the oncoming vehicles. "Either way, we'd have to start shooting our way out of here."

Hawk pulled at the duffel bag strapped to her. "Time for the toys, sweetheart."

This was Hawk's arena. Running teams, moving into position, and executing firefights. But he didn't know how experienced Amber was. He started running back into the shadows and she followed quickly. He knew weapons could only buy them some time because Dilaver's men would be coming from all directions once shots were fired. He deliberately placed himself in front of Amber.

He aimed at a headlight of the closest oncoming vehicle and pulled the trigger, then sweeping the weapon left to right to get both of them. The high-pitched shatter of glass mixed with the rat-tat-tat sound of machine gun fire cut through the air. He aimed lower. The smell of burning tires was immediate as the car zigzagged out of control.

Hawk turned to the other vehicle. Amber nudged his elbow. "Wait," she yelled into his ear. "It's signaling. Cover me from the rear!"

Before he could ask what the hell she was doing, she started running toward the oncoming car. Fuck. There was no time to think, just do as she ordered. He ran behind her, turned, and fired again at the first vehicle. It had finally come to a stop, the doors flinging open as Dilaver's men jumped out. They ducked as Hawk started firing his weapon.

Amber had better know what she was doing because they were in the direct line of fire. Hawk became aware of the other oncoming car screeching to a halt right behind them. Someone killed the lights. Someone was shooting at Dilaver's men, besides him.

"Am I glad to see you!" he heard Amber say.

"Got your message. Can't miss the action. Hop in."

It was Lily. Hawk turned to find her behind the driver's door, using it as a shield, as she shot at their pursuers. He ran toward Amber, who had pulled open the back passenger door. She aimed and popped off a few shots before sliding inside.

Hawk went behind the door. "I'll keep them down while you get back in," he yelled to Lily.

"Yeah."

Hawk pulled the trigger again and found his weapon out of ammo. "Fuck!"

Amber stuck hers out of the car. "Here, Hot Stuff. Mine's still loaded."

Hawk grinned. "I have something to show you later," he promised as he turned his attention back to the thugs. He discharged a series of shots as Lily jumped back into the car. He did the same, slamming the door. "Go, go, go!"

20

Amber looked at the pile of clothing on her bed. By now Lily and Hawk would be halfway to the safe house. Lily had dropped her off so she could get her vehicle out of the alley and come back to the house. Amber would meet them later.

Hawk hadn't liked the idea one bit, but it was the only logical thing to do. Dilaver was going to show up looking for Hawk, and Amber didn't want them tearing the place apart. There were things there she needed to take care of first.

"Call Sun," Hawk had ordered gruffly. "Let him show up if Dilaver drops by. Promise me, Amber."

"All right," Amber said. She looked at Lily. "He's injured."

"We'll take care of it. You be careful," Lily said.

"Okay. Take care of the duffel bag, Hot Stuff. We'll need it for our vacation coming up." What she really wanted to do was check out Hawk's injuries for herself, but she had to do this. "Be there soon."

"You have three hours or I'll come looking," Hawk had told her.

She smiled at the memory of the ferocious stare he'd

given her. She had taken care of herself for so long that it made her feel giddy to see a man act so protective. Was it possible that she had only just met him? She felt as if she had known Hawk a lifetime.

The commotion outside her window interrupted her reverie. She peeked, then went out of her bedroom to look through the other window. Her little building was surrounded by cars. She could see Dilaver stepping out and giving some commands.

"Showtime," Amber muttered.

By the time they reached her upstairs apartment, she was pulling out huge suitcases from the little closet by the stairway. She turned. Two men stood at the connecting door, weapons drawn, their eyes searching the small apartment.

"Can I help you?" she asked calmly.

The men ignored her. One of them walked to the kitchen door that led to the deck and opened it. Dilaver strode in, leaning heavily on his stick.

"The restaurant isn't open today, Dragan," Amber said.

"I'm not here for a meal, Amber," Dilaver said, and nodded to his men. "We're looking for Hawk."

"You could have called on the phone," she said. Her apartment was suddenly filled with men. "I'd have saved you time. He isn't here. I thought he was with you."

Dilaver sat down in the sofa and looked around him. "Very small place. It's hard to hide a man in here."

Amber raised her eyebrows. "Hide? Why would I hide a man? Are we talking about Hawk still? Because I thought you were both friends."

"As of this morning, we're not, my dear. He's an informer." Dilaver leaned on his walking stick, cocking his head. "As if you didn't know."

Amber shrugged. "No, I wasn't sure. He's a careful man,

that Hawk. Doesn't reveal much about anything." She walked around her suitcases. "Are you really looking for him here, at my restaurant? Why would he come here to hide? This would be the first place you'd look, wouldn't it?"

Dilaver nodded. "True, but you have been seeing him a lot lately. He couldn't have gone far, though. He escaped not too long ago."

Amber noticed Dilaver didn't mention Hawk's injury. She sat down on the arm of the sofa. "Excuse me, are you telling me that a man escaped from your compound? I find that hard to believe, Dragan."

A grim expression finally crossed the Slav's face. "It was a dramatic escape. He and a few others killed and injured a number of my men there."

"So there were others involved?" Amber asked. She smiled. "Come on, now, you're pulling my leg, aren't you? How can anyone go into your compound without your knowing it? And then mount an escape after killing your people? I know you better than that, Dragan."

A voice interrupted from the kitchen doorway. "You seemed awfully calm about the news that Hawk's in danger." A smartly dressed small middle-aged woman stood there. She surveyed the apartment. "Are you sure you know nothing about his background?"

Amber shrugged. "I knew he wasn't telling me the whole truth, but then this is Velesta. You must not know much about this town." She cocked her head, studying the woman curiously. "Which part of the States are you from?"

"Don't tell her anything, Aunt Greta," Dilaver warned from the couch. "Amber sells information. This is my aunt, Amber, and that's all you need to know."

Amber crossed her arms. Here was a chance to find out exactly what everyone was after. "We can make a deal.

You're after Hawk for something big. I can see that now. What does he have that you don't?"

"And what will you do for me if I tell you?" Dilaver asked. His eyes narrowed. "Can you tell me where Hawk is?"

Amber shook her head. She gestured toward the suitcases. "I'm leaving town for a vacation very soon," she said, "and last night was my goodbye with Hawk." She sighed loudly. "I didn't want it to end, but a woman has to make some tough choices."

"A vacation with the CIVPOL chief, right?" Dilaver leaned closer. "Good choice. Your going away might help me. Hawk won't have one more place to hide. It won't be easy for him to get in and out of Velesta without my knowledge. I'll have people posted at every crossroads looking for him."

"It really sounds like he has something very important that you want," Amber said. "Now I'm really curious. Is this information going to make me a lot of money?"

"Miss Hutchens," Greta cut in, still standing in the doorway. "I deal with information myself. In fact, I can give you all kinds of classified information to sell that will make you a very wealthy woman. Now, if you can locate Hawk for us, maybe we can do some business. But there's a time limit. Hawk won't be of use to me after the seventeenth of this month."

Amber noticed Greta said "me" and not "us." "Why the specific time?" she asked.

"Some information will just be old news after a certain deadline, Miss Hutchens. Now, do we have a deal?"

Amber looked at her watch. "We have a deal, but Brad— that's Chief Sun, if you don't know who that is—will be here very soon to pick me up. I don't think he'll be too happy to see all your cars around my place, Dragan."

"I'm not so happy with him, either. He raided my *kafena*

this morning. One of these days, my dear, you'll find another one of your boyfriends gone."

"Then they will send another one and this time he might not be someone I can get close to, Dragan." Amber glanced at Greta. "I like the sound of the word 'classified.' You're either American or have lived there a long time. I'm guessing you're privy to so much information because you're either married to a diplomat or you're working inside. Someone like me can't run a café forever, so please explain to Dragan here how our line of work progresses."

"She certainly does sound more concerned about this chief than Hawk," Greta said to Dilaver. She nodded at him, a satisfied expression on her face. "All right, tell her about the bomb and the decoy."

He refused the painkillers. Where the hell was Amber? She was late.

"What time is it?" Hawk asked. He scowled from the bed. "Can I get up now?"

"It's five minutes since you last asked, and no, you can't get up till Amber's here," Lily said. She sat at the far end of the room, by the door, with a gun pointed at him. "Be good, will you?"

"I've eaten. I've subjected myself to being prodded by women who don't really know me. And you took a shot at me and I haven't retaliated." He scowled at the dark-haired woman. She had really used that weapon when he had tried to get out of the house. "Haven't I been good enough?"

"Obviously not, or I wouldn't have had to use this," Lily said, waving her gun. "You just sit there and rest up. How am I going to explain to Amber where you are when she shows up and you've gone off?"

That had been his plan after sitting there at the safe house for a while. He just couldn't wait any longer. What if

Dilaver . . . ? He didn't want to imagine what Dilaver might do to Amber.

"She's okay, Hawk," Lily said quietly. "Brad was going over there to pick her up for their vacation, remember? Dilaver wouldn't hurt her."

"How can you be sure?" Hawk challenged.

"Not so calm and cool about not killing the scumbag now that he has someone of yours, are you, Mr. McMillan?" Lily asked softly.

Hawk became still. "Meaning?"

Lily leaned back, resting one arm on the back of the chair. "You know what I mean. You and Brad. Both of you wouldn't take down Dilaver when he wasn't hurting someone you know. Look at you now. You look like hamburger meat, yet you want to go after him and his men. Brad, too. He took off like a maniac the moment he heard that Amber might be in danger from Dilaver."

If he didn't know any better, he would have thought Lily was jealous. But surely not of Brad and Amber? "That's what happens when a friend's in trouble, Lily," Hawk said, eyeing her closely. She appeared relaxed, as if she were trying to distract him with conversation. "Wouldn't you take off after Dilaver if he had Amber?"

Lily smiled. "Are you trying to get me all defensive about my friendship with Amber?"

"Not at all. But I notice you still haven't answered my question."

She looked at him seriously for a moment. "For me, it all depends on the situation," she said. "I mean, sometimes you have choices to make, you know. I love Amber very much, but what if one of the girls is in trouble at the same time? I can't be at two places at the same time, can I?"

Hawk reached for the peanut butter sandwich by the bed,

carefully chewing it, since his gums seemed to have swollen. "So what are you saying?" he asked in between bites. "Sounds like you're saying you might abandon Amber."

Lily's smile widened. "I'm saying that everyone has priorities and they rewrite their rules around them. For example, Brad won't arrest Dilaver. I'll bet you, if Dilaver had Amber as a prisoner, he would break all sorts of laws to rescue her. Then there's you. You're on a special mission to retrieve something and won't get rid of Dilaver because that isn't part of your operation. But you'd help Amber by sneaking in the two reporters, which probably was what got you caught. And now you just want to go after Dilaver because he might have Amber, too. So the two of you rewrote your rules when it suited you. I, on the other hand, have very few rules and try never to break them." She cocked an eyebrow. "Do you want to know why?"

"Why?" Hawk finished the sandwich. He was still worried about Amber, but at least the conversation was making time go a little faster.

"Because when you break a rule, there is no more order. The center doesn't stand without order and the world around you collapses."

"You know, Lily, that's too damn profound for a beat-up guy right now. I'll tell you something, though. I don't know what your rules are, but life isn't order or chaos because of people who make or break them. And if you were in trouble with Dilaver, Brad would do the same thing for you. More, I suspect." Hawk carefully sat up. His whole body was stiffening up from not moving about. "Are you going to shoot at me again if I take a piss?"

"No. I just don't want you to attempt rushing out of here like before. Looks like you're in too much pain now, though. Are you still not going to take the painkillers?"

Hawk shook his head. "Nope."

"Why? It'd make you feel better."

Hawk got off the bed. "One of my rules," he said with a smile. "Never take medication when someone in the room is pointing a gun at you."

"That is, if you have a choice," Lily pointed out.

"That goes without saying," he said.

The door opened. Amber walked in, taking in Lily, the gun in her hand, and Hawk with a sweeping glance. She didn't seem surprised at the weapon pointed at him, heading straight into his open arms, although she was very careful how she hugged him.

"Tried to come after me, didn't he?"

Brad came in and he briefly exchanged glances with Lily.

"He won't be sedated. Then he got impatient and I had to get all philosophical with him," Lily said, putting away her gun.

"Oh no, she didn't start one of her long tracts about choices and rules, did she, Hot Stuff?" Amber went over to the bed, her smile disappearing. "You look even worse in this light. What did Marisa say about your injuries?"

Marisa was one of the housekeepers, who also appeared to be the nurse around here. "Nothing serious," he answered, and looked over Amber at Lily. He nodded at Brad. Those two didn't even address each other anymore. "So all that stuff about choices and rules was to distract me? Did you mean any of it?"

"Absolutely," Lily said, not indicating which question she was answering. "Marisa said he has bruised ribs, nothing broken. The pretty face is going to heal. But he really needs to go to a hospital just in case he's hurt inside. There's also a lump on his head, so probably a concussion."

"Shouldn't you be in bed?" Amber tried to step out of his arms to get a better look, but Hawk wouldn't let her. She frowned. "Hawk, I need you in bed. Oh, stop grinning like that. You don't know how awfully swollen your lips are!"

"Ah, in case you haven't noticed, they are attached to me, so I do know they are swollen, thanks." He just wanted to bury his nose in her hair, inhale her scent. It was good to have her in his arms again. "Did Dilaver give you any trouble?"

"Yes and no. We'll talk about this once I get you back in bed."

Hawk looked at the other two occupants in the room. "You're going to embarrass Brad and Lily, sweetheart, the way you keep suggesting bed."

"I'd punch you if you weren't hurt already," Amber warned.

Hawk sighed. He was going to have to show her how tough a SEAL was. "First Lily shot at me, now you're going to punch me. I think I just escaped one torture chamber for another. I was heading for the restroom when you came in. I'll get back into bed after taking care of business, if you don't mind."

Lying down for so long had cramped up his sore muscles. Since he knew she was watching him, he tried not to hobble too much as he made his way to the john.

"Look at him pretending to limp," he heard Brad say as he closed the door.

Hawk leaned heavily against the door, willing the burning in his ribs to go away. Bruised ribs were better than broken ones, he reasoned. It was going to hurt a lot while he hiked around in the country looking for weapons.

He looked at his face in the mirror, turning slightly to the left to check out the cut that was courtesy of a bottle. The housekeeper had sewn up the wound. There was another cut above his eyebrow and he had a nice black eye.

"Frankenstein," he breathed out, baring his teeth to look at his gums. His swollen lips made the task more difficult than usual and even stretching his face that way hurt. He hoped the swelling would go down fast. It was easier to remember a battered face and it would make walking around incognito a bit tougher. He'd have to think of a good plan to protect both of them from Dilaver's men.

Amber tried not to look too worried. Hawk needed to be checked out by a doctor and there was no way she could get him to a hospital without Dilaver finding out. Maybe when they made it out of Macedonia . . . She frowned when she heard his breathing again. She wished she had been here when they had taken his shirt off. Those bruised ribs must make moving around very painful, yet he hadn't taken any of the painkillers.

They had to come up with a plan and she was glad Brad and Lily were here this time, and apparently holding a truce. After she had checked with the housekeepers and some of the girls, they pulled a table into Hawk's room and gathered around it, with a map of the region spread out. She ordered Hawk to stay in bed, and placated him by sitting on it herself. He wanted her near him and the heated look in his eyes made her feel all warm and funny inside. She knew he was only obedient because he didn't feel like arguing at the moment. She was beginning to understand how he was—always biding his time.

"The most important thing is to get out of here," she said. "Sooner or later, Dilaver will get wind that I'm still in town. Right now he thinks Brad is taking me on vacation, so we have to stick to that part of our original plan."

"I'm more interested in this Aunt Greta that suddenly appeared," Hawk said. "You said she was at the apartment making a deal with you. I'm going to have to ask my contact about her. If only we had a last name. . . ."

"No reference to her last name in our conversation," Amber said, frowning as she took a sip of her coffee. Hard to believe it was still barely noon. "She has no accent whatsoever, very chic, and knew a lot about information and how it works in the system."

"Maybe I can contact someone to check the airline logs, see whether any American woman around her age came into Macedonia recently," Brad said.

"Good, but according to her, something big happens soon. Why didn't you tell me it was a bomb, Hawk?"

"I was only told that the weapon was a trigger," Hawk explained. "My contact told me he'd tell me what to do when I get to the right location."

Amber put down her cup and drew a circle on the map with her finger. "Jed probably didn't want me to get the information. Anyway, from the coordinates, we're going all the way to Serbia. Each weapons cache was dropped so Dilaver didn't have to transport them to the different groups controlling the region. So why is Greta so adamant about getting her hands on a bomb? Anyone can make a bomb, right?"

"The correct question is, what is the bomb for?" Hawk asked.

"Well, you're the one after it. Don't you know?" Lily countered.

Hawk shook his head. "I have only two tasks. Destroy the weapon caches at the different locations. But most important of all, retrieve this specific one. I can see now why I can't just destroy it—it's a bomb." The first mission was for his SEAL commander, who brokered the deal to work with GEM and the COS commandos. Admiral Madison didn't want any more weapons given or sold to anyone who might be shooting back at them in future covert ops. The second mission was to retrieve the secret weapon for GEM and the COS commandos, who weren't exactly talkative types.

"Don't you know anything else?" Lily persisted.

"Need-to-know basis," Hawk said. "That's the nature of the business, Lily. Thought you knew."

Lily shrugged. "Surely there's a big picture. There's always a big picture."

Amber caught Brad looking at Lily as if he were going to say something, then appeared to change his mind. He turned his attention to Amber instead. "So," he said, "we're going on this romantic vacation."

She smiled at him, knowing what it took for him to avoid starting an argument with Lily. "Yes, but we'll have to detour because Dilaver will be keeping tabs on us to make sure we're actually going somewhere."

"Where are we actually going?" Brad turned to Hawk. "We can't stop at every place they dropped off shipments. It'd take more than a week."

Hawk nodded. "I'll confirm this later, but the main plan is to get out of here without being spotted. Too bad you're dark-haired, Lily, or we could use you as a decoy with Brad. Both of you can drive off in the opposite direction."

"There's such a thing as a wig, you know."

"There's that possibility," Hawk said, looking at Brad, who kept silent. "Amber and I will head off to retrieve the bomb. We can keep in touch by cell."

Amber found it interesting to see how these two men were becoming sort of friends. They hadn't talked that much with each other, but she could tell that they were backing each other up in a way only males did, by diverting attention.

"What are you going to do with the bomb when you get it?" Lily asked.

"I call my contact and wait for instructions."

"Then the mission is over? That's it?" Lily hid a yawn behind a hand. "Where's the glory? No payoff, nothing?"

"We get to save the world, Lily, or some part of it," Amber said, amused. "Guess that isn't a big enough payoff?"

"I'd much rather save a bunch of girls' lives than some bomb that might be used somewhere. Who knows? It might explode in Dilaver's face before he sells it, killing him and his buyers, and that's a good thing."

"I think Dilaver and his aunt have very big plans for this particular bomb," Hawk said. "First, they don't even know what it looks like, which makes me think it's a new weapon of some sort. Second, they have a deadline of a week, which points to the possibility of them using this bomb in a big way."

"That's how it sounded when Greta talked to me. She offered me a big sum of money for you," Amber said, smiling wryly at Hawk's raised eyebrows. "I'm to call Dilaver if you contact me and to try to get you to tell me where you are. Huge sum of money."

"Glad to know my price tag is so high," Hawk said.

"I suspect they let me off so easy because they want to see what I'm going to do next. If I put the word out on the street looking for you, they will hear of it tomorrow. They also know that if they cut off your sources of help, they might get to you sooner. They didn't mention to me how injured you are, by the way."

"Wouldn't want you to feel sorry enough to help me, now, would they?"

Amber reached over and lightly touched his bruised cheek. "He's going to pay for this," she said softly. "I'll think of some ways to really hurt him back."

"This is tolerable. You came just at the right time, sweetheart," Hawk said, covering her hand with his. "This boy would have been quite badly injured if Dilaver had started on me. Thanks to you, I only get to limp around like him for a while."

The knowledge of how close he had been to dying hit her like a bull's-eye. She had avoided that very thought all morning. She had lived in Macedonia for four years. Lives were cheap here and many people she knew had either gotten hurt or had died. She had grown to accept that as part of her current job.

Somehow Hawk had become important to her. She had fallen hard for him and had put his life before hers, running off to save him on her own. And what she was going to do now could also jeopardize her future here in Velesta. Lily was right. She couldn't have it both ways—going off on a tracking mission *and* rescuing girls from Dilaver's clutches. Dilaver's suspicion could put the whole venture in danger. When this was over, she and Lily would have to talk things over. She had a feeling it was going to be a sobering conversation.

"Hey, you okay?" Hawk nudged her with his leg.

"Yes. Just thinking about everything." When she caught Lily yawning again, she added, "I vote we take a break before we get our final plans together. We can get going easier in the dark, anyway. Hawk, you need to rest up or we can't go anywhere."

"Yes, ma'am. I second the vote."

"I have a few of my most trusted men stationed outside," Brad said. "I get the feeling that Dilaver will soon be on the way out of town, though."

"He didn't seem too affected by the tear gas last night," Amber observed.

"CS gas isn't long-lasting," Hawk explained. "But he does have a lot of injured or dead men to take care of this morning, so that gives us a little time."

"Too bad neither of you killed him in there last night," Lily quipped. "It'd save us all this trouble."

Amber sighed. "I didn't get a long enough look to see where he was in that room."

"That's because you were looking for Mr. McMillan here." Lily stood up, stretched, and took her empty cup with her to the door. "Oh well, another wasted opportunity there, that's all. Why can't anyone see how easy it is? Kill this Greta bitch and Dilaver and we solve all these problems. But no, we'll go off and find the bomb while they chase us everywhere. See you all later."

After she left, Hawk remarked, "Bloodthirsty woman, isn't she?"

"Lily and the army of one," Brad said, looking at the closed door. "You take down Dilaver, there'll be another in his place in a matter of days."

"And all the factions would start another civil war to grab land and power, and more UN and U.S. soldiers will be deployed," Hawk said. "So we're back to square one. Get the bomb before the KLA does. It's got to be a different kind of bomb, Brad, or they would just rig up some ordinary plastic. I'm going to try to find out what it is when I call my contact."

Brad got up. "You do that. I have a few things to take care of before we leave, too. Call me."

Amber followed him out and then locked the door. She turned to Hawk.

"And now, before we talk, I want to see every little bruise and cut," she said. She had this need to touch him all over, feel his heat under her hands, make sure he was truly all right.

"Come here," Hawk said, patting his front. "I'll let you be on top."

Smiling, Amber shook her head. If the man had a concussion, it hadn't affected his libido.

Lily slipped into her jacket, pulling the collar up. She pulled the gloves out of the pockets, turned, and bumped into Brad.

"I thought you were tired."

She noticed that he always kept his distance when he stood by her, which should make her happy. So why did it irritate her? "I can't. Need to walk off some of my energy."

"Be careful."

"I'm the only one no one's looking for, remember?" she pointed out. "But I'll be extra careful. You aren't going to sic your guys out there on me, are you?"

"One might follow you, make sure you're okay."

Lily rolled her eyes. "Oh, please, Brad, that's so secret-agent. Haven't I proven that I can take care of myself?"

Brad moved a step closer, his eyes studying her closely. "I know you can. Why do you do that all the time?"

Lily frowned. "What do you mean, why do I take care of myself all the time?"

"Yes. You always act so independent, like you don't need anyone. Is it to push people away or to keep yourself safe?"

The hair on the back of her neck stood up. He was suddenly standing way too close. "I don't know what you mean."

"What's Project Precious?"

Lily blinked. "That's none of your business," she hissed sharply, then wished she had kept her cool. He was studying her reaction.

"I just wanted you to know that I know," Brad said quietly. "Lily, it doesn't matter to me what that CIA file says. If nothing else, it makes me admire you even more."

A part of her wanted to kill him for knowing. Yet another part was relieved. Maybe he would understand her for what she was. But she couldn't allow him to share the information. Not yet, anyway. "You don't know anything. Those are just words written down by somebody. What I have is in here." She tapped her forehead. "Don't dig up information on me, Brad. I don't need your or anyone's pity. The last thing I want right now is to have Amber worried about me."

Brad searched her eyes and she stared back into his, willing herself not to show her fears. "I understand," he finally said, "but I also want you to know that my feelings for you haven't changed, Llallana. You're special to me."

His smile was so tender, she wanted to walk up to him and lay her head against his chest, have him wrap his strong arms around her and take away the loneliness. But there was always reality. And it was buzzing for her in her coat pocket.

"Thanks, Brad," she said, smiling back. "I'll think about that during my walk."

She could tell he was disappointed that she didn't invite him along, but she needed to take this call. She was the only person left who could help the girls.

"Physical functioning at seventy percent. Mental at ninety," Hawk said wryly. He knew Jed would figure that if he could joke about his condition, then he wasn't too seriously injured. His tone of voice became more serious. "At least my legs aren't broken, so I can do a lot of hiking."

"You're fortunate Amber came to get you when she did, then," Jed said. "Our observer contacted us and said that they took you down at the brothel."

"I suppose an observer can't lift a finger to help out, can they?" Hawk asked. He watched Amber set up the links to his laptop, sitting in bed beside him. She had even managed to snatch that from Dilaver's man. What a woman. He caressed between her shoulder blades and she looked up at him inquiringly. He shook his head. "She's almost ready to link."

"He was too far away to help, Hawk, and wasn't even sure whether you were alive. He did say you took down fifteen of Dilaver's men before shots were fired. There were several fights happening and he thought he saw someone shoot you. We were hoping it wasn't you, but since we had no contact from you for a while, we had to accept the possibility." There was little emotion in Jed's voice. "Tell Amber I'm ready whenever she is."

"She's almost there." Amber was enabling a direct video link with Jed so they could consult back and forth using visual aids such as maps. Hawk could do it himself, but he wanted to let Jed see how much he trusted Amber at this point without going into a full discussion in front of her. He knew the other man would get his not-so-subtle message. "How long before you can get back to me about what Dilaver and this new person, Greta, are planning?"

"Give us a couple of hours. Probably this evening, before you leave the area."

"Good." By then he should be a bit more rested and able to process all the new information. To be honest, his mental state wasn't at ninety percent. He needed to be very alert, especially during the first leg of their journey, when they had to sneak past Dilaver-controlled road posts.

"Link's ready," Amber said.

"Okay, Jed, everything's secured at our end. We're ready to transmit."

"Hang on." There was a pause. "Ready to link up here. There we go."

Hawk leaned closer to Amber. A moment later, Jed's face appeared on the screen of his laptop. To his surprise, instead of his usual attire of jeans jacket, the COS commando team leader was wearing a tuxedo.

"Did we interrupt something important?" Hawk asked. Like all computer linkups, it took several seconds before his question was transmitted through to wherever Jed was.

"I always dress up for dinner," Jed replied with a straight face. "You don't look so good, Hawk. Hello, Ambrosia, long time."

"Jed, it has been a while." Did he imagine it or did her

voice lower a notch? Hawk resisted the urge to turn his head to look at Amber. "How have you been?"

"Good. Can you handle this route?"

"It shouldn't be a problem." Amber tapped on the keyboard. "I'm transmitting the map I've prepared. Hawk's coordinates match a few areas. Time being the key thing here, which of these routes should we head for?"

"We're printing it right now. Hang on."

Jed disappeared off-screen for a moment, then reappeared with a piece of paper. He studied Amber's map, then talked to someone off-camera to the right of him. It sounded like French, but Hawk couldn't make out the words. It totally fascinated him to see how comfortable the other man looked all suited up, looking so civilized. He looked far from the "Stefan" he knew in Asia, a jeans-clad weapons dealer, carousing with the local kingpin's sister and making shady deals with dangerous characters. Hawk would never have imagined Jed McNeil would even fit into surroundings that required a dress code.

Jed looked up, his silvery eyes unerringly directed at Hawk. "First, I agree that you should abandon the initial plan to destroy every cache of weapons shown here. The most important thing is to get to the target weapon. Once you have it, you can contact me again and I'll send a contact to pick it up. Second, we have compared your coordinates with the aid and relief dropoffs by manned and unmanned U.S. aerial vehicles the last six months. Although your physical description of the woman doesn't fit, we have reason to believe that Greta is the same handler that had worked as a secretary to Deputy Director Philip Gorman's task force in the CIA for the past ten years, so we have a paper trail. We're transmitting a file photo. We have computed that the target weapon is in the cache between Elbasan and Tirana at ninety percent.

"The third factor is still an unknown. We're concentrating on all political activities in that part of the world in the next seven to ten days and putting out a code red alert. From what little Dilaver hinted to Ambrosia, the target weapon is to be used after a decoy has been activated. There's an international summit going on in Skopje right now and the main meeting with certain world leaders present in two days. That, however, will be off the seven-day deadline, so we're assuming that either the event or threat is a decoy and there's another target. Keep your cell or your watch close by, Hawk. Someone will contact you. Check for messages whenever you can."

"Will do," Hawk said.

"Still the same prepared guy, aren't you, Jed?" Amber asked.

Jed gave her the barest of smiles. "Still trolling for information, Ambrosia?"

"I can't help but notice that little pin on your collar, that's all. You're at this summit already, aren't you?"

Hawk frowned. "Wait a minute. You're here in Macedonia, Jed?"

Jed's expression remained blank. "It's just a pin. We'll talk soon. Any messages for Admiral Madison?"

Hawk straightened up at the mention of his commander's name. "Please let him know that I'm standing and ready for the team."

Jed nodded. "Talk to you soon. Amber, consider your *veza* settled."

A favor. So, there was a history between Jed McNeil and Amber. He turned his head just in time to catch her smile at Jed.

"No more free rides for you, Jed McNeil," she told him.

"Don't be too sure, Ambrosia," Jed said. The screen turned to snow as the transmission was cut off.

"Are you two close friends?" Hawk asked as Amber closed the laptop.

"We've known each other for a while," she said.

He didn't like her vague reply. "How close?" he insisted.

She put the laptop on the nightstand and turned to face him. "He saved my life," she said.

Hawk let her push him back against the pillow. "Oh," he said. Well, hell, what was a man to say to that? "I guess that's why you feel you have to help him in this operation."

Amber curled up next to him. She buried her face in his neck. "No, you're the reason why I decided to help him in this operation. Satisfied your curiosity enough for now?"

Hawk smiled. "Yes," he said, and obediently closed his eyes. They both needed to rest. They could talk more later.

"Who's Admiral Madison?" she asked.

"Not an ex-lover," he assured her sleepily. "Satisfied your curiosity for now?"

She chuckled and snuggled closer, sliding a hand around his waist. So much to tell her. And with the imminent danger ahead, Hawk was determined to see it through so he could have all the time in the world to tell her everything.

21

"**Don't worry, I'll take care of everything** here," Lily said, giving Amber a quick hug.

Amber held her friend tightly for a second. They were going separate ways—Brad with Lily, acting as Amber's decoy by wearing a blond wig, were heading back to his place to get "her" things, whereas Amber and Hawk would start for the western border, toward Albania.

"I'm sorry about this," Amber said. She felt bad, as if she were abandoning Lily. "I have passports for each of the girls ready in the large envelope. If you need cash—"

"How many times have I done this? Don't worry so much."

It wasn't that she worried about Lily, but it was her responsibility to do the paperwork in their operation. Whereas Lily's skills had always been on the survival side, rescuing the kidnapped girls and guiding them safely out of Macedonia, Amber undertook all necessary detail work to prepare the girls for their new lives. It was she who got the fake passports ready, double-checked all the tickets for the girls going overseas, and, most important of all, made sure the girls understood what they had to do to make it safely to their destinations.

With Hawk's escape, Lily was afraid that Dilaver might go house to house looking for him, and would come upon the safe houses. She suggested she would take the current group of girls out of Macedonia immediately. Amber had agreed. She felt she had let Lily down.

"We do what we have to do," Lily continued. "Call me so I don't worry."

"I will."

"Here's the map to where Dija is," Lily said, giving her a piece of paper. "I've already talked to him and he'll let you guys through somehow."

"Can we really trust him?" Amber looked at the drawn map doubtfully.

Lily shrugged. "It's a risk you'll have to decide. Hawk saved his life back there at the hills and this is a simple return favor. Dija has always kept his word to me."

"Okay, thanks." Amber gave Lily another hug. "It's dark enough now that they can't really see your face. You look gorgeous as a blonde, by the way."

"Yeah, watch me scoot down in the car so I look petite like you."

Laughing, Amber stuck a tongue out at her friend before turning to go back upstairs. Hawk was having his ribs tightly bandaged by one of the housekeepers. When she opened the door, she found several of the girls keeping him company, fussing over his injuries. They had heard about what had happened and had been worried. It astonished her to see how these girls, most of whom had grown to dislike men, had warmed up to Hawk.

He looked up and his puffy lips attempted a crooked smile. Her heart did a slow somersault at the look in his eyes. Sexy. And dangerous. The man must be superman. A few hours of rest just couldn't be enough for an ordinary guy to look so ready for battle again.

One of the girls touched his shoulder. "Be careful and good luck," she said.

Hawk nodded. He glanced back at Amber. "Don't worry. I've got Amber to take care of me," he said.

Brad was surprised Lily had agreed to this part of the plan. Going back to his place couldn't be comfortable for her. Hell, he wasn't comfortable, either. But he was going to try to be a gentleman and not force himself on her.

"You're still angry with me, aren't you?" Lily surprised him by bringing it up.

He congratulated himself silently at not braking the car to a dead stop. "I'm not angry," he said quietly. Not now that he understood her, anyway.

"Why? Because you feel sorry for me?"

There was the slightest hint of bitterness in her voice. He couldn't see her face in the evening darkness.

"I'm not sure how I feel at the moment," Brad said honestly. He checked the rearview mirror. "We're being followed, by the way."

Lily sat up a little straighter, fluffing her hair. "Probably Dilaver checking to make sure Amber and you are doing what you both said you were doing."

They came to a stoplight and the car pulled next to Brad's. Lily looked down, then turned away so they could only see the back of her head.

"What are they doing?" she asked, casually leaning over to flick something off his collar.

"Two men. Watching us." He turned and gave her a smile. "Can I kiss you before we turn into my garage? It'll make it seem like we have romance on our minds."

"All right," she whispered.

Brad leaned down and softly brushed her lips with his. To his surprise, she opened her mouth, inviting him to taste her.

He slid his tongue into her mouth and she nudged closer, eagerly responding. It was more than he had expected and he didn't want the kiss to end, taking his time to explore her softness. For his part, he wasn't pretending.

A honk from behind jolted his consciousness and he released her lips. The light had turned green. He looked over Lily's shoulder and caught the occupants from the other car looking at them, grinning. Another honk, more impatient this time, from the driver at the back. He turned and started the car moving again.

They didn't say anything as he turned into his street. He checked the rearview mirror. They were still being followed. As he activated the garage door opener, he turned and pulled Lily into his arms. She came willingly and he briefly wondered whether she was still playing the part of Amber. Of course she had to be. But he no longer cared.

"I want them to see how much I want you," he told her, and kissed her again.

The ride to the mountain pass was uneventful. No one paid attention to the old van used to transport the girls. Hawk had made sure they weren't being followed as he followed Lily's map. Just before they reached the border, he pulled over so Amber could get into the back.

This was perhaps the most important part of the passage. Dilaver controlled many of the border gangs and he was sure to have everyone on the lookout for them. Through the years, Amber and Lily had mapped out which were the safest routes in and out of Macedonia, "safe" being a relative term here, as all sorts of shady characters resided in the mountains. Lily had many contacts and she told them that there was a price on the Americans' heads. Alive.

When they stopped at the roadblock, Hawk gazed directly into Dija's eyes. In spite of all this *veza* stuff among the locals, he much preferred to trust his own instincts. The other man had told Lily he would let Amber and him pass through because Hawk had spared his life in the firefight. He supposed that was the mercenary's way of returning the favor. Fair enough.

Still, he didn't put all his trust in the man's word. Dija was, after all, a mercenary, someone who put a price on lives.

"What are you transporting at this hour?" Dija asked.

"Fruit." Amber had assured Hawk that she would be ready back there if Dija decided to betray them. "Market day tomorrow."

Dija turned to the man next to him. "I'll look in the back. You stay here."

Hawk didn't turn his head as he listened to Dija's footsteps leading to the back of the van. The sound of the back door opening. He smiled at the other man standing by his side of the vehicle. The back door slammed shut. Dija trotted back to the front, his weapon pointing down at the ground.

"Okay, you can go," he said crisply.

Hawk met his eyes one last time. "Thank you," he said.

"Not a problem," Dija answered.

Hawk drove about ten kilometers before he found a good place to hide the van. He got out in the dark. He could hear Amber getting out of the vehicle from the back. They had to abandon it and go the rest of the way on foot. They didn't have the paperwork to show to the authorities and the Serbian police were no better than Macedonian thugs, except that they had prisons in which to beat people.

"Well, that was easy enough," he said, half joking. The country roads that connected Macedonia with Albania were sort of a no-man's-land where two sides were at war. The KLA was determined to take control of as much land as possible and sporadic battles broke out without any provocation. "He didn't give any hint of having seen you back there at all."

"Dija moved some fruit around, but it was obvious he wasn't going to look too closely," Amber said.

"What are you looking at?"

Amber had pulled out something from her bag. "Another map. I want to get our bearings right." She pointed to several spots on the map. "These are places to avoid. More gangs or checkpoints. We'll have to move around them and try not to get caught in a battle. Oh well, at least we still have my handy bag of weapons."

It amused him to listen to her talk of the operation ahead as casually as the way she followed one of her recipes. In a way, she reminded him of Jazz, who could talk strategy and make it sound like music. He knew that she would get along with his SEAL brother.

"If we follow the trail around this lake," he said, "then we'll get to Elbasan first." The cache they were looking for was between Elbasan and Tirana.

"It's a long hike from here. Most of Tirana is hilly, perfect to hide a weapons dropoff. It's going to take at least a day." She rubbed his arm. "Or more, with your injuries."

Hawk knew she was concerned about his bruised ribs. He ran a finger down the curve of her cheek. "I can do this, sweetheart. Trust me." He had to tell the truth now. "I'm a Navy SEAL, so I'm quite used to a lot of pain."

"A what?"

"Navy SEAL," Hawk said. "It stands for sea, air, and land, and I—"

"I know what a SEAL is," Amber interrupted. "You said you're one."

He stroked her soft skin again. "Yeah." He didn't blink when she shone her flashlight at his face, looking at him closely. He cocked his head. "Don't look any different, do I?"

"You're a soldier?"

Hawk shook his head. "See, you don't know what a SEAL is. I'm a sailor, sweetheart. You know . . . *Navy* SEAL."

She waved the flashlight away. "What's the difference? You're military." There was disbelief in her voice.

"Don't let my frog brothers hear you say that. Plenty of difference. When I have time, I'll have to teach you."

He waited as she stood there thinking about what he had just told her. He knew she had thought he was a part of Jed's outfit and, being Amber, had him all figured out in her head. Or so she had thought.

"Frog brothers?" she muttered. "So you can swim?"

Hawk chuckled. "Yeah, I can swim. I'll take you sometime, too."

"But I can't swim, except doggy-paddle."

He hadn't thought of that. "Okay, then I'll teach you." He took hold of her hand. "What I was trying to say was that I've been trained to do this."

"Hmmm. I knew there was something about you. I guess I can teach you to cook."

That was his girl. Always had to compete. Hawk grinned. "Deal," he said.

Lily put away her cell phone. "That was my contact telling me that he's waiting for Amber and Hawk," she said. "He'll call me again when they cross the border."

"Good," Brad said as he poured himself a glass of wine. "What would you like to drink?"

"The same thing," Lily replied. It would help relax her.

"To Amber and Hawk," Brad said, holding up his glass for a toast.

"To us," Lily said, smiling.

Brad studied her for a moment, his eyes searching. "This teasing has to stop eventually, Llallana."

"Eventually," she agreed, and finished her wine in one gulp. "I want more."

"More . . . wine?"

"More . . . everything. Call me Lily, Brad."

He carefully put down the glass. "What are you doing, Llallana?"

She didn't want to tell him that he'd won. That she yearned to feel something besides hatred and fear one more time in her life. That she was tempted to give in to this need for him. She knew that if she went through with this, she would hate herself in the morning, but she wanted him and couldn't deny it any longer. For once in her life, she wanted a man to satisfy her.

"I'm not teasing any longer, Brad," she said softly. To prove that she wasn't, she undid the zip at the side of her silk top and slowly pulled the blouse loose. "We have to kill some time, let Amber and Hawk get out of town. Why not spend this time doing what the men outside think we're doing?"

She walked to him and started to unbutton his shirt. He didn't stop her, his eyes, full of questions, searching hers. She felt excitement surging through her as his shirt parted. She laid her cheek on his bare chest, listening to his heartbeat.

This was the easy part. She was in total control, just the way she liked it. "We're going to finish what we started the other night," she told him. "I promise."

"We don't have to do anything you don't want . . . Lily."

"I want . . . this." She ran her hand down his chest toward the waistband of his pants. "I want this." She unhooked the belt and pulled on the zipper. "I want this." She put her hand inside and grasped his hard arousal. It pulsed with heat. "Inside me."

Brad let out a soft groan as she stroked his penis. He abruptly took her hand and pulled it out of his pants, then turned, taking her along with him. She assumed they were heading for his bedroom. Her feet suddenly felt weak. She was really going to do this.

Lily didn't even have time to register what his room looked like. He had her on her back, on his bed, and started kissing her face and her neck. She gasped when his mouth covered her nipple, sucking and licking it. His hand reached between her legs and she felt his fingers rubbing her through her panties. She almost choked from the shock. How could she be so near to coming from just that? She fought for control. No.

"Not yet," she said. "Slowly, Brad."

"I'm sorry," he said, moving up and kissing her lips. "I can't think straight when you're around me. When you took off your blouse just now, I think I about lost it. I'm going to make this good, Lily. I promise you."

She was dying from forcing herself not to move. He let her take her clothes off, heard his compliments through the buzz in her head, and watched as he removed his. He was so handsome. So big. She stared at his arousal. He climbed on top of her.

She wanted to be on top. She always wanted to be on top. Not this time. She could do this. She opened her legs. "Come inside," she invited, and forced a smile, even though she was fighting the growing fear. She was screaming inside. *No, no, no.*

"Not yet," he said, and his smile was so beautiful. His hand reached down again and he intimately explored her. "Slowly, Lily. I want you to feel very good. You're so wet now, baby. I want you to lose yourself like I'm going to lose myself in you."

Lily shut her eyes tightly. She didn't want to lose herself. She always had them come in her and lose themselves as she rode them. They were the ones out of it; she was the one using them. Except that she hadn't felt the same sharp pleasure that Brad was giving her now. It was the same building pressure from the other night, the one that took all her control to stop.

She was so close. She held her breath, fighting the need to pull his hand away. A sob escaped her lips.

"Yes, baby, so close."

She felt him slide down and gasped at the first feel of his tongue where his hand had been. He pleasured her with rhythmic strokes, strong and hard, his sure fingers opening her folds wide for his tongue. She was melting, losing all thought. She fought it even as she felt herself getting wetter and closer.

No! She couldn't be this easy to conquer, could she? She chased after that elusive tension mounting inside her even as she fought to let go. His fingers joined his tongue. She sobbed harder. She couldn't lose control.

His weight came back on her and she wrapped her legs eagerly around him. This she could do. She would make him come inside her, and she would watch him. Instead of plunging into her, he rubbed himself against her clitoris, over and over, until she felt her legs falling onto the bed as she helplessly squirmed.

And then, suddenly, he was inside her, filling her. She was so wet that he went all the way in, stretching her to the point of no return. And still she fought not to let go.

"It feels so good to be inside you," Brad whispered into her ear. "I want you to come with me, Lily."

His strokes were long and hard. She heard his breathing as he neared his climax. She gritted her teeth and clenched

her insides so that he would come sooner. A few more
strokes. He would be a useless soft pile of nothing in a few
more . . . She gasped as he changed angle, jerking upward in
swift, hard thrusts. He reached down and opened her again,
his knuckles slithering over her most vulnerable spot. He
thrust harder. His knuckles slid in time.

Lily tried to raise her legs. If she wrapped them around his
waist, she could control his . . . Brad sat up on his haunches
and plunged deep. The first wave of her orgasm hit her.

No. She tried to stop it. She felt him pulling out slowly.
Felt the long, slow stroke of him filling her all the way. The
tightness started to uncoil. *No!* His finger pulled at her clitoris and her whole body quivered as everything unwound
inside her. She had no control left. The pleasure was unbelievable, almost painful, every wave taking away all her
fight. She heard Brad give a moan and felt him shuddering
as he fell on top of her body. He was right. She was lost in
him and she was falling apart. She hated herself for losing
control.

Afterward, Lily stared up at the ceiling in the dark, listening to Brad's breathing. They both fell asleep afterward. He
held her close, one hand covering her breast. She had to get
up soon. Find her pants. Get the hypodermic needle.

For some reason, after so many years, she had wanted to
feel an orgasm with a man. So tonight she had done it successfully. It had felt wonderful and wrong. Brad had made
her lose control and now she truly hated him. He deserved
the needle.

Her cell phone's muffled ringing came from somewhere
near the foot of the bed. Brad stirred. "Shhh," Lily said. "I'll
get it."

They rested till dawn broke over the mountains, then resumed their climb down the mountain pass. It had been a

while since Amber had hiked like this. She had grown up doing this with her parents, going from small village to small village, some of which were reachable only on foot. She had learned to appreciate the local culture of each country and to use the resources to make traveling easier. It wasn't the first time she had to walk like this in the dark. There were times in Africa when her parents and she had to run off with many other villagers from advancing militia.

She looked at Hawk. She didn't care whether he was a SEAL or not. The man was injured and any kind of strenuous exercise had to aggravate those bruised ribs and Lord knew what else. His breathing still didn't sound right, although it didn't seem to stop him as he kept a pace that would down most ordinary men.

But she was fast learning that Hawk McMillan wasn't an ordinary man. She had always admired that well-sculpted body, thinking that he must work out a lot. As a SEAL, she now knew, he had undergone training in conditions that would test his spirit and endurance. She had seen television shows on SEAL training in which young men were deprived of sleep and made to train in extreme conditions in the ocean.

Sailors, she corrected herself. She looked up at Hawk climbing above her. She recalled the way he had tested her, the sure way he had learned the city alleys. How could she not have noticed how calm he had been in the middle of a battle? Her lips twisted when she remembered how she had teased him, saying he was probably hiding in a bush. She suspected now that he had been doing a lot more. That sailor body had been sculpted to be a fighting machine. How strange that she, who had thought she would never meet someone who would understand her way of life, would meet a man like him.

Hawk looked down. "What's the matter? Are you tired?"

"I'm fine. Do you need to stop for a rest?" She grinned at his snort. He didn't even bother to answer her. "You keep forging ahead like you know where you're going."

"I wanted to make sure there's nothing over this ridge, that's all. You're back to point man once you get up here."

She grinned up at him and resumed her climb. He had been teaching her all these military terms as they hiked through the night. "Point man" was the one walking point, looking for wires and bombs as he led the way.

"I kind of like checking out your cute ass from behind," she told him.

Hawk frowned down as he offered a helping hand to pull her up. "That's not very professional," he said. "You're supposed to be looking around you to make sure we don't come under attack."

She had been doing that, but she wished he hadn't taken off his jacket. His soaked T-shirt molded his pumped body like a second skin and it was distracting. She had better change the subject before she showed him how unprofessional she could get.

"There's a farm a short way from here," she told him. "We'll try to hitch a ride. That will give us more rest time."

"Won't the farmer think it odd to have two strangers drop in like that?"

She shook her head. "No, this area is full of foreigners, refugees, and aid workers. During the height of the war, refugees were pouring in from Kosovo and Macedonia, so strangers are nothing new to the locals around here. It's the Albanian authorities we have to worry about. We'll tell the farmer we're heading for Tirana. It's one of the oldest cities, with famous castles, and we can have them drop us near there. And if nothing else, money talks around here."

"Tirana. That's one of the cities near the weapons."

Amber nodded. "It's roughly fifty kilometers between

Tirana and Elbasan. Let's hope your coordinates are correct, because that's a lot of area to go looking for a hidden cache."

"Jed told me that they had all the coordinates for the UAVs as they flew over the various drop points. The problem from his end was to distinguish between regular food aid and weapons that are being illegally smuggled into the theater."

Amber coughed. "Umm . . . UAV? Theater?" He had definitely reverted to military mode, with all this talk. "Can we talk English?"

His lips quirked. "Unmanned Aerial Vehicle. "Theater" means the battle zone."

She chuckled quietly. "You guys. How about stopping for some TQL from the WHD?" She pointed to their pack. "You know, thirst-quenching liquid. Water-holding device?"

Hawk pulled her close to give her a quick kiss, his stubble rubbing her face. "ILY," he said quietly into her ear.

She looked up at him, the morning sun just breaking into a tiny red streak in the sky. Standing on a mountain. Heaven above and mere men below. Her parents would certainly approve. She smiled joyously.

"ILY, too," she said, and it felt so right.

Everything seemed to fall according to plan after that. They didn't see any border authorities or roaming mercenaries. The farmhouse. A curious but helpful farmer and his family. American dollars bought them some breakfast, the use of the facilities, a new change of shirts and some straw hats, and a ride toward Tirana. They took turns napping as they sat in the back of the little truck, bouncing uncomfortably, though still it was, Amber noted with satisfaction, much better than spending the next two days hoofing it. It was a risk, but time wasn't on their side anymore. Dilaver had transportation, and sooner or later he would catch up.

She watched Hawk give the farmer another tip when he dropped them off, frowning as she noticed Hawk limping.

"How're the ribs holding up?" Like he was going to tell her truth. "I know, I know, you're a SEAL, blah, blah, blah, but you're a limping SEAL right now."

Hawk surveyed the dusty path. "We have to get off the main road, if you can call this one. Do we go to the left or the right of it?"

He had changed the subject, so he was in pain. Amber frowned. His eyes were a little red and there were lines bracketing his mouth. She probably looked just as rough, but she didn't have to deal with bruised ribs. They probably had another ten kilometers to cover and then they still had to conduct a search of the area. "Hawk?" she prompted.

"I'll make it, sweetheart," he said. "The thing is to keep moving. It's the resting that's killing me."

She stared at him for a moment, then shook her head. "Is that what they teach you in SEAL school?" she asked incredulously.

He grinned. "We have a saying. The only hard day is yesterday, baby. Come on, I'll race you."

To prove his point, he took off running. Amber stared after him. "I'm in love with a madman," she muttered.

The morning sun broke through the canopy of trees, dappling the path with speckled patterns. They made their way through the woods, then a clearing, and then another patch of rocky woods.

"According to the coordinates, the drop zone should be east of here," Amber said. "I need a quick break before we get out into the open again."

"All right. I'll stand guard right here." Hawk looked around. "Don't go too far. There might be ugly bears or something."

"There aren't any bears in Albania," she said. "Are there?"

Hawk nodded solemnly. "Albanian bears are noted for their stench."

Amber glared at him over her shoulder before disappearing behind a clump of shrubs. He was such a tease sometimes. Looking around, she relieved herself quickly in a shady area. As she readjusted her clothing, the sound of crushed twigs behind her gave her warning that she was no longer alone. She turned and ducked at the same time, lunging forward and using her weight as an element of surprise.

She knew Hawk had been setting her up with that stupid bear story. Her "assailant" toppled onto his back with a grunt. She climbed astride, careful to avoid the rib cage. Leaning forward, she gripped his hips with her thighs. Strong hands came up to hold her waist.

"Ha! What do you think of th—You're not Hawk!" She sat up, too startled to attack. But she could have sworn it was—

"No, ma'am," the stranger said, amusement in his voice.

"What the hell are you doing, straddling my husband?" a woman's voice cut in.

Amber had barely registered the similarity between the stranger and Hawk before the woman charged at her. No time to think. Rolling off, she kicked out at the new assailant.

"Hawk!" she called out.

22

Hawk heard the thumps first, then the
voices. He limped over to the clump of vegetation that
screened his view. He was in no hurry. He had known for
some time that they were being watched.

Pushing through a leafy shrub, he came upon a sight that
brought a grin to his lips. Hell, who would have thunk it? He
approached the man standing nearby. The man didn't turn.
Both of them watched the two women going at it for a few
seconds.

"Mine's going to win for sure," the man said.

"Sorry, Kisser. I have the winner. Why do you think I let
you attack her? I knew she could take you down."

They finally exchanged glances. The other man looked
him up and down.

"Sorry, cuz," he drawled. "She had other things on her
mind when she jumped me. That's why Lena is a bit . . .
ah . . . mad. Your companion was overly enthusiastic about
straddling me."

Hawk narrowed his eyes. Amber on top of Steve, he could
take. Amber being amorous with him was a different matter
altogether. "Did she tongue you?" he asked, remembering a

certain incident when Marlena, Steve's wife, had mistaken Hawk for Steve and had been rather amorous herself.

"She was about to," Steve said, a corner of his mouth lifting.

Marlena must have stopped her just in time. Good thing. Steve would have gotten revenge, even at the risk of being beaten up by both his wife and cousin. Hawk's grin widened. "Well, then, I still win," he mocked. "M. will never let you near Amber now."

A small branch flew over Steve's shoulder. "That's the way to do it, babe," he called out approvingly. "Ohhh. Nice move there. Trust you to end up with a woman in the middle of the woods, Hawk."

"She's my guide," Hawk said. Among other things.

Steve glanced at him briefly. "Since when have guides in Albania lost their bad breath and facial hair? Did she do that number on your pretty face, by the way?"

Hawk grinned. "Why, you afraid my woman's gonna do the same to your wife?"

Steve gave a snort and looked back at the two fighting women. "Lena will kick my ass if I jump in there and stop her in the middle of a cat fight. *Your* woman, huh?"

Hawk crossed his arms and leaned back against a tree trunk. "Yes." And it felt good saying that. He had seen the possessive looks his cousin had given Marlena the first time he had met her in D.C. and had wondered at what made a man feel like that about a woman. Now he knew. He looked at Amber, busy dodging Marlena's kicks, and felt a rush of masculine satisfaction knowing that they belonged together and there was no doubt in his mind that he had every right to call her his woman. He wanted to be with her more than anything else. And if it meant staying in Macedonian hell awhile after this was over to convince her, he would do it. The decision was made just like that.

He straightened from his pose. "Come on, shark bait," he said to his cousin. "We'll be brave SEALs and go in there together."

"But Lena's winning," Steve protested as they walked into the fray.

Both of them parted the women. Steve wrapped his arms around Marlena from behind; Hawk blocked one of Amber's punches and swung her over his shoulder. Both women immediately turned their attention to their captors.

"Put me down right now," Amber said, her voice breathless from exertion.

"Can't have you girls making all that noise, babe," Hawk said. "Now, now, you don't want to kick my injured ribs, do you?"

She gave a rude snort but stayed still, letting him stride a few steps away from the other couple. He had to smile. She really didn't want to hurt him.

He looked over at his cousin, who seemed to be having a more difficult time placating Marlena. "But Lena," he heard Steve say, amusement in his voice, "she attacked me."

"You didn't have to enjoy it so much when she was on top of you trying to lick you off."

Hawk slid Amber off him and brushed twigs from her hair. "Lick?" he murmured. "You licked another man in front of me?"

"I did not lick him! And I thought . . . never mind what I thought. Who are those two?"

"He's my cousin and she's his wife. She was just mad to see you licking her husband, so I don't blame her." He cupped Amber's face. "Am I not enough for you, that you have to attack some other woman's husband?"

Amber stuck a tongue out at him childishly. "He looked like you," she said, and cast a glance at the squabbling couple a few feet away. "Well, in these shadows he did."

Hawk and Steve had been mistaken for each other since they were kids, so he couldn't blame her. His cousin was more like a brother to him, and they had both had their share of pranks blamed on each other through their childhood. "He's uglier," he told her.

Steve glanced over. "I heard that, Rocky Balboa. You're the one with cuts all over your face."

Lena turned to look at Hawk, too. "Are you injured, Hawk?" She sounded surprised, her anger gone. "Who hurt you?"

"Good question," Steve said, and released his wife now that she was no longer trying to hurt him.

"But why would you suddenly bump into your cousin in the middle of the woods in Albania?" Amber asked.

"That's another good question," Hawk said, looking at his cousin. "Strange coincidence."

"It's part of our honeymoon," Marlena said, smiling, as she and Steve walked over. "We thought since you didn't show up for our wedding, we'd come see you for our honeymoon."

Marlena Maxwell—Marlena McMillan now, he supposed—was one of GEM's premier covert operatives. She was known in the underworld as the world's most glamorous assassin. When Hawk had first met her, they were in the middle of a gun battle. Steve had asked him for help to save her, but from the way she had coolly picked off the enemy, she seemed able to take care of herself quite well. Hawk liked her. She was definitely a good match for his cousin.

"Well, then, I'd better make some friendly introductions," Hawk said. "This is Amber, Marlena. Amber, this is Marlena, and Steve, my cousin."

Marlena's smile dimmed a little as she studied Amber. Hawk noticed Amber was doing the same thing to the other woman.

"Nice form," Marlena said.

"You're okay, too," Amber said, eyes narrowing just a fraction. "Are you always so impetuous about starting a fight?"

Marlena deliberated for a second, then her face broke into a smile. "Yes," she drawled, "but only with the worthy ones."

Amber blinked, then laughed. "Good to know I'm one of them."

"I'll have to teach you other ways to get rid of the flies," Marlena said.

"Flies?"

Marlena's expression was mischievous as she looked at Hawk. "Don't tell me you don't know how delicious the McMillans can be," she drawled, and comfortably leaned against Steve when he wrapped his arms around her. "Trust me. You'll need to talk to me about the flies."

Hawk grinned back at Marlena. "You haven't changed a bit since I last saw you." Always teasing. Never boring.

"Darling, you have." The other woman looked critically at him. "Now tell me who beat you up like that so I can take care of them for you."

Hawk felt Amber nudging his side. "I can take care of him," she cut in smoothly.

He grinned at Steve and shrugged. "What are you good for these days, Kisser?" he asked.

Steve shrugged back. "If I tell you, you'll be deathly afraid," he deadpanned.

It was definitely great to see familiar faces from his real life. However, it also reminded him of why he and Amber were there. "So, seriously, you two didn't just appear in this no-man's-land to honeymoon, *and* happen to bump into me. Tell me."

"It *is* our honeymoon, just a bit late. We decided to do a

little side trip, that's all. Remember Harden, my old OC from the CIA?"

Hawk recalled that Rick Harden was the operations chief of a CIA task force Steve had been sent to infiltrate a while back. He was the one who had almost had Marlena killed. "Yeah. He causing you trouble again?"

"No, he's actually turned out to be a hero of sorts back in D.C. Admiral Madison likes him." Steve shifted and pointed south, toward where Hawk and Amber had been heading earlier. His expression sobered. "We're here on a side mission for ourselves and Harden. Cam and Patty have been missing for a few months now, and after looking through all the possible avenues, we've concluded that they or their bodies were dumped out of the planes."

Hawk frowned. "Cam? It's that mouthy dude in your task force, right?" Steve and Marlena nodded. "Why would he and his girl be dumped out of a plane in Macedonia?"

"Long story. They were tracing hidden illegal air shipments and weapon dropoffs by certain elements in the CIA that were supposed to be relief aid. There were multiple shipments going out when they disappeared, so the difficult part was trying to pinpoint which was legit. Harden and I traced one of the moles who disappeared and managed to find her background connecting to the old German system and the KLA. She was the connecting piece to all the moles, giving orders on what went where. Some sort of double-agent handler." Steve looked at his surroundings. "Hard to believe old Greta would be walking around in this place, running weapons. Anyway, Lena and I are only concerned about Cam and Patty, so that's why we're doing this on our own. Needle in a haystack, but we're close."

There was one thing that caught Hawk's attention. "Greta?" he mouthed quietly.

Amber turned to him. "She has to be the same Greta."

"What, you've seen her? Where?"

"About this tall, brown hair, stylish. She's supposedly a relative of Dilaver's," Hawk said.

Steve frowned. "Don't think we're talking about the same person. The Greta I'm talking about was Harden's secretary, and had been working as one for over a decade. And she had white hair. Kind of old-ladyish in the way she talked and walked."

"Darling, appearances can be deceptive," Marlena chipped in, canting an eyebrow.

"I saw her in and out of that office for a year and never thought of her as more than a secretary," Steve said.

"And it's positive that she's a double agent?" Hawk asked.

"A handler," Steve corrected.

"What's the difference?" Amber asked.

"A double agent is an asset. A handler makes sure an asset remains one," Marlena explained.

"Thank God I'm in the contracting business, then," Amber said with a wry expression.

"Oh, me, too," Marlena said. "What do you do?"

"I collect info and sell it for money," Amber replied sweetly. "And you?"

Marlena cocked her head. "I cancel people. Sometimes for money."

"And other times?"

"Other times I do it when they're straddling something that doesn't belong to them." Her blue eyes were challenging.

Hawk cleared his throat. He didn't have to be standing where Steve was to know that Amber's eyes would have that dangerous sparkle in them that meant she was thinking of some form of revenge. He could tell Marlena was in her GEM operative mode, testing Amber, and he didn't particularly want to have to explain about her agency and its ways to Amber right now.

"It's a high probability that it's the same Greta," he said, smoothly segueing into using GEM's love for percentages. "Dilaver's always talking about drop shipments from D.C. that are disguised as relief aid. Then there's an Aunt Greta who's a handler who knows about these shipments, or at least some things in them. She seems to be waiting for someone else to show up, though, because she doesn't know what the weapon I'm looking for looks like."

"I bet it's the missing CIA director from the Directorate of Administration. Remember, Lena? Harden told us the director from Administration had disappeared along with Greta," Steve said, then turned to Hawk and explained, "Administration is a department at the Agency that distributed weaponry among its many functions."

Hawk nodded thoughtfully. "Makes sense to have a mole in that department, then, distributing weapons under the guise of relief aid. No one would check too closely if the director was also involved. I have a bunch of coordinates of each hidden cache for the KLA and there's one around here, between Tirana and Elbasan. Amber's very knowledgeable about this area, but the concern is we'll get to the cache too late."

"We know where it is," Marlena said, affecting a yawn. "If I'd known you were after something in there, I'd have taken care of it while we were looking for Cam and Patty."

"You know the location?" Hawk asked. He looked at Steve. "Why didn't you contact the admiral? Or GEM?"

"Like we said, we're officially on our honeymoon. Except for Harden, nobody knows we're here," Steve said, a corner of his mouth lifting. "Nobody told us you guys were after weapons caches. We didn't even know what was in the crates. Most of them had 'U.S. Relief Aid' in bright blue and red on them. We planned on reporting this, but we found things that we think belonged to Cam and Patty and we're heading off to Tirana for more clues."

"Then they're alive," Hawk said.

"We don't know," Steve said, concern creeping into his voice. "We do know they were in one of those crates. I wish I knew for sure, Hawk. I can't let it go when I don't know what'd happened to them. Anyway, we'll take you two back there. It'll be faster."

Hawk tapped Steve's shoulder. "Sorry about Cam," he said. Cam had been Steve's closest friend when he was alone, a fish out of water, in D.C. "You guys can go ahead to Tirana. Just give Amber and me the directions. Tracking is tracking, after all."

Marlena gave an exaggerated sigh. "Get the job done and follow us back to Tirana. Why would anyone track on foot when they can rent a Land Rover?"

Hawk grinned. He couldn't imagine Marlena tracking up a mountain, either. "We had to cross a border without papers, for one thing. And then for some reason there weren't big signs saying 'Land Rover Rentals' up in the mountain villages. Can't figure out why."

"Keep my cell number with you, darling. Call me whenever and I'll arrange to pick you up one way or another."

"I'll keep that in mind," Hawk promised, and didn't blink when Amber bumped into his painful ribs. He'd have to teach her not to take Marlena's baiting so easily. "Give me a few minutes to talk to my partner."

He gave his cousin a telling stare, to which he received nothing but an amused quirk of the lips for an answer. It wasn't lost on him how relaxed and happy his cousin appeared to be now. Apparently, keeping up with Marlena Maxwell's lifestyle was good for him. He glanced at Amber, who was looking in the duffel bag, as if she wanted to use some weapon in there. Well, if Steve could manage a handful like Marlena, he could adjust to Amber and all her shady deals. She was doing something that he wanted to help with, anyway.

He bent down. "Land Rover?" he asked, leaving it to her to decide.

"You're letting me decide?" Amber gave Hawk a sideways glance. Did he know how good he made her feel when he consulted her?

"You're the guide. That's what being a team means, sweetheart. We do everything together—like those two."

He did know. She had to remember that he was a SEAL team commander. He would be the kind of man who liked to make sure his team, no matter how small in number, would know they were needed for the job.

Amber didn't know what to make of the other couple. The man was very obviously related to Hawk. He had the same facial features, though he was a bit more clean-cut and stood a bit taller than Hawk. The woman reminded her a bit of Lily, with her sardonic humor and dark beauty. Amber wasn't sure about that tidbit of information regarding her background, but from their fight, she could tell Marlena Maxwell wasn't just a pretty face.

"You okay about this?" Hawk asked, pulling her up and taking her to one side.

Amber shook her head and spoke confidentially in his ear. "It's too weird to think how we managed to bump into your cousin and his wife right in the middle of nowhere and they know the exact location of what we're looking for. I mean, can you really trust them?"

"With my life," Hawk answered, his eyes that dark gold color that always reminded her of sunlight reflecting on a bright ocean. "If they say they are down here looking for their friends, they are. Cam and Patty were their good friends. If it helps, the timeline checks out. I was in Asia when the drop shipment records were discovered and that was why we set up Dilaver. My commander wants me to map out the caches for destruction and GEM wants to make sure I get hold of one particular weapon for them. That's this bomb."

Amber looked over to where Marlena was talking to Steve. "GEM?" She should have known. "GEM is working with Jed now?"

"Isn't Jed part of them?"

She looked at Hawk in surprise. "No. Jed is part of COS Command. GEM is an independent contractor agency."

"They are working together now, Amber," Hawk said, "and have been for some time. They were part of my mission in Asia. Jed runs part of GEM's operations."

"Well, the things a girl finds out in the wilds of Albania," Amber muttered. "I don't like GEM operatives."

"Why? I've seen them at work a few times. They're good."

Amber leaned forward, making sure her words wouldn't carry. "We call them witches."

Hawk's gaze turned quizzical. "Witches?"

"That's info-world lingo. Some agencies get a reputation. When you want information personally extracted, hire a GEM witch. They're programmed to seed suggestions to the subconscious." She glanced at the couple not too far away again. "This one has probably infiltrated your cousin."

Hawk slowly shook his head. "He works for them. Actually, now that I think about it, Jed probably has a hand in them being here. He's a manipulative son of a bitch. What you're talking about is NOPAIN, by the way. I know a little about it. It's just a mental strategy technique."

Amber snorted. "Mind control techniques, more like." Amber studied him skeptically. "They taught you? Impossible. They only pick certain profiles."

"Like what?"

"If you have been around them, haven't you noticed? They're mostly females. And orphans. I've been trying to get info on this agency for ages. Every operative that I've encountered or researched was an orphan and very carefully chosen. Info about GEM is an expensive item in some circles." She met Hawk's gaze levelly, then shrugged. "That's my job. Even the CIA's ultra-interested in GEM."

To her surprise, he didn't make fun about the information on the Agency or get angry at the notion that his cousin could be in trouble. He considered for a few seconds. "Will it make you mad if I tell you that too much info kills action? It's not my area. Right now—"

Amber sniffed. "Yeah, yeah, yeah. Bomb, retrieve, remove, whatever. All this cool info and all you want is to save the world." She smiled. "I'll just grin and say 'I told you so' when you realize *she* isn't just in Albania for some side job. She has another assignment."

"Then that's Steve's problem."

How like a man. She rolled her eyes. She would have loved to find out more about any new assignment. Information was money, and . . . She let it go. She realized that he wouldn't understand how little bits of knowledge added up to make big money, thus paying for expenses incurred by her and Lily's venture. Anyway, she was in this for him.

When she nodded, Hawk turned his attention back to his cousin. "Jeep it is. You guys aren't afraid of a bomb, are you?"

"A bomb? Let's go for it."

Marlena sighed again as she fell into step with Amber. "You know about their penchant for explosions and destruction, don't you?"

"Besides other things," Amber replied.

"Oh, of course. They are SEALs," Marlena agreed. "How did you and Hawk meet?"

"I own a café in Velesta."

"Oh, I have to drop by sometime. Do you do your own dishes there? Stash adores my cooking," Marlena said, suddenly looking mischievous again. "Don't you, husband, dear?"

"Absolutely," Steve said without looking back at them.

"Stash?" Amber prompted.

"Personal nickname. You have to have one with the McMillan men, darling. They are all named Steve."

"I don't understand," Amber said with a frown.

Marlena tsk-tsked. "Hawk, darling, you really should tell her." She turned back to Amber. "It's a shock to the system to find out that not only is Stash Steve McMillan, but every damn male in that family is also Steve. Or Steven. Or, if I remember, there was one named Stephanus. Stupid family tradition."

"You mean, Hawk's name is . . ." She had never really thought about asking him.

"Steve McMillan," Marlena sagely finished for her. "And if you have a kid with him, he's doomed to be called Steve. Oh, quit looking at me like that, Hawk."

Climbing into the vehicle, Amber returned Hawk's amused gaze. A kid. She definitely hadn't thought that far ahead. She didn't tell Marlena that she already had a nickname for Hawk.

Hawk squeezed her hand gently. "We'll sort it all out when this is over," he whispered into her ear. She smiled back at him.

She had to admit that the Land Rover was a good idea. It covered the rocky terrain in no time and it felt great not to be on her feet. She was in good shape, but it had been a while since she had done such strenuous exercise. Besides—she glanced furtively at Hawk—she was glad Hawk was resting, too. She didn't care that he hadn't said one word about his injuries; she knew they had to hurt him, especially when tackling the steeper paths.

Feeling her eyes on him, he turned. The sunlight reflected the deep brown shades in his hair. His eyes had that golden glow that always fascinated her, and they had that heated expression that never failed to make her insides clench in anticipation. She kept her hands in her lap even though what she really wanted to do was reach out and touch that scruffy handsome face, pull him by the collar, and kiss those lips.

Her eyes moved to his mouth. Masculine. Sensuous. She blinked and looked back up. He was watching her silently, but she knew he was reading her mind. His eyes lazily roved down her face and to the V opening of her shirt. A small quirk lifted the corners of those lips. Then his eyes went lower and she unconsciously squeezed her thighs tightly together. He was driving her crazy by just looking at her. It just wasn't fair what the man could do.

She was about to do the same thing, let her eyes travel where her mind was leading, to see whether she could get a reaction, when the sound of vehicles from behind them caught her attention. Hawk and she turned around at the same time.

"Two vehicles behind us, Kisser," Hawk said.

"We're going to turn into that small road. If they follow us, start shooting," Steve said.

Marlena had already turned around, weapon ready. Amber caught the Uzi Hawk tossed and positioned herself against the back seat.

"Not much protection this way," Amber said.

"I have some grenades to do the job," Marlena said.

"That definitely ups our protection," Hawk said quietly.

The Rover turned. So did the other two vehicles. Sunlight glanced off the weapons pointed at them.

Marlena didn't wait. She tossed the first grenade just as

Steve made another sharp veer into the side road. Steve pushed Amber's head down as he also hunkered down. The loud explosion hurt her ears and she felt things spraying over them and into the vehicle. There were shouts and screams.

Something fell on top of the Rover, blanketing them. Amber blinked, trying to focus even as Steve braked hard. The material was heavy, ropelike. She heard Steve cursing as the vehicle ground into whatever it was and smelled tires burning as they tangled with the rope.

"That was a fucking decoy!"

Hawk pushed up with the muzzle of his weapon. She did the same. The gauze broke easily, but the ropes binding it weighed a ton. Something sharp hit her in the back and she cried out.

"Amber?" She heard Hawk yell.

"Stash! Don't come over here!" She heard Marlena call urgently. "I've been—"

The world turned woozy and the voices slowed down like a recorder in need of a fresh battery. Amber felt as if she were being choked. She needed air. She reached out and felt Hawk slumped down against the back seat, struggling, too. Drugged. Whatever had hit her had gotten the others, too, and they must all be feeling disoriented like her.

They needed air. She pushed out of the cut material, the thick rope bindings wide enough for her to squeeze through. Sunlight flashed blindingly as her focus blurred and cleared and blurred again. A figure stood not too far away.

Amber frowned. "Lily?" she asked, her voice sounding hoarse and strange. The last thing she saw was Lily walking toward her, a grim look on her face.

23

The voices sounded distorted, as if he were underwater. Hawk opened his eyes and everything was white, without shape. He found it hard to move his arms and his head felt as if something heavy was holding it down. The glaring white light hurt his eyes and he had to blink hard to focus.

Maybe he was dead. They always talked about a bright white light at the end of a tunnel. But there was no tunnel and the sounds weren't angelic. In fact, it sounded like . . . a very, very pissed-off woman, using a lot of words he was sure wouldn't be present in heaven.

"This time I'm going to kill her! I'm sick and tired of being poked by these tranqs every time we go for a drive. Stash, don't move, so I can cut the ropes, babe. These things are heavy."

"I'm okay. Go check on Hawk and Amber."

Amber! Hawk jerked up with a start and his head hit something hard. His chest exploded in pain.

"Hawk, are you hurt?" he heard Marlena somewhere beyond the white light. There was the distinct sound of a slicing knife and suddenly he saw a glimpse of trees and sky, then Marlena's face. "Hawk?"

"I'm alive," he said, pushing away the rest of the material. It tore easily enough once there was a cut. "Amber?"

There was no reply.

"Amber!" He struggled up, squeezing out between material and ropes.

"Careful, Hawk," Steve said. "The ropes can get you tangled up even worse. Almost like a commercial net of some kind."

"Where's Amber?" Hawk asked, moving toward where Amber had been sitting. She wasn't there. "Amber!"

"She's gone. They must have taken her," Marlena said.

"Dilaver," Hawk said grimly.

Marlena nodded. "It's Greta, for sure."

"How do you know?"

"Stash and I were tranqed in a similar fashion in D.C. when we were driving. Darts. Same effect. Since Greta was the handler in D.C., of course it must have been she who authorized our capture then. We have to get out of here and call Center." She turned to Steve. "We don't have a choice."

"No, we're going to go after Dilaver right now and get Amber," Hawk corrected.

"Don't think so, cuz," Steve countered. He was out of the vehicle, looking down. "All the tires have been slashed."

Hawk determinedly cut through the rest of the material, making the opening wide enough for his body. He jumped out of the Land Rover. Like Steve said, the tires were flat as pancakes. He kicked the rim in frustration.

"We've got to get to Dilaver." He looked at Steve and Marlena. He tried to say it as calmly as possible. "You don't know what he'll do to her."

In reality, his whole being was frozen with fear at the

thought of what could be happening to Amber now. He had to get to her. Dilaver would be taking revenge on her because of Hawk's betrayal.

"Hawk, we'll have to call Center to get help here," Marlena said quietly. "You know they'll ask us to go check on the weapons cache first."

"She's right," Steve said. "They will ask for the status on the bomb."

"Fuck the bomb." Hawk meant it. "I need a vehicle and we're going back to Velesta."

"Look, there's a note." Marlena pointed to the windshield.

Steve snatched the note that was stuck between the glass and wiper. "'Bring the bomb to me and you get her back,'" he read. He glanced up. "What do you want to do, cuz? I'm with you, whatever you need."

Hawk nodded. He knew Steve understood what he was going through. When Marlena was missing in D.C., his cousin had enlisted his help and had even gone off to destroy an entire luxury sailboat to get his woman back.

"This is going to be more than a dozen armed thugs," he said quietly. "Dilaver's got an army in Velesta and he should have the compound fortified by now."

"Draw it up. Let me see it. Then we'll make plans," Steve said.

"My darlings," Marlena interrupted. "Can I interject here and make a suggestion? Like, let's go to the weapons cache and then call Center?"

"Lena, we can worry about the bomb later. We have to find a way back to Tirana to get . . ." Steve paused and smiled wryly at his wife. "Sorry, love, my bad. . . . Hawk, we have weapons nearby—that cache itself. It makes sense to go there."

Hawk frowned as he figured out a way to get out of there.

Marlena slipped in between Steve and him and stood quietly till he gave her his whole attention. Her blue eyes, a little darker than Amber's, didn't have their usual flirty sparkle. They were cool and assessing as they caught his gaze.

"We need Center to get us transport out of here," she said. "It's the quickest way. And you'll have all the weapons you need."

Hawk returned her gaze levelly. "Tell me the truth, Marlena. You know Center doesn't give a hoot about Amber. They will want the bomb and won't let me use it for an exchange."

Marlena nodded. "Yes, you're right, but we can use a decoy."

"That's fine and dandy, but they didn't even allow me to cancel Dilaver because he's still an asset. I'm not going to endanger Amber to please them." Hawk turned to the Jeep. "If I have to I'll go there myself with what weapons I have."

Marlena laid a hand on his shoulder. "Call Jed, then," she said. "He'll find a way, Hawk. Jed's Number Nine in his group and it's his job to finish up any operations. He makes the final decision for the COS commandos. He won't leave anyone behind if he can help it."

Hawk stilled. That was right. Jed and Amber had talked as if they were good friends. "Okay," he said. He pulled out the cell phone from the duffel bag. "Since you two aren't supposed to be here, I'll try not to mention your presence."

Marlena's smile was classic Marlena—sly and sultry. "If you have to, do it. I can have my honeymoon anywhere I choose," she told him, then turned and walked back to Steve.

As the other two pulled out their gear from the vehicle, Hawk dialed the numbers and went through the usual indirect routing. He finally got hold of Jed McNeil. He gave an account of what had happened as quickly and succinctly as he could, then waited as Jed kept silent.

"We'll get Amber," he finally said, "but you have to go to

the cache and get the bomb. When you're there, activate your watch. I'll find you."

Hawk frowned. The watch had been a recording and uploading device. "I'm not sure what you mean. I activate it to steal the coordinates from Dilaver's system. How would you locate me?"

"Ask Marlena to show you," Jed said, and cut off.

Hawk put away the cell. "I didn't mention your names, but he knows you're here with me," he told the other two. He showed them his watch. "He said Marlena would know how to use this to let him know how to locate us."

Marlena crossed her arms, then turned and glared at Steve. "I hate those commandos."

Steve grinned at Hawk, then showed him his wrist. He was wearing the same watch. "Wedding present," he said, trying not to laugh. "His and hers watches."

Hawk frowned. "What is it?"

"It's obviously some kind of tracking unit," Marlena said angrily. "Sneaky bastard. I'm going to kill him too. Right after I kill those who got us."

"No," Hawk said. "Dilaver's mine. Now let's go get the bomb and wait for Jed."

"I didn't find the weapon on them. Time's running short, so I revised the plan. I have Amber Hutchens with me and left a note. He'll bring the bomb in exchange for the hostage. Make sure you keep her alive till Hawk McMillan shows up. He'll want to see her before he gives you anything in exchange."

Amber didn't move as she listened with her eyes closed. It was useless anyway. There wasn't any way to loosen the ropes around her. She couldn't believe that this was Lily speaking. It was her voice, but there was something different about its tone. It was flat, without emotion.

"They would have known I was following them. This way

is better. Let him bring the weapon." There was a pause, and Lily's voice was very sure. "Of course he will come for Amber. Are you afraid? He's just one SEAL against so many of you, and this time you'll be ready for him, right? There will be no surprise ambush."

There was a longer pause this time and Amber had to strain to hear Lily's whisper. "I will do what I have to do. Things fall apart."

"Someone's been here since we left," Steve said.

Hawk looked at the scattered branches and brush that had once covered the crates. "Didn't you touch any of them before? How did you know Cam and Patty had been here then?"

Marlena pointed to a crate behind a big shrub. "That's the one we looked at because it wasn't hidden very well. It was as if it had been pushed back into place by someone else." She walked over to it and slid the top aside. "It wasn't nailed and it looked as if things had been taken out of it. Then we found a few articles of clothing that Stash said were Cam's."

"Definitely Cam's," Steve agreed. "A truly classic Cam tie. I checked around and noticed the hidden crates but opted not to open them. I had a feeling about what they were anyway. But we needed to find out about that particular one because Cam's things were in there. It looked like he and Patty had opened it and taken things out. But then why leave his stuff inside?"

Hawk walked closer to the exposed crates. "Don't know, cuz. Right now, my concern's more on these. Whoever's been here opened them, too, but left all these weapons lying around. I guess they were after something else."

"I don't think your target weapon's going to be here anymore, either," Marlena said.

"I'm going to look anyway while Jed sends us help."

Hawk watched Marlena pull on Steve's arm so she could glare at the watch he had on. "There's no need to activate your watch," she said, "since someone's activated something on his wedding present that let *everyone* know where we were *every* moment of the day."

"How was I to know?" Steve shrugged. "It's just Jed, that's all."

"Oh yes, control freak king. Obviously, Hawk never activated his, so tell me, what did you do that's different?"

Steve frowned, his fingers playing with the watch. "He showed us the recording and uploading feature." Then he grinned sheepishly. "I asked him whether it took pictures underwater. And he told me to find out for myself."

Hawk shook his head. "I don't want to know," he said. Marlena was staring at his cousin as if she were going to attack him any minute. Hawk shook his head again. Newlyweds. He added, "I really don't want to know."

Marlena didn't seem to have heard him. "Is that why you took me swimming after . . ." She paused, the expression on her face somewhere between outrage and amazement. "I'm so going to kill him."

"We'll have a talk with Jed later, babe, but right now . . ." Steve looked around.

"I know. Sorry, Hawk. When we get Amber back, are you going to marry her?"

Hawk looked up. And he was suddenly very sure. "Yes," he said simply.

Marlena smiled. "Well, then, don't accept any wedding presents from Jed McNeil." She looked up at the sound of a far-off chopper. "Do you think that's for us?"

"Knowing Jed, yes," Steve said.

"There's nowhere to land except way out in the open," Hawk said.

"Can't tell you what Jed's up to, cuz." Steve swung his

weapon over his shoulder. "But if it's not him, we have plenty of toys and ammo here."

Hawk looked up, trying to gauge where the chopper was heading. "We stay exactly where we are," he decided. "If someone finds us, then we know it's through . . . your wedding present."

Marlena made a rude noise, then gave Steve a nudge. "Did you at least delete those pictures?" Hawk heard her ask in a low voice.

"Of course," Steve said with a straight face as he headed toward Hawk.

Newlyweds. Hawk looked down at the weapon in his hand. He knew they were also bantering to distract him from worrying too much about Amber. The SEAL in him knew that he could do nothing for now, but the man in him knew the danger she was in and was howling in silent fury. He knew Dilaver would take great pleasure in hurting Amber. He prayed that he would somehow be in time to save her. And for the first time in his life, he was deathly afraid that he wouldn't be.

They used the crates and shrubs as a barrier and waited in silence. Twenty minutes went by after the sound of the helicopter flying by had stopped. Hawk was about to say that maybe they had made a mistake when a shadow emerged from behind a tree. Hawk immediately took aim, quietly noting that the intruder hadn't made a sound to betray his approach.

"He's wearing white," Marlena said. "That's Alex Diamond, Number One."

There were nine COS commandos. Hawk stood up from where he was. He'd seen this one before. After he and Steve had saved Marlena that time in D.C., Alex Diamond had shown up to debrief her.

The man stopped, giving the area a sweeping glance. He

was either confident or arrogant, because wearing white wasn't conducive to camouflage. He waited till Hawk reached him.

"Where is it?" His voice was as cold as his light blue eyes.

"It isn't here," Hawk said. "It might be with the same people who took Amber Hutchens."

Diamond shook his head. "Then why the exchange note? Something's wrong." He turned to Steve and Marlena. "Congratulations. I heard you got married."

Steve slipped a hand behind Marlena's waist. Hawk suspected it was to stop his wife from making one of her usual rude comments. "Thanks. Anything to stop you from assigning her to work with you as a married couple," he said with a slight smile. "Did you get hold of T.?"

Diamond's eyes narrowed a little. "Have you seen her lately?"

"I did a few months ago," Hawk said.

The other man pinned his gaze on him immediately. "We'll speak more about your last meeting with her on the chopper. Leave the crates here. I'll take care of it. The target weapon is more important."

"But we don't have it," Hawk pointed out.

Diamond turned toward where he had come from. "You have twenty-four hours to find it," he said. "We'll get hold of Jed on satellite inside the chopper."

The older man moved as if he had been trained in jungle warfare. Hawk admired his fluid speed and eerie silence. Even hiking with his SEAL team, Hawk would hear certain sounds from weapons and clothing. He looked at Diamond's back ahead of him and wondered at the COS commandos' training program. He had to find out more, not just for Admiral Madison, but to satisfy his own curiosity.

Not turning around, Diamond said, "You're injured. I can hear you breathing. There's fluid in your lungs. You'll need medic care very soon or you'll get an infection."

"I'll take care of myself after the mission," Hawk said quietly.

"Good."

The chopper was military-issued. An armed man waited nearby, saluting Diamond as they approached.

"Better you than me," Marlena whispered to Hawk.

"What?"

"He'll want to know every little detail about T. She's determined to avoid him."

Hawk frowned. "Why's that?"

"You really don't know?" She looked at Diamond talking to his man outside the waiting chopper. "He and T. had some kind of falling out and now she won't see him. She's my operations chief, so of course I won't tell him anything I might know when he asks me."

Hawk shrugged. "I'll tell him anything he wants to know about T. Somehow, I think she can take care of herself." He studied Diamond for a moment. There was a certain polished danger around the man that reminded Hawk of T.'s elusive quality. "A woman like that is hard to catch, anyhow. More power to him."

Diamond turned at that moment. If he had overheard their conversation, he didn't show it. "We have Jed on satellite. He's at an international summit where we suspect this bomb was going to be used. It's small and flat and can be hidden very easily in a tiny suitcase. It's also totally undetectable because of its covering."

Amber had been right. That was why Jed McNeil was all dressed up on the video link. "But why this particular bomb?" Hawk asked. This had been bothering him. "Anyone can rig up a one."

"It's the mother of all little bombs," Diamond explained. "Virtually undetectable by all the modern sniffers. Because so many heads of state are attending this summit, it's going to be very difficult to smuggle any arms or devices into the area. The surrounding streets have been cordoned off to stop vehicular suicide bombers. Air traffic has been reduced."

"Only a person who is authorized or invited can get in there, then," Hawk said.

"Yes." Diamond turned. "Jed will fill you in on the details."

Hawk's cell phone buzzed. "Hang on," he said. Very few people knew his number. He frowned. It was Bradford Sun's ID. "This is Hawk."

"Lily's gone."

Hawk waved Steve and Marlena over. "What happened? Were you ambushed?"

"No," Brad said grimly. "She drugged me."

Hawk's frown deepened. "What do you mean, she drugged you?" He looked up. All the others' eyes were on him. "Tell me exactly what happened, Brad."

"We were followed to my place and, to give you and Amber more time, we decided to stay longer. Everything was fine, or so I thought, until she stabbed me with a needle full of some kind of powerful drug. Whatever it was damn near killed me. She nearly OD'd me. My housekeeper saved my life." There was a pause. "She tried to kill me, Hawk."

"Are you certain it was her? We were drugged here, too. But it's Dilaver who did it."

"I'm sure. We were sleeping in . . . my bed," Brad said. "I . . . still can't believe it."

Jesus. Hawk didn't need Brad to paint a picture of what had happened. "I'm sorry, man," he said. "I'm not sure what's happening. Amber and the bomb are missing, too. Look, I'm meeting my contact via video and have to go, but I'll bring this up. We'll figure out what's happening here. I'll call you as soon as we have a game plan. Are you doing okay?"

There was a short bitter laugh from Brad. "Barring the fact that I'm still at the hospital, I suppose I am."

"I'm sorry," Hawk said again.

"Not your fault. I should have gone after the details in her file more. I had a gut feeling about her CIA background, so I did another check with another source. I found out recently that she was saved by the CIA after being abused for two years in the whorehouses, and the file mentioned that she was part of Program Precious. I had assumed that was the name of the rescue operation, but now I'm not too sure. You do have CIA connections, right? Maybe you can find out what this program is and get a tie-in. There's something wrong with her, Hawk. I woke up when she answered her cell phone. I thought it might have been you or Amber calling. Then she stabbed me with that thing and . . . she was muttering the same line over and over again."

"What was it?"

"It's that poem. 'Things fall apart' . . . do you know it?"

Hawk took out a pen and jotted down the line. "That's it? Things fall apart? I think I know it. Sounds familiar."

"It's from a famous poem. I swear I heard her saying that line as I tried to understand what was happening."

"Okay. Keep your phone by you. I'll be in touch." Hawk ended the call. He turned to Diamond. "There's another woman missing and I think she's betrayed Amber and me."

"Give Jed the details."

Hawk and the others climbed into the huge chopper. There were two systems technicians, in familiar fatigue greens, working and monitoring the computers.

"We're clear, sir," one of them said.

"Good."

The large LCD screen was state-of-the-art. Jed's image was clearer than the one Hawk had talked to on Amber's laptop. Now he could even see the flecks of silver in the other man's eyes in the close-up. He was back in his usual faded jeans jacket but the background was a sumptuously decorated hotel room. His expression remained impassive as Hawk gave a detailed account of the state of the crates and Brad's phone call.

Hawk waited after he was done. He was getting used to Jed McNeil's odd long silences. The others standing with him must be, too, since they kept quiet. He always had a feeling that Jed was computing and simplifying, because when he spoke up after these silences, he always seemed to be able to reduce to bare bones the most complicated facts.

Jed looked down and Hawk could hear him shuffling some papers. "The summit meeting took place successfully, with only one minor incident. A woman was caught with an exploding device. It wasn't our target weapon," he said quietly. "Computation of seventy-five percent success of our operation, but that's without the detail of Llallana Noretski. The woman in custody was obviously the decoy Greta mentioned to Amber Hutchens in their meeting. Llallana was the one going in with the bomb."

"But the note demanded the target weapon and if they had it, why take Amber?" Hawk asked.

It was just a trick of the camera setup, but Jed's light eyes seemed to turn colder. "McMillan, you like Miss Hutchens. It's the only way to get you to do what they want—that is, go back to Velesta without finishing your mission. Meanwhile, Llallana takes off to the summit with the bomb."

"One question. How's Lily going through all the security without a pass?"

"There's a very famous art exhibit unveiling in eighteen hours. I'll let you make a guess as to who might be part of the entourage."

Hawk took a deep breath. "Too coincidental."

"There was a reason they didn't kill you, Mr. McMillan. While you're busy saving Miss Hutchens, the bomb will go off. You can't be at two places at the same time." Jed looked down at his papers again. "Granted, there's something else going on here that would explain Amber's girlfriend's motives. Bradford Sun dug up something important that had been left out of previous classified files. Project Precious."

"Brad said he thought it was a CIA-headed operation to rescue underage prostitutes."

Jed shook his head. "Negative. This was a super-classified project. Very short summary—it's short for Project Precious Gems. The last word sounds familiar to you? The CIA wanted trained operatives with the same talents unique to GEM operatives, except totally under its control. GEM, as you know, is independent, and the CIA was interested in finding out its secrets. Project Precious failed in copying or modifying NOPAIN, the GEM system, but things don't go to waste in the CIA. Project Precious has morphed into what I know is a sleeper cell program. Trainees aren't exactly operatives; they are embedded with sleeper commands that are activated with a repeated phrase."

"Things fall apart," Hawk muttered. He was beginning to feel the whole cloak-and-dagger world ought to explode with a certain undetectable bomb. Lily—a sleeper? He couldn't even wrap his head around it right now. "So she's been around Amber all these years waiting to be . . . activated?"

"She probably wasn't aware of it, or only vaguely. Sleeper commands come in slowly, each one triggering the operative into a deeper state of awareness. By the time she's fully activated, she'll be ready to finish her assignment."

Hawk shook his head in disgust. "I don't even want to know how they did this to Lily."

"Project Precious Gems picked up victims who are ideal for this type of program. Sleeper cells are manipulated through their emotions—hatred, fear, and a deep belief in a cause. I don't have to point out Lily Noretski has all the requirements."

"She's heading your way, then," Diamond interjected at this point to Jed.

"Apparently. I'll be at the art show."

"Get T. to bring the other weapon."

Jed's lips quirked. "I'll let you know as soon as I take care of Llallana Noretski and have the device in my hands."

Hawk understood what "taking care of" meant. Jed was Number Nine, the one who finished the job. "I'll head off to Velesta now," he said grimly. There was nothing he could do to save Lily. He could only pray that all these crazy calculations were wrong, that it was somebody else.

"Do what it takes to wrap up," Jed said. "Diamond, there's a message in your decoder for you. Hawk, any questions?"

He was going back to Velesta for one thing and one thing only. "Permission to take care of Dilaver," he said.

"He's no longer an asset," Jed said, and nodded to someone off-camera. The screen went blank.

"This chopper will fly you to an airstrip by Velesta," Diamond said. "While we're on the way there, you can brief me on T. and your activities with her."

Hawk didn't say anything when Marlena winked at him as she passed him. "Stash and I will go to our seats and map out an attack plan," she said.

The helicopter was faster than any he had ridden on. He didn't bother to ask questions about permissions and international borders. Let them take care of those details. He had a personal war to wage against a certain Slavic warlord and he knew it would just be him, Steve, and Marlena. Three against a small army. He refused to think of what was happening to Amber. He and Steve were SEALs and they would get Dilaver one way or another.

After answering Diamond's questions to his satisfaction, Hawk looked outside the chopper. He frowned. A familiar blue.

"That's the ocean we're heading toward," he said. "We aren't heading to Macedonia."

"We have to make a stop," Diamond said.

"I don't have much time," Hawk said, getting impatient. Amber. "Turn back now."

"I suggest you sit down and wait. Fifteen minutes won't make any difference at this point."

Hawk resisted the urge to punch Alex Diamond and ruffle up his nice white shirt. He didn't care for waiting fifteen minutes. Fifteen minutes could mean getting to Amber in time before . . . He looked down at his clenched fists. Save energy. He needed to direct his anger for the battle.

The helicopter landed and Hawk was the first to jump out. The first thing he noticed was the smell of the ocean. Fresh. Clean. Something that he had missed a lot the last few months. Then his eyes followed the direction Diamond was heading.

Waiting by the beach was a very familiar sight. A rubber ducky, the boat with which SEALs transport inland from a larger ship or submarine. And by that boat, six very familiar men. Jazz. Cucumber. Mink. Zone. Dirk. Joker. His brothers-in-arms were here.

For the first time since he had woken up from the drug, Hawk felt a measure of relief. Oh yeah. This was going exactly as he'd prayed for.

"Thank you," he said to Diamond, then approached his team. They saluted him and he snapped back a salute. "About time. Where's Turner?"

"He's out of commission for a while. We need you back for a wedding," Jazz said. "Best man's missing."

"Been missing too many damn weddings. Won't miss this one," Hawk said. "Are we ready?"

"Standing and ready, sir!"

24

"**I know you can hear me, Amber,**" the voice whispered in her ear. "I know you hate me and I'll have to live with that. But I need you here. Hawk will come for you and that will keep him from following me. I didn't give them that high a dose, so he and his two friends can get back here in time. But just in case . . . I've made sure that you don't feel anything. I know what it's like to have your legs spread out while they maul you one by one and I don't want you to feel the pain and anguish I did. I don't have time to get more of the stuff that puts you out, but this will work just fine."

Amber felt a jab in her arm. Tied up as she was, she had never felt so helpless. Her eyes flew open and met Lily's dark ones, except they didn't seem like her friend's eyes at all. There was a far-off look in them, as if she weren't really looking at Amber.

"Dilaver will rape you," Lily told her matter-of-factly, "and Hawk will kill him. I'll finally get what I want—the bastard gone. Meanwhile, I'll be at the art show and I'll wipe out the rest of those bastards who think they can run the world by selling weapons and women. I'll show all the

CIAs and World Health Organizations and humane watch-dogs how it's done. They think they run everything, but they are wrong."

Although her mouth was taped, Amber tried to say something. The sounds she managed to make were weak and took too much effort. Lily shook her head.

"You can't do anything, Amber. No one can stop this. I have to do it. Things fall apart, you see. Even friendship. The ceremony of innocence is drowned. There is anarchy. I will destroy the slouching beast. It is my duty and my revenge."

Amber blinked. The drug must be affecting her. Lily was murmuring some familiar lines that sounded like one of her father's speeches when he preached. Things fall apart . . . yes, she remembered now. It was Yeats, her father's favorite poet. Her brain was getting addled. She was hallucinating Lily talking like her father.

"That's right." Lily's voice was growing soft and drifting. "Don't fight the drug. Let it take you somewhere so you won't see or feel anything. I wouldn't wish that on you or anyone. I don't want you to end up like Tatiana. If Hawk is too late, you won't remember more than blurred images. No pain. Not like me, always remembering the pain. Always seeing their faces in my head. I wouldn't want you to not let Hawk or Brad or anyone make love to you again without feeling like you're a helpless victim. I wouldn't do that to you. This way is better. You won't need to constantly want to be in control of everything, even sex.

"Listen to me. Hawk is coming for you. There is hope. Don't let me down, Amber. You and he belong to each other. Maybe I'm selfish, but I don't want you to think of Brad. Just remember, what they do to you is nothing. Dilaver will be killed and so will every one of those bastards who hurt us and our girls. You will finally be one of us, Amber."

Amber shook her head, but even that felt like it took too

much energy. It made everything spin around, as if she were at the edge of being drunk. The sensation wasn't unpleasant at all. Part of her mind was screaming, trying to stop what was happening, but the floating sensation was so soothing, so relaxing. She wanted to tense up. But why? It was nice not to feel anything. She knew what was coming. Dilaver. His men. And she should be . . . She didn't even feel it when Lily kissed her forehead.

"Things fall apart. The blood-dimmed tide is loose. I must do this, Amber."

"The countryside looks like the Middle Ages here," Jazz noted. "Oxen-drawn carts and wooden wheels. Not quick enough transportation to the city. Look at those walls. Are they guarded? Once we're inside, we have to find transportation to the target area."

Hawk looked at his best friend. It was definitely good to stand beside him again. He had missed the easy camaraderie between them. His fake "friendship" with Dilaver only emphasized how much his friend meant to him.

Jazz was the strategist in their team, always mapping out a plan of attack, always looking for the weakest points of the enemy. With his quick foresight, he protected his team from surprises ahead of them.

"Dilaver has chosen one of his favorite *kafenas* for the exchange," he told his team quietly. "Not the compound, which is fortified by an even bigger wall. What does that tell you?"

"He wants you to get to him easily," Cucumber replied.

"These *kafenas* are crowded with UN soldiers," Hawk continued.

"He's also making sure he's surrounded by the blue army so you can't simply throw in grenades," Dirk said, referring to the blue uniforms of the UN forces.

Hawk nodded. He had supplied them with details of his capture and escape.

"He wants an exchange and then he'll have his men capture me again. This time, he has Amber." Hawk paused, glancing away for a second before meeting his men's eyes. "Look, this is personal to me. It's not for glory or country or any of that stuff. My woman's in one of those whorehouses and . . . and if anything happens to her, I'll kill every fucking one of them, blue army included."

Cucumber spat to the side. "If they're in there doing what I think they're doing, then they have no right to hide behind any uniform. Let's go get them. I'm with you."

Jazz laid a hand on Hawk's shoulder. "We aren't here just to help you destroy those caches, buddy. We're here for you. We'll go save Amber and you can take down Dilaver any way you please. Just save a little piece of action for me. He owes me something for the wallop he gave Vivi."

Hawk recalled how hard Dilaver had punched Vivi, which reinforced his urgency to get to Amber. "I'm very familiar with all the back alleys and pathways in Velesta," he said. "During the months here, I had thought of destroying these whorehouses before I finished up, so I've explored a lot in the dark, waiting for this moment. I have C-4 and wires ready in certain weak spots. All I need is to activate the fuse and every fucking one of the walls will fall down like cards. We start doing this at the same time except for the target area."

"Surprise attack," Jazz said, nodding. "Everyone would panic inside. Each of us will go to different points and will keep in contact through intercom and wire."

"Estimated time thirty minutes," Hawk said. He showed them the map he had drawn. "I'll use a word when I give Dilaver the decoy. Pick one."

"Kaboom?" Mink suggested helpfully.

"Make it a phrase to be sure," Jazz said. "How about 'It's over'?"

It's over. "Yeah," Hawk agreed.

"Let's party! We're going to have what the Americans call a freebie. A *very* special freebie. Some of you might even know her and I'm going to be the first to show you how to have a good time with a blond bitch. Bring her."

"Hey, it's the café lady!"

Amber felt light as a bird. The voices didn't frighten her. She recognized one of them but couldn't quite place it. She didn't care, although she knew she should. Something bad was going to happen to her, but it was all right. She wasn't afraid.

"Hey, Dilaver, that's our boss's woman you're doing, man. We can't let you do this."

"You're going to have to. Look around you. You're all surrounded by my men. And what's more, you're going to watch and report back to that son of a bitch what happens to people that raid my places."

"Fuck this, I'm here for a good time, not to watch you rape a woman."

A shot rang out. "There, you're no longer watching. Gentlemen, you're young. Got to toughen up a little. This woman is nothing. There will be more of her kind. After I show you what she's got underneath those clothes, after you hear her moan from my taking her right here on our favorite whore table, you can all take turns. Who's going to complain? Look."

Amber tried to focus. Something was happening.

"You're all gathering around, aren't you? Come on, get closer. Come and watch. See? Lovely breasts. And you can all have her for free tonight. Let me get to the pants now.

Don't you want those long legs spread for each one of you? Amber, can you hear me? You're going to feel something big and hard inside you."

It was as if she were floating above somewhere watching herself on the table. She should struggle. But she just lay there. She focused on Dilaver's hand pulling at the zipper on his pants. She wanted to kick him in the groin, but she couldn't remember how to move her legs. And she didn't feel a thing. Shouldn't she scream, like that girl she had seen not so long ago? Then she thought she heard more shots.

"Well, if it isn't another one of Amber's men. Good to see you again, Hawk McMillan. How do you like my hand on your girlfriend's breast?"

Hawk! Hawk would come and save her. Didn't Lily say that? Hawk was here. Amber moved her head, trying to see, but there were arms and legs and blue stuff in the way.

"Let her go."

That was Hawk's voice. She would know it anywhere. She strained upward.

"Oh, look, she heard her lover. Come get her, lover boy. She's lying here all lovely, waiting for you. Or me, ha! She can't move very well, though. The other bitch delivered her full of drugs, something I hadn't agreed to. Should have known I couldn't trust a woman. These pants have got to go, what do you say?"

"Make another move and I'll detonate this and everything here will be gone."

"Sacrificing yourself for a woman? What kind of warrior is that? Aunt Greta said you're probably a Navy SEAL. You know what? This is for your killing two of my best men. I'm going to fuck your woman and kill her in front of you. Here, let me hold her head up and you can see her pretty face one last time. Take him, men. Shoot his legs."

Amber still couldn't see what was happening. Gunshots

reverberated around her. "Nooooooo!" she managed, struggling against whatever that was holding her down. He was here for her. And suddenly panic rose in her and everything seemed to speed up, even her heartbeat. Hawk was in danger. "No!"

It took every ounce of her energy. She turned her head. And bit down hard.

She didn't even know what exactly she was biting on, but Dilaver's howl sliced through her consciousness like a wakeup call. Her head was shaken back and forth, but she refused to let go. Another hand grasped her throat, cutting off her air.

There were more shots. She could hear men shouting. Gunshots. She didn't care about them. She concentrated on Dilaver instead. He had hurt Hawk and he was going to pay.

Hawk had been told fury could fuel a human bomb ticking and he would always remember the moment of explosion. That was all he could recall for debriefing, even months later. The moment he laid eyes on Amber on that table, everything important ceased to exist except to get to the man standing there, his filthy hands mauling her.

He had hated that table worse than anything else in the *kafena*. There were so many times he had to walk by it, following Dilaver out, and not look at the girls left there after a "free" night. Sometimes, when he did look at an empty table, he would still see glimpses of faces and hear the screams. And there had been nothing he could do then.

Not now.

Not this time.

It didn't seem possible, but somehow he reached Dilaver across the expanse of the room without getting shot. Maybe some of the UN soldiers present had their conscience pricked at seeing a woman they knew laid out there on the table for them. Maybe someone up there was protecting him. He got to the big Slav as he was bending over Amber, screaming, trying to shake her off. A part of his mind registered that her mouth was clamped on some part of Dilaver's hand.

Hawk curled an arm over Dilaver's beefy throat from behind and snapped his head back. The snarling man immediately released Amber to pry Hawk's arm from his throat.

"It's over, pig," Hawk said into Dilaver's ear. "My turn to show you how to have fun."

The Slav was strong, pulling at Hawk's arm as he jammed his elbow into his injured ribs. Hawk felt the pain but forced himself to apply more pressure.

The roar of multiple C-4 being set off added to the confusion around the table. There were shouts as people fell to the ground, covering their heads in fear. Screaming girls ran out from the back. Hawk felt the ground shake from so many explosions around the city. His SEAL brothers were doing what they did best.

"I've wired every one of your places in Velesta and they are coming down tonight," Hawk said as he swung a punch into Dilaver's face. He punctuated each blow. "Every. One. Of. Them. Gone."

Dilaver wasn't going down easily. He matched Hawk's blows with several of his own. He had gotten free of Amber, blood splattering all over as he went for Hawk's throat, pushing his thumbs inward.

Hawk let out a roar and rammed his body against Dilaver, pushing forward until the other man hit one of the supporting beams in the room. The blood made everything slippery and the hold on his throat loosened. Dilaver landed a vicious fist on the side of his face. Hawk straightened up and resumed punching at his target like he did to his punching bag in his room, going for the face and neck area. He cut upward into the groin. He head-butted him. Dilaver roared and struck out one last time. Hawk smashed a fist into his face so hard, the other man's head whipped backward and hit the beam with a loud crack. Even then he continued pounding as Dilaver slid down the beam.

He was still beating and kicking when someone pulled him off. It was Jazz, holding him from behind, cuffing him from the underarms.

"It's over, buddy, hey, it's okay, he's done."

Hawk finally stopped. He looked down at Dilaver. He had just killed a man with his own bare hands. "Let go," he said. "I'm fine. Where's Amber?"

Jazz released him and he turned to the table, stumbling over debris and bodies. He caught sight of her blond hair.

"Amber! Amber!" He turned her over. There was blood all over her chin and the front of her shirt. Her eyes were open. He pulled his precious package into his arms, hugging her tightly. "Where are you hurt?"

"I'm . . . okay. I think I bit off part of Dilaver's thumb. Hawk . . . Lily . . . oh God, Hawk—"

"Shhh . . . it's going to be okay. I know, I know," Hawk told her, wiping her face and mouth with his sleeve. She wasn't hurt so far as he could see, thank God. He lifted her and started to head out toward the entrance. "We'll talk as soon as we get you taken care of. Jazz, we're snatching a vehicle and going to the hospital. Call headquarters. They can land something at the UN base or wherever, I don't give a fuck. Get them to transport her out of here!"

"Aye, aye, sir!"

"You came for me, Hot Stuff."

Hawk looked down. "Of course I did. Don't you know I love you yet?"

She smiled weakly. "I love you, too. Don't leave me alone at the hospital, Hawk. I don't think I can stand being without you."

"I'll never let you go," he told her.

* * *

Lily looked at the buzzing cell phone on the passenger car seat. It lay there beside the small explosive device. She picked it up to check the ID. Brad. She frowned. Not who she was expecting. He shouldn't be calling her. Dropping it back on the seat, she ignored the sound and continued driving. The cell kept buzzing. She glanced at it several times as the minutes continued. Finally, she reached for it again. Why would a man who should hate her call? Just to tell her he despised her?

"Shouldn't you be in the hospital?" she asked levelly, keeping her eyes on the mountain road.

"Surprised I'm not dead?" His familiar voice was low.

"I called your housekeeper to make sure she showed up early, you know. I couldn't let you die."

"I know what you're doing, Lily. You can't do this. I know what you are."

"What am I?" she asked calmly.

"You're a CIA sleeper. They used your anger and hatred and programmed you. They channeled all your emotions into looking for a sister you don't have so you could have a purpose in life, and then they put a trigger in that they could set off when the time's right. All those cell calls you have been taking . . . don't let them use you, Lily!"

"I don't know what you're talking about."

"You don't have a sister. It's you all along! You know this! Stop lying to yourself, Lily."

Lily frowned. "Llallana," she corrected. No one was to know about her sister's identity or—"*Things fall apart; the centre cannot hold.*"

Brad's voice was very sad. "*The blood-dimmed tide is loosed, and everywhere the ceremony of innocence is drowned.* What comes next, Lily? Say it and be free."

He had changed the order of the code. She obeyed. "*The*

364 \ Gennita Low

best lack all conviction, while the worst are full of passionate intensity."

Her consciousness zapped her like electricity. Lily blinked, trying to understand. That line had never been spoken. She was not to say it until she was told to. Something unlocked inside, like an old creaking drawer, and she was drawn to it. There was something waiting for her in there. Open it. Open it. She pulled at the image in her head. The cell phone fell from her hand as she continued driving, staring into the darkness.

She thought she heard someone calling her name. But it was too late. She had to stop what she was doing. There was only one way to obey and disobey. Detonate here. Now.

She veered off the road and drove a short ways away. She braked to a stop as she came close to a cliff. Darkness out there. Like the darkness in her heart.

She deserved what was coming to her. She released the brake.

25

Amber looked up eagerly as the door opened. Her nurse pushed her wheelchair forward a little as another nurse followed Hawk, also in a wheelchair. She hadn't seen him for two days since the initial checkup at the hospital. Not that she had been able to talk much anyway. Her drugged body needed time to get rid of the toxins in her system.

"We really have to stop meeting like this," he said, a small quirk to his lips. His eyes devoured her, taking in every detail. "Like the similar outfit."

She grinned back. "You look good in a hospital gown. Nice legs."

He stretched one out, looking down at it with interest. "Oh yeah? I knew there was a reason why the nurses wouldn't let me put on my clothes for this. What do you think, Nurse Hill?"

"Nice legs, bruised ribs, bad internal injuries," Nurse Hill summarized from behind him. She smiled at Amber. "He was quite a petulant child the last few days when he couldn't get to see you. Like you, his body needs rest, but he doesn't seem to understand that. And he threw a tantrum about his outfit and the wheelchair. Fortunately, he calmed down quickly."

"Yeah," Hawk said, "they threatened not to let me see you today. How are you feeling?"

It was so good to hear his voice again. Amber wanted to jump out of her chair and kiss him. "A bit weak," she replied. "I'm just glad to see you."

It had been a strange two days, coming in and out of her drugged sleep. When she was finally cognizant, she had found out that she was in a medical facility in a military base. There were visitors, but she didn't know any of them. She just wanted to see Hawk.

She had heard all the details of what had happened from Lieutenant Jazz Zeringue, Hawk's close friend from his team. Dragan Dilaver was dead. All his *kafenas* had been destroyed by fire. Hawk was all right, but he had some injuries that needed to be taken care of. She knew some of those came from being Dilaver's prisoner.

"We'll let the two of you have a few minutes alone after the meeting," Amber's nurse said from behind her. "Here is some water, and if you need us, we'll be outside the door."

"Thank you," Amber said. She looked up when the door opened and a familiar figure, clad in faded jeans and jacket, walked in. "Hello, Jed."

Jed McNeil always made a room feel smaller. The man had the kind of presence that was quietly forceful, speaking volumes without actually having said a word. She had forgotten how those light silvery eyes could gaze with an intensity of a hunting animal. Right now they were assessing, taking in both her and Hawk's physical condition. She was pretty sure that he had already read the medical reports.

"Hello, Ambrosia. Long time." He looked at Hawk. "Lieutenant McMillan. Good job."

"I haven't completed my assignment," Hawk said quietly. "There's still those caches."

"Your team will take care of it. We're combing the different locations right now." Jed took a seat. "Except for one factor, we have everything under control."

"What's that?"

Jed glanced at Amber. "Llallana Noretski."

Hawk also turned to her. "Lily took the bomb with her, Amber."

"I know," she said softly, trying to keep the sorrow away. Lily was, in all likelihood, dead. "Lieutenant Zeringue told me about it. She had been programmed by the CIA to follow certain orders. I'm still not sure what they are, though. Why was she with me all these years? Was she waiting for this particular weapon?"

Jed shook his head. "No. She's a sleeper cell, which means that the CIA intended to use her for a target. A sleeper lives a normal life until their trigger is activated, so Lily didn't really know much of anything except that she had undergone some kind of psychological evaluation from the CIA. From what I gather talking to Mr. Bradford Sun, she had been brainwashed into a separate identity. She identified her missing self as her sister, which the CIA used as a cause to channel her hatred and distress. That way, whoever activated the trigger would have the key to manipulate her."

Amber frowned. "So, someone from the CIA did this to set off a bomb at an international meet?" She was still in shock at all this stuff about Lily and her conditioning. She had heard about these topics but had never really thought about it happening to her in real life. "Why this particular group of people? Wait, I remember Lily's last words to me. Something about finally getting rid of all those responsible. Does that mean she had been programmed to think all the political figures at that summit were her enemies?"

"That makes sense," Hawk said. "She hated those who had power to stop the trafficking of women. I think that's why she acted so oddly with Brad. Her feelings were in conflict with her conditioning. At the same time, those phone calls started."

Amber sighed. She still couldn't believe what she had been told the last few days. Yet, looking back, she could see how out of character Lily was, and how she was always mentioning calls on her cell phone. Amber had misunderstood, thinking it had to do with the girls' transport in and out of the country. How was she to know that those calls were activating whatever embedded commands that were dormant in Lily's psyche?

"We found her car," Jed said.

Amber bit down on her lower lip. She wasn't sure whether she wanted to hear this. Hawk pressed a button on his wheelchair, moving him forward and closer. He held out his hand. She put hers in his. It felt so good to touch him again.

"It was at the bottom of a cliff," Jed continued. He opened a file and leaned forward to hand them some photographs. "It's not easy to recognize, but you can see the license plate. Is this her vehicle?"

Amber squeezed Hawk's hand as she checked the photo. "Yes."

"There's no body in the wreck," Jed said.

Hawk jerked forward. "You could have told Amber this right from the get-go," he said, then paused. His eyes narrowed. "You son of a bitch, you were testing her."

Amber looked at Jed steadily. "Did you think I would lie about Lily?"

Jed ignored Hawk's glare. "I wanted to see how prepared you are for her death," he said calmly. "Because eventually she will die."

"Why?" Amber asked. Despite what Lily had done to her, she didn't want her dead.

"Because she still has the bomb," Hawk said.

"We need you to work with us to understand how Lily's mind works—what would be her next target, if she uses the weapon. We need to find her and eliminate her."

"I don't want her . . . killed," Amber said.

"Time is running out for her," Jed said. "Mr. Sun released her mind, but the trigger is still there, waiting for someone to reactivate. She's a time bomb, Amber. If we don't find her, Greta will. Greta, as you know, is the mole who was the handler to a few very important CIA higher-ups. She wanted the weapon for some agenda, but Llallana's actions changed everything. Apparently, we have another problem with the CIA having a different agenda." Jed's expression hardened as he added, "Which will be dealt with when I get back to the States. But the point is, someone at the CIA knows his plan to eliminate a number of political figures at the summit has gone awry. He'll be after Llallana, too. Or worse, find a way for her to actually use the bomb the next time. We have to find her first. And eliminate this problem."

"I'm not working for the damn CIA again," Amber told Jed coldly. "I don't like what they have done to Lily and they can kiss my ass."

"You'll be working with my agency," Jed said. He cocked his head. "Who knows, with your input, you might be able to save your friend."

Amber stared at Jed for a moment. Then turned to Hawk. "He's a son of a bitch," she declared. Jed knew that would be the perfect bait to get her to cooperate.

Hawk lightly squeezed her hand again. "You don't have to do anything you don't want to," he told her.

"I'll do anything to save Lily," Amber said. Lily had been

her best friend the last four years. How could she not help her? She made a face at Jed. "I hate your innovative negotiation technique, Jed McNeil."

Jed inclined his head. A small smile entered his eyes. "You've always wanted to know more about NOPAIN," he said. "No charge this time, Ambrosia. Bradford Sun is outside, waiting to talk to you. Want to see him?"

"Of course!"

"Then I'll leave you two now. I'll be in touch. McMillan, Admiral Madison will call you today sometime. You and I will talk soon. It was a good joint venture."

"Yes," Hawk said. "It was . . . different."

Amber watched as the two men exchanged glances before Jed slipped out of the room. "What was that about?" she asked.

"He'd told me a while back that this would be the hardest assignment I'd ever have because of the length of time it would take me to live in Dilaver's world, that I would come out of it different," Hawk explained. "And it had been tough for me because at that time I couldn't do what I wanted to do—take down every piece of mortar and brick of those *kafenas* and destroy Dilaver. But . . . I found you, too. I'm glad I did."

Amber could imagine the toll it took. Fighting one's natural self all the time. And Lily did that for so long. "ILY," she mouthed softly as the door opened and Brad came in.

Hawk's lips curved and his eyes caressed her. "ILY backatcha," he mouthed back.

A man either had to learn to let go of something out of his control or be driven out of his mind by it. It was late at night and Hawk couldn't sleep. Once again, images haunted him. He wished Amber were here with him.

Hawk thought of Bradford Sun and couldn't help but feel sorry for the man. He had appeared his usual unruffled self today, but Hawk could tell that the man was suffering. There were shadows under his eyes as if he hadn't slept well lately. They lit up when Amber told him that there was a possibility that Lily wasn't dead. He had come to tell them that the girls at the safe houses were gone, along with the two nurses. It was now very probable that Lily had gone back to take her girls to safety.

"She couldn't just trust them to you or me. I freed her mind with that damn trigger, but she still hadn't freed herself."

"What are you going to do, Brad?"

"Let her go. She and I weren't meant to be, Amber. I'm not even sure whether I ever reached the real Lily." His voice had turned bitter as he added, "Except maybe those last few minutes. But that was her turning point, not mine, and she chose to continue on without me or anyone close to her. I could stop my life and go off hunting for her, but I don't even know where to start. If I keep at this, I'll end up like that line she kept repeating—I'll fall apart. I'll have to learn to let go. It's out of my control."

Brad's words made Hawk think. He had to learn to let go, too. He couldn't let what he had seen and not been able to do the past few months living under Dilaver to destroy his own view on life. In a chilling way, Lily had been right. Things *would* fall apart if one's core beliefs didn't stay strong. He had to find some way to anchor his own dark fury.

His laptop by the bedside beeped him. This was how they communicated while they were apart.

Hot Stuff. I have something for you.

He smiled in the dark. He knew who his anchor was. He placed the computer on his lap. *We aren't talking till you agree to marry me.*

Oh, all right, if that's the most romantic way you can think of to propose. At a stupid hospital. In a wussy white hospital gown that barely reaches your knees.

He chuckled. *Something else to remember us by along with the sumo wrestlers.* He would never be able to watch *that* particular activity again without remembering what Amber did to him on her couch. *What do you have for me, love?*

Something to add to our collection of memorable moments. Remember the message you scrawled on my thigh?

How could he not? *Yeah. You cooking me another hamburger?*

No . . . I have this.

A window popped up on the left top corner of the screen. It was Amber in front of her rigged-up laptop camera. She patted her hair self-consciously, then smoothed her hands down her naked breasts to her hips. Hawk stared, his mouth falling open. Was she wearing . . .

Well? Are you going to find a way to get in here to eat this? Or aren't you hungry? It's strawberry-flavored, by the way.

Hawk didn't even bother answering, shutting the system down in a hurry. He scrambled out of bed. Hospital rules be damned. He was a SEAL. He would find a way into her room tonight. He had more memorable moments to make.

Don't miss the heat in these sizzling new August releases from Avon Romance!

Love According to Lily by Julianne MacLean

An Avon Romantic Treasure

Lady Lily Langdon is ready to take matters of passion into her own hands. With lessons in flirtation from her American sister-in-law, Duchess Sophia, Lily means to seduce the object of her affection: the Earl of Whitby, a man who up to now has only seen Lily as a troublesome girl. He'll soon find that though she is still troublesome, she is no longer just a girl . . .

How to Marry a Millionaire Vampire by Kerrelyn Sparks

An Avon Contemporary Romance

Welcome to the dangerous—and hilarious—world of modern day vampires. There are vampire cable channels, a celebrity magazine called Live! With the Undead, and just like the living, vampires have dental emergencies. That's how dentist Shanna Whelan, a human female, meets the smolderingly undead Roman Draganesti, and finds her life turning absolutely, well, batty . . .

Daring the Duke by Anne Mallory

An Avon Romance

She once lived a secret life. He, a reluctant duke, once pursued that secret to the ends of the earth. Could he know her identity—and if he does can she trust the aid he offers? And what will happen to their growing passion when he discovers her final secret—the one that proves how powerfully they are connected?

Courting Claudia by Robyn DeHart

An Avon Romance

After a lifetime of chafing under her father's high expectations, Claudia Prattley is determined to please him by marrying the man of his choosing, but a dashing rogue is bent on foiling her plans. That rogue is Derrick Middleton, and he's so drawn to Claudia's enchanting combination of passion and trust that he knows he must take a chance on winning her love.

Avon Romantic Treasures

 Unforgettable, enthralling love stories,
sparkling with passion and adventure
from Romance's bestselling authors